*SET UP*

# Other Fiction
# by Cheryl B. Dale

## *Romantic Suspense*

Intimate Portraits
The Man in the Boat

## *Paranormal/Gothic Romance*

The Warwicks of Slumber Mountain
Treacherous Beauties

## *Light Mystery*

Taxed to the Max
Overtaxed and Underappreciated

## *Vintage Mystery*

Losing David

This book was previously published in 2012 by MuseItUp Publishing.

Copyright Information
Copyright 2012-2014 by Cheryl Dale
Published by J&H Press
Previously Published by MuseItUp Publishing
Cover Art by J&H Press
Content editor: Barb Wilson
Line editor: Val Haley

ISBN: 978-0-9908695-1-1

www.cherylbdale.com
cherylbdale.blogspot.com
cherylbdale@hotmail.com

# SET UP

## by

## Cheryl B. Dale

J&H Press

# CHAPTER ONE

AMANDA SAW HIS double-take when he noticed her.

The henna rinse might have caught his eye—everyone knew he was a redhead junkie—but the black dress cut to the waist stopped him cold. Across the small theater, he craned his neck.

Oh, yeah. He was circling the bait.

*Can I do this?* She swallowed nervously.

Onstage, two big-name singers, imported for the grand opening of the McIntyre Grand Tartan Resort Inn near Houston, stood in the spotlight. Voices soared through the dim auditorium.

In the opposite box, sleepy eyes focused on her with an intensity that allowed her plenty of time to take in his broad forehead that blended into defined cheeks and solid jaw. Not exactly handsome but all male, with a laid-back air that said, *I'm easy to get along with. I'll let you do whatever you want with me. Everything about me is easygoing. My mouth, my hands, my . . .*

Not the place for these thoughts. Her stomach fluttered.

And no reason for jitters.

*You may be rusty but you've played the game before. This one's for Noelle, for little Teddy.*

A deliberate breath emphasized her breasts.

He liked that. The mouth parted, looked ready to smile.

As it did.

She'd forgotten how easy flirting was.

*You aren't here to renew bad habits.*

Lifting her brows, she turned away but not before a sidelong glance showed his smile widen. He edged forward in his seat.

Nibbling at the bait. She almost had him.

Conscience flared.

She shouldn't be here. For once in her life, she should have refused to help Noelle.

No, maybe someday she could stop being the protective big sister but not now. Not with Noelle's marriage and child at stake.

Across the auditorium, he watched her.

She made sure he saw the glance flicked his way, and then snubbed him.

Contrived, every movement. She knew exactly what she was doing because when it came to men, she'd always known what to do.

But that was the old careless Amanda, who'd delighted in excelling at the game and breaking hearts galore.

No time to dwell on the past. *Play him till he bites.*

The performers finished their duet. The crowd at the newest gem to adorn the McIntyre Resort Inn chain burst into applause. When Amanda followed suit, a rebellious curl escaped and refused all attempts to tuck it back.

With a shrug, conscious of the man's scrutiny from across the way, she removed the hair clasp and shook out the red strands. While desultory fingers raked them back, she checked out his reactions.

He leaned forward, his lips parted like primitive man stalking a fat deer for the kill.

Amanda's hand clutched involuntarily, her heart leaping into her throat. He didn't look like the irresponsible playboy Noelle had described.

He looked like someone a woman would be foolish to dupe.

No, nothing to worry about. *He's a man, isn't he?*

She scowled at him.

He didn't stop staring.

She sighed and swung her head back and forth as if to ask, *what's the world coming to when a woman can't let her hair down in peace?*

His sudden grin was charming. You're wonderful, it said. Fascinating. Irresistible.

When he kissed his fingertips to her, she let her chin drop but not until one corner of her lips turned up.

Way too easy. And heady to find she could still send out the old signals.

*Stop being so pleased with yourself.* If it weren't for Noelle and little Teddy . . . *If you're caught, if anybody finds out* . . .

Fear dried her mouth.

*Calm down, calm down.* No one would find out. No one would connect Atlanta's sedate Amanda Jane with a seductive redhead in Texas.

He remained riveted, sitting on the edge of his seat, his box filled with men in formal tuxedos and women with glittering jewels.

Noelle had mentioned he occasionally loaned pieces from his antique jewelry collection. Surely to goodness he wouldn't have lent Noelle's ring out tonight. It was impossible to see the women's hands clearly in the dim light, but one of the men in the back looked familiar. Where had . . . ?

No matter. Someone to avoid.

The vivacious blonde seated beside Amanda's quarry laughed at something he said before giving him her opera glasses.

He aimed them toward Amanda.

Hooked.

Now to reel him in. She sank back into the plush seat to lose herself in the music. Her nerve was back.

If only it was over.

\* \* \* \*

THE SHOW WOULD never be over.

Across the small auditorium, Callaway Mills McIntyre, III used the redhead as an antidote for boredom, chuckling silently at her pointed snub.

What a knockout. A ripe peach. Ready to be plucked, savored and slowly devoured. Damn, she was tempting. Almost tempting enough to make him forget the last fiasco.

Too bad he'd sworn off women like her.

Didn't hurt to look though, especially when he'd seen this play a half-dozen times.

At the end of the interminable act, the chorus came onstage for a rousing number. The lights in the ornate sconces brightened before Cal handed the opera glasses back to Miles de Graffen's wife.

"Thanks, sugar."

Sapphire rings sparkled as Patrice took the glasses. "You needed them more than I did." Her cute French accent didn't make up for her smirk. A shame she was so snotty, but that was Miles's problem.

Cal got up and stretched. "I'd rather look at her than listen to what's-his-name howling. She's a lot prettier."

Patrice swatted at him. "Howling? He's one of the best-known tenors in America!"

"Cal, stop teasing Patrice." Meek Lynette de Graffen couldn't hide a smile at her stepmother's irritation. In a pale yellow dress, with small diamonds in her ears and minimal makeup, she looked like a clean-scrubbed teenager rather than an assistant art professor. "You know he's her particular friend."

Cal winked at Lynette before assessing the opposite box.

Red hair spilled to creamy shoulders. His peach pretended to be engrossed in a program, but he spotted the glances sneaked his way.

She was interested. Should he go over?

Probably not. As the official McIntyre representative for the opening, he'd written the night off as one more family duty until Sonny pointed out the redhead.

Though he'd have eventually seen her himself. He always found women like her.

Or they found him.

"How do you come up with such trashy women?" his exasperated mother had once asked. "Don't you know they're only out for money? Find yourself a girl with character. Or do you even know what character means?"

"Girls with character are invariably plain and have never heard of makeup," he'd apologized. "No sense of humor, either. They don't much turn me on."

Mother had snorted with her usual contempt.

But those kinds of girls still didn't turn him on. Give him a brassy, butt-swinging female with big hair and big tits. One who could laugh.

He bet the redhead across the way had the kind of body he relished. If he . . .

*Forget it.* Why bother?

If she were willing, she'd be airheaded. Or worse, deceitful. Nope, he understood her kind of female only too well. He'd keep his distance and play the obedient genial host so he could earn his salary and keep Robert off his back.

Melancholy threatened, to be impatiently staved off. Women might help, but he'd finally learned they weren't the answer to his restlessness.

Robert Winslow, Cal's brother-in-law, pursed his lips. His ramrod posture reinforced disapproval. "If you've got any sense, you'll pass on her."

Robert always expected the worst.

Okay, maybe sometimes Robert had justification.

"Just going out for a cigarette," Cal said.

The men hooted while the women exchanged knowing glances.

Why the hell did they all think he was headed for the redhead's box?

Because they knew what he was. Miles and Lynette, lifelong friends, might overlook or excuse him, but they and the rest still knew. He was a hanger-on, as unessential as any minion in the corporation. Even though he was a McIntyre.

Robert opened his mouth for the inevitable rebuke, but his aide, Sonny Kirkman, ran interference. "Cal, the plane's set to leave after the bigwig brunch tomorrow. You need to be up and at 'em by ten at the latest."

"I'll make it."

Sonny held up his watch. "That gives you thirteen hours." He glanced toward the redhead. "A hundred says she'll turn you down flat."

Cal started to shake his head.

Robert burst out with, "For pity's sake. Leave the woman alone. Your flings always mean trouble. I begged Claire to come along and keep the reins on you," he added bitterly, "but she wouldn't listen. She never listens. Her little brother walks on water."

Cal tensed, hot retort swallowed at the last minute.

Since he would do anything for Claire, and that included avoiding a quarrel with her husband, he made himself relax. "You know why she couldn't come, Robert. She had to be home to deal with Johanna's wedding."

Robert, stubborn man, acted like a dog with a bone. "Stay here. The last thing we need is the press digging up the *ménage a trois* with your last—"

"Yes, I know." *Fool. Don't let the pompous ass get to you.* "Don't worry about me."

"Someone needs to," Robert snapped. "You certainly don't."

"I can look after myself."

"Since when?"

Dammit to hell, he didn't need Robert of all people to dictate what he should or shouldn't do. If he decided to go over to the redhead's box, he'd go.

*Screw you, Robert!*

"Stop worrying," he said. The lady in question languidly fanned herself with a program. *Whoa. Sexy.* "I won't do anything to embarrass the family."

Sonny threw up his hands. "All I ask is that you be here for the brunch."

Robert muttered something under his breath.

Weariness enveloped Cal. Why shouldn't he do what everyone expected? One hook-up wouldn't spin the world off its axis. Why shouldn't he give Robert something else to carp about? "A hundred bucks. Right, Sonny? If she comes to the party after the play?"

"Uh-uh, not nearly enough, buddy." Sonny shook his head. "The whole nine yards or nothing."

Might as well light Robert's fuse. Cal yawned, straightened a diamond stud on his cuff. "I'll collect at brunch tomorrow."

Two pairs of eyes belonging to Miles de Graffen and his daughter fastened on his wrist.

Miles, an old family friend, had introduced Cal, as well as Lynette, to the joys of antique jewelry collecting. Both de Graffens openly envied Cal his studs because Miles's jewel assortment, though more voluminous, didn't include a set of legendary diamonds.

"Watch your Antoinette diamonds," Miles said. "I intend to have them one day. And there are women who—" he looked across the auditorium, "—wouldn't think twice about stealing them."

Lynette laughed. "Too true, Dad. I'm one of them."

Cal touched a glittering stone. "That's why I keep them away from you, sugar. Don't worry, Miles. I'm always careful with my good luck charms. But I promise you'll get first crack at them. If I ever decide to sell."

"I'll hold you to that."

The chorus finished its number. The house lights brightened.

As Cal left, Sonny called, "Remember the brunch. You can stay another day if she's worth it, but don't forget the brunch."

"Ten thirty, right? I'll remember."

Robert started in on his assistant. "He can't stay, Sonny. You'd have to be here to keep an eye on him and you know I can't spare you. You've got to get to Las Vegas tomorrow to do the groundwork for the new resort."

*Keep an eye on me.* Cal gritted his teeth but kept going. He hated confrontations as much as he hated lectures. Especially lectures from Robert.

He'd liked the serious student Claire brought home, the man putting himself through college by working as a mechanic. But one accounting degree and fifteen years later, Robert Winslow had turned into a prick. How could Claire stand him? No wonder resort managers were complaining about his high-handed tactics.

No matter. Robert was the Board's problem, not his. He had no say in running his family's corporation. His mother had seen to that long before her death.

In the lobby, Cal gave indolent waves or nods to familiar faces eager to catch his eye. Men stopped him to shake his hand or clap him on the shoulder while effusive women called his name before engulfing him in hugs and clouds of perfume. Despite pauses to respond and give sincere smiles in return, he didn't deviate from his destination.

Some of his popularity, he was smart enough to understand, was due to money. But people fascinated him. He genuinely enjoyed them. Claire insisted he ought to be in purchasing or public relations, but he knew his limitations.

Robert would be resentful if the black sheep tried to horn in on company affairs after all these years. And they couldn't afford to lose Robert. Claire's husband might have his faults, but he knew his stuff.

No, best to leave running the business to Robert and the Board. That gave Cal plenty of time to plan next month's vacation in Greece or schedule a business trip coinciding with a horse race in England.

Or relax in the company of a tantalizing redhead.

His attentions had piqued her curiosity. He grinned, thinking of her expression when he'd thrown her that kiss.

Yep, she was the type woman who could be persuaded, and he was the man to do it.

Damn his vow to leave all women, especially redheads, strictly alone. A little flirtation never hurt anybody.

At her door, he entered without knocking.

"This box is taken," she said. Her voice was husky and low. As enticing as her looks. "Oh!" The quick gasp conveyed recognition, surprise, and imperfectly concealed interest.

Mid- or late twenties. Her halter dress plunged down the "V" of her cleavage to where nipples nudged the thin black silk.

Sexy. Real sexy. The familiar need stirred.

"Don't you think I know it's taken?" When he stepped behind a chair at her left, a scent of oranges drifted by. "I've been watching you watching me all evening, sugar. I'd be ashamed, if I were you, flirting with me that way when I was trapped in my seat till intermission. You've got to stop ogling me."

"Ogling you?" Breasts mounded with a disbelieving gasp. "I wonder why you'd think that. If you'd bothered to look anywhere else in the building, you would certainly not be under the mistaken impression that I was ogling you."

"I couldn't possibly have looked anywhere else. I was too busy watching you." Uninvited, he sat down beside her. "You're the most beautiful woman I've ever seen."

The same old words he always said. He always meant them, too.

"You must not know many women, then. Go away." Red-tipped fingers tightened around a beaded evening bag. The diamonds at her throat—not very good ones, though the lighting might have accounted for the off-tint—couldn't hide the rapid pulse beating in one of the tiny hollows. Brows were delicate arches nearly hidden by red curls falling over her forehead. A dignified nose showed off a short upper lip that peaked delectably.

Made for kisses.

A pink tongue licked the peak. "I hate ugly scenes so don't make me call an usher to throw you out. I don't know you, and I don't want to talk to you."

Strange. Oranges were common, but on her their fragrance was intoxicating. "No, you don't know me, but if I leave, how'll we ever get to know each other? You'll enjoy talking to me. I promise."

Her complexion was the unblemished cream redheads sometimes possess. Her eyes, accentuated by green eyeshadow and fake fringes half an inch long, were large and emerald and abnormally bright.

Contact lenses, probably. Nearsighted with astigmatism? Maybe dull intellectually and ordinary conversationally, but irresistible physically. Packaged just the way he liked.

Cal moved closer. "I'll tell you who I am, and you tell me who you are. Then we can sit and talk. I'm Cal McIntyre. And you're . . . ?"

The corners of her mouth tried to curve upward. After a full five seconds, she giggled. Not a titter, a breathy gurgle. "I'm astonished."

"Hello, Astonished. How quaint. Is that an old family name?" He held out his hand. "How do you do?"

Ignoring his hand and execrable humor, she looked around for help. "I'll do much better when you're gone."

Good. Not a hint of annoyance or impatience. The sweet thing was curious. "I'll leave but not until you tell me your name. Come on, fair's fair. I told you mine."

"You've got a lot of gall. I'm calling someone to get rid of you." The infectious grin wouldn't be restrained, belying her words.

"Oh, I'll leave. I promise. If you tell me your name. Please. If you don't, I'll be up all night wondering. And how can I ask you to dinner if I don't know what to call you?"

"I wouldn't go to dinner with you. I wouldn't walk out of the theater with you. I don't like men who stare at a woman all evening and then burst in on her private box uninvited."

Said in the friendliest way imaginable.

Oh, yes, the lady was definitely interested.

He moved his chair a half inch toward hers. "If I promise not to stare any more, will you tell me your name?"

The delicious mouth tried its best to present a prim line. "You can call me Scarlet."

"As in O'Hara?" Mild derision couldn't be contained. "Is that what you are? A vain, opinionated, spoiled heroine?"

Her quick withdrawal made him backpedal. Stupid. Not playing the game lately had made him forget the rules. Scarlet apparently didn't care for blunt men.

The puppy dog look should cover his mistake. "Not that you're spoiled or opinionated. You're perfect."

His beseeching eyes didn't allay her suspicions. "Scarlet because of my hair." She held up a strand, revealing a long rhinestone earring, before drawing enchanting brows together. "You'd better go."

He loved gaudy dangling earrings. "I wasn't making fun of you, sugar. You didn't tell me the rest. Scarlet what?"

Two white teeth caught her bottom lip. "Scarlet . . . Smith."

Smith. Yeah, sure. No matter. That luscious mouth, the orange scent, her whole flamboyance made him want to sigh. Later. Afterward.

"Okay, Scarlet Smith. The Resort is having a small reception upstairs after the show for all the cast."

Her face lit up. "Will Jeanne Picarde be there?"

So she had a thing for New York divas. "Along with the others. Would you join us?"

She drooped. "I can't. I'm expected at home."

"Surely you don't have to answer to Mother."

"I don't have to answer to anybody!"

"Good. Tell whoever's expecting you that you'll be home later."

"I can't. I have a car scheduled to pick me up."

Sweet Scarlet could be persuaded. "I can tell you really want to go. Cancel your car. I'll take you home afterward."

The breathy laugh returned. "You're persistent. You make it seem easy." One hand pushed at the necklace, drawing attention to the swell of her breasts, the sketch of her nipples. When she moved, the silk whispered suggestively. "I *would* love to meet Jeanne Picarde. Her voice is amazing."

He knew what she was doing, but the flaunting of her body still worked. "Then come. Please. If you don't, you'll spoil my evening." Her shoulder where it curved into her neck invited a light caress. *No, don't spook her now.* "Call and tell them you won't be home tonight."

"That won't do."

A husband somewhere? Another messy scene for Robert to growl about?

Forget sanctimonious Robert.

"Then say you'll be a couple of hours late. I promise I'll take you home whenever you're ready."

Another enchanting gurgle came. "All right. I can call home. I'll come to your party, but I won't stay."

"Just long enough to meet the actors. I'll come for you when the play's over and take—"

"No. I'll meet you there. In the . . . Where did you say the reception would be?"

"Upstairs in the small ballroom. The Lady's Hall."

"I'll come up after I see my driver."

He pulled out a card. "Give this to the doorman so he'll let you in. I'll be waiting."

When she took his card, her fingers were careful not to touch his.

Maybe he should ask her over to his box.

No, better wait. She might still flee. Before he could make any headway, she'd have to trust him and that meant patience.

A good thing patience was one of his few virtues.

"Promise me you won't back out."

She shrugged. "I'll see what I can do."

When he caught her wrist, her pulse rippled beneath his fingers. "That's not good enough. Promise me you'll be there. I won't leave till you do."

"A promise under duress isn't much of a promise." Long lashes lowered.

He adored false eyelashes on a woman. Along with bright eyeshadow, low cut dresses, swinging earrings, and five-inch stilettos. All the female trappings condemned by his sisters and his mother as tawdry, he loved.

"You'll keep your word."

"Yes, I'll keep my word." She twisted her wrist away. "I want to meet Jeanne Picarde."

They took each other's measure for one long second before he left, breathing hard, despising his weakness.

He was too frigging susceptible to redheads.

After a cigarette, he entered his own box in time to seat himself before the lights dimmed and the music began. The others looked at him with amusement.

Except for Robert. Cal winked at his brother-in-law, making Robert's pout deepen. *Yeah, I am what I am, boss man. So lump it.*

Sonny, whose banter had brought a becoming blush to Lynette de Graffen's cheeks during her father's absence, asked, "I guess you got what you went after, huh?"

"We'll see."

She'd taken the bait. Hook, line and sinker.

The evening wouldn't be a total bust.

\* \* \* \*

WHAT HAD SHE hooked? A minnow or a shark?

Her skin tingling where Callaway McIntyre had held her wrist, Amanda stared resolutely at the stage.

What if Noelle was wrong? What if he wasn't the careless womanizer the paparazzi made him out to be? He'd shown an alarming quickness. If he realized what she . . .

Sick waves roiled her stomach. Her mouth dried.

He wasn't what she had expected.

Not at all what she had expected.

What had she let herself in for?

# CHAPTER TWO

WOULD SHE SHOW or not? Cal hung around the entrance to the Lady's Hall as melodies from a dance band covered the crush of animated people trying to get from the door to the bar, the bar to a table, a table to the dance floor.

"Cal, sweetie!" A woman in hot pink grabbed his arm. Her other hand held a glass of white wine. "This place is so-o-o fab. Everybody who didn't get an invitation will be livid."

A Texas heiress whose father had helped swing the land purchase for the new resort. What the hell was her name? It'd come, but for the moment: "Sugar!" He hugged her.

"Reeely big turnout." Her unprepossessing escort boasted a fringed leather dinner jacket with matching boots. He looked for a place to discard a wooden skewer that had held lobster. "Now who woulda thought about a theater troupe based in a hotel?"

"My sister. Claire's full of weird ideas. There's a table here for empty drinks and plates."

Thanks to his late mother's coaching, the couple thought they held his full attention. Lila McIntyre Lathen had been strict in bringing up her children. Though Claire and Johanna never disappointed her, Cal always did. But she had succeeded in beating manners into him. The heiress and her date never once suspected he was staking out the door.

He went on easily, "Claire felt guests who didn't want to go into Houston should have something to do besides drink. An acting troupe and dance company in the hotel seemed a perfect fit."

Sonny Kirkman appeared out of nowhere with a barely touched glass. "Of course Robert executed the idea. He dealt with the logistics and negotiated with both groups. Even had the original architectural plans changed to accommodate the stage."

*Yeah, after I rustled up enough votes to keep it in the plans.*

Claire's husband had adamantly opposed the theater, but Cal had roused himself long enough to ensure Claire's pet project would survive.

He said nothing, though, because Sonny was okay and as Robert's right-hand man, he was only doing his job, trying to put his boss in the best light. Loyalty was a rare commodity and should be encouraged.

As the dance floor filled, Cal nabbed champagne from a white-coated server and entered into the social niceties slicing the air like light from the flickering wall sconces. Two hundred selected guests decked out in party clothes milled, laughed and talked. Tables with ice sculptures and displays of fruits, veggies, cheese, sushi, paté, caviar, and the other usual finger delicacies lined one end of the room. Over the entire room hung the convivial bonhomie that marked the affair as a rousing success.

Cal mingled but didn't stray far from the entrance. He kept checking his watch.

Ten forty. Eleven o'clock. Nearly eleven thirty.

The play had been over for an hour and a half.

He'd hoped she would come but wasn't too disappointed that she didn't. Those were the breaks.

*Probably just as well. I can use an early night.* Her no-show ought to please Robert. Might as well give Sonny his money.

When he strolled toward where Sonny and Miles de Graffen stood, Sonny saw him and broke away. "Whatsa matter, buddy? Your girl not coming? Still time, but not much. Oh." His head swiveled.

The redhead walked in the door. A white satin cloak covered her dress, its feathered collar framing her face so that she looked like a flower.

The lights brightened, the music mellowed, the crowd livened.

No going to sleep right away tonight.

"Talk to you later, Sonny. Let's not plan on leaving for the brunch too early."

A white-toothed smile enhanced Sonny's good looks. "So long as you're dressed by ten twenty-five, dude. We're only entertaining the governor and one U.S. senator and three representatives along with the entire city council and mayor. Don't let my puny concerns spoil whatever plans you've made for tonight."

"I won't."

Sonny rolled his eyes. "Damn, you're so predictable. Bring on a slutty redhead and you forget everything but your pecker."

Cal made his way to the arched entrance where Scarlet surrendered her cloak to a doorman.

Her shoulders were as smooth as he remembered, but her figure was better. Average boobs, but a tiny waist and round hips a man could clutch.

From the top of her shining hair to the black stockings glimpsed under the slit of the clinging dress, she was perfect.

This was going to be a good night. For a few hours he could forget his deficiencies and satisfy someone.

When he came up, she was straightening the strap of a tiny evening bag hanging off one shoulder, the movement swishing the aroma of oranges toward him. "I kept my promise." Her voice was musical, sultry.

"I never doubted you would," he lied. "Come meet some of the people you saw on the stage. If you want to."

"Of course I want to. That's why I'm here, isn't it?"

She knew as well as he why she was here. This prelude was a required part of the game he could dispense with, but a part that women expected. He wouldn't disappoint Scarlet because he tried never to disappoint people.

Taking her elbow, they moved across the ballroom where couples swayed under light reflected from a thousand chandelier prisms. Citrus filled his nostrils, blotting out the odors of food and every other perfume. In front of mirrored panels, he stole champagne from a passing waiter and handed her a flute. "To us."

"Us?" Delicate brows arched. "There's no such thing."

"There will be." He lifted his glass to her and drained it.

Her own rim touched a mouth that didn't object to his certainty.

Thinking to impress her, he pointed out some dignitaries but drew no reaction. Was he amusing her? Boring her? Antagonizing her?

The de Graffens came up and were duly introduced. Patrice, brilliant with huge sapphires from her husband's jewelry assortment, murmured in accented English, "Scarlet? How American. I've heard mothers hope their children live up to their names. What do you suppose your mother had in mind for you?"

Scarlet didn't blink. "Running a sawmill. Patrice translates to Patsy in the south. What do you think your mother had in mind for you?"

Patrice stepped back, flushing. "There's someone we absolutely must see. Come, Miles."

"Yes, my love." Miles shrugged at Cal and followed.

Scarlet gazed after them. "She's a walking jewelry store."

"I suspect Miles married her so he could have a place to exhibit his collection."

"She makes a good backdrop. I thought she was his daughter."

"No, Patrice is not his daughter. But his daughter was in the box with us tonight."

"The girl over there? The cute one in yellow?"

He looked in time to see Lynette beam as Sonny Kirkman caught her up and whirled her onto the dance floor.

Sonny was too experienced for Lynette, but Miles had noticed and scowled after the dancing couple.

No need to worry about Lynette. Miles would take care of his daughter.

Good thing Scarlet wasn't a sheltered innocent.

As he introduced her to the singers he'd promised and several local officials he hadn't, he laid on the charm. Later, when he reached for more champagne, her hand covered his.

"We both need clear heads." She looked him straight in the eye, pulling him into green depths he was more than ready to experience. "Let's leave the bubbly for later."

So there would be a later. He set down the flute and took her hand, soft and warm, a sign of what was to come. "Whatever you say, Miss Scarlet."

When acquaintances stopped them, he held onto her. Across the room, Sonny had abandoned Lynette for Robert, and the two men looked at him and Scarlet. Cal maneuvered her in the opposite direction. He didn't need any interference from them, not when he and Scarlet were getting along so well.

He told her about a painting hung prominently in the ballroom before closer inspection revealed a knight's armor unfastened over a strategic area best left covered. "Unfortunately, an early open house for a Baptist youth group brought it to light."

She told him about a friend who was supposed to come to the opening with her, but fell down a spiral staircase and broke both legs. "So I had to come by myself."

Her pretty pout begged him to kiss it away. "I won't say I'm glad, but if he'd been with you, I'd never have met you."

"Did I say it was a he?" Lowered lashes didn't hide the gleam behind them. The sensuous black dress shifted and clung and sighed with each tiny movement.

How the hell could a dress look so demure and reveal so much? "For you to bring a woman friend would be a crime." As the orchestra began a slow number, he turned his back to someone vaguely familiar marching their way. "Dance?"

He didn't wait for an assent but pulled her close and moved into the forest of suits and tuxedos, silks and satins. She didn't resist. Against his chest, her breasts and hips beneath the fabric were supple and unbound.

Images of white skin and tangled red hair against his naked body clogged his throat.

The old craving surged.

He pushed his need against her, murmured into her hair, "I could dance this way the whole night, but I'd rather be alone with you."

"Alone?" The throaty voice hinted at moonlight and candles,

crisp-sheeted beds perfumed with orange. She tilted her head, amused, understanding, expecting what was to come.

Exactly like all the others.

Disgust threatened to sabotage the evening's sweet obliteration, but he pushed it aside. "Alone. I have a nice suite upstairs. Ten minutes away in a lovely glass cage with twinkling lights that floats us away to wonderland."

Her head bent back, her chin neared his.

Encouraging. "In the elevator, you can look out over the lake while we ride upstairs. My suite is quiet and peaceful. One whole wall is windowed so when we're in the dark, we can look out over the lights of Houston. They're beautiful. You have to come up and see for yourself."

The champagne made her eyes gleam.

"Please," he coaxed.

"Can you leave your guests?"

"They're not my guests. They're guests of the resort."

Lips pursed. Forehead creased. For one long second, while he held his breath, she considered. "All right."

Later, he'd be sorry. He'd think of her, if he thought of her at all, as one more liability to be shed with a minimum of money and publicity. Once again, he would wonder why he'd let his prick make him forget everything he knew about women like Scarlet.

But that would come afterward.

Now he wanted her, and he'd do whatever was necessary to get her. Maybe he'd be lucky. Maybe she'd get him through the dreariness of Johanna's wedding, till he could go back to his normal routine.

*My stale arid routine.*

Damn this funk. Tonight Scarlet would make him forget. "Shall we go?"

It was so easy for him.

\* \* \* \*

IT WAS SO EASY for her.

From experience, Amanda guessed his seduction wouldn't take long. But when he'd clasped her wrist and she'd felt that jolt of recognition, her confidence had plummeted.

And her conscience kept nagging. She hated feeling like a criminal, no matter how underhanded he'd been with poor Noelle.

If he'd been devious, callous, calculating, she wouldn't feel so bad. But he was engagingly frank about his intentions, delightful in his efforts to amuse her.

Then there was his sleepy-eyed smile, reminiscent of a mischievous boy. Disarming, hopeful, eager. Endearing.

*He's a womanizer, a cheat, a user. He deserves this.*

No need to suggest stopping for a bottle on the way to his suite. He plucked two glasses and a fifth of champagne from one of the serving trays as they left the ballroom, saying, "You wanted to wait till later for the bubbly."

"Yes, and this is later, isn't it?"

He flashed a grin, the one that was jaded, appraising, and almost contemptuous.

That grin disturbed her.

"It will be." Confidence oozed from him. He wore it like an entitlement and why not? He was a McIntyre, used to taking whatever he wanted.

After she collected her cloak, they went out on the best of terms. He was taller despite her heels so she had to tip her head back to see the chiseled cheekbones, the upturned nose, and the strong chin. An oblong mirror by the elevator reflected a striking, well-matched couple. No one would have guessed tonight marked their first meeting.

Waiting for the elevator, they talked about the play and its cast, but the game they played had nothing to do with the musical, and they both knew it. When he touched her back as they entered the elevator, she recognized the desire, naked and unabashed. For a terrible moment, her own appetite surged.

She should pull back, escape while she could.

*Crazy. You're crazy. He's only a man like every other man you've ever known.*

In the hushed suite, he moved faster than expected. Once he set down the bottle and glasses, he pulled her to him and found her mouth. Before she could pull away, his tongue slid over her lips, opened them, delved inside.

No time to think. She had to get control.

*Relax, relax. Keep him at arm's length.*

His tongue lingered over each tooth before he came up for air. "God, I've wanted to do that all night. You have no idea how much I've wanted to do that, sweet Scarlet."

"I'd never have guessed." She dropped her cloak and evening purse, and then wrapped her arms around his neck and a leg around his thigh, molding herself to him, feeling his muscles shift. His fingers touched her cheek, trailed lower till they skimmed the line of her neck to her breast. His lips followed, a beginning beard rough against her throat.

A familiar twinge tightened her most private place.

Time to retreat. Breathless, she used the flat of one hand to fend him off.

He wavered between irritation, doubt, wistfulness, and lust.

There was also anxiety, but since she was the manipulator, she understood. He'd taken her retreat as rejection. Time to use the secret face she'd put away years ago. An inviting smile, lips caressed by the tip of an unhurried tongue.

As a teenager, she had spent hours practicing the look that promised so much and guaranteed so little.

Because he didn't know the promises were empty, his taut body relaxed. "Would you care to see the bedroom?"

"Yes." Recovering from her misstep, she donned the dewy-eyed mask of passion. "I would love to see your bedroom."

Her agreement brought back his confidence.

Poor little gullible boy. *I can handle him.*

They walked together, arms around each other's waist.

The sitting room with its opulent Victorian furnishings and quantities of plush carpet made the barest impression on her. In the bedroom, all she saw was the large bed, its plum colored comforter overcast by a dim lamp dangling crystals and fringe. The wall behind it, covered with floor to ceiling mirror tiles, reflected the two of them as shadowy, dreamlike apparitions.

One of his hands steered her toward the bed, the other unbuttoned his coat.

Her stopping short brought out a frown. "I know you want me." *Make it plain now, while he's just exasperated, before he gets angry.* "But you have to do it my way, Callaway. Slow. I won't be rushed. We have all night, don't we?"

Her frankness dispelled the crease in the broad forehead.

"Sure, sweet Scarlet. I have as long as you want. All night, all week." His fingers caught her hair, sifted through it before he cupped the back of her neck. "We have all the time in the world to discover what turns you on, what turns me on."

The hazy light softened his features so he looked young and trusting. Even his mouth looked innocent.

She wanted to touch it with her fingers, taste it with her tongue.

*He's a man. Like any other man. You're off men, remember?*

"Good. So we'll go slow."

"We'll go slow." He pulled her to him again. His hands clasped her hips and pressed her against his sex, kneading her as if he would pierce through clothing and take her right there. When his fingers worked their way up, sliding into the top of her dress to search for a breast, she moved away.

"Don't rush me." There was no need to pretend breathlessness. "You agreed."

He took off his coat, laughing, sure of himself and her, but pleasant, always pleasant. "All right, pretty lady. Do you want a cigarette to slow things down? Do you smoke?"

"Yeah, let's have a cigarette. And where's the champagne? I thought you were going to toast me in champagne." Knowing full well he'd left the bottle in the other room, she pretended to look around.

When he started toward the door, her hand caught his cummerbund and tugged suggestively. "Stay here. I'll get it." Along with something that would put an end to his casual devastation of her body. "Take off your clothes, turn down the bed, and light me that cigarette."

"Yes'm, Miss Scahlet!" he said with an exaggerated drawl and unexaggerated alacrity. "Ah'm yo-ahs to command."

She felt his eyes on her as she went into the sitting room.

\* \* \* \*

HE COULD TELL she knew he was watching her. The sassy swing of her butt gave her away.

Damn, she was something. Clever, too, at least about man-woman things. She had understood his unspoken meanings, voiced her approval. Maybe there was more to her than he suspected.

Nope, he was wishing again.

Undoing his tie, he went into the dressing area where he took out both cuff diamonds and the four smaller shirt studs, all made from a necklace Marie Antoinette never purchased.

His Antoinette diamonds. Priceless.

In London, an impoverished peer who knew he collected antique jewelry had approached him.

The man was dying and wanted to give them to someone who would care for their history; someone who could pay. A ledger over two centuries old supposedly proved the studs came from the infamous necklace that some historians claimed led to the unfortunate queen's beheading.

True or not, the peer had spun a fascinating tale, and the studs, once acquired, had brought Cal good luck. After winning at roulette and blackjack more often than not while wearing them, he used them for a talisman.

Tonight all six studs went into their leather case before he opened the electronic safe in the wall.

It contained only two other items, one a book and the other a ring purchased that afternoon from a frantic woman sent by Miles de Graffen.

"I know you don't share my prejudice against emeralds," Miles had said in his aristocratic way, "and this would make a nice addition to your collection. The ring's late Victorian, with a rather unusual cut and setting. Pretty little bauble. She's desperate to sell. You can get it for a song."

Cal had never been as serious a collector as his mentor, and the ring wasn't particularly attractive.

But he, softhearted chump, could never withstand a tearful woman. Not only did he buy the ring, he'd overpaid.

No matter.

His father had left him plenty of money, and the weeping blonde had needed some for her sick child. Content with his good deed, he pushed the emerald aside before placing the leather stud case on top of the book.

His mother's journal.

When they'd found out it existed, Claire had already begged off the Houston opening. A change in her plans would have made Robert suspicious.

So Cal had volunteered to retrieve the journal. He adored his sister, and there was little enough he did for her.

Usually it was the other way around.

His fingertip slid down the spine of the journal and its betraying pages.

They'd destroy it, but first Claire wanted to read Lila's innermost thoughts about that crazy year in Italy herself.

He'd scanned it himself, been surprised that his mother would admit herself so vulnerable. Claire would be, too. Lila had always been in control. Of herself, of her family, and of the business once she took the reins.

While his sister didn't often ask for his help, occasionally he could be of use.

Humming, he patted the book, closed the safe and locked it up. Then he emptied his pockets, turned off his cell, and stripped to his boxers. Full frontal probably wouldn't scare Scarlet but . . .

Condoms. He rummaged in his shaving kit.

In the bedroom, he folded back the bedcovers. No sound from the next room.

The redhead was taking her time. A little late to pretend modesty, wasn't it?

Perhaps her game called for force. Some women went for the rape scenario. Rough sex wasn't much to his taste, but he'd give

Scarlet whatever she asked for. Obliging women was one of his other few talents.

Twelve thirty.

He'd forgotten to remove his watch but no matter. He would light cigarettes to give her another minute before enticing her to bed.

* * * *

AMANDA FUMBLED AS she pressed the lid on the small ibuprofen bottle and replaced it inside her beaded evening bag. A pill that was not a pain reliever had already disappeared into one of the filled flutes.

Better hurry. He would wonder what was taking so long.

According to her research, a couple of glasses of champagne before taking the drug shouldn't be life-threatening. It might even hasten the effects.

*I hope Noelle got me the right stuff.* She must have. Edward was a pharmacist. She couldn't help but soak up something from him in three years of marriage. Besides, the pill looked like the one on the Internet.

As she picked up the flutes, her hands shook, but by the time she reached the bedroom, they were steady.

The lamp revealed him waiting, stripped down to boxers and lounging against a stack of pillows. A few dark hairs littered the tanned chest and muscular legs. His eyes gleamed through slitted eyelids.

Her stomach lurched. Her mouth dried out.

He patted the sheet beside him. "Do you intend to join the party in all your clothes? You're a trifle overdressed."

"I like this dress." She walked toward him, swaying her hips, activating the sultry smile. "Don't you?"

"Take it off and I'll tell you."

Two cigarettes glowed red. She noted them with the same detachment as she noted the bulge in his boxers.

He didn't miss her glance. "Yes, he's excited. But I think I can control him long enough so he can do his job."

He drew on one of the cigarettes before laying both in the ashtray. Then, while smoke escaped from his mouth and nostrils in a sinister manner at odds with his engaging frankness and mischievous smile, he put out his hand for a champagne flute. "If not, I promise I'll make him keep trying."

For a split second, her mind left her.

Which glass had the pill? The one on the right. *Yes, this one.*

She gave it to him. "I think we should drink to us first."

With one hand he took the flute and pulled her down beside him with his other. "Miss Scarlet," he drawled, "Ah'd purely love to drink to us."

Her hip nestled against his waist. She held her champagne in one hand and put the other on his chest for balance.

Heat shot through her fingertips. All the secret places burst to life.

Glasses touched, tinkled. When he caressed her shoulder, so near his breath warmed her arm, her chest constricted. "To us."

"To us." As in the ballroom earlier, he drained his glass.

Noelle had told her about the way he tossed back alcohol, persuaded her the disconcerting habit would make things easier.

Amanda's sister might be handicapped in understanding the big picture, but she had an uncanny ability to pick up on details that normally didn't matter.

This one did.

Bent on seduction, Callaway noticed nothing.

Amanda drained her champagne, too. She needed it.

When he reached across to set his empty flute on the nightstand, his arm brushed her silk-covered breasts. "I lit you a cigarette. Want it?"

"Sure. Give me a minute." Setting her glass down beside his, she took two small packets from her evening bag and tossed them onto the sheet.

His hand with a cigarette paused. "A modern female."

"I like to be prepared."

"Ummmm," he purred. "I like a woman who's prepared. A woman who's prepared is a wise woman."

"Most people would call her something, but I doubt it would be wise."

After the first moment of surprise, he laughed, really laughed. He threw back his head and roared.

She waited for him to sober. "It wasn't that funny."

"No?" He put the cigarette in his mouth and leaned over. Again his arm nudged her breasts while he opened a drawer of the nightstand. "I have my own, you see." He dropped several packets beside her two. "I also believe in being prepared. Whose shall we use?"

"Neither right now. Is this my cigarette?" Inhaling didn't make her dizzy, but his hip pushing at hers did.

She shouldn't be here, taking part in this farce. Why hadn't she told Noelle no?

Right. And let Noelle's marriage and little Teddy's family

disintegrate. Besides, nothing was going to happen with Callaway McIntyre. In a few minutes, he'd be asleep and she could get Noelle's ring and never see him again.

Maybe he'd think the flush in her face was from sexual tumult. Partly true.

But he wasn't looking at her face. Settled back against the stacked pillows, he studied her bare shoulder. The cigarette dangled from his mouth as his hand stroked her skin. "This will be an evening we'll never forget."

Her smoke rings rose, perfect circles reminding her of college, when she'd been young and frivolous before . . . "Not for a long, long time."

"Never." He shifted his attention to her mouth. "Have we talked enough? Or are you one of those tedious women who want to dredge up every childhood memory before doing it?"

His eyes on her lips made her nervous. "Yes to your first question." Every word she spoke would be remembered later, analyzed and dissected for clues as to her identity. "No to the second. I won't tell you my history if you won't tell me yours."

Reaching over, he put out his cigarette. "Come here." He grabbed her forearm and turned her toward him. A muscle twitched in his jaw. "You're driving me crazy. This is worse than when I tried to climb up on the refrigerator to get to the cookies when I was four years old."

Taking her time, she crushed her own cigarette in the ashtray. A few more minutes and the drug would work. A shame she hadn't encouraged him to talk. "Did you get them?"

"No. I fell off. Got five stitches in my chin." He grew impatient and pulled her down on him where his lips found hers, claimed them, and threw her into headlong confusion. Noelle's diamonds lay against her collarbone, prickly and heavy, and her lungs fought to breathe. Her breasts strained against him.

What was wrong? Why did a kiss bring on such turmoil?

Because it had been so long since she'd kissed a man. *And he is a man.* She repeated her mantra as she felt her will slipping away. *I'm in control. He's just a man.*

Then he shifted her so she sat on top of him. He rolled the bodice down to her waist and exposed her to his hands.

Panicked, she rescued her gown and covered her breasts.

He laughed, holding her, keeping her on top. "Fair's fair," he mocked, rubbing her nipples under the silk. "I'm undressed. I want you undressed, too."

"You're going too fast." Her voice wasn't under control. It

sounded husky, sex-drugged. Her dress was hiked up to her waist, only her panties and his boxers protecting her from penetration. She couldn't keep from cradling him. "You said you'd be slow."

"I'll be slow, I just want to look." He turned persuasive. "That's all I'll do. I promise I won't do anything but look at you until you say I can. Let me see you. Please."

With no small effort, she forced herself to perch docilely astride him as he drew down the top of her dress again. The cool air made her nipples bud, but his heat rose to envelop her.

Too much stimulus for someone who led a nun's life.

His breaths lengthened, either from the drug or his desire.

Her desire. Her breaths lengthened, too, until she was giddy from oxygen that sent her heart drumming in her ears like too much bass. The fire of his sex met hers, kindled when she rubbed against him. How long since she'd given in to this mindless frenzy?

"See?" he murmured. "That wasn't difficult, was it? Notice I'm not touching anything vital."

"No," she panted. "It wasn't difficult at all."

His eyes, wide-awake, locked with hers. "You're making me crazy, did you know that?"

Not as crazy as he was making her. "Maybe you were crazy to start with."

"No. You're doing it. I'm still not touching anything."

But he was. She was acutely aware of her thighs around his waist and his solid chest under her hands, of his hard length against her center. It wouldn't hurt to move, grind against him. Just for a . . .

*No, you're going too far.*

He lay back, plainly aroused but on alert like a dog waiting for his master's command. Unlike her, wrestling with her lust.

*Get hold of yourself.*

He should be unconscious at any time. She could contain herself long enough for the drug to work. Of course, she could. But did she want to?

His watch band snagged in the tatting as he worked with her dress.

*He's looking at the label.*

Oh dear God, the label!

The tatted border and embroidered A. Jane, Atlanta were too distinctive. A minute with sharp scissors could have seen the label cut out, but she hadn't planned on going this far. Now there was no withstanding his scent, his touch. It was too late.

Too late for everything.

Did it matter? What would it hurt to give in? One time . . .

Before she could throw caution to the winds, he let out an impatient sound and freed his watch from the tatting. In one swift motion, he pushed the silken bodice down past her navel.

When he ran one hand down over her hip, the other caressed the curve of her breast.

"I can't stand this." His whisper was provocative.

Her hands stopped his. "It's too fast." Was that hoarse voice hers? "I don't, I need . . . You need to slow down." No, he didn't need to do anything of the kind.

She needed him in her. Now.

"I know what you want." His thumb traced her navel's circle, wandered down, down, inside her panties.

Down through the curls.

The place bloomed under his thumb, drawing a moan.

"I'll make sure you get there, sweet Scarlet. I won't leave you hanging, I promise."

"Stop it." Somehow she found the strength to slap at his hand, stop the circling thumb. "We need something before we go any further."

"Ah, protection. I'd forgotten. You did that to me." He gave a long shuddering sigh. The little boy's smile spread with delicious slowness. "We'll take care of that right now. Mine or yours?"

"What about another cigarette first?"

"I think, if it's all the same to you, I'll skip the cigarette, and no, I don't want more champagne either," he said gravely though his eyes began to dance. A dimple, unsuspected before now, broke out into the open. "Thank you just the same, but the only thing I want is for you to pick up a condom and put it on me. Or are you too shy? Should I do it myself?"

"Now? I don't want to rush it, Callaway."

"We won't rush." As he spoke, a small yawn escaped. "But we can't put it off all night either."

His guard dropped, revealing complacency and something else.

He was a user who saw her only as an object to be possessed and discarded.

Desire fled even as she moved closer and pushed her breasts against his face. "Let's make this night special."

"It's already special." The light in his eyes had faded so the brown irises were opaque. "You made it special the moment I saw you at the play." He yawned again.

He'd soon be out.

*I'm not sorry. I'm not.*

"Lie back," she whispered, stretching and letting her length cover him and force him down into the pillows. Cheek against cheek, breasts against chest, stomach against stomach, sex against sex. "Close your eyes and think of me."

"I am thinking of you." A drowsy arm tightened around her. "I thought . . . all night . . . you make me . . . I'm lightheaded . . ."

"Lie here and imagine what we'll do together." Her hand reached up to cover his eyes. "Close your eyes and think about what you're going to do to me, what I'll do to you."

"I want . . ." He gave a heavy sigh, his mouth twitched. "I can't think . . . Something isn't . . . something's wrong." His eyelids fluttered. His eyes were trusting and uncomprehending. "You . . ."

For one terrible moment before the drug took him, his credulity stabbed her. She should never have let Noelle talk her into coming here like some despicable hustler.

His arm relaxed as his breathing became slow, steady. The long lashes rested dark against his cheek.

Defenseless as a sleeping child, he lay.

Beneath her ear his heartbeat remained strong and regular. Her head relaxed on his chest, allowing her time to stamp down the passion, calm her thudding heart. Noelle and Teddy were all that mattered.

Callaway McIntyre had brought this on himself when he took advantage of Noelle.

"Sorry, Callaway," she muttered as she slid out from under his arm and got up. "It's dangerous picking up strange women. A big boy like you should have learned that long ago. You're lucky I'm not a thief or worse."

After settling him into a comfortable position—he really did look like a little boy with his upturned nose and soft mouth and tousled hair—she tucked the covers beneath his chin. The packets on the night stand, hers and his jumbled together, went into her purse.

What else? Wipe the flute glasses along with the champagne bottle and whatever else she'd touched so as not to leave anything incriminating. Her fingerprints weren't on record, and please God, they never would be.

In his bathroom, she dressed before punching in the numbers Noelle had given her. Holding her breath, she tried the handle.

The safe opened.

Hah. So stupid to talk about the combination in front of people. Callaway McIntyre should be smarter, but then a smart person wouldn't have trusted a stranger.

He hadn't loaned Noelle's ring out, thank goodness. It lay to the side by itself, waiting to be slipped on her finger.

Wiping down the locked safe took only a moment. Going back through the bedroom, she avoided looking at the unconscious man while checking one last time for anything overlooked. He was still breathing easily so she grabbed her cloak and evening bag from the living room, and fled.

Only when her driver dropped her at the airport did the tension dissolve. It was over. She'd never see Callaway McIntyre again.

So why did she feel like a criminal?

# CHAPTER THREE

*WHAT'S THAT NOISE?* After a while Cal realized that it came from a telephone. He opened his eyes only to squinch them against brilliant light peeking through cracks in the heavy draperies.

The ringing continued.

*This aching head.*

He groped for the receiver by the bed, managing a grunt.

Sonny Kirkman's cheery voice assaulted him. "Rise and shine. It's ten o'clock. Our meeting's in half an hour."

Cal groaned.

What the hell had he done to deserve this mother of all hangovers? His head felt as if an ax were striking between the eyes and coming out through the crown.

"Cal?" Sonny sounded suspicious. "Are you awake?"

"Yeah." He somehow got the words out through his mouthful of cotton. "I'm awake. Be right there." The phone didn't want to fit back on its cradle, but it finally settled.

A hungover head had never been this bad before, not even when he was a freshman in college.

The woman.

He turned to check the other half of the bed, but the tiny movement caused his head to explode again. Everything blurred.

Finally, the pain subsided enough to see she was gone. All he could remember was her hair, a thick red cloud tumbling over creamy white shoulders.

What the hell had happened? Could he have passed out before the big event? Had she left in disgust? No, he hadn't drunk that much. He distinctly remembered bringing her up here.

She showed no reluctance about entering the bedroom, drinking champagne, and kissing him.

Now everything was coming back.

They'd made it as far as the bed. The pillows were cool against his back, her gown silky under his fingers.

Lying on his back with her straddling him, he'd fondled breasts that were smaller than he'd expected but round and perfect in his hands.

She'd played shy before letting him caress her, kiss her. Cupped by her spread legs, he'd wanted to tear into her, but . . .

What had happened? He'd been excited one moment but then had to struggle to keep from yawning while listening to her whisper stuff about . . .

What?

Her breath had been warm, tickling his ear. When she'd pressed his eyelids closed, he'd . . .

He sat up cursing.

Which was a mistake.

Not only did he feel like a colossal sledgehammer had slammed the top of his head, but the worst nausea he'd experienced in his entire thirty-five years attacked.

Gritting his teeth, he made it to the bathroom before throwing up. Once he was able to wash his face and rinse his mouth, he staggered out to check his wallet.

About five hundred dollars was gone.

A common thief. He should have known.

Damn the conniving tramp and damn him for being so gullible. He should have put the wallet in the safe. His head pounded.

Damn this frigging head. He'd have to scrounge up some ibuprofen. Staggering back to the bathroom, he raided his shaving kit and found two tablets he managed to keep down.

What about the safe? No, it was all right. A girl he'd met one time might find the hidden safe in the dressing room closet, but she wouldn't know the combination. Still . . .

He punched in the numbers: the date of his mother's graduation from Agnes Scott.

The door swung open.

The emptiness hit him like a blow in the stomach.

He forgot the nausea and the headache. Blood rushed from his brain and left him so dizzy he fell against the wall.

When he could stand unaided, he reached inside the safe for physical confirmation of what his eyes relayed.

Not only was the case containing his lucky studs missing, but so was the journal he'd picked up the day before.

The emerald ring was gone, too, but that was nothing. The bauble wasn't worth half what he'd given Blondie for her sick baby.

No, only his studs mattered and more than the studs, his mother's journal.

He and Claire hadn't known it existed until the past week. Lila's trusted secretary had died in her retirement home near Houston, and in sorting her things, her daughter had come across Lila's journal from twenty-three years earlier and wondered if the McIntyres would like to have it.

Would they ever. There was no telling what intimate family secrets it might—and did—contain.

Claire had delegated Cal, already scheduled for the Grand Tartan opening, to pick it up.

Which he'd done. Except now it was gone, along with the pages revealing all the details of Lila's rushed marriage to Tip.

He cursed for several minutes.

Why the hell had he been so willing to shoulder the responsibility? Everything he really wanted always fell apart when he went after it. He knew that. God, he knew that.

He should have destroyed the pages when he had the chance. Now the redhead could be reading them, could have read them while he slept.

Still in last night's boxers, he went through the suite he shared with Sonny. Robert always made Sonny babysit him, but Cal was okay with it because Sonny was easy to get along with.

When he knocked at the other bedroom door, there was no answer.

He opened it to a neatly packed and closed overnight bag on the unmade bed.

How like Sonny. Efficient and punctual in his business persona, discriminating in his sex life. Everything that Cal was not.

Sonny would never cause a scandal by drinking too much or losing his temper and decking his rival. Sonny would never let some two-bit whore take him for a ride. Not Sonny.

Padding back through the suite, anger growing every second, Cal found Mr. Perfection seated on a sheltered outside patio with cigarette and coffee. Dressed in gray slacks and white shirt, Sonny leaned over an open newspaper spread on the table. A navy blazer hung on the back of his chair.

Robert's aide was showered, shaved, and dressed. Clear-eyed and ready for the morning ceremonies, Mr. Perfection reviewed news reports from last night's gala so as not to waste time while he waited for Cal.

Frigging paragon.

*Don't be so damned petty. You're just jealous because he's good at his job.*

Cal stepped out.

Sonny saw him and crackled his paper before glancing toward the deserted pool below. "Shit. Don't you effing believe in clothes? All we need is some photographer snapping a picture of you in your skivvies."

"When time did you get in last night?"

Sonny blinked. "What time did I get in? To Houston? About six, I guess. In time for the show. Why?"

"Not to Houston. What time did you get to bed?"

Sonny blinked again.

A handsome man about Cal's age, he had a debonair air rivaling the movies' James Bonds. Women liked Sonny, and Sonny liked women. Though he sometimes juggled two or three, he was always discreet.

A lot different from Cal and his messy affairs.

Now Sonny smirked. "Bed? Checking up on me, Papa? I'd think you'd be the one to do the explaining. We're having guests for brunch this morning, remember?" He blew smoke toward Cal.

"Was the girl gone when you came in?"

"Girl? Gone?" Sonny shifted a blank gaze behind where Cal stood as if expecting to see someone there. "The redhead? She didn't stay all night? Whassamatter, buddy? Losing your touch? Don't tell me I made an easy Benjamin after all."

Cal clenched and unclenched his hands. "When did you get to bed, dammit."

"Hey, don't get your skivvies in a wad. It was about two thirty, maybe three. Robert and the de Graffens wanted to go down to the pub. I figured I'd give you time to do your thing and get off to dreamland. What's wrong?"

"The bitch made off with my studs."

"Your Antoinette diamonds? You're kidding." Sonny pursed his lips in a soundless whistle. "The redhead?"

At Cal's furious assent, he gawked. "I'll be damned," he said at last. "She didn't look the type to me, Cal. I swear she didn't. How did she open your safe?"

"It doesn't matter how. I've got to find her."

Sonny got up. "Of course, of course. The publicity will be awful, but we'll get the police in right away."

"No police!" He couldn't let the contents of his mother's journal be laid open to every two-bit tabloid reporter.

Sonny gaped. "No police? But what . . . ?"

Cal ground his teeth. *Damn this splitting head.* "It's bad enough to be made a fool of without having the whole world know. Use hotel security and if they can't turn up anything on her, hire detectives. But keep it quiet, Sonny. No police."

"Sure. I understand." Sonny closed his mouth, obviously not understanding at all. "No police. Keep it quiet. Okay, if that's what you want."

Should he confide in Sonny? No, Lila's journal was his and Claire's business. No need to bring more people than necessary into this, at least not until he'd talked with his sister. "Yes, keep it quiet."

As Sonny whisked away to set things in motion, Cal forced himself to think.

The redhead had not only known exactly where to look for the valuables, but she must have known the combination. How the devil had she got it? Or could she be a safecracker?

That seemed pretty far-fetched, but it would be one explanation. She couldn't know that his family always programmed the same combination into all the safes they used so anything inside would be available in case of a business emergency.

Unless he'd told her the combination himself under the influence of whatever it was she'd used on him. Would he? He didn't think so, but he couldn't remember.

Damn, why couldn't he remember? Groaning, he sat down and dropped his head into his hands.

He'd been a fool, taken in by the oldest trick in the book. He'd let the pretty face and voluptuous body turn him on.

But this was worse than marrying some twit who cost the earth to get rid of or getting arrested for loitering while intoxicated. This was even worse than when the psycho football player coerced him into a fistfight at a crowded charity function and beat the shit out of him.

He cursed softly and vehemently. "I'll kill her with my bare hands. I'll grab that mane of red hair and yank it till she screams bloody murder. I'll take that pretty little neck and wring it till it breaks."

He wouldn't rest until he found her.

* * * *

SHE WAS ALMOST home where she could finally rest.

About the time Cal woke up in Houston, Amanda Jane got off the bus shuttling her to a park-and-fly lot near the Atlanta airport. In blue jeans, dyed red hair hidden by a brown wig and gray eyes covered by sunglasses, the woman who threw her carryon into the back of the small sedan was a far cry from the temptress of the night before.

As she started her car, she sighed. Part of the sigh was for what she'd done and part for relief that it was over. But the biggest part was for the truth she had discovered about herself.

The old urges hadn't been vanquished. They still lay dormant. Twelve years she'd fought to eradicate the impulses that had led to Tommy's death but she'd failed. They'd emerged at the most inconvenient time to crow in triumph over her weakness.

If only Callaway McIntyre hadn't been so ingenuous.

From Noelle's description, Amanda had expected a spoiled, callous sophisticate. At the least, he should have looked jaded. But his unexpected small boy's smile had breached her detachment to let her in for that roller coaster ride of emotions she'd vowed never to climb on again.

Her impulses may have been contained, but at what cost?

On the expressway leading to her home and shop near Lenox Square, the past night played over and over in her head.

She was contemptible, not only for deceiving him but for allowing—no, encouraging—him to reawaken the unwanted sexuality inside her body. There should have been another way to help Noelle.

Wallowing in guilt, she was nearly home before noticing the smoke curling from the hood of her car.

Her heart sank. What now?

Maybe she could nurse the car a few more blocks.

No, it was getting denser. Better not try it. Ignoring angry horns, she pulled across two lanes of traffic into a strip mall at the side of the road and turned off the key.

At least it had happened near enough home for her to walk the rest of the way and call a tow truck. Grabbing her purse, she got her bag from the back seat.

Not twenty feet from her car, a tremendous whoosh erupted behind her. Heat lashed out. The force hit her so hard she stumbled and fell to one knee.

When she clambered up, she looked back in disbelief.

Her car was engulfed in flames.

"My car!"

People gathered to join her in watching the car burn.

"I got 911," said an old woman, snapping her cell closed. "They on they way. That yo' car, lady?"

"Yes," Amanda said faintly. "My car is burning up."

"No shit," a scrawny African-American guy with earring and tattoos said. "Wha' happened?"

"I don't know. I pulled over because there was smoke coming up and after I got out, it exploded."

"Some fire," a Hispanic woman in spandex and tee said. "Lucky you got out."

A police car pulled up, blue lights flashing. Amanda's shoulders, drooping with fatigue and maybe shame from her charade of the past evening, needed squaring before she could go over and claim ownership.

The registration was in the dash of the fiery car, but she dug out an insurance card from her purse with a vehicle ID the policeman could run through his computer and prove the car was hers. After she got everything sorted out, which took far too long, the police officer didn't offer her a ride home.

She felt safe, walking the three tree-lined blocks of the Lenox area in broad daylight, but the weather was warm and her legs trembled from the unexpected fire.

By the time she reached the old house that was her home as well as her place of business, she was cross, sweaty and happy to see the modest sign by the driveway that said A. Jane, Dressmaker.

Plodding through budding azaleas and monkey grass lining the flagstone path to the basement, she rang the bell three times to let Noelle know who it was, and then used her key. The cool tranquility of her apartment greeted her, soothed her. Every muscle in her body relaxed.

Pulling off her wig, she put her purse on the entry console and dropped the carryon bag onto the parquet hall floor.

How wonderful to be home safe and sound.

Well, safe and sound except for her car being totaled.

"Manda, is that you?" Noelle Parham, hair mussed but fully dressed in leggings and oversized tunic, rushed out from the back. One cheek had lines in it from where she'd been asleep on a pillow crease. In a childish gesture, she brushed back a blonde strand from one eye.

To Amanda, Noelle would always be nine years old, bewildered and scared after their mother abandoned the family. Because of an emotional disability, Noelle was the little sister who had to be looked after and kept out of trouble. Their father had been alive then, but it was still Amanda who'd dealt with the teachers, doctors and other people necessary to keep Noelle on track.

When Edward Parham had asked Noelle to marry him three years earlier, Amanda had explained about Noelle's borderline personality disorder. He'd assured her he was prepared to assume responsibility for Noelle and had promised to look after her.

Amanda was thankful. And relieved Noelle had someone else to depend on.

After the wedding she had tried, not always successfully, to work herself to the periphery of her sister's new life.

Then last week Noelle had showed up.

Edward had warned her to curb her gambling habits, but she'd taken one last trip to Las Vegas and lost her engagement ring that had belonged to Edward's grandmother.

Begging for help, she'd expected Amanda to fix everything.

Amanda had wanted to turn her sister away but couldn't. Though twenty-four and a mother for nearly a year, Noelle was mentally a child. So Amanda had agreed and now . . .

"Did it go all right?" Noelle sounded half-fearful, half-eager.

"I got it."

Noelle screamed and fell on Amanda's neck. "I knew I could count on you. I've been on pins and needles since I got here last night. Manda, if Edward ever found out, he'd divorce me. I know he would." She frowned. "It's not a pretty ring, either. It's clunky and ugly."

"Here, take it." A bit of green flashed in the light as the emerald ring changed hands.

Noelle clasped her engagement ring to her heart. "Oh, thank you, thank you, thank you! I don't know what I would have done."

A blonde, courtesy of her beautician, Noelle had delicate features that conformed to the classical notion of beauty. Despite the straight nose and pretty lips, though, Noelle managed to look like hundreds of other women.

She'd never learned the knack of making herself unforgettable.

Not that she needed to. Being unforgettable only led to tragedy. Noelle had enough problems.

"How can I ever repay you?" In the small hallway beside Amanda, Noelle surveyed the ring on her finger the way a child might admire a new toy.

Time to be brutal. "You can start by never doing anything like this again."

Noelle looked up with stricken eyes. "But, Manda, I didn't mean to bet my ring. I just got caught up when I went to that casino with Em and Stef. They said if I let him loan me his chips for it, I could always buy it back. And I tried. I went to the ATM right away, but he was so horrible. He wouldn't even talk about giving it back. He wanted it for his jewelry collection. And I didn't know what to do." Her face clouded. "Em and Stef weren't very good friends, I guess."

"No, honey, they weren't. I keep telling you, be picky about your friends. You've got to choose people you can count on."

"I thought I could count on them."

"Well, this proves you can't. You need to stop hanging out with them. And you mustn't ever bet that ring again."

"Oh, I won't, believe me. Cal McIntyre was so . . . You should have been there. He wasn't nice. Not at all." Noelle's bottom lip poked out, trembling. "He's a hateful person."

As always, Amanda soothed her. "It's over, honey, but you can't keep doing this kind of stuff. You're going to have to think. And what about Edward and Teddy? You shouldn't go off all the time and leave them. You could end up losing both of them."

The blue eyes widened. "Losing them? I know I shouldn't have gambled but . . . You think because I go away with my friends for a few days, it makes Edward mad?"

"I think Edward gets lonely without you."

Noelle chewed on her lip. "I'm sorry, Manda, I won't do it again. Not if you think I shouldn't."

"Good." Amanda stroked her sister's hair. Noelle would never understand what she'd done wrong.

Dear God, she was tired of looking out for Noelle. Until this moment, she hadn't realized how tired she was. "Go on home, honey," she went on. "It's time for me to stop babying you and for you to start being a mother. You have to settle down and stop doing things like this."

Tears glistened. "I'm sorry I'm so stupid, Manda."

Amanda took her sister's hands. "You're not stupid. You're not. You just don't think. It didn't matter before, but now you have a husband and an adorable baby. You're going to have to quit doing stuff like using your engagement ring for collateral."

Noelle mumbled, "I know. But nobody thought Cal McIntyre would be mean enough not to give me the ring back. I got the money to pay him back with, didn't I?"

Why couldn't Noelle understand? Amanda wanted to shake her. "You shouldn't have been gambling to begin with. Then you wouldn't have had to borrow money on the ring."

"I wasn't going to. But Em and Stef invited me. They've been so good, getting me in the junior league and the country club and everything. I thought it was okay."

"Just because people are nice to you doesn't mean they're doing the right things for you," Amanda said. "We've talked about this before. You have to be the one to decide what's right for you, not let other people talk you into doing things you know are wrong."

Like she followed her own advice.

Noelle hung her head. "I'll try, Manda. Really. I'll do better."

She dragged into the bedroom and came out with her overnight case.

"I guess I'll go on. Edward's expecting me back today. I don't want him to think I've left him." Her mouth twitched, wanting to smile at such an absurd notion.

Amanda, thinking about Callaway McIntyre, tried to smile back.

*I'm drained. Worrying about Noelle takes so much time and effort that there's nothing left for me. If I'd gone out to a dinner or movie with some of the men who've been interested, Callaway McIntyre's body wouldn't have turned me on the way it did.*

"No, you don't want Edward to worry about you," she said. "Kiss little Teddy for me."

Noelle paused on the threshold. "I will. And thank you again. I don't know what I'd have done without you."

Amanda went over and hugged her. "You did fine, honey," she said. "I'm still amazed you thought of such a complicated plan to get your ring back."

Noelle glowed at the questionable praise. "I just thought you could charm him out of the ring. The boys always used to fall all over themselves to please you."

And a pair of trusting brown eyes would plague her forever.

"But then you got those pills from Edward." Amanda frowned. "And remembered the safe code. After meeting Callaway McIntyre, I'm surprised he boasted about the combination."

Noelle looked uneasy. "Yeah, well, anyway, it worked. I can go home now." She kissed her sister and left.

What was that about? Noelle got that same uncomfortable expression when she was hiding something. For the umpteenth time, Amanda wished Noelle were normal.

As if wishing does any good. Noelle couldn't help it. *We were lucky she didn't have a baby when she was fifteen or get hooked on meth or run away. The only real problem was her anorexia, and we resolved that.*

Noelle's condition was nobody's fault. It was simply how things were.

The apartment seemed unnaturally hushed.

# CHAPTER FOUR

"TO SUM IT up, Mr. McIntyre, I'm no closer to discovering who she is now than I was when I started."

In a borrowed office at the McIntyre Grand Tartan, Cal lounged behind a gleaming cherry desk and listened to the conclusion of the recital given by the man across from him. He stared at his outstretched ankles and shiny wingtips, but didn't see the shoes at all. He had flown into Houston that morning, hopeful of better tidings.

In the lengthening silence, the clean-shaven man who looked more like a college professor than a private investigator slid some photographs of the opening night party across the desk. "We got these pictures from the media shots of the opening, but they aren't enough to go on. She was smart in covering her tracks."

The redhead was indistinct in most of the prints, appearing to have deliberately shunned the photographers. In the best one, a profile shot taken unawares, her nose was too long and the short upper lip not nearly so charming.

Why had he lost his head over such an ordinary woman?

The investigator said, "A bellman here remembered her getting into a taxi. We traced her to the airport and are working the flight lists, looking for solitary women leaving. Do you have any idea how many flights leave Houston, even at that time of the morning? Not to mention she could have left the airport and gone somewhere else. Or she might have met an accomplice there."

"She certainly had an accomplice." Bitterness with himself made Cal snap at the other man. "She couldn't have got the ticket to the opening if she didn't have an accomplice. So after ten days and thousands of dollars, you've come up with exactly nothing."

"You knew the rates when you hired us." The investigator must have been used to dealing with disturbed clients because his amiable smile didn't flag. "If you insist, I can keep a man on it, but it might be a waste of our time and your money."

"At least you're honest. Keep on it anyway."

"All right. You're paying. Look, I know you're reluctant, but I think we need to tackle it from your end since we've come up against brick walls everywhere else."

"My end?"

"Like who knew the combination you used for the safe."

"No one who would take those studs," Cal said shortly.

He got up and paced the room, ending up by the balcony door. Opening the blinds, he could see the enclosed swimming pool and its fountains below him, and beyond, past the ornate granite walls, the distant skyline of Houston. Inside the main building's boundaries, people filled the walkways, guests leaving and arriving. Some hurried as if late for appointments, others meandered as if they had all the time in the world.

The investigator wouldn't let him off the hook. "Look, Mr. McIntyre, someone had to be familiar enough with the invitation list for the opening to know whose invitation would be declined. That same someone had to arrange for the woman to use that particular box. You couldn't help but notice her seated right across from you. To me, that says someone inside the organization planned it. Someone who knew about your thing for redheads."

Cal snorted. "Who doesn't know about my thing for redheads? You'd have thousands of suspects if that's your only clue."

"That's why we've got to narrow the playing field."

"I see your point."

The redhead couldn't be traced from her reservation of the box in the theater because it had been booked in the name of a leading citizen of Texas who, with her husband, had embarked on a three week tour of Japan during the opening of the Grand Tartan. What's more, that august lady swore she'd neither made nor confirmed a reservation to the charitable event.

Someone had done both in her name, however. Someone had paid for the ticket with an untraceable cash card and picked it up from the box office at the last minute, when none of the workers would remember a single face among the crush of people filing in.

"Scarlet Smith," he said aloud, "came prepared to take me for a ride."

"Looks like it."

Cal rubbed the back of his neck. All the time he had thought he was the stalker, and instead he was the prey. What a fool.

He faced the detective. "Okay. Only my sister, her husband, and my stepfather know the safe combination. We all use the same sequence in case any of us need to get to papers or keys involved in the business. None of them would be involved."

"You sure one of 'em might not have confided in someone?"

Claire wouldn't and Robert was paranoid about security. Tip had never been able to remember the numbers, even when Lila was alive. "No. None of them would have."

"Not even for diamonds worth five million dollars? Look, Mr.

McIntyre, somebody knew you would wear them and somebody knew where you'd put them. Maybe if I talk to those three people and see what they say—"

"No, I don't want you bothering any of them. They don't know anything. I've asked." The last frigging thing he needed was this man to involve Robert, start him nosing around asking questions that might lead to the journal.

"You're the boss," the investigator said as he rose to go. "But right now we have piss-all to go on."

She had to be after the studs, Cal told himself as he flew home on a company jet. He closed his eyes, but the redhead in her slinky dress with her hair cascading down floated before him. Something nagged at him, something about the way she had leaned over to kiss him in bed. He wished he could remember what it was, but he couldn't.

He would, though. Give him time and it would come back. He had a pretty good memory.

The woman hadn't come for the emerald ring or the journal. Neither had been in his hands before the day of the opening, and the theft had been carefully planned beforehand. She'd come for his studs and taken the other things because they were there.

What if she read the journal? What if she figured out what those sections meant?

God, why hadn't he torn out those damned pages when he first retrieved the book? It would have been so easy to rip them out and burn them or flush them down the toilet.

But Claire had wanted to read all the intimate details herself. All their mother's hopes and plans after Tip's wonderful offer, the hurried marriage and their refuge in Italy.

He stared out the porthole. How the hell could he go back and tell Claire there was no trace of their mother's journal or the redhead?

Taking a deep breath, he leaned back in the cushions. *Let's try it another way.* The studs were Scarlet's original target, and she probably had a buyer. Only someone willing to take stolen goods would purchase them without authenticated papers, someone who knew he couldn't show them in public.

Miles de Graffen.

No. Not Miles. Miles might covet the jewels, but he wouldn't go so far as to steal them. Besides, Miles didn't know the safe combination.

But what if he was offered the studs? Would the acquisitive Miles ask questions about how the seller got them?

Hah. Miles would snatch up the frigging studs with no questions asked. Everyone knew Miles coveted the Antoinette diamonds and wouldn't care how he got them.

Perhaps he should call Miles, say the diamonds were of no consequence but that he wanted his mother's journal back.

He ground his teeth. He couldn't do that, much as he'd like to. A plea based on suspicion alone would do no good. Miles would never admit to being involved with anything illegal.

For the moment, Cal couldn't do anything except curse the woman, whoever she was.

\* \* \* \*

AT FAIR MEADOWS, the old plantation east of Atlanta that Lila had bought and restored, Cal stopped at his cottage on the outskirts.

He'd moved into the guest house after Claire and Robert married, using their need for more space in the mansion as an excuse to get away from his mother's critical oversight. The cottage had turned into his sanctuary, but today his guilt allowed him no respite in its quiet.

He threw his clothes bag down. Might as well get it over with.

On a walk lined with fading daffodils, he trudged up to the mansion without regard for the pink azaleas, purple wisteria and red rhododendron.

It had been humiliating to come home the day after the gala in Houston and admit to Claire what he'd done. Telling her the detectives had found nothing would be as bad.

She hadn't blamed him—she never blamed him—but he knew where the fault for losing the journal lay.

Mere days till Johanna's wedding, and they were no closer to catching the redhead.

He found his sister alone in the study, a comfortable room she used as an office. Chintz-covered armchairs stood on an Aubusson carpet among cherry bookcases and small tables with bronze lamps.

Claire sat at her writing table, checking some sort of lists against each other. At his entrance, she threw her pen down and jumped up. "I told you to call."

She shared his wide forehead and pliable mouth, but her determined jaw came from their mother. His older sister, the one person he depended on, was usually unflappable. Not today.

Cal closed the door. "There was nothing to tell. He hasn't found out anything that will help."

The hope in her face died. She bit her lip.

Cal walked over to the mantel, picked up a wooden mask

brought back from Africa, checked a sconce for dust, and looked at the painting of Amsterdam's river district.

Anything not to have to face her.

If only she'd accuse him or yell at him. He wouldn't say a word if she hit him.

But she was Claire. Reproach was never her style.

He put down the mask and went over to where she'd sunk into an armchair by the fireplace. One hand covered her throat. It would have been a melodramatic gesture had it not been Claire making it.

"Hang in there, Bags." He called her by the childish nickname and patted her shoulder awkwardly, her pain another nail in his heart. "It's been nearly two weeks and there's been no attempt at blackmail. Maybe there won't be."

"What if the woman's approached someone else?" Claire moistened her lips. "What if she's approached Matt?"

He stiffened. "Matthew would have told us." Walking over to the bookcase, he studied the volumes through the glass. "Matthew can't afford to be blackmailed. Not in his position."

"He's too fine a man to be blackmailed."

Too fine a man? Hell. He shouldn't care that she forgave Matthew Swift so easily. After all, she never censured Cal for his lifestyle. But her shielding the man after all this time . . .

Damned annoying. "Come on, Claire, Matthew's no better than the rest of us."

"Don't start that. Not now, not when everything's such a mess." She stood, took a few paces. "I can't bear it. I can't bear to think that it might come out after everything everyone went through to cover it up. You, Mother, Tip . . . After all this time, for this to happen now. With Johanna so happy, her wedding so close."

"Steady, steady." He came over and put his arm around her.

Claire, always so strong and confident, leaned on him in a way she'd never done before.

Under the slacks and neat shirt, her waist felt thinner while her whole body seemed so fragile the bones might crack like dry twigs if he hugged her too tightly.

Remorse coursed side by side with anger at the redheaded witch.

Of all the people he cared about, Claire was the last one he should have let down. She'd been the big sister who picked him up when he fell skating, the one who wiped his nose and dried his tears and gave him candy, the one who protected him from Lila's rigid expectations and punishments, often by drawing their mother's anger toward herself.

Claire pulled away. "It's a nightmare. I didn't have to see the journal. I should have made you destroy it right away. What if the woman goes to the tabloids? Or Johanna? Or Robert?" She wrung her hands. "If Robert finds out, I can't bear it."

Robert Winslow was single-minded almost to intolerance, but Claire could manage him. "Robert may be more understanding than you give him credit for. Maybe you should tell him."

Her eyes, the same melted chocolate color as his, widened. "Never! I can't. He'd . . . I don't know what he'd do. You don't understand, Cal. Don't you dare speak of it to him."

He'd guessed his sister's marriage wasn't as smooth as it seemed, but she was almost incoherent talking about it. "Okay. But I don't know of anything else to do. We have to wait for this woman, whoever she is, to make the next move. Come on, Bags, you can make it. Is Robert due in from California tomorrow?"

"He's been detained, but he'll be home in time for the rehearsal dinner Saturday. I mean it, Cal. He can't find out. He'd leave me if he knew."

"No way."

"Maybe not. But even if he forgave me, he'd hold it over me. You know how he hated me coming to work after Mother died. He wanted me to stay home with the boys and only gave in when you and Tip insisted . . . No, if Robert finds out, I won't be able to work with him. I'll end up like some of my friends, taking to drink or a younger lover because I don't have enough to do."

"Not you. You've got too much character." *And no way I'd let him browbeat you.* What if the SOB was already doing just that? Cal's teeth clenched. He'd . . .

"Cal." Their stepfather, golf shirt hanging loose over plaid shorts, wearing loafers with no socks, interrupted. "I thought I heard you."

Travis Isaacs Penn Lathen, long retired from the state department, was seventy-eight years old and not in good health. He was one more person who'd be hurt if Lila's journal became public.

"The detective wasn't able to find her," Cal answered the unspoken question.

Claire put on a brave face. "We're not giving up, Tip. We'll get Mother's journal back."

"My dear, I know what anguish you're going through." Tip patted her shoulder before turning to Cal. "I still can't imagine why you let yourself be taken in so easily."

Cal flushed but Claire, fiercely loyal, spoke out. "Don't start on Cal. Blame won't do anybody any good right now."

"I do know it's my fault," Cal said.

Tip's grave face looked out of place over his small rotund figure.

"I'm only glad Lila isn't here. After all she went through to protect you and Johanna, my dear," he said to Claire, "she would be devastated if everything comes out now."

Chagrin fled and affection swelled. Despite never being around children, Tip had accepted Cal and Claire without condition when he'd married their mother, taking on a paternal role and even acting as a shield between them and Lila. They could never repay Tip.

"Well, it isn't public yet." Cal forced himself to speak cheerfully. "With luck it won't be."

"And you mustn't worry. With your heart condition, you don't need to get upset." Claire slipped her arm through Tip's and kissed his cheek. "We'll pay whatever we have to pay to get it back. Cal will take care of it."

"You still won't go to Robert?" Tip asked her.

The stricken look reappeared. "No. He mustn't find out."

"I suppose that's best. The fewer who know, the better." Tip hesitated. "What about Matthew?"

Cal turned up his lip.

Claire turned away. "Cal says if Matt's approached, he'll come to us and he's right. Besides, if the woman does plan on blackmail, we'll be the logical first target."

Tip looked troubled but didn't reply. On her way out, Claire patted his shoulder and said again, "It'll be all right."

Cal followed her. "We'll work it out."

"I know." She took a ragged breath. "Go upstairs and see Johanna. She was asking for you this morning. I think she's getting a case of jitters now that the wedding's upon us."

He forced a smile. "Will do. One of my meager talents is calming down nervous women."

# CHAPTER FIVE

IN HER MUTED peach and beige bedroom, Johanna wasn't a bundle of nerves after all so instead of launching into a pep talk, Cal teased her a little. "Oooh. Are you sure Jeremy will approve of this?" He picked up a filmy teddy off a bed stacked high with clothing.

Johanna didn't look up from her packing. "He'll love it."

"But he's so prudish. I don't want you to shock him on your wedding night and have him annul the marriage. Good grief, you'd have to come back home. Don't you have a nice flannel gown more his speed?"

Johanna threw a stuffed bear at him. "Stop making fun of Jeremy."

He caught the bear, lifted aside Johanna's cat sleeping on a coral-colored skirted chair and sat down. The cat yawned reproachfully from its new spot on the floor. Cal stroked its head with the toe of his shoe. "I'm not making fun of Jeremy. I want your marriage to get off to a good start, Princess. I like Jeremy a lot more than that Lassiter boy who was always around, eating three meals a day with us and sleeping over every weekend. He even washed his clothes here."

"You've been listening to Dad." Johanna mimicked Tip's dulcet voice, "Is that boy boarding with us? Are we charging enough to cover his grocery bill?" She unloaded the contents of another drawer onto the bed. "For your information, Larry's father ran off when he was eight. He had a hard time."

"No harder than his mother, I bet. And don't make fun of Tip. The father of the bride deserves all the respect he can get. Never mind me." Cal hugged the teddy bear. "I don't know why I bother to give advice. Nobody around here listens or respects me. That's for sure."

"Stop with the pity party. You don't deserve any respect." As if agreeing, the yellow cat whipped its tail back and forth, and stalked away. "You're a bum. If you and Dad thought I'd marry Larry, you're both crazy. Unlike my big brother and his raging hormones still stuck in the pubescent stages, I have good sense."

"Ouch." Johanna had the same high standards as Claire but didn't view Cal's failings with Claire's loving equanimity. "You know all that happened when I was young and idealistic, Johanna. I thought if you slept with a girl, you ought to marry her. So I did."

"Three times?" Holding up a stack of lingerie, Johanna shook her head sternly, but couldn't suppress a smile. "Come on, Cal."

Cal tossed the bear aside. "I have a learning deficiency when it comes to women."

"You have a learning deficiency when it comes to sex."

In many ways, Johanna reminded Callaway of Claire. She had Claire's way of making a person feel she was laughing with him rather than at him, but while Claire was forgiving, Johanna, under Jeremy's influence, was heading toward puritanical.

Cal hoped she wouldn't turn into another Robert.

Her standards were part of the reason this business with the redhead hit so hard. He didn't want either Claire or Johanna hurt by the nasty publicity that would follow if the journal was made public.

A satin robe sailed by, missing the bed and landing beside him on the exact spot where the cat had taken refuge. "Pick that up for me, will you, bro? It goes in my honeymoon bag, too."

Ignoring the cat, which emerged from shiny folds puffed up with outrage, Cal lifted the robe and idly fingered the lacy trim.

And half-forgotten memories of the lost night flashed.

His watch stem catching in lace.

Heavy woven threads of lace edging an elaborate label on an expensive dress.

A designer dress label with embroidered letters.

He marshaled runaway thoughts. "Johanna."

"What?"

"Do you have a pencil and paper?"

"Why? Can you write?" But she found them for him.

"Thanks." He started sketching. "You're a real clotheshorse, up on the latest styles and all, aren't you?"

She made a face. "What does that have to do with the price of coffee? You're going to fuss at me about how much I've spent on clothes for this wedding, aren't you?"

"What? Don't be silly. You only get married once. Well, most people do. No, I saw a great dress the other night. The label was unusual, kind of a satiny oval thing in a bunch of lace. Kind of like this." He thrust the rough drawing at her. "I think a name was embroidered on it, but I can't remember. Maybe it had an A in it? Where would I go to find out who made this dress?"

"You?" Johanna's chin dropped. "Found a great dress?"

"What?" He spread his hands. "You don't think I could tell a great dress when I see one? I happen to be as interested in clothes as much as the next guy, thank you very much."

She snorted. "Since when have you started buying dresses?"

"Well," he stalled, trying to think of a plausible lie, "since, um, since, um . . ." Inspiration came. "Since Claire saw this dress and raved over it. You know her birthday's coming up next month and I thought this year I'd get her something she actually wanted."

Johanna narrowed her eyes.

He rushed on, embellishing on the fly. "I can't get the dress if I don't know the designer. I don't remember where we were when we saw it but we weren't at a store. And Claire was so enthusiastic." He let his shoulders sag. "Oh well, if you won't help me, I guess it's perfume like last year."

"And the year before." Johanna took the sketch. "Okay, bro. Strangely enough, I might be able to help you despite your totally inadequate skills as an artist." She went to the closet and pulled out a beaded top. "Was this the label?"

There it was. The satin oval, the lace. "You are a witch."

She laughed and turned back to her packing. "I'm not so bad when you get to know me. Besides, Jane's doing my wedding dress."

Cal read the embroidered script, the curlicues so embellished that it took several minutes to puzzle out the words. A. Jane, Atlanta.

"Doing your wedding dress, eh? Where did you buy this top?"

Johanna was intent on the large open suitcase. "From Jane's shop, silly."

"Jane's the designer?"

"Yep." Johanna folded a sweater and put it in a pile on the bed before pulling out another drawer of clothes. The cat strolled over and inspected the items on the bed before making a leap into the open suitcase.

Cal pretended not to see. "So tell me about Jane."

Johanna held up a garment. "This shirt doesn't fit right. I ought to get rid of it."

"If it doesn't fit, yes. So where's this Jane's store?"

"It's not a store." She held the shirt to her shoulders. "I hate to do away with it. It was the last thing Mother gave me. Maybe I can get it altered."

Cal gnashed his teeth. "Jane. Where's her boutique?"

"She calls it a dressmaker shop. It's near Lenox."

The cat curled up in the suitcase and closed its eyes. Johanna didn't notice. Cal ignored it. "Lenox Square in Buckhead?"

"That's where it was there the last time I looked." She shook out slacks. "Jane's great. Everyone in Atlanta uses her."

"I don't."

She gave him an indulgent glance. "She designs for women, Cal." She folded the slacks, turned to the case, saw the cat. "Snick, get out of there."

The napping cat, amber eyes blinking in feigned bewilderment, was picked up and set aside. "Look at those damn cat hairs all over my good pants."

"Tell me about Jane."

She brushed yellow fuzz off jeans. "What's to tell? Jane, like, personalizes things. She's great for giving clothes that extra little oomph. Her stuff costs the earth. You and Claire are springing for her to do my wedding gown, though."

"We are?"

"Y'all offered to go thirds with Dad on the wedding, remember?" She replaced the jeans and glared at the offended cat who sat on the floor cleaning white tipped paws and ignoring the open suitcase. "It's the most romantic dress ever, an absolute miracle. I have my last fitting this afternoon."

"Your last fitting, eh? Near Lenox. I'll go with you."

"You?" Johanna forgot the cat. "Are you sure you're looking for a dress for Claire?" Her eyes narrowed. "You're not tangled up with another woman, are you?"

"Me?" He put on his virtuous face. "You know I gave up women after my last divorce."

"Hah." Johanna slapped her hands on her hips. "So what were you doing with that French model when she threw you in the fountain? I thought Robert was going to have a heart attack when he opened the morning newspaper."

"Robert worries too much about my business." Cal waved a negligent hand. "No, really. I have given up women. Except for an occasional fling," he amended under her skepticism. "Come on, Johanna. Give me a break. I really want to do something nice for Claire."

Good thing Johanna's entry to adulthood hadn't changed her. She was easily diverted where Claire would have been tenacious. "Well maybe . . . Claire loves Jane's things but doesn't buy many. She hates shopping and never spends money on herself."

The cat seized on Johanna's distraction to sneak around and jump onto the bed from the other side.

"So we'll buy one of Jane's dresses for her." Cal saw the yellow cat, eyes on Johanna's back, put one cautious paw over the edge of the suitcase.

Live and let live.

The cat snuggled down among Johanna's folded clothes.

"If I go with you this afternoon, you can help me pick something out. Tell me more about this Jane."

\* \* \* \*

AMANDA WAS WORRIED about her sister.

She hadn't heard a word from Noelle since their conversation two weeks before. Though she'd left a message on Noelle's cell several times, Noelle hadn't called back. Maybe everything was going all right at home and she'd simply forgotten. Forgetfulness was a symptom of Noelle's disorder.

Maybe it was time to call Noelle at home.

She picked up the phone but put it back down. Edward didn't work set hours and he might be there. If he didn't know about Noelle's indiscretion, Amanda didn't want to inadvertently let anything slip. Surely Noelle would call soon. Besides, Noelle would have let her know by now if everything wasn't all right with Edward.

If only everything was all right here.

Until Callaway McIntyre, Amanda had never done anything illegal, and now her conscience, already burdened with memories of Tommy, had a new reason to hound her.

At the drafting table, she twirled the drawing pencil between her fingers while her part in Noelle's scheme gnawed at her insides. She ought to be figuring how much she could afford to pay on her loan this month, or estimating how many dresses she had to sell to keep her lovely business with its stark white wallboard and varnished wood safe from the bank.

Instead, she couldn't stop worrying about Noelle.

Her workroom, normally a sanctum with its different swatches of new-smelling material, had white walls covered by drawings representing her latest ideas. A few were complete, needing to be taken down and filed after having been constructed by the three full-time seamstresses her growing clientele now allowed her to employ; but most of the drawings were unfinished, lacking some detail or other that would come to her after hours of staring at them and pondering.

Amanda loved her workroom but today her eyes came back to the solid pine desk, adorned by a single photograph of Noelle, Edward, and Teddy, that never failed to warm her. In it, the baby burbled with laughter while his parents beamed proudly over him. The little family was safe, thanks to her, but Noelle should have let her know that for sure.

She threw the pencil down.

How could she work?

Maybe she should go ahead and call. Even if Edward was home, he wouldn't think it unusual.

Yes, he would. Edward knew she was always too rushed to call Noelle from work.

Taking off her reading glasses, Amanda closed her eyes and

pressed them with her fingertips. All her problems were getting her down: Noelle's future, her complicity in drugging an innocent, well, a nearly innocent man. Her car.

It was ridiculous to believe anyone would put a bomb in her car, but that's what the detective had told her when he came by the day before. "It was set to explode when the engine reached a certain temperature but the thermostat was off. If you hadn't seen the smoke and stopped when you did, you would have been inside. Are you sure you don't have any enemies? A jealous ex-husband? An angry ex-boyfriend?"

No. There was no one who wanted to harm her.

"Gangs," the detective had suggested. "They're into everything nowadays. Maybe it was an initiation. Or maybe they got the wrong car."

That was the last time she'd park overnight at that particular shuttle lot, even though there had never been problems in using it before. Of course, if it hadn't been for Noelle, she would never have parked there to begin with.

Which brought her back to her more immediate concern. Should she phone Noelle or not?

Her assistant stuck her head into Amanda's office. "Jane, Johanna Lathen is here for the final fitting."

"Thanks, Melissa. I'll be right out." Johanna was a nice child. The fitting would mark the end of a long day and leave Amanda plenty of time to call Noelle when the shop closed.

Getting up without undue haste, she inspected herself at the full-length mirror beside the door.

Looks were important, and her severe image let customers know they were dealing with a professional. The loose jersey fell gently to mid-calf, with only a white lace collar to relieve the austere gray. A stray hair needed tucking into the knot at the nape of her neck before she headed toward the door to meet Johanna.

She froze.

Beyond the glass wall of her office, Johanna and a man talked to one of the clerks. A man with a wide forehead and prominent cheekbones.

Callaway McIntyre.

In her shop.

Her legs threatened to buckle. Instinctively she stepped back, out of sight of the couple in the front room. Her shoulder, propped against the wall to hold her upright, wrinkled a drawing of an unfinished design destined to go to the governor's niece, but no matter.

Panic welled, was pressed down.

Callaway McIntyre couldn't possibly know who she was. There was no way he could know.

*Then why is he here?*

Sick at her stomach, she made her rubbery legs carry her over to the corner desk and its intercom. "Melissa, will you come back here, please?"

Her assistant returned, raised brows questioning.

"Who is that man?"

"Ooooooh." Melissa's eyes sparkled, widened. "He's hot, isn't he? That's Cal McIntyre, Johanna Lathen's brother."

"Her brother?" Amanda repeated faintly.

Melissa frowned. "Half-brother, I guess. Do you remember Claire Winslow? She's bought one or two things from us. She's his sister, too."

"Claire Winslow?" Johanna and another customer? Callaway McIntyre's sisters? Dear God, what was she going to do? "I can't quite place her."

"She's only been in a couple of times. Anyway, he and Claire had a different father. He left them the McIntyre hotel chain. Johanna's father was a mere diplomat." Melissa flapped one hand in exaggerated downplay.

She was going to throw up.

"You've probably seen him in the newspapers," Melissa went on. "He and his girlfriend had a falling out a while back and there was a picture of him on the front page of the Atlanta Journal-Constitution, soaking wet after she pushed him into a fountain at some fancy party in Paris. Boy, did he look annoyed."

"I'm sure," Amanda murmured, managing to breathe.

Melissa lingered. "He wants a dress for his sister's birthday. Claire, not Johanna. I could show him what we have while you're with Johanna."

"Yes. Have her go back to the fitting room and I'll meet her there."

"Are you all right? You're awfully pale."

"I'm fine."

Brother. Callaway McIntyre was Johanna Lathen and Claire Winslow's brother. Brother to two of her customers. Claire owned part of the McIntyre hotel chain.

Calm down, calm down. She would stay in the back, fit Johanna's dress, and let Melissa help Callaway. With any luck, he'd never see her, though it wouldn't hurt to disguise herself a little.

Reading glasses would help hide her face and wasn't there some cologne in her desk drawer an elderly customer had given her? Yes. A liberal spritzing of the awful stuff should make him think of wrinkled old ladies instead of sexy Scarlet Smith.

There. The very essence of a discreet salesperson. Even if he saw her, Callaway wouldn't be expecting the wanton Scarlet in the prim woman with brown hair pulled back in a spinster's knot.

Purely coincidence. It had to be.

\* \* \* \*

"WE CATER TO a clientele from all over the country," the attentive clerk told Cal as a clarinet's haunting notes showered them from a hidden sound system. "We provide antique lace and hand-sewn beading and anything else the customers require. Jane herself goes to Europe periodically and picks up materials at special auctions."

Pete Fountain's magic didn't distract Cal. "How long have you worked here, Melissa?"

She stuttered, flustered. "F-four years. Since I got out of high school."

"Ah. A mere baby."

She managed a nonchalant shrug, but a blush gave her away. "Hardly. I've been on my own all that time."

"How long was Jane's here before you started? I've never heard about her till now."

Recovering her poise, Melissa was happy to enlighten him. "She opened about three years before I came, but she was at Macy's before that. Everyone knew her. Since I came, business has tripled. Even Jane says she can't believe the way it's grown. Something black, you said?"

The abrupt transition back to the object of his visit threw Cal. He had to think. "Oh. Yes. Black. Strapless and straightish, made out of that kind of clingy stuff. Silk or chiffon, maybe? Long, with a slit on the side. And a kind of halter top."

The fifth dress she showed him was The Dress.

When she held it out, the mellifluous sound of the fabric moving against her arm recalled the whispered rustle as he slipped the dress over Scarlet's head. He took the thin material in his hand and could have sworn it smelled of oranges.

Oranges.

The scent brought back the softness of small breasts and rounded hips. Despite himself, inside the cold ashes of anger, something akin to desire flickered.

He extinguished it, along with the tiny ache that always showed up whenever a woman disappointed or betrayed him.

The redhead had done both. She'd duped him easily and coldly. "How many of these do you sell?"

Melissa showed her shock. "I assumed you wanted an original. We have some styles in several sizes, but this dress is one of a kind. It will be fitted to the customer."

He brought the dress to his nose. That was definitely a faint citrus odor. "So there's only one dress like this and it's this one?"

"Yes."

This was the actual dress Scarlet had worn. If proof other than the sales clerk's assurances was needed, the scent provided it. Unless an orange aroma permeated all Jane's dresses.

"This has perfume in it." He held it out to Melissa.

She sniffed. "It does, doesn't it? Perhaps a customer tried it on, or one of the models." Another sniff, and she said, "I don't recognize this particular fragrance."

"Nice scent." Scarlet could have been a model. That would explain the eye-catching aura, the arrogance that demanded adulation. "You use models here?"

"On weekends we have college girls come in and wear different outfits. That lets customers see what's available. You'd be surprised how many clothes a pretty girl can sell." She added hastily, "Not that Jane's designs need a hard sell."

Scarlet was no college girl. He'd lay odds on that, but he'd check the lead out anyway.

He was about to ask about customers from Houston when Johanna reappeared, a vision in ivory satin and lace. "Come here, Cal," she called imperiously. "I want your opinion."

Cal turned. "Oh, so now I'm good for something?"

Johanna spotted the dress he still held. "Oh, jeez. You don't mean that for Claire."

"You don't think she'd wear it?"

She shook her head emphatically. "Nothing skimpy or sexy. Definitely no slits. This is Claire you're buying for, not one of your fancy whores."

"Johanna. Mother would have washed your mouth out."

"Cal, look at my dress. Does it fit all right?"

"Perfect. I never knew you could look so good. Jeremy'll faint when he sees you. I'll bet he never knew you could look so good either."

Johanna posed in front of the mirror wall. "I thought I wanted a cutout back, but I feel indecent with the point all the way down at my waist."

"You'll only be in it a few hours," He was anxious to send her off.

"True. How about the hem. Is it too short?"

"Let it down and you'd be stepping on it."

"Does the long waist make me look fat? I loved it when I first saw it but—"

"No, not a bit. Looks great. What d'you mean by long waist?"

"Cal!"

"Why are you asking me all this stuff? What do I know about women's clothes?"

Johanna huffed and flounced away. "Obviously nothing. I should have made Claire come with me."

Cal asked Melissa if someone might have bought the black dress and returned it.

"Returned it? We seldom have return items and when we do, they're marked as such."

"But you do occasionally? Someone could have taken this dress and worn it, say to a dinner party where she got perfume on it, and brought it back without you knowing the difference?"

Melissa smile became strained. "No, no. Not this dress. Jane only finished this dress a week or so ago and it's been right here in the shop since then. In case you're concerned someone else wore it, set your mind at ease. No, that perfume came either from a customer trying it on or from one of our models."

Unless Jane herself had lent it out to a favored customer. "Any chance of meeting the great lady herself?"

Melissa looked puzzled.

"Jane," he clarified. "Maybe she loaned it to a friend." Melissa was cute but a little slow. Callaway preferred a woman with a livelier mind and a touch of mystery about her, a woman who knew what was what. Like Scarlet Smith.

Not like Scarlet Smith, damn her.

Melissa's brow cleared. "I'm sure she didn't, but I'll check. Jane's with your sister right now. Maybe she can see you when they're finished."

Depending on his impression of Jane, he might confide part of the truth, ask about her models. He pulled out a cigarette and was swiftly herded down the hall into an isolated smoking room where a comfortable sofa and chairs circled a coffee table filled with magazines.

A television was tucked away to the side. A fan whirred above, pulling air outside.

"The smoke gets into the material and stays," Melissa said. "Jane absolutely abhors cigarettes and cigars. Naturally we can't allow them in the sales or design area."

From the sports magazines, this was where trapped husbands awaited their wives. Jane was prepared for everything.

Callaway curled his lip. He'd be damned if he'd ever be so docile as to hang around this cubbyhole while his wife tried on dresses. Poor suckers, hooked by sex but ending up gutted and spineless and tortured the rest of their lives. Not for him the marital ordeal. No way would he go through that again. He'd have his freedom to do as he liked and . . .

Wait patiently for Johanna to be finished.

He laughed at himself. All right. He was no better than ninety percent of the other men he knew. Now, if he could only get on Jane's good side—and there was no reason why he couldn't; he was always good with older women—maybe he could chase down Scarlet.

Johanna's voice from the sales room brought him out of the lounge. "I don't dare leave it to Cal. He's trying to buy something a Vegas showgirl would feel right at home in."

Melissa said, "I'll be happy to pick out a few things," before smiling at Cal. "I'm so sorry but Jane has an important phone call from one of our bead suppliers and can't talk to you right now. I did ask about the dress, but I was right. No one has borrowed it. It's been in the sales room since it was put out."

"Thanks." That dress had definitely been on Scarlet. Maybe an employee had sneaked it out without anyone knowing. He'd call his investigator and put him to work on Jane's staff as soon as he got rid of Johanna.

Johanna turned back to Melissa. "So Jane'll steam my dress whenever she brings it out Sunday morning, right?"

He'd have to drop Johanna off at home before he called the investigator. "Let's pick out a dress for Claire so we can go."

Johanna exuded infinite patience. "Cal, I'm trying to make arrangements to get my wedding dress delivered."

He looked around. "How about that green dress over there? Think she'd like that?"

"With pink paisleys all over it? I don't think so." Johanna took a deep breath, holding her temper in check. "Ignore him, Melissa. He's brain-impaired. Back to my wedding. Jane'll be there early Sunday, right?"

"Yes, eight thirty or nine. We'll call the day before to finalize and get directions."

"I think Claire will like that green dress," Cal said.

Johanna threw up her hands. "No, she'll hate it. That burnt orange gauze is more her style."

"Orange gauze it is, then. Wrap it up."

"I'm sure we have Claire's measurements on file," Melissa said. "Do you want to wait for it to be altered?"

"No." He wanted to take Johanna home and get his investigator started looking at Jane's employees and models.

"Let Jane bring it when she comes down for the wedding." Johanna looked at her watch. "She won't mind, will she?"

"Of course not," Melissa said.

Cal herded Johanna toward the door. He had a lot to do.

# CHAPTER SIX

CAL DROPPED JOHANNA off at Fair Meadows, but Claire had taken her twin boys on an overnight trip to Atlanta for a school project. He couldn't relay his discovery to her.

He did talk to Tip, who recommended a private investigator in Atlanta.

"He'll be faster than the one in Texas. And he keeps his mouth shut."

Pleading urgency, Cal got an appointment that afternoon. As he got into his car to drive into the city, his brother-in-law called.

The connection from Virginia was tenuous but Robert's annoyance was plain. "Claire doesn't answer her phone."

"She's at that junior whatever thing with the boys. I'm sure they want cells turned off. Leave a message."

"I did, but I want to make sure she gets it. I had to drive five miles to pick up a signal. Tell her we've hit a snag with the zoning so I can't leave here till Saturday. I'll have to go straight from the airport to the rehearsal dinner. Tell her she needs to schedule me a ride from the airport to the restaurant. And tell her to bring my dinner clothes."

Cal wanted to tell Robert a thing or two. "Why can't your secretary handle it?"

"She's off for a couple of days. Claire can call. It won't take a minute. Four thirty is when I get in. Remind her I hate waiting."

*Don't we all.* "I'll tell her."

Robert wasn't through complaining. "I don't have Sonny here to take care of stuff like this. It looks like I could at least depend on my wife to be home when I need her."

Cal bit his tongue, but Robert went on. "If she insists on working, I wish to God she'd do her job."

Okay. One barb too many. "As I understand it," Cal drawled into his cell, "you won't assign her any specific duties. She can't do her job if she doesn't know what it is, can she?"

Silence.

Robert spoke first. "If you hear from her, have her call me tonight when I'm back at the hotel." He broke the connection.

Cal pocketed the cell. Christ, the man could be such an asshole.

\* \* \* \*

"NONE OF THEM can possibly be the woman."

The Atlanta investigator recommended by Tip had been worth every cent. After less than twenty-four hours, Cal sat in the shabby offices looking at several photographs of Jane's employees, including models.

"You sure?" Hilliard, with his seamed mahogany face, looked like a balding workman with few smarts, but Tip had vouched for his integrity. "These are all the seamstresses, the salespeople, and the models they use."

"None of them is the woman I'm looking for." Cal lounged wearily back in the beat-up visitor's chair. Another dead end.

"Okay." Another picture slid across the desk. "Amanda Jane doesn't have any close female friends, but she has a sister. How about her?"

Cal bolted straight up. "I recognize her."

"Awright." White teeth grinned.

"She isn't the one I want though." Cal picked up a wooden pencil and tapped the picture. The blonde simpering from the color photo had a pretty face partly hidden by a drooling baby.

When she'd sold him the emerald ring, the pretty face had been splotchy from crying.

Hilliard leaned forward. "Does it help then, your recognizing her?"

"Maybe. Is there another sister?"

"Just the two of 'em. No brothers. Parents both dead. This one's the youngest. Noelle Christina Parham nee Jane, aged twenty-four. Lives in Alabama, married to a pharmacist twelve years older who inherited money. They got one son, ten months old. She don't work, but she's got a full-time nanny and stays gone a lot. Neighbors say the marriage ain't in great shape."

An image of a woman's profile with short upper lip and slanting brow returned. "What about the older sister?"

This answer was as prompt as the other. "Amanda Lee Jane, thirty-three. Never married. Dropped out of college to purchase clothes for Macy's. Three customers there—women ve-er-y big in Atlanta society—encouraged her to go in business for herself seven, eight years ago. She paid off her loans last fall except for the long-term mortgage on her shop. She's trying to borrow more to expand."

"Is she?" Coldness swelled from his stomach. He turned the pencil over and over in his fingers.

Hilliard waited a moment. "You thinking maybe your diamonds'll cover her expansion costs?"

"That's about the size of it."

"That's all I had time to find out. If you want more, I can get on it."

"Yes, do. And I need to see a picture of her."

"I think there's one in here." Wheeling in his chair, the man fiddled on his computer before rolling back to let Cal see the screen. "Can you tell anything?"

Cal got up to look.

The woman wore black-rimmed glasses with brown hair pulled back in a bun. He started to shake his head then looked closer.

That top bowed lip, that full lower lip, the slender neck . . .

He felt like he'd been punched. When he could speak, he said, "That's her. Find out everything you can about her."

The investigator picked up a pen. "The older sister?"

"Yeah. The older one."

Scarlet Smith. Amanda Lee Jane, who was conveniently occupied when he asked for her yesterday; who was coming to Fair Meadows Sunday morning to dress Johanna for her wedding and deliver the dress for Claire.

*Well, Scarlet-Amanda, you're in for a big surprise.*

"Uh, you broke my pencil," the investigator said.

Surprised, Cal looked at the two halves he held.

Wait till he got hold of this Jane woman.

\* \* \* \*

THE WHINE OF an alarm blared.

Amanda jerked awake. Her interrupted dream had her cowering behind Johanna's wedding dress and trying to keep Callaway McIntyre, brandishing the black dress, from seeing her face.

A second's orientation before the noise made sense.

That was glass shattering. Someone was trying to break in.

She lay petrified.

Scuffling noises came from her apartment's front door.

*Do something!*

Rolling out of bed, she retrieved her .38 revolver from the bedside table.

It was bound to happen. A shop in this section of Atlanta. Cash deposits.

For seven years, there'd been the fear that one day a robber would try to get in.

Her fingers shook. Willing them to stop, she gripped the handle tight. Then she crept into the living room.

Moving shadows by the doorway materialized into an arm and

hand snaking through the broken sidelight. The hand found the deadbolt and fumbled with it.

She flicked on the lights.

"Go away or I'll shoot." Her voice didn't quaver. It sounded quite calm.

This had to be a bad dream. But the gun's weight was real and so was the hand, now motionless.

An actual person, invading her home.

Dear heaven, a man had been killed the past year in a home invasion a few blocks over.

Training from a woman's firearms course kicked in. Both hands gripped the gun and pointed it. Her stance steadied. "I mean it."

The gloved hand disappeared through the broken pane. A dark form outside melted away.

Quiet descended.

Was he going around to the bedroom window?

Amanda didn't dare go see. He might return to the living room and finish breaking in. Putting her back to a wall, she watched and waited, too terrified to do anything but guard the door.

The phone rang, scaring her so she almost pulled the trigger.

It was the security firm checking to see if she was all right.

"No, I'm not all right." She wanted to cry but she never cried. Never. "Somebody tried to get in."

Luckily she had splurged on the security system when she first outfitted the old house near Lenox Square for use as a shop and home. Still, the few minutes before a blue light pulled into the yard and a uniformed policeman got out, seemed like hours.

"You got a license for that gun, lady?" was the first thing the policeman asked. He didn't do it politely.

She was a victim, dammit, not a lawbreaker. "I certainly do." Bristling, she dug into her purse for her carry permit.

That was only the beginning. The rest of the night flew by as she dealt with the surly policeman and a detective who arrived later. Her unsympathetic rescuers seemed doubtful of an arrest while the discovery that the intruder had worn gloves decided them against trying to lift fingerprints. They perked up when hearing about the car bomb but in the end, only took notes.

"After all," a detective said, "your intruder didn't get in, did he? I don't expect you'll see him again now he knows you're armed. And your car . . . The bomb might not even have been meant for you."

Afterward, there were more questions to be answered and forms to be filled out, all of which took longer than Amanda thought a few minutes of terror warranted.

The men did not finish until nearly five in the morning.

Almost time to leave for Johanna Lathen's wedding. No need to go back to bed for forty minutes.

She made herself a pot of coffee and took a hurried shower, all the while listening for strange noises. Before loading her minivan, she checked that her enclosed garage was empty and locked.

Break-ins weren't everyday occurrences, but they also weren't uncommon. She'd been expecting something like this since she'd moved to the area. One attempted burglary in eight years wasn't too bad. Part of the price for living near Lenox.

But the car explosion and the break-in together worried her. Neither could have anything to do with Callaway McIntyre, but nothing like them had ever happened to her before.

She stowed her appliance case in the back and shut the tailgate.

There, loaded and ready to leave.

Maybe she should beg off. No, Callaway might have recognized the black dress, but he couldn't know it was the same one or who had worn it. She'd just stay out of his way at the wedding and he'd never figure out she was Scarlet.

It was too early to call Melissa at home and ask her to find someone to repair her door. She'd call from the road so as not to waste time.

How horrible the past few weeks had been. Her attempt to help Noelle had unleashed a torrent of bad luck.

What else could possibly happen?

\* \* \* \*

FROM NOW ON, he was controlling events, Cal McIntyre told himself. No more jumping through hoops for a pretty woman.

At his cottage on the edge of the Fair Meadows estate, he had arisen early. A bright puddle of sunshine on the patio warmed the morning and made it pleasant enough to sit at the wrought iron table and drink his coffee outside.

Wisteria scented the air. A squirrel scurried halfway down an elm, beady eyes hopeful of crumbs. Birds called overhead. It promised to be a good day for Amanda Jane's downfall.

Sipping coffee, Cal re-read a typewritten report picked up the night before.

When Amanda was eighteen and Noelle nine, their mother had died in a car crash after abandoning her family. Eleven years later, their father had died from cancer.

A neighbor where they grew up called Amanda a second mother

to Noelle. Another said Noelle had some kind of disability that meant Amanda or her father was always taking her around to doctors and psychiatrists and therapists.

One of Noelle's teachers was quoted as saying the girl, while sweet, was impetuous and prone to do stupid things. "Emotional disability. Borderline personality disorder, I think they called it."

The consensus was that Noelle wasn't very smart.

As for Amanda, she was engaged while a junior in college, but her fiancé accidentally died. Friends, neighbors, one and all, said his death had devastated her. A co-worker of her father said he'd never seen anyone change so much so fast.

No one who talked to Cal's investigator had anything bad to say about the sisters.

*Except that they're con artists and thieves.*

Noelle must have been casing his suite the entire time she hawked her ring and gave him the sob story about needing money for her sick baby.

He threw the report down. *And I fell for it.*

Same old stupid, gullible Cal. When would he learn?

They'd both pay. Especially Amanda Jane.

By seven o'clock, when Amanda's minivan became one of the many vehicles on the interstate heading out of the city, Cal was showered and dressed in the striped pants and starched shirt mandatory for ushers in the wedding.

Carrying his coat on a hanger, he whistled as he came up from his isolated cottage for breakfast. His tune ceased at sight of the usually fastidious Claire descending the stairs. Her slacks were rumpled and her T-shirt had a big stain on the front. "You look like crap."

"Thanks loads." She walked like a sleepwalker, moving through dust motes that danced and glittered in sunshine streaming through a round window on the landing. "At least we won't have to cope with rain on top of everything else."

"Did the rehearsal dinner wipe you out after that big bachelorette party the night before?" He'd left early to pick up the report on Amanda Jane.

"No, I was in bed by eleven but I couldn't go to sleep. Then when I did, I dreamed Johanna's dress was lost and the caterers had set up for a Halloween party instead of a wedding reception. We had pumpkins and corn stalks instead of ferns and candles. I kept saying, it isn't Halloween, but they didn't listen."

Cal hung his coat in the hall closet. As Claire headed toward the back of the house, he fell into step.

He hadn't told her what the investigator had found. No need in getting her hopes up. But from the looks of her, maybe he ought to say something.

At the breakfast room, Claire touched his sleeve. "Robert's already down here."

That explained the car that woke him up this morning. "I thought he went back to Atlanta after the rehearsal dinner. He made a big deal out of meeting Sonny at the airport. I figured they'd stay at the apartment overnight."

"He picked Sonny up, but then they came on here. I don't know what time they got in, but he was up early."

In the breakfast room, Robert sat at the table, dirty dishes pushed to the side. Casual in khaki shorts and a golf shirt, with the Wall Street Journal propped up before him, he put down his cup. "What, Cal, not wearing your lucky studs for the wedding?"

Claire stiffened.

"One of the stones was loose," Cal said easily. "I'm having them all cleaned and checked."

Trust Robert to notice, he thought as Claire gave her husband a perfunctory kiss.

Across the table were the remains of someone else's breakfast, probably Sonny Kirkman's.

Sonny, who thrived on little sleep, had doubtless got up to eat with Robert and discuss more developments, more mergers, more whatever.

"I was so tired I didn't hear a thing after my head hit the pillow," Claire said to her husband. "What time did you get in?"

Robert made a face. "I don't know. Late. Too late. Sonny's flight was delayed. I should have let him take a cab instead of going back to pick him up."

Cal went over to inspect the breakfast buffet. "I heard your car go by. You got here about five." Eggs, grits, bacon, country ham, gravy and biscuits on one side. Muffins, pastries, and bagels on the other.

"Five?" Claire frowned. "You and Sonny should have slept in. We have a few hours before the wedding."

"Sonny's never needed much sleep," Robert said, "and I'm not that tired. We used the time in the car to go over this zoning thing in Virginia. Sonny says we may have to go directly to the state legislature to get . . ." He droned on about red tape.

Cal tuned him out and poured himself and Claire coffee. He opened the lid of the warming pan. "Want a muffin, Bags?"

She shook her head. "I'm not very hungry."

"Come on, have one. They're blueberry, the kind you love."

"No, thanks. I can't eat a thing."

He winked at her. "Everything will be all right. Trust me." He put a muffin on a plate and took it to her. "Eat. I promise you'll feel better tonight," he said meaningfully.

"Oh." Hope lit her face. "All right." She began to pick at the muffin.

Robert noticed their exchange. "What's going on? What are you two plotting?"

Claire laughed without humor. "A wedding, I hope."

Robert examined her. "You're nervous."

"We're all nervous," Cal put in, to take the heat off Claire. "Aren't you?"

Robert's eyes narrowed, but Cal smiled pleasantly.

Too bad the Board was probably going to name Robert CEO. Too bad there was no one else they could name. Cal sure couldn't do the job.

Claire could. She'd be ten times better than her husband, but forget asking. She'd never emasculate Robert by taking a job he'd worked so hard to get.

Robert shrugged. "I suppose you're right, the pressure of the wedding's getting to all of us."

"We've had the auditors in all month, too. They've been a pain." Claire pinched off a blueberry. "We're always having to dig out junk for them. I wish the timing had been better."

"I know." Robert's face softened. He leaned over to take Claire's hand. "Perhaps when this wedding's over, you can relax. Why don't we take some time off, go on a cruise or something? Somewhere without the boys. Tip would babysit if we asked him."

Claire showed surprise, then pleasure. "That would be wonderful."

"We'll do it then. Let's have Sonny, no . . ." Robert's forehead creased. "Sonny's taking off on vacation right after the wedding. Talk to my secretary next week, darling, get her to make arrangements for us."

"Yes, I will," Claire said, beaming. "It'll be good for us to get away together, won't it?"

"A second honeymoon. Have Martha check my calendar."

Damn. Even a tiny bit of Robert's attention made Claire glow. *She deserves better.*

\* \* \* \*

AMANDA DESERVED EVERY bit of this uneasiness for what

she'd done. But she had nothing to worry about. Her nervous stomach had to stem from conscience.

Callaway McIntyre would have been on her like a shot the other day had he suspected Scarlet was the designer Jane. Instead, he had gone away without a backward glance.

But he still saw the dress and questioned Melissa about it. He'd even wanted to ask her about it.

She'd almost gotten Melissa to attend Johanna's wedding in her place but had reluctantly decided against it.

Her reputation rested on personal attention to the elaborate and costly bridal gowns she designed and sold. Sending Melissa might have caused people to wonder or started rumors circulating that Jane was slipping.

No, she would steam the gown and dress the bride and adjust the lace and straighten the train and flounces before Johanna started the march to the altar, the same way she did for every other bride she costumed. Any variance in her routine would only draw attention.

The last thing she needed was Callaway McIntyre's attention.

A few minutes before nine, she reached Fair Meadows. The large antebellum home east of Atlanta was an imposing venue for Johanna's wedding.

At the rear entrance, Amanda stopped at the intercom and showed identification to a camera. When the gates opened, she drove by a small white cottage half-hidden by rhododendrons and wisteria, and continued down a graveled drive lined with cherry trees profuse with flowers.

According to instructions, she bypassed the full circle lined by crepe myrtles that would have brought her to the front of the house with its six-columned, two-tiered portico, and pulled around to the back.

Of white frame construction similar to the cottage she'd passed, the main house had been enlarged by two additions, one on either side of the boxy two-story middle. The only vehicle in sight was a caterer's van at the main rear entrance, its doors open.

Amanda pulled her minivan up beside it.

A blue-jeaned Johanna skipped out. "Hi, Jane, I'm glad you're here."

Behind the greeting, excitement sparkled. She looked as excited as Noelle when she'd married Edward.

Amanda had been so relieved to see her sister settled, so happy. Thank heavens she'd managed to save Noelle's future.

She wouldn't think about Noelle now, nor worry about why she couldn't get hold of her. There was no time. Johanna was talking.

". . . Bring in my dress but could you possibly drop Claire's dress off at Cal's cottage on your way out this afternoon?"

"Cal's cottage?" Amanda's throat threatened to close.

"The little frame house you passed coming in. Nice and secluded. Cal can't stand noise, believe it or not." Johanna laughed as if the idea of her brother not liking noise was hilarious.

When Amanda said nothing, Johanna's laughter died away. "It would be such a big help if you can drop it off," she coaxed. "After all, we can't have Claire seeing her birthday present, can we? If it's anywhere in the house, she's certain to find it, and that would spoil the surprise."

Amanda gathered herself together. "Will your brother be there to take it?"

Johanna's smile grew brilliant. "If he could, I wouldn't have to ask you to help us out. No, Cal will be tied up here all day but he's leaving the door open. He said you can go right in and hang it in the living room coat closet. You're so sweet, Jane, to do this. And you look so elegant. Can I help get your things out?"

Johanna was a nice girl. "Yes, please. Come take the veil bag, and my appliance case."

*He won't be there when I drop off the dress,* Amanda reassured herself. Still, she didn't trust this twist, not one bit.

\* \* \* \*

WHEN CLAIRE WINSLOW put in an appearance later that morning, Amanda forgot her own worries.

Johanna's half-sister looked tired. More tired than could be blamed on the approaching wedding. Perhaps the peach and beige of Johanna's bedroom made Claire's complexion seem sallow, or perhaps it was the lack of makeup. Though neatly dressed in slacks and sweater, she seemed dispirited.

Amanda wondered why, but she had too many problems of her own to worry about Claire's. She still hadn't been able to talk to Noelle, and the possibility of meeting Callaway McIntyre scared her to death.

Also, the insurance adjusters had yet to decide whether or not to total her car, and she couldn't do anything about replacing it until they did.

To top everything off, last night's burglary attempt had left not only a damaged entrance at her apartment but the prospect of a visit to police headquarters to finish filling out yet more forms. Not to mention the repair bill for the sidelight and door still to come.

Too much paperwork entirely in life. Maybe the same thing was wrong with Claire.

"Your dress is gorgeous," Claire said to Johanna as Amanda finished steaming the silken creation. "Those pearls make the gown. Oh, gosh, I'm going to miss you, Princess."

"I'm only moving to Charlotte," Johanna said. "Not Timbuktu."

"I know. But it's a four-hour drive." The sisters looked at each other. Tears glistened, threatened to fall, but conscious of Amanda's presence, the two women laughed shakily and embraced.

An elderly man looked in, dressed in striped pants and dress shirt. "Claire, Johanna. Will one of you help me with these dratted buttons? My fingers are so stove up I can't fasten them."

"Let Johanna. I need to get dressed myself," Claire said. "Jane, this is Tip Lathen, my stepfather and the father of the bride. Tip, this is the Jane you've heard Johanna and me raving about. Hasn't she given Johanna a magnificent dress? You will forgive me, won't you, Jane, if I run on to change?" With a smile slightly askew, Claire left.

Tip was a kindly old soul, the sort of man who'd make a good father and grandfather. Though like Claire, he seemed too solemn for the occasion.

A cellphone rang. Johanna looked indecisively from her father's sleeve to the purse on her bed.

Amanda put down her steamer. "Let me finish that."

"Oh, thanks," Johanna said, running to pull out her cell. Her voice softened. "Oh, Jeremy. Hey. Don't you know you aren't supposed to speak to me till the wedding?" She carried the phone outside onto the balcony.

Tip Lathen chuckled. "I remember when she was born," he said as Amanda took his cuff. "She was the tiniest, most perfect thing I'd ever seen. I was assigned to a small town in Italy, and the nurses didn't speak English. They couldn't tell me if she was a boy or a girl, but she was so beautiful, I knew right off she was a girl."

Amanda finished one cuff, started on the second. "I believe I heard someone say you were in the diplomatic corps."

"Yes, but I resigned when Johanna was three and Lila took a greater role in the business. Johanna used to complain, very vociferously at times, I might add, that she missed out on a lot of exciting travel."

"Whenever I complained, Mother always told me I was lucky to be here at all." Johanna floated in from the balcony. "She said that you and she were out of your minds, starting a family at your ages. She said I was an embarrassment, coming along when Cal was nearly fourteen years old and her in her forties."

Tip mistook her needling for a real grievance. "My dear, you were a blessing. You know the teasing was just her way."

"Of course I do. I'm the luckiest person in the world. I just wish she could be here." Johanna threw her arms around her father and kissed him.

Amanda hesitated. "Do you need help with your tie, too?"

"Would you mind?" He turned back gratefully. "My hands are so arthritic that I can't do a thing for myself. It's a burdensome thing, growing old."

"The photographer should be here any minute," Johanna told Amanda as her father left, studs securely fastened and tie neatly tied. "It'll take an hour to get the photographs and then it'll be time to go down. It's going to be so beautiful."

Her sister might be under the weather, but Johanna was deliriously happy. Again, Amanda stanched memories of Noelle on her wedding day.

A car horn sounded from outside and Johanna ran to the French windows opening onto the balcony to wave. She came back inside, laughing. "That's my maid of honor," she said, with a lilt in her voice. "Lynette introduced me to Jeremy." She danced over to the door where Amanda steamed the lace veil. "The rest of my bridesmaids should be here soon, too. I need to make sure they stay away from Cal! One of them's a redhead."

"Oh?" Amanda felt constrained to say something. "Does he like redheads?"

Johanna snorted. "I'll say. Actually, he likes anything in panties." She laughed again. "I never thought I'd be so happy. Now where, oh where, did I put my bridesmaids' gifts?"

# CHAPTER SEVEN

THE GARDEN WEDDING of Johanna Maria Lathen to Jeremy Bartram Carruthers, scion of an old banking family from North Carolina, went off as planned, with but a few minor deviations.

Tip Lathen, the bride's ailing father, was suitably subdued, blinking to hide the moisture in his eyes as he handed Johanna over to her groom. When he pulled out a handkerchief and loudly blew his nose, every woman and several fathers smiled with sympathy.

Then there was the charming moment as rings were being exchanged, when the bride's pet cat strolled out from behind a fern and batted at a bead on the train. The flower girl stepped aside and picked it up, reproving it in a loud whisper. She held onto the squirming feline for the rest of the ceremony and carried it out at the end, still audibly scolding.

Many guests chuckled out loud.

On the lawn, the lunch reception was blessed with spring sunshine and blue skies. The dogwoods and cherries were at their height of color in the background, while fading iris and drifts of daffodils set off the pink azaleas leading to the formal gardens.

Eating at small tables near the patio buffet, people laughed and exchanged remarks about how well the ceremony had gone. They talked about how the adorable flower girl handled the cat's faux pas, how lovely the bride looked, how well-behaved Claire's twin sons were as ushers, and wasn't it a pity poor Lila hadn't lived long enough to see her youngest daughter looking so radiant?

Amanda moved among the chattering guests, dodging Callaway McIntyre.

"There's Senator Swift," she overheard one fortyish woman say to another while nodding toward a handsome man near the fountain. "Isn't he luscious? If my husband could look half that good when he's that age, I'd die happy."

"Honey, if my husband could look like that now, I'd die happy," came the quick retort.

They roared with laughter.

Amanda felt ancient.

Had she ever been so carefree?

She studied Matthew Swift. Okay, he did have a certain appeal about him. Straight of figure and courtly of manner, he was the epitome of a southern gentleman. Still, to go around rhapsodizing about him or any other man was not her style.

Images of Callaway McIntyre's laughing face came to mind to be hastily discarded.

She felt very virtuous and superior. There was no reason at all for her to feel she had lost something, somewhere, somehow, during the years she'd been struggling to succeed.

*I made my choices. I can live with them.*

While the obligatory wedding pictures were staged, she sipped on a cup of punch and stayed out of the way. Once the reception luncheon was over and the bridal gown safely put away, she could leave. She'd drop off Claire's dress in the cottage and be done with the McIntyres forever.

Thank heavens Callaway McIntyre was occupied with the photographer. She had no desire to come face to face with him again, watching in agony for that flicker of recognition that might or might not come.

He, she couldn't help noticing as he posed in his gray striped pants and morning coat, had more than his share of masculine appeal. Long legs, wide shoulders, easy smile. The chocolate eyes that told a woman she was fascinating.

Senator Swift's genteel manner was all very well, but there was something about Callaway McIntyre's insouciance that Amanda preferred.

If she had to choose between the two.

Which she didn't, because she wasn't interested in any man. Not even one whose remembered touch sent chills tumbling around her stomach.

Firmly expunging thoughts of Callaway McIntyre, she edged toward a secluded corner of the sunny garden and sat down on a wrought iron bench placed against a high boxwood hedge.

A man's voice, smooth and apologetic, came from behind the hedge. "Of course it could be a forgery. I only know what I got in the mail, but if you feel—"

"I feel threatened," a second voice, precise and mellifluous, interrupted. "I'm a politician, remember? How do we know this person hasn't made more copies?"

Matthew Swift. Who did the senator feel threatened by? Who was he talking to? Amanda looked over her shoulder, but the boxwood hedge was too dense to see anything or anybody.

"Copies aren't worth the paper they're printed on," the first man answered. "Anybody can forge something and make a copy. The original diary is all that could hurt any of you, Senator. I hate to say it, but if the papers get hold of this . . ." The words trailed off into a pregnant silence.

"The papers would almost certainly get hold of it, wouldn't they?" Contempt rasped the senator's tone. "Even if I agree, it's Sunday. I can't get that amount of cash today."

A burst of hilarity came from a noisy group approaching from the side. The footsteps behind Amanda's seat retreated.

The loud group went by her and toward the pond below. She crossed her ankles.

Hmm. Sounded like Senator Swift was being blackmailed, but that had to be an occupational hazard for politicians. Too bad. From everything she'd read, he was a decent man.

His wife had developed Alzheimer's in her thirties, but he'd dealt with it till she died some years back. He hadn't remarried, but finished raising their son by himself. Thoughtful and informed on big issues before Congress, he never displayed himself to disadvantage on television or press conferences, an almost impossible achievement for anyone in this Internet age.

Oh, well. Everybody had his secrets.

Including her.

Maybe Noelle would take her near-disaster to heart and find some new friends who were nice and sensible.

A pair of familiar faces came into the garden, and Amanda's bowels knotted up.

The maid of honor and her father.

The de Graffens had been in the box with Callaway that night in Houston. She'd actually met Miles. What if one of them recognized her?

Why, oh why, had she come here today? She was a fool for not sending Melissa.

Father and daughter followed the rock walk without noticing Amanda. Lynette de Graffen, in the jonquil-yellow attendant gown that flattered her dark eyes and skin, said, "I don't understand why you're so against him."

Her father was blunt. "He's after your money."

"You have no reason to think that."

"I know it. Believe me. Please. He's not someone you want to get mixed up with."

The girl's face clouded. "Dad . . ."

"Trust me in this, sweetheart. Please."

Lynette looked away.

"I love you too much to see you hurt." Miles touched her arm gently. "Think about it." He looked over her shoulder and heaved a sigh. "There's Robert waiting for me. I'll see you at home later. We'll discuss it then."

Lynette lowered her head, a mulish look on her face.

Uh oh, that girl wasn't about to listen to her father.

*She's not my problem, thank heavens.*

When Lynette wandered along the path toward Amanda's haven, Amanda picked up her punch cup and fled, following the flagstones round the hedge into an adjoining garden with a small gazebo on one end. Choosing a vantage point on one of the gazebo's wooden benches, she tried to enjoy the vista of meadow and sparkling pond in the distance but found herself continually monitoring the entrance to the garden for intruders.

She was in turmoil, and had been ever since Callaway McIntyre walked into her shop.

No, she'd been in turmoil since long before then.

From the time he'd grasped her wrist in the theater box and every nerve in her body had jolted to life.

She wouldn't think of her body's betrayal now. She had to stay out of sight. There was no sense in flaunting her presence in front of people who might remember her.

Would the day never be over?

\* \* \* \*

CHRIST, THE DAY would never end.

In between greeting guests, Cal found a moment alone with Claire.

She grasped his elbow. "At breakfast, did you mean you've found out something?"

"I'll know by the end of the day but it looks promising. We'll talk later. Robert looks like he could murder me."

She glanced over to where he stood watching them. "He's under a lot of pressure right now."

"Yeah. He thinks once this audit's over, the Board's going to name him CEO."

"Cal, let's not discuss it now. He's been really pleasant this morning, almost as nice as he used to be."

"He's coming this way and so is Miles. Two people I don't want to talk to. I'll catch you later."

"Sonny!" he heard Robert call. "Where've you been? Do you know where I left the file on the Las Vegas project we were going over this morning? Miles might have a tenant for one of the spaces."

Sonny, Sonny, Sonny! It was always Sonny. Immediately after the thought, Cal laughed at himself. He was jealous because Sonny played an important part in the business while he was—yeah, might as well face it—a screw-up.

Claire did her usual tactful thing. "I saw the file up in the sitting room, Robert. I'll get it for you."

Sonny, neat in a navy pinstripe suit and maroon tie, with a smiling Lynette on his arm, wandered up in time to hear. "No, no, I'll go, Claire. I'm sure you're needed here."

"Yes." Miles's grim eyes swept past Sonny to his daughter. "Let Sonny get them, Robert. In fact, why don't I walk upstairs with you, Sonny? All I want is a quick look at the estimates."

Cal turned his back to the men and Claire, and found a group he could hide in.

* * * *

AMANDA HID AT the fringe of the crowd.

It had to be past time for Johanna to change into her going-away outfit.

Where was Callaway? Ah, over there dancing with a lively bridesmaid and, from their raucous laughter, enjoying himself immensely.

Amanda's stomach lurched and her temple gave the little twinge that signaled a headache coming on. She moved far away from Cal, toward the protection offered by a rose-trellised patio.

A familiar voice caught her ear. "So everything's okay with our contract? I told you you'd be pleased, Miles."

She turned, recognized Lynette's father with another man heading toward her.

Merciful heavens, could she never escape those people from Houston? Even Claire's husband had turned out to be one of them. Was she doomed to keep running into reminders from that horrible night? Was this some sort of purgatory?

As she hid behind a column of ferns, she heard de Graffen say, "We're good there, you've done the job. But I want to talk to you about Lynette, Sonny."

Only when they went into the house did she realize the younger man's voice was the same one that had subtly threatened Senator Swift.

Another man from Callaway's box.

*Wonder what he's doing trying to blackmail the senator?*

Johanna had her groom in tow and was beckoning to Lynette de Graffen.

The newlyweds were finally going inside to change clothes. The end of her nightmare was in sight.

Thank goodness.

\* \* \* \*

ABOUT TIME.

Cal watched Johanna and her groom disappear inside the house. The afternoon had been interminable.

Claire was near to collapse. She'd always been the strong one, buffering him from their mother and standing up for him when he failed, as he had always failed, to meet Lila's expectations. Since Claire had protected him all his life, it hurt to see her this way because of his damned weakness for redheads.

Never mind. He would make it right.

He whirled the girl in his arms around and around, teasing and flirting until he barely knew what he said. It didn't matter. She'd had too much of the champagne punch to care whether he was coherent or not. When he remembered the last time he'd danced with a woman, rage threatened to overwhelm him.

Later, he promised himself as he towed the bridesmaid toward the gate where the bride and groom would be leaving. Later, he'd deal with his anger and the woman who'd caused it.

As the bridal couple reappeared in travel clothes, Johanna kissed Tip and Claire, and then Cal.

Amanda Jane would be upstairs, packing up the wedding gown and getting ready to leave. He would see Johanna off and go to his cottage.

The bridal bouquet reeled toward Lynette de Graffen, who caught it, looked directly at Sonny Kirkman, and turned pink. Cal tossed his birdseed at the couple rushing to the limo.

*Keep your cool.*

This was not the time or place to make a mistake. He'd soon have little Miss Scarlet-Amanda in hand and then he could give way to anger.

He intended to savor every minute.

\* \* \* \*

EVERY MOMENT BROUGHT Amanda more assurance. It was going to be all right.

The clock hands were both past four before she went down the stairs with her tool case. The afternoon sun slanted through the mullioned windows in the back of the house and laid a rich golden gossamer over the hardwood floors and oriental runner.

With the burdens of the world off her shoulders, she practically danced out to the minivan.

She'd made it. She could leave Claire's dress and get out of here, go home and try again to reach Noelle. Callaway McIntyre might have seen the black dress but it hadn't led him to her and with luck, it wouldn't.

As she rushed to load up paraphernalia, she would have sung if she'd been able to carry a tune.

Her ordeal was over.

# CHAPTER EIGHT

NO INTIMATION OF danger emanated from the deep pink rhododendrons and azaleas ringing Callaway McIntyre's neat cottage. Beyond them Amanda could see the gate marking her escape route from Fair Meadows.

Soon as she dropped off the dress, she'd be gone. Far, far away where she'd never have to see Callaway McIntyre again.

A cobbled path led to the door, unlocked as promised.

Still no hint of anything wrong.

In the vacant house she headed toward the closet door beyond the sofa. She'd hang up the dress and get out. Pronto.

Not until she passed the field-rock fireplace did a creaking door make her pivot.

Callaway McIntyre, coat unbuttoned, filled the entry. His face was no longer easygoing. He looked more like a rampaging bull.

He slammed the door. Its crash reverberated.

A dead bolt key, its ominous click filling the room, turned.

Amanda's mouth fell open. "I-I-I . . . What are you doing?" *No, no! He doesn't know. He can't know!*

One corner of his lips turned up in a half-smile neither polite nor pleasant. "Getting back what's mine, Scarlet." The key slid into his pants pocket.

Scarlet. *He knows.*

Sanity fled. She backed away, tongue dry, ears pounding. Her mouth opened, but no sound came out.

Eyelids narrowed to slits, he parted the front of his morning coat as if readying for combat. The smile that wasn't a smile stayed in place.

How could he possibly know? He couldn't. Why was . . . ?

His coat slipped off. He balled it up in a deliberate movement defying comment and torpedoed it to the side. Then he marched toward her one step at a time. "Where is it?"

Amanda retreated toward the hall.

The first door led into a closet, the second into a bedroom. She whirled but too late.

He was at her elbow, his hand shooting out to imprison her wrist. She yelped.

"You sure can find your way to the bedrooms, can't you? Strange house or not. Guess you've had plenty of practice." His tone was level, he still wore the tiny smile, but his eyes flashed. "All right, Scarlet. You've got a hell of a lot to explain."

"Get away." Amanda backed away. No matter how she tried, she couldn't yank her wrist free.

He followed, step for step, through the short hallway.

She reached a wall.

He blocked her in, so close she could smell the champagne punch on his breath. "Where's the journal?"

Something, a small hard object, punched her between the shoulder blades. "I don't know what you're talking about."

Wrenching to one side, she escaped the gouging thermostat but not him. He held her fast.

"I d-do know you're going to be in big trouble for this," she stuttered.

Infuriated, he caught her chin, trapped her head against the wall. "What did you do with the things you stole from me?"

"I didn't steal anything!" This couldn't be happening. No man had ever gotten physical with her. She abhorred violence. Especially after Tommy . . .

"The hell you didn't. Where are they?" He held her against the sheetrock. "Where. Are. My. Things."

When she writhed to the side, his chest pushed her back. The muscles against her breasts radiated anger.

"You bastard! I never stole anything from you." Taking Noelle's ring wasn't stealing. Not really. "I didn't."

He grabbed her wrists, pulling them over her head. His body kept her pinned to the wall. "A thief and a liar."

The air whooshed out of her. Her arms were stretched too far. "You're hurting me."

"But I knew what you were, didn't I? Listen to me, Scarlet. You're going to tell me where my things are and you're going to tell me now."

"Let me go." She struggled, but he was too strong.

"I don't like being made a fool of. I hate it almost as much as being lied to." He gritted his teeth. "Now. One more time. Where are the things you stole? Where is that book?"

*Don't fight him. Go along with him until you can escape.*

She went limp. His body was all that held her upright. "I don't have your book." The ruffles of his shirt pressed into her cheek. Woodsy aftershave mingled with a musky masculine odor. Buttons cut into her skin. She couldn't breathe, caught between him and the wall. "I didn't steal—"

He jerked her wrists higher.

She whimpered.

He released her so abruptly she would have fallen except that he caught her by the shoulders.

"Where's the book?" Fury smoldered beneath the control, a fury that, once unleashed, would roll over her and obliterate her. His fingers on her shoulders tightened, dug into the bones.

She wouldn't cry, she wouldn't. She'd keep her head upright, look him in the eyes. "I don't know what you're talking about."

Enraged, he shook her.

"Stop!"

Grunting, he took his hands off her and clenched them as if to keep them from crushing her. "All right, Scarlet. I didn't want to involve the police, but we'll do it your way."

"The police?" Her reputation, her clients, her entire business would be lost. Everything she'd worked for during the past eight years. Her physical fear vanished under his new threat.

He reached for the phone.

She started to run.

His arm shot out, blocking her, forcing her down the hall.

A different door. A bedroom. Large bed. Large painting. White walls. Browns and blues. French windows opening to the outside. Greenery, splashes of purple, red flowering bushes.

If she could reach the window . . .

He stayed on her heels, close enough to catch her elbow.

Whirling, she kicked out.

He shunted her foot aside, throwing them both off balance so that they stumbled and fell onto the bed in a tangled heap. His knee caught her dress and fabric ripped.

"Get off me!"

He rolled off but held tight to her arm. "You may as well stop your sniveling. Before you leave this house, I'll know who hired you and what you did with my things you stole. The quicker you tell me, the quicker you can leave."

"I'm not sniveling. And there's no reason for you hurting me." When she tried to sit up, her wrist bent backwards too far. "Ouch! I told you I didn't take—"

He shoved her flat. "Don't bother repeating yourself. If you think I've hurt you, you're wrong. You don't know what hurt is, but you keep on and you're liable to learn."

His contempt was so palpable, he practically smoldered.

Scared witless, she stayed perfectly still. There had to be something that would pacify him, keep him from going to the police.

What could she say?

"That's right, sugah," came the hateful drawl. "Just lie there. I'm sure you know how to do that real well."

The gibe pierced her fear, made her stiffen.

He got up. "Better practice your wiles. You're about to tell your story to the police."

"You can't call the police." Her dress, caught beneath her, held her immobile.

"No?" He stood at the foot of the bed. His eyes that long ago had been warm and admiring were cold. "Do you have other ideas? We could put off calling them for a while if you want. You prefer your sex slow, I believe."

"You don't know anything about me." Freeing her dress, she used her heels to scoot toward the top of the bed and away from him.

"I know enough." His eyes narrowed, his nostrils flared. "Where is my book?" He took off his tie. Slowly. Deliberately.

"I don't know anything about any book." There was no room to run. Not that running would do any good. He would simply call the police and have her arrested. Why hadn't she told Noelle she wouldn't do it?

Holding up a sleeve, he removed a cuff link. "They say you can catch more flies with honey than vinegar." Leisurely, he loosened the other sleeve. "You believe that, Scarlet? Want to see if it's true? We could finish what we started the other night. It might put us both in better moods." He tossed the links on a table and began undoing his shirt. "We were having a pretty good time, as I recall."

His tone was seductive, his face terrible.

"You . . ." When she scooted up some more, her head banged the headboard.

The shirt came off and fell to the floor.

Dear God, he meant it. "You can go to jail for this. You're going to be in big trouble if you don't let me go."

A lightning movement brought him onto the bed, kneeling beside her. "Trouble?"

She turned to escape but he caught her, rolled with her so that he lay stretched out on her, his length molded to her back, her butt. "You're the one in trouble. You're damned lucky I haven't already gone to the police."

His body exuded an all-over heat. The spread rustled beneath her ear. When she turned her face to free it from the suffocating pillow, her cheek and nose pushed against his silk undershirt. His masculine scent mingled with woodsy cologne. "I c-can't breathe."

His chest pushed into her back. He murmured at her ear, "This is about where we were, wasn't it? When we were interrupted in the middle of our good time? By one roofie. Or a relative. You remember?"

Shame filled her. "Get off me."

"Do you remember how far we'd got that night when you stopped the game in the middle? Want to start over? After all, you owe me."

The scumbag. He was lower than dirt. "I don't owe you anything." The words sounded too defensive. She hardened her voice. "Get off!"

"No way." His fingers threaded her hair. Almost like a lover's caress. "You're going to tell me all about our night together. You're going to tell me who put you up to it, and why, and then you're going to tell me where my things are that you stole . . ."

"I didn't steal your things." His thigh was close enough to hit with the side of her fist.

He caught that fist and then the other. ". . . from me, and you're going to start now. If you don't . . ." His voice at her ear softened, became insinuating in a way more terrifying than his anger. "We'll call the police. But we can put that off awhile if you prefer. I've waited weeks for what you promised, Scarlet. We have some time now."

One of his hands clasped her wrists above her head while the other slid underneath her to pass through the front opening of her dress.

"No!" Outrage helped her free one wrist.

When she swung her elbow at his face, he dodged and laughed. "You like it rough?" The hand inside her dress tightened on her breast. "I'll give you whatever you want. Just say the word."

"Get away from me, you bastard! It was only a ring. You can buy a million rings." When she threw her weight to the side, he held tight. Terror filled her. She couldn't fight him off. He was too big, too strong.

"You can buy a million rings," she sobbed.

Her sudden lack of resistance must have surprised him because his grip loosened. He leaned back.

Taking advantage, she rolled to the side and fell off the bed. Carpet burned her knees, but she barely felt the sting in her scramble to stand up and push hair out of her eyes.

She had to keep away from him.

He slid off the other side of the bed, gulping for breath. They watched each other across the mattress, two hostile animals waiting for an opening.

"You took more than a ring." His words were flat. "And you

know it. I don't give a damn about a frigging ring. You could have had it that night if you'd asked me. But the journal and my diamond studs are a different matter. I want them back and I want them back now."

Journal? Diamonds?

"What are you talking about?" What did he think she took from him?

He couldn't mean . . .

Her jaw dropped.

\* \* \* \*

CAL DIDN'T MISS Amanda Jane's shock. Though her mouth softened so that it resembled that of the redhead who had first beguiled him, there was no trace of coquetry about the woman before him.

Her bewilderment took the edge off the fury that had seethed for days.

"I, I don't know what you mean. I only took Noe . . . I only took a ring." The words between gasps were so low he almost missed them. "The emerald ring was all I took. I swear that was all I took. It was."

His own lungs struggled for air, but he'd already dropped his guard once when she'd whimpered beneath him, when he realized he was hurting her.

He couldn't afford to drop it again. He had to be alert, ready to catch her if, when, she made a break for it. "Then why am I missing a set of diamond studs and a book?"

She shook her head vehemently. Tresses of brown hair clung to one cheek and fell to her shoulder. A part of him took in her dishevelment and exposed breast, noted how defenseless, how trapped she looked. It was hard to remember what she was, what she'd done.

Hard to maintain his rage. "Well?"

"There were other things in the safe, but I didn't take them. Why should I? All I wanted was her engagement ring. If you'd given it back to Noelle, I'd never have come. Her ring is all I came to Houston for, and that's all I took."

He curled his lip, for his benefit as well as for hers. "Liar."

"It's true." She brushed back strands of hair with trembling fingers, poise long since fled.

No longer the cool and collected businesswoman, she was as terrified as a colt cornered by a wolf. "It is true. If you'd just returned Noelle's ring after you took it as a gambling pledge . . ." Her words tumbled out. "If you'd returned it when she begged you, I'd never have been there."

"Noelle? Your sister? She said that?" Despite his efforts to whip up anger, he failed as a piece fell into place.

He sorted facts and tried to match them, all the time wondering if he could believe her.

Damn it to hell, of course he couldn't believe her.

He knew better than to trust somebody like her.

"I got the ring from your sister, yes, but I got it in Houston. I bought it outright because she needed money." He sneered. "She said she needed money for her sick baby."

"No, that's not . . . Noelle wouldn't . . ."

He watched her already pale face turn white.

Maybe she didn't know.

* * * *

*WHAT'S GOING ON?*

Doubts filled Amanda, doubts stemming from memories of other instances when her sister had twisted the truth. Because of those doubts, denials were bit off.

She couldn't panic, not with Callaway McIntyre so furious.

"I understood," she said, choosing her words with care, "that you made Noelle a loan at a Las Vegas casino when she was low on cash. She gave you her engagement ring as collateral, and when she went to pay you back, you wouldn't give up her ring."

He shook his head. "The first time I saw her was in Houston when I bought the ring from her. There was no question of it being collateral. She never tried to get it back. I bought it outright one morning and by the next day, it was gone. Stolen." He scowled. "By you."

Could it be true? Could Noelle have lied to Amanda, used her? But why?

Her hands twisted together in a nervous habit long ago broken. She unclasped them.

This was ridiculous. Noelle wasn't a thief. Self-absorbed and silly sometimes, but she wasn't a thief.

Then why had Noelle lied? Or had she lied?

No, the man before her was toying with her. "I don't believe you. My sister isn't a thief."

"It doesn't matter what you believe. I want my diamonds and that book back, and you're going to give them to me or talk to the police."

Her heart sank. "You don't want the ring?"

His face turned red. "I'm sick to death of hearing about some trumpery ring. I don't give a good goddam about that ring. I never wanted the frigging ring to start with. What I do want are my studs and that book, and I want them now. If you don't tell me where the hell they are, you'll be an old woman when you get out of prison."

Amanda's last hope shattered. He didn't care about Noelle's ring. He had never cared about it.

Her legs failed, depositing her on the floor with no will left for battle.

He wasn't lying. Her sister had been the liar.

Numb, she realized something else.

She was in trouble. Big trouble. "So I'm a thief. I'm sorry. I don't know why you should believe me, but all I took was the ring. I don't have it now."

Her hands clenched and unclenched. The magnitude of her crime paralyzed her, but overriding that was anger with Noelle.

Why had Noelle lied? Had she planned to steal the diamonds? No, Noelle wasn't that dishonest. Or that intelligent. Maybe Noelle hadn't lied. She could usually tell whenever Noelle wasn't being completely truthful. Although when Noelle had taken her ring at the apartment and left, there had been something . . .

"All right." His tone was milder. His eyes were back to chocolate. While he stood next to her, he made no move to manhandle her. "Noelle planned it, did she? Your hooking up with me and robbing me, I mean?"

Amanda nodded, the words choking in her throat. "I was trying to help her recover something you took from her illegally. Well. At least immorally."

He looked down his nose.

"That is, I thought you had taken it. I'd never have done it if she hadn't, if I hadn't thought she . . ." The tears were too close to the surface. She put an elbow over her face. "The ring was Edward's—her husband—his grandmother's ring. He would have divorced her if he found out she'd lost it gambling. He'd never have forgiven her."

Then his explanation for possessing the ring penetrated. His story didn't make sense.

When she tried to stand, he didn't move to help so she used the bed to pull herself up. "I can't believe Noelle sold it to you. Edward would be bound to find out."

"Maybe she doesn't care." He waved impatiently. "Anyway, she got it back, didn't she? Who told you the safe combination?" He read the answer in her face. "Noelle again?"

She wet her lips. "She said you boasted about it. I suppose that was a lie, too."

"I suppose you're right. You're quite sure you didn't take the other things?"

"No. Though why you should believe me, I don't know." She spread out both hands, palms up. "I've never done anything like that. Never. And I wouldn't have this time except that Noelle was about to . . . Dear God, if Edward finds out about this, he'll, he'll . . . What do you intend to do?"

He chewed on the inside of his jaw like he was brooding over thoughts other than her muddled excuses.

"So your sister talked you into going through that little performance in Houston to get her ring back." The quiet words belied the simmering air between them.

Amanda nodded. "You don't believe me, but it's true."

"I'm not sure what I believe. When you opened the safe, did you see anything else in it?"

"Yes." She tried hard to remember. "Some kind of box." The image was at the edge of her consciousness, almost within grasp. "Brown. Leather, maybe."

"Is that all?"

She balled her hands into fists.

He closed his own hands over them. Not with hostility but not with comfort either.

Her legs trembled again. "I wasn't going to hit you. It's a habit I have."

"Is that all you saw?" He kept hold of her fists.

What had been in the safe when she looked inside? "There was a little box or book or something underneath the leather case. I remember Noelle's ring was lying right beside them. That was what I wanted. I didn't care about anything else."

He let her go. "I suppose the next thing to do," he said almost to himself, "is talk to your sister."

"Noelle? She won't know any more than me about your other stuff. If you're missing anything besides the ring, then someone took them while you were . . ." She stopped.

"Knocked out," he supplied helpfully.

"Yes." She swallowed. "But I didn't take them. Noelle doesn't—"

"Someone stole them while I was under the influence of a drug you fed me, Scarlet."

*Why did I think he was easygoing?*

"It would be," he ruthlessly pursued the train of thought, "someone who knew I'd be unconscious. Someone who meant you to take the blame. If that's true, it means you're wrong about your sister. It means she set you up. Like you set me up."

"Not Noelle." Amanda's legs nearly buckled again. To keep from falling, she sat down on the bed. "All she wanted was her ring. Noelle wouldn't do that to me."

"Wouldn't she? Oh, no, Scarlet, if you're telling the truth, Noelle will know a lot more about this. What the hell did you give me to knock me out so fast?"

"That date rape stuff." Miserable, she rested her head in her hands. "Edward's a pharmacist. He told Noelle what it was one time. She got some and we figured out how to use it."

"Christ. You could have killed me."

"No." She lifted her face, aghast. "I looked it up on the Internet and it . . ."

Under his outrage, she faltered. "We thought it would be all right."

The lash of his unspoken contempt mocked her. She saw her exposed breast and straightened her bodice. The seam was ripped, but she folded it together as best she could.

He was quiet for a long time. Did he believe her?

"Okay," he said at last. "Assuming for the moment you're a victim, too, how did you get a ticket to the opening?"

"Noelle. She knew someone who wasn't going."

"Someone in Texas?"

"I don't know. She said it was a friend."

"The lady the invitation went to wasn't even in the country and I bet Noelle never met her."

She didn't answer. There was no need.

He went on, "If you're telling the truth, and Noelle talked you into that moronic stunt, she had an accomplice."

"An accomplice?" Her hands and feet felt as numb as her mind.

"Someone who knew I'd be at the Houston opening." He threw out one finger. "Someone who had access to ticket information, to reserve your box." A second finger went up, followed by a third and fourth. "Someone who knew I'd bring my studs. And someone who knew my combination. Your sister couldn't have guessed all that."

"Noelle did know your combination," Amanda said, still dazed. "Maybe she overheard you mention it to someone."

"I don't talk about confidential things. And certainly not in front of a woman I met once in my life." He snorted. "If there's one thing I've learned in thirty-five years, it's how to keep my mouth shut. How do we get in touch with your sister?"

"I can call her." Or try to.

No wonder Noelle had been avoiding her calls.

He followed her back through the cottage to her van. Under his vigilant eyes, she got out her purse with her cell and hit Noelle's number. A computer-generated voice answered.

Her breath went away.

The call ended. Her breath came back. "Her number's no longer in service."

"Give that to me." He took her cellphone and ushered her back into the cottage.

There was no need to resist.

"I kind of expected your sister wouldn't make it easy. I guess we'll have to go to her. She lives in Birmingham?"

"What do you mean to do? You can't bother Noelle. Edw—"

"Can't I?" His mouth was ugly. "Watch me."

"It'll take four or five hours to drive there." *That's right. Speak reasonably. I'm good at reasoning with people.* "You can't go barging in at ten or eleven o'clock. Edward will wonder—"

"The hell with what Edward wonders." He glanced out the window at the darkening sky. "I don't care. But you're right. It's too late to drive, and I'm too beat. It's been an, um, exciting day. We'll wait till morning."

"I have to get back to Atlanta. I have a shop to run. I can't be away from . . ."

The single raised brow stopped her words.

"You're no fool, Scarlet. You're not leaving my sight till we find your sister and she tells me where my things are. You're going to be damned lucky not to land in jail, the both of you."

"I can't stay with you. I have to get back to my shop."

His voice grew silky, but his mouth twisted unpleasantly. "Of course you can stay with me. We've practically spent the night together already. As I recall, we were very intimate."

He let her stew before letting loose a mocking laugh. "Don't worry, Scarlet," he threw over his shoulder as he pulled out his cell. "I may be a fool, but I do learn from experience. You aren't very appetizing anymore." He pushed the screen. "Claire, your dressmaker is going to stay the night with me."

Amanda stiffened with impotent outrage.

"Yes, Jane knows about my mystery woman and is anxious to help. Isn't that nice of her? Could the kitchen send over some food? Yep, more than cooperative. She and I are going to Birmingham, to visit her sister. Will you see if the helicopter's free tomorrow and let me know?"

Once he listened, his voice became gentle. "I hope so. Try not to worry, Bags."

"Claire will think you and I are shacked up together," Amanda flung at him after he hung up. "You'll make her think I'm a tramp. You're deliberately ruining my reputation." Her protests might be useless, but she had to try.

Callaway didn't bother to answer.

"My business is built on my reputation. If it gets out that I spent the night with you . . ."

He spared her one cynical shrug. "You'll sell twice as many dresses, sugar. Relax and enjoy the free food and lodging, but don't look to me for entertainment."

It might be prudent to remain silent, Amanda decided.

\* \* \* \*

GOOD THING SHE shut up. Cal was beginning to feel sorry for her the way her sister had worked her. If she was telling the truth. Which he kind of thought she was.

Yeah, right. Like he would know when a woman was lying or not.

Claire called back in a few minutes. The helicopter was booked, but she had reserved one of the company planes to pick them up at eight the next morning. "What do you think about Jane?" she asked.

Cal recognized her tone. "Do not try to fix me up with your dressmaker. You know I'm not husband material."

"If you could find someone as nice as Jane instead of those usual bimbos you run around with, you'd be a perfect husband."

"No way. She's, ah," He glanced at the stiff form sitting on the sofa. "She's simply being kind enough to help with our problem."

He ought to tell Claire exactly what Jane was, but for some reason, he didn't.

"You and Sonny and your women. I overheard him talking while ago, giving some girl his usual line. Don't you sweet-talk Jane and get her hopes up, Cal. She's nice."

"I think the last thing she'll do is get her hopes up."

Nor was she nice, he could have added but didn't. Amanda might be telling the truth or she might not. He'd find out the next day.

Damn, wasn't it just his luck to get tangled up with another calculating, deceitful female? Interfering in her sister's life, running roughshod over him and then whining because she got caught.

Now she expected him to believe she didn't know a thing about what her sister was doing.

Well, he was through being a sucker. Like he told her, she wasn't getting out of his sight till he found that book.

# CHAPTER NINE

AMANDA PICKED AT leftover reception food with Callaway McIntyre while a baseball game played on television. Smoke clouded the air as cigarette after cigarette filled the ash tray to overflowing. He might appear oblivious, but she could tell he watched her every move.

Later, he put her in a bedroom across from the one where they had scuffled. "I had that bolt installed especially for you, Scarlet. You should be flattered."

She bristled and he grinned. At least, his mouth did. "Better learn to deal with it. I don't trust you an inch, and until I have my things back, you aren't getting out of my sight unless you're under lock and key."

Damn the man. There was a large Chinese vase on a table next to her hand, probably terribly valuable. Her fingers itched to break it over his head, but she kept herself from seizing the vase and hurling it.

Instead, she entered the bedroom and slammed the door.

The bolt turned on the outside, leaving her alone and, courage dissolving, traumatized. The one window was closed, secured by a shiny key-lock that looked recently installed. "If there's a fire and I burn to death, he'll be liable."

Muttering defiance didn't help.

There was no phone and he had taken her cell, but she found a bathroom with a tiny window of circular stained glass sealed shut. A new toothbrush lay on the marble sink while a robe hung beside thick towels on an ornate corner rack.

Callaway McIntyre had made careful arrangements.

How long had he known?

The dress. The label. She should have realized once he'd seen it, he'd chase it down.

In the shower, she let hot water massage her tense shoulders. How could she have been attracted to him? He was rude and hateful as well as a sadist. She'd love to take him down a notch.

Not that he didn't have a right to be all those things, if he was telling the truth about Noelle.

Amanda cringed beneath the spray. Somehow she knew he was telling the truth.

There must be an explanation.

Perhaps Callaway's plan to confront Noelle was for the best.

Edward should be at work and need never learn about his wife's duplicity, and Amanda wouldn't be missed at the shop since Monday was her off-day.

After showering, she wrapped up in the robe and checked the bedroom window. Just to see, she told herself. A gentle tug proved it immovable. The room was a prison.

Pulling out the sewing kit she always carried in her purse, she repaired her torn dress so that it was presentable. Then she brushed her teeth, put her camisole and panties back on, and slid between the sheets.

Sleep didn't come.

What would Noelle say? If she didn't have a good explanation, and if Callaway pressed charges, she and Amanda would be in serious trouble. Noelle had brought this whole mess on herself, but Amanda had agreed to help. They deserved any punishment Cal devised.

Except jail meant Noelle would lose Edward and Teddy for sure. And if Amanda went to jail, she could never rebuild her clientele. Her chance for success would be gone, along with every ounce of self-respect.

*I let protecting Noelle cloud my judgment. I knew better. If we go to jail, it'll be my own fault.*

* * * *

THIS MESS WAS his fault, but Cal was trying his best to salvage something. For Claire's sake he had to.

She'd sent breakfast over to the cottage. French toast, muffins, bagels, and orange juice. Nothing tasted good, but he forced down a bagel slathered with cream cheese.

Amanda toyed with French toast until finally she pushed her plate away and spoke for the first time that morning. "Do you have anything for a headache?"

He hadn't said anything since unlocking her door and telling her to get up. Nor was speech necessary now. He found a bottle of pain reliever and watched her take two tablets with her coffee.

As they left the cottage, he gripped her arm.

"Don't worry," she said, pulling loose. "I'm not going to run away. I'd be foolish to let everything I've worked for be destroyed because of a misunderstanding."

"There was no misunderstanding, Scarlet."

Her eyes, gray instead of green and devoid of makeup, looked weak, but she didn't flinch. "When we find Noelle, she'll tell us why she got me to steal that ring and who gave her all the information."

"Fine. In the meantime, I'm not taking chances on you running off."

"I told you I won't run away."

"Yeah. Right."

Once in the car, she laid her head back against the headrest and closed her eyes.

At the airfield, he nudged her toward the red and white Cessna waiting to take them to Birmingham. "Come on. We're late." He greeted the pilot, but saw no need to introduce the two women.

Amanda didn't seem to care. The ibuprofen must not have helped because she still looked white around the mouth, the way Claire did whenever she had a migraine. He started to ask if her headache was better, but held his tongue. He shouldn't care about her headache.

Once they were airborne, she closed her eyes, still looking sick.

Well, hell. His head hurt, too, from the sleepless night spent reviewing what she'd told him.

He was pretty sure her sister's accomplice was a man, and he suspected the man was Sonny Kirkman. Sonny was persuasive with women, and as Robert's assistant, had opportunities to get the safe combination. Much as Cal liked Sonny, he couldn't come up with any other possibilities.

Shooting a glance at the haggard woman beside him in the small plane, he found himself wanting to believe her story and absolve her. After all, if she was willing to break the law to help her sister, shouldn't her misguided loyalty be commended?

Sort of?

He knew firsthand the desperation engendered by a sister's cry for help.

*Damn it, I'm letting a pretty face get to me again.*

By now he ought to know how gullible he was when it came to women. Not that she looked pretty this morning, without makeup and with her mundane hair slicked back in that hideous knot. Unhappy, sick, and worried, but not pretty.

Damn her. He would make her sorry for what she'd done, and not simply because she had turned his and Claire's lives upside down. He wanted to make her sorry because she had flirted and led him on for her sister's sake. Because she had never been attracted to him. He wanted to make her sorry so as to soothe his wounded pride.

How petty, he jeered. Male ego. That's all it was. He ought to be too damned experienced to let ego color his reactions.

*We'll find her frigging sister and get Mother's journal back,* he promised himself, *and then I'll never have to see Amanda Jane again.*

* * * *

MAYBE THEIR TALK with Noelle would pacify Callaway. Maybe he'd learn what he wanted to know and get through with them. Maybe she'd never have to see him again.

Amanda wished.

Outside a small airport near Birmingham, a rental car awaited them.

He was thorough in his arrangements, she thought as she gratefully slid into the passenger side. The pain reliever had alleviated her headache, changing it from a steady hammering to a dull throb.

Callaway drove, his only speech regarding the GPS directions to the rolling area of Alabama where Noelle lived. His tense shoulders proved him geared up for mutiny on her part despite her assurances that she had no intention of running away.

For heavens' sake, how did he think she could possibly run away with his threat of prison hanging over her?

At Noelle's house, one in a subdivision of large homes with steepled and broken roofs, he stood at Amanda's shoulder when she rang the doorbell.

Her brother-in-law opened the door.

"Edward." Oh, no, he was supposed to be at work.

Noelle's husband, a slight man with a mustache and thinning ginger hair, was dressed in undershirt and slacks. The smell of soap attested to a recent shower.

"Amanda?" He blinked owlishly, uncertain whether or not she was really there. He eventually decided that she was. "Amanda." His perplexed gaze took in Callaway and came back to her. "What are you doing here? It's awful early."

He didn't sound happy to see them, and she had no excuse prepared. "Why, w-we, I, um, you know I always, um, take Mondays off, and—"

"I took Amanda flying," Callaway McIntyre's smooth voice rescued her, "and she suggested we visit her sister." He draped a friendly arm around her.

Surprised, Amanda suffered his arm without protest. She even managed a craven smile, so gratified was she that he wasn't spilling all the wrongs suffered at her and Noelle's hands. His cover-up made her feel almost kindly toward him.

"So here we are. I hope we haven't come at a bad time." Dispelling any gratitude he'd earned, Callaway added, "I felt we should call first, but Mandy said it would be fine to drop in unannounced. Insisted on it, in fact."

"Don't call me Mandy," she snapped before remembering Edward's presence. She banished her frown. "I knew Noelle would be here. Is it a bad time, Edward?"

Her brother-in-law didn't smile back. "You're always welcome, Amanda, but Noelle isn't here."

"She isn't?"

Callaway interceded again. "Where is she?"

Edward hesitated, looked at Amanda. "She didn't tell you?"

Apprehension prickled in Amanda's stomach. "Tell me what?"

"You'd better come in." Edward stepped back.

Callaway raised inquiring brows as they followed Edward through the silent house.

Amanda mouthed, "I don't know."

In an airy, sky-lighted kitchen, Amanda's nephew sat strapped into a high chair with portions of eggs, grits, toast and bacon around its base. Teddy himself was squeezing some indistinguishable edible object in one grubby fist.

The sight of his big blue eyes and rounded mouth made Amanda forget her worries. She went straight to him.

"Hello, Teddykins." He crowed as she bent to kiss the crown of his silken hair that was the one clean spot on him. "My goodness, aren't you a mess?" Laughing, she fended off the offerings of food. "No, thank you, sweetie. Auntie's already eaten this morning."

Callaway eyed them with jaundiced disbelief.

His scorn annoyed her. Why should she care what he thought? "Isn't it late for breakfast, Edward?"

Edward was rinsing out a pan. "The nanny's sick."

"Where's Noelle?" Callaway asked.

Edward put the pan in the drain. "Gone." While he caught Teddy under the arms and swung him out of his chair, holding him well away from his trousers, he avoided looking at his guests. "Let's wash you off, fella."

Callaway and Amanda exchanged glances. A jerk of his head urged her to question Edward further.

Stripping the squirming baby, Edward set Teddy in the sink and sprayed him with the hose. Water flew everywhere, on counters, on the floor, on father as well as son. Teddy howled but his father kept washing.

Amanda gaped, but Callaway gave no indication he deemed Edward's bath methods incongruous. He caught Amanda's eye, jerked his head toward Edward again. Impatiently.

Highhanded arrogant bully. "So Noelle isn't here. Where's she gone?"

"She left me." Edward lifted up the still-objecting Teddy, and wrapped him in a towel. "When she went to Las Vegas a few weeks ago, she said she wasn't coming back." He took a deep breath and looked directly at Amanda. "I guess she didn't tell you. We're getting a divorce."

*No, impossible!* The room whirled. Holding onto the table kept her from falling.

She hadn't heard correctly. Edward had not said what she thought he had said.

Teddy's howls, that had tapered off once he was wrapped in the towel, started up again.

"Did you say you and Noelle are divorcing?" Amanda enunciated each word with special care.

"Yes." Edward joggled Teddy to quiet him. "That's why she went to Las Vegas, to establish residence and file."

"But you can't be getting a divorce. You promised me you'd look after her."

Amanda had talked to Edward bluntly before the marriage, telling him about Noelle's emotional handicap and explaining what her care entailed. Edward, mature and comfortably settled in his native Birmingham, had still wanted to marry Noelle.

Edward might not be as handsome as some, but he was dependable, and his determination to look after Noelle had reassured Amanda. She'd been certain marriage to the sensible, older pharmacist was in Noelle's best interests. And Noelle had wanted to marry him.

Now this.

"You promised me," she repeated, wanting to cry.

Edward met her accusing gaze without flinching. "I know. I'm sorry, Amanda."

"You couldn't have tried hard enough."

"I tried. Believe me."

"Let me talk to her, make her see what she's giving up," Amanda begged. "You know she doesn't always realize how things are until they're spelled out."

Edward shook his head. "It's too late. I have to think of Teddy now. He doesn't deserve a mother who's never at home, who always puts her interests before his."

How could she repudiate that?

"Edward, I'm sorry." Her words were inadequate, not only for him, but for herself.

"I'm not." Edward paused, debating how much to say. "I thought I could look after Noelle, give her a normal life, Amanda. But being married to someone with her problem is exhausting. With

Teddy to think of now, I just can't do it anymore. I don't know how you stood it all those years."

Noelle had left Edward and Edward wasn't sorry.

Amanda pulled out a kitchen chair and sat down heavily. The headache battled earlier returned in full force. Behind her, Callaway's vague form took a position that offered support.

Or reminded her she was a prisoner.

She was a prisoner.

No, she mustn't think about her situation. Noelle's problems were more important. Amanda had drugged and deceived a man to keep Noelle's family intact, but Noelle's family had disintegrated anyway.

*Pull yourself together.* "Edward, you love Noelle. I can't believe that you'd let her go."

"I do love her, but it's her choice. I won't fight it. I'm tired. I can't work and look out for her every minute." Once Edward started, discontent poured out. "I thought when Teddy was born, she'd settle down, but she got worse. She met these women who're, uh, jet-set-wannabes, and she goes off with them all the time. Lately, she's taken up gambling and God knows what else. I can't keep up with what she does anymore."

"She seemed so happy with you." Amanda thought a minute. "What about Teddy? Noelle wouldn't abandon Teddy?"

Edward's mouth tightened. "Teddy's been left with the nanny so much he cries for her. I told Noelle she couldn't have him, and she agreed it was best if he stays with me."

"She left him? I can't believe it."

Edward's sad smile wrung her heart. "I've tried. We both have. But much as I love Noelle, and as much as she's tried, I don't think she's capable of being a wife and mother. Now I have Teddy to worry about and I have to do what's best for him."

Amanda opened her mouth but was forestalled by a throat clearing behind her.

"I suppose there's a third party involved," Callaway McIntyre said. "There usually is."

In the shock of Edward's bombshell, she had forgotten Callaway. The weight of his hand settled on her shoulder. At first it felt comforting. Then she remembered why he was there.

"Another man?" Edward looked surprised. "You think Noelle went off with another man?"

"Do you know who it is?" Callaway prompted.

He didn't have to blurt it out.

Although there was no way to phrase the question tactfully.

Edward knitted his brow. "She's never said anything but then she wouldn't, would she? I suppose there might be someone else. I've been so busy with work and Teddy that I never thought about it. Why do you care?"

"Where in Las Vegas is she?"

Teddy had managed to shed his towel and wriggle over Edward's shoulder.

Edward retrieved him and got the towel back in place. "I have no idea. She called yesterday to see if I'd received the divorce decree, so that I would put money into her account." He addressed Amanda. "I agreed to a lump sum settlement. All I asked was for her to relinquish custody of Teddy and to return my grandmother's ring. She sent me the ring, but I won't give her the money until I have the final divorce papers in hand confirming that Teddy remains in my custody."

"Smart man," Callaway commented. "With my first wife, I made the mistake of signing all the paperwork before my attorney saw it. Paid through the nose getting out of that one, let me tell you. If I'd only—"

Amanda cut off Callaway's marital reminiscences. "You're sure Noelle called from Las Vegas yesterday? I tried her cell today and it was out of service."

Edward shrugged. "That's where she said she was. I'm sure she went there. The papers came from an attorney there."

Amanda persisted. "She didn't give you a phone number when she called?"

He pointed to a pad beside the kitchen telephone. "She gave me the number of the hotel where she's staying." Teddy started grumbling.

Callaway whipped out his cell, punched in the information.

Amanda said, "Edward, are you absolutely sure there's no chance you and Noelle can get back together?"

"No. I'm sorry, but I don't want to go through this again. I have to do what's best for my son." Edward's expression was unyielding. "I hate to rush you off, but I have to get him over to Mother's. She agreed to keep him today."

Callaway, cell put away, bumped her chair. "We're in the way, Mandy."

Her reproof was automatic. "Don't call me Mandy."

"Okay." He pulled her to her feet. "Let's go. Amanda."

His directive reminded her of her precarious position. If he couldn't find Noelle, he would hold her liable for the theft of his valuables as he had every right to do.

And now Noelle's marriage had fallen apart despite her efforts.

*Oh, Noelle, how could you? How could you leave Teddy? How could you lie to me?*

That last was the big thing. A younger Noelle had occasionally fibbed, but this was a deliberate, calculated lie.

Someone had talked Noelle into this, coached her. Otherwise Amanda would have recognized the signs that her sister was not telling the truth.

She plastered on a smile and said her goodbyes to Edward and little Teddy. She had to find Noelle.

# CHAPTER TEN

SO NOELLE HAD flown the coop. He still had to find her.

As Cal drove the rented car back to the airport, Amanda stared out the window at the Alabama scenery.

He noted her withdrawal as he tried to remember where he had heard Las Vegas mentioned. Someone had been there recently or was going soon. Who had been speaking? And in what context? He couldn't remember.

Oh, well. It would come to him. He had a better memory than most people gave him credit for.

Amanda sat still and quiet, head laid against the headrest with her face averted.

Was she brooding? A different kind of silence lay over her from the one coming out. That silence had radiated hostility. This one was subdued.

He didn't understand what was going on behind this kind of silence, and things he didn't understand bothered Cal.

Not understanding meant failure.

He had failed his mother because he'd never understood her expectations and so couldn't live up to them. He had failed at his first job because he hadn't understood the importance of paperwork. He had failed his wives because he'd never understood they wanted the perks of being his wife but didn't want him in the bargain.

But the worst failure was with Claire because he'd misunderstood Amanda's come-hither act.

Since he couldn't chance losing the journal because he didn't understand her silence, he probed. "You weren't much help in finding out who Noelle's accomplice was."

"I didn't know Noelle's marriage had gotten to this point. If I'd known, maybe I could have done something, made her see divorce wasn't an option."

He noted the stiff set of the shoulders and back of her head. Was she about to cry? No, he thought, she's way too tough for crying, especially about her sister's divorce. If she didn't cry when I cornered her, she isn't about to cry now.

He hadn't treated her very nicely. He'd never lifted a hand to a woman till Amanda, but with her, he'd given way to anger.

Like a bully.

To allay his guilt, he talked. "Noelle's an adult. Her choices are her responsibility."

"No. You don't understand. Noelle's never grown up. She doesn't realize how people can be hurt, how she can hurt herself. Until she married Edward, I always watched out for her."

Cal had been around enough females to hear the throaty quiver signaling that, despite her toughness, Amanda Jane was very near to crying. So she cared about her moronic sister. Empathy rolled in. "Why do you worry about her so?"

"She's my sister." The hand that had rested on the door's armrest went up to shade her eyes. "Sometimes she isn't very smart, but she's still my sister and I love her."

He had a sister, too, dammit, one a hundred times more deserving than Noelle. This whole frigging mess was Amanda's fault. Amanda had let herself be duped by her lying sister and in turn had duped him. Amanda was responsible for all his problems.

He fanned indignation, but indignation refused to flare.

Hell, it was his own damned fault for being so weak when it came to his penis.

He had let Claire down, and that was the bottom line. After all the years when she'd listened and advised and protected him against Lila, he'd let Claire down. His problems were caused by him and nobody else.

He saw Amanda furtively wipe at a cheek, but he didn't care. Amanda could shed a thousand tears and he wouldn't care. No doubt they were fake, anyway, as fake as Scarlet Smith.

Still, a weeping woman bothered him, even one who was a thief. He made an effort to revive irritation. "Huh. From what I've seen, your sister can look out for herself. She got you to do her dirty work for her while she left her husband holding the baby. Literally."

When Amanda didn't answer, he taunted her. If he could get her to blow up, he could dispel his misplaced compassion. "Ten to one her boyfriend helped set you up so they could get their hands on my diamonds. You would have balked at stealing them, I assume. Or would you? Would you have balked at outright theft?"

Damn, how frigging nasty he sounded.

But his taunts accomplished what he hoped.

Her head whipped around. Her eyes blazed. "Of course I would have balked at stealing them. What do you think I am?"

His own impotence brought out a mirthless laugh. "I know what you are, sugar, and don't you forget it."

The gray eyes clouded before they turned back toward the window. A delicate pink stained her neck.

Tough, he told himself. She brought it on herself, letting her frigging sister talk her into conning me.

He wished he didn't feel like the guilty one.

* * * *

*WHAT DO YOU think I am?*

Humiliation brought on by her own ridiculous question remained as they drove into Birmingham. Amanda knew perfectly well what Callaway thought she was. A thief and a slut. What else could he think?

Noelle had a lot to answer for. Amanda couldn't rationalize her sister's behavior this time or blame it on her handicap. There was no excuse for what Noelle had done.

Nor was there any excuse for what Amanda had done.

Callaway broke into her self-castigations. "Nearly one o'clock our time. We'll have lunch near the airport." He wasn't suggesting. He was telling. At one point she might have protested his autocratic ways, but now she meekly submitted.

In a restaurant's parking lot, he used his cellphone to call the number copied off Edward's pad. "She's been at the Las Vegas Mont Grande," he told Amanda when he'd finished. "She isn't there now."

He'd regained his laidback, sleepy air but she noted the strained mouth, the tense shoulders. "It's not a cheap place to stay." He dialed again, and repeated the information to an unseen confederate. A third, unsuccessful call, maybe to his sister, was made before they went inside the restaurant. When she came out of the ladies room, he was putting his cell away again.

Amanda, hoping her ordeal was almost over, tried to ignore the pounding in her head so that she could carry on a civil conversation over lunch. The memory of their first erotic encounter lay as a tangible reminder of their unwanted alliance; but in spite of their mutual distrust, a sort of armed truce prevailed.

The more accommodating she was, the less likely he would be to file charges against her and Noelle, and criminal charges were her main worry. She would figure out what to do about his stolen valuables later.

If there was anything she could do. How much would a set of diamond studs cost? Ten thousand dollars? Fifty thousand? A hundred thousand? That much money would take years to repay, but she'd do it if she had to sell everything she had.

"What would you say your diamonds are worth?" she asked when an opportunity arose.

"Why? Thinking about claiming a finder's fee?"

There was no hostility; his response seemed automatic. She pushed the food around her plate, appetite gone.

He didn't eat much either. His head might be aching as much as hers.

At the cashier's stand, small boxes of pain relievers lay stacked alongside the mints and toothpicks. She bought one and swallowed two tablets, dry, in the car, not bothering to offer him any. Let him suffer.

Instinct prickled when they drove up to the Birmingham airport instead of the smaller one where they had landed.

Why were they here? She already knew Callaway McIntyre was organized, a trait she could appreciate because to manage her business, she cultivated it. Still, she was unprepared when, on leaving the rental car counter, he took her elbow and steered her into the crowd saying, "Let's pick up our tickets."

She forgot her headache. "What tickets?"

The smile that transformed him into a brute appeared. A jaw muscle clenched and unclenched. "The Cessna had to go back to Atlanta so we'll have to fly commercial to Las Vegas."

"Las Vegas." She stopped in midstride.

"Didn't I tell you?" he drawled. "Yep, we're going to Las Vegas, Miss Scarlet. Won't we have fun?"

After one stunned moment, Amanda forgot her resolve to be agreeable. "I have to get back to my shop." She stayed in the middle of the crowded lobby, her voice rising. "You told me we'd be back this afternoon."

A man bumped into her and muttered apologies. Two women pulling large cases made a production of getting around her. Amanda stood her ground. "You told me!"

Callaway dragged her aside. His grip was businesslike. His shoulders concealed her agitation from passers-by. "Any time you say the word, I'll file charges. And don't think I'd mind putting you and your sister in prison."

Amanda balled her trembling hands. His woodsy scent drifted around her.

He released her arm. "I did tell you we were able to lift fingerprints from my room the night you . . ." his voice lowered, "umm, took advantage of me, didn't I?" When she made no reply, he added, "It's your call. Las Vegas or jail."

Anger gave way to despair. Looking down, a bruise on her wrist reminded her of their encounter the day before. No need for rough stuff, not with the threat of jail. "I'll come."

"Somehow I thought you might."

"I need to call Melissa, have her cancel my appointments tomorrow."

"As soon as we pick up our tickets." He nudged her forward. "And better cancel your appointments for the rest of the week."

"The rest of the week?" She stopped again. "Look, I can't be gone the rest of the week. I have a business to run."

"I don't know how long it'll take to find your sister. You heard what Edward said about depositing her settlement. She and her boyfriend aren't raising money to squander in the casinos, sugar. With what they get for my diamonds, they can retire to South America."

"South America?" Dear God, Noelle couldn't leave the country. "How much do you think your diamonds will bring?"

"If they have a buyer, and I suspect they do, five million is the least they'll take."

Her mouth fell open. She ignored the crowd around them. "Five million," she repeated faintly. Her surroundings began to spin, darken. She swayed, felt his hand bracing her and was glad of its support. The terminal came back into focus. "Dollars?"

His expression was curious. Appraising. "Nice bit of pocket change, isn't it? Enough to live on in South America for a while. Not that I wouldn't give every cent to have that book back," he muttered. The harsh smile glinted as he pulled her into the crowd. "Don't worry too much, Scarlet. I've got people down there, too."

They'd better get somewhere they could sit down soon, or else her shaking legs would give completely away.

Five million dollars.

\* \* \* \*

CAL WORKED TO whip up the old anger, but her dismay caught him off guard. What the hell had she thought a set of stones like that would be worth? And why was she looking so sick? She was conniving, deceitful and a liar.

It didn't work. His eyes involuntarily returned to her wrist and its bruise. He knew the cause. He wanted to beg her pardon here in the airport but clamped his teeth together.

*She doesn't deserve any apologies. She doesn't deserve any consideration at all.*

Claire was the one he needed to worry about.

He hoped his sister wasn't brooding. He'd tried her twice today and not been able to get her. The more he thought about it, the more convinced he was that Sonny was Noelle's lover.

Sonny had worked closely with Robert for years. Robert wasn't careless, but he trusted Sonny. Hell, they all did. Sonny could easily have found out the combination. And Sonny knew what the diamonds were worth and how much a collector like Miles would covet them.

Come to think of it, Miles and Sonny had had their heads together at the wedding yesterday.

But that didn't mean anything. Miles wouldn't stoop to theft to get them. At least, the Miles he thought he knew wouldn't. But if Sonny approached Miles with diamonds in hand, that was a different story.

Didn't matter. He needed Noelle to confirm who was behind the scam before he confronted Sonny and made him tell who had the diamonds. Then, he could recover the book.

He'd find Noelle one way or another.

# CHAPTER ELEVEN

THE HOTEL LOBBY in Las Vegas was dark, so dark that Amanda had to strain to read the signs. This was as bad as being inside a cave. How did they expect people to see? She would have complained, except that Callaway McIntyre obviously wanted to hear as little from her as possible.

Not that she blamed him.

Five million dollars' worth of his diamonds she had helped steal. Along with a book that he valued more than his jewelry, if she hadn't misheard.

Her head ached intolerably. A tiny sigh escaped as he arranged their accommodations, attracting his tiny searching glance, not unsympathetic.

She focused on a nearby urn at least three feet high filled with large purple and small white flowers among glossy green foliage. Anger and pride had gone with everything else, leaving only shame tied to an insistent pounding behind her eyes. All she wanted was a bed where she could plop down and hide.

No space was available, a disinterested desk clerk told them. Callaway, naturally, asked for someone by name.

It didn't take two minutes after Cal spoke to his contact before the clerk, suddenly very attentive, found a room for them after all.

So he had connections out here, too, did he?

Some people always knew the right person in the right place to help them out. Some people always had everything go smoothly, without bumps or setbacks. Some people led charmed lives, damn them.

Amanda's annoyance at Callaway McIntyre's ease in circumventing the system almost made her forget her headache.

Unaware of her resentment, he picked up the keycard. "We have a room but it's probably not much of one." He led her down steps, up steps, and past crowded shops into an alcove that broadened into the mouth of a wide corridor. "With the broadcasting, home, and poultry conventions all in town this week, we're lucky to get anything."

When the corridor forked, they veered left into the North Tower and passed more sparkling shop windows. Dresses, furniture, artwork, toys, jewelry . . .

All the well-lit displays looked stylish and expensive.

Under different circumstances and with her head not pounding, she would have enjoyed window-shopping.

After covering an interminable distance of thick carpet, they came to a side alcove containing elevators. Quiet doors opened onto an empty cage. She stumbled getting in.

He caught her elbow, steadied her. "Tired?"

She summoned up her reserves. "It's too dark. I can't see where I'm going. Your influential friend who got us the room ought to replace some light bulbs."

He chuckled as he pushed the button for the eighth floor. "Ever been to Vegas?"

"No, and I don't plan to come back."

"The hotels want their customers to gamble, and for some reason, people prefer to gamble at night. You won't find any outside windows in the casinos or any bright lights. You won't find any clocks, either. When customers don't know what time it is, they keep gambling, the casino keeps winning, and everyone's happy."

"Except the losers." Bitter thoughts of Noelle ran through her mind. Her head was splitting. She pressed her forehead.

"You really are tired, aren't you?"

That couldn't be compassion. She gave a weary nod.

"Me, too. At least we have a place to sleep. With the conventions, everything's booked. I took whatever was available."

"Whatever was available" proved to be a wallpapered and modish room with a huge window overlooking Las Vegas and distant mountains. A king-sized bed sat in the center of the room and a short, strangely-shaped sofa stood in front of the window.

He'd had a hard time wangling a room so she couldn't object to the one bed. Besides, her head hurt so much she had to concentrate to put one foot in front of the other. All she wanted to do was turn down the bedcovers and climb between them.

Callaway mistook her grimace for criticism of his arrangements. "It's all they had, Scarlet," he drawled with the old mockery. "If you're worried about being ravished, don't be. I've never had a taste for plain women, particularly when they're thieves and phonies."

Plain!

She relaxed the fists unconsciously balled. "I'm not worried." She most certainly was not plain. No one in her entire life had ever called her that.

"You can sleep on the sofa if you're scared. You'll have to sleep drawn up in a knot, but I'm sure you can manage."

"I'm not scared of you."

He fell down on one side of the bed on his back without turning down the covers. "You ought to be." He closed his eyes. "You ought to be damned scared. I eat little girls like you for breakfast."

"I'm thirty-three years old," she said dryly. "Hardly a little girl. And you don't frighten me one bit."

She wasn't lying. Somewhere along the line, she'd become too numb, too exhausted to be scared of Callaway McIntyre.

A smile flickered on his lips. The copper hair had fallen away from his broad forehead. Tiny lines of weariness fanned out around the closed lashes and made the raw cheekbones stand out sharply. He looked as tired as she felt.

She wondered what was in the book that made him so anxious to get it back, and whether it belonged to his sister. She wanted, for some ridiculous reason, to smooth out the wrinkles in his forehead and whisper to him that it would be all right.

*I'm exhausted. I don't know what I'm doing.*

When she fell down on top of the covers beside him, not even her pounding head kept her from dozing off fully clothed. At some point, she was awakened by his muttered, "Sonny came out here from Houston," and felt the bed shift. She heard him dial his cell and ask for Claire, but he sounded distant, very far away. Sleep reclaimed her as she heard him say, "No, no message."

\* \* \* \*

CALLAWAY CAME WIDE awake at the first chime. He blinked at fading daylight coming through the window, remembered he was in Las Vegas, and became aware of the sleeping woman next to him, all in the single instant before he spoke into the cell. "Yes."

Claire was on the other end. "I don't have long to talk, Cal. The sheriff's people just left."

"The sheriff? What's happened? Are you all right?"

Claire sniffled, obviously under stress. "I'm fine, but Sonny's dead."

"Sonny?" How the hell could Sonny be dead?

"Yes. He was in the pond."

"The pond." *Has Sonny drowned? How does this fit?* "Was it an accident?"

"No. He'd been shot."

"Christ. Do they know who did it?"

"No, but listen, Cal, there's more and I've got to get back before Robert misses me. Sonny and I were eating breakfast this morning and he told me he got a crank call last week. He said he didn't think anything about it until he got an envelope in the mail. It . . ."

Claire's voice wavered.

Amanda Jane did not stir as he carefully got out of bed. "What was in it?"

"Copies of pages from Mother's journal."

"Damn him. I suspected it might be him but I didn't really believe he would do it."

"No, no, Cal. I don't know that Sonny's the one—was the one. He said someone is—was using him as a go-between."

"Hah." He glared at the sleeping woman. "I've heard stories like that before."

"But he urged me to go to the police. He wouldn't have done that if he was involved, would he?"

Cal tried to think. "That could have been a ploy."

"Maybe, but listen, Cal, he all but asked me to leave Robert and run away with him."

"What?"

"It was so strange. I've always known Sonny liked me. I've always teased him and he's always carried on with me. But that's just Sonny. *Was* Sonny."

Over the connection, he heard her blow her nose. "Are you saying he thought you'd leave Robert for him?"

She gave a shaky laugh. "I was tempted. For a few minutes, I was really tempted. But you know how Sonny is. Was. I never thought he meant anything, just that he was flirting like he always does. But this morning . . . I think he meant it, Cal. He was kind of sad, not kidding at all. I think if I hadn't turned it into a joke . . . It was after I laughed it off that he brought out the copies."

"Bullshit. What did he say?"

"That someone, he didn't know who, had called him. Whoever it was told him to get five hundred thousand dollars in cash or bearer bonds from me or Matthew, and that he'd be instructed as to where to exchange the money for the book."

"Has he . . . Did he talk to Matthew before he died?"

"I don't know. I was stunned at first, and since then I haven't had a chance to see Matthew. There's worse. Robert's sick and stayed home."

"Robert? Mr. Don't-Let-Pneumonia-Keep-You-From-Work stayed home from the office?"

"Don't be sarcastic. Robert has a bad case of flu. Anyway, Sonny and I were having breakfast out on the terrace under our bedroom when we talked, and I thought I saw the blinds move. Robert may have heard."

"You think Robert murdered Sonny?"

"Now you're being ridiculous. But I'm sure he suspects I'm keeping something from him. The thing is, I liquidated funds today to get the money. I wanted to give it to Sonny, but I couldn't find him. Then the boys did."

"The boys?"

"The twins found him in the pond. They were riding bikes and saw him in the water."

Images of his nephews' innocent faces flashed through his mind. They must have been traumatized. "Are they okay?"

"They're ten-year-old boys. They're more excited than anything else. But I'm worried the investigators will find out I cashed out the treasury notes. What do I tell them when they ask?"

"Hell." His mind went blank. "If they ask, tell them you planned on giving it to Johanna for a wedding gift."

"All right." She sounded dubious, but it was the best he could come up with. "What about Matt? Should I check to see if Sonny approached him, too?"

"No. Wait before you talk to him. If I can find this woman, we'll have a better handle on what's going on."

"All right, Cal. I'll wait till you get back."

Amanda didn't stir so he said softly, "I'd already guessed Sonny must be in this up to his eyeballs, Claire. I guess you didn't say anything to the authorities about the, you know, the studs and journal?"

He heard her negative reply. "Good. Don't. I've a man working on a new lead at this end."

Claire wasn't through. "One more thing. After breakfast, I overheard Sonny on the phone. It sounded like he was planning to go away with a woman. I thought it was strange, when he'd just asked me to run off with him but figured he was flirting with me after all. Do you suppose whoever he was talking to is the one who stole the book from you?"

Denial was on the tip of his tongue, but he glanced at the sleeping Amanda. "Could be. He didn't say anything we could use? Maybe her name?"

"No. I just heard a couple of sentences," she said regretfully. "If Sonny's the one behind the theft, who killed him? Do you think the woman did it?"

"I don't know, Bags." He didn't want to think about what her question implied. Not yet. "We'll talk about that later."

Why was he shielding Amanda's part in all this?

He closed his cell and moved softly back to where she lay sleeping in a fetal position. From the window overlooking the front of the hotel and the outskirts of the city, a last afternoon sunbeam drifted in and fell on her brown hair. Reddish highlights, unnoticeable before, sprang to life.

Aha, she had some redhead in her.

Her shoulder rose and fell. From here he could see the mouth softened by sleep and the dark smudges beneath the lashes. Something stirred inside him. Longing tempered by revulsion.

He swallowed.

He still wanted her.

Redhead or not, hot as fire or cold as ice, enchantress or thief. Whatever Amanda Jane or Scarlet might be, he still wanted to take that luscious mouth and run his finger round its curve and press his own against it. He still wanted to stroke those smooth shoulders and run his hands through the sleek hair and plunge himself into her ripe center.

He shuddered.

Damn, what in hell was he thinking? Hadn't he learned anything? The extent of his carnality made him sick. That he could be aroused by the woman after what she'd done to him was disgusting.

She'd never cared anything about him. The sole reason she'd come on to him had been because of her sister.

Careful not to wake her, he walked away. He might be a fool, but he wasn't that big a one. He'd best stay far away from Amanda Jane. In mind and in body.

The clock radio said it was nearing six o'clock. That meant nine in Atlanta. Poor Claire must have had an awful evening, and no one deserved it less. She'd long been Cal's hero. He could never live up to her.

More unprofitable thoughts. He'd let her down royally this time. The one person who'd never failed him, and he'd repaid her by being unable to keep his pants zipped.

Him and his damned libido. His mother was right. He was a weak fool.

Unwilling eyes went back to Amanda.

His libido that he couldn't repress.

He dropped into the armchair by the bed. *Stop beating a dead horse. Figure out what to do next.*

Right. He already had an agency calling hotels, searching for Noelle. If she was still in Las Vegas, he'd know her whereabouts by morning. Once he found her, he'd get the answers to his questions, in particular, the identity of her accomplice who, as now seemed apparent, had been Sonny Kirkman.

The problem was the one Claire had raised. Who killed Sonny?

With Noelle here, that ruled her out. And where was the journal and Cal's studs? With Noelle?

The studs could be a separate thing from the book. If Sonny, assuming Sonny was the thief, had found the journal when stealing them and decided to make a little money on the side by taking it, too, then the diamonds may already have been sold.

Which made sense. Plenty of collectors would buy stolen gems without batting an eye. Miles, for instance. But he'd worry about the studs later. The big question was what Sonny had done with the journal.

For now, his hopes for recovering it lay in Noelle.

Amanda shivered in her sleep.

The room was chilly. The gray dress was made of some thin stuff that couldn't be warm. He folded his share of the coverlet over, cocooning her between its top. She stirred and sighed, but didn't wake.

After turning up the thermostat, he sat back down and started to light a cigarette despite the non-smoking ban.

No, the smoke would wake her up. He put the cigarettes away. She was tired. Let her rest.

He leaned back wearily, watching her sleep as he waited for his phone call.

\* \* \* \*

CHIMES WOKE AMANDA.

She heard a man speaking, recognized him as Callaway and opened her eyes.

His back was to her, cell phone to his ear.

Noelle. Someone was calling about Noelle. She sat up, joints hurting from sleeping so hard.

"So she left without a forwarding address. All right. Keep at it."

He pocketed his cell and turned to meet her inquiring look. "Noelle was in this hotel until early this morning. She's gone now, not in the city." When he drew up the Roman shades, gray light with garish streaks from flashing fluorescents and neons filled the room.

"What time is it?" Amanda's mouth was dry and cottony.

"Seven thirty."

Her stomach growled. "In the morning?"

"No, sugar. There are three hours difference, remember? Seven thirty in the evening. Ten thirty at home. Time for dinner out here."

She started to get up, pulled the place in her back where the thermostat had gouged it in the cottage.

He saw her flinch. "What's the matter? Sleep the wrong way?"

She wouldn't complain of her injuries at his hands. "Yeah. It'll go away."

Callaway picked up the hotel phone to make flight arrangements to Atlanta while Amanda went into the bathroom. After washing her face, she felt better.

He stopped pacing when she came out and scowled. "The first plane we can get on leaves at seven tomorrow morning."

For some reason, she felt like crying. Another day away from the shop meant disgruntled customers, disturbed personnel, and nasty rumors to deal with when she returned. And she still had Noelle to worry about. Everything was closing in.

She blinked back tears. "Then I need a toothbrush."

"The concierge is supposed to send up some things in a few minutes." He glanced at her wrinkled dress and away as if embarrassed. "Along with clothes from one of the shops."

"Oh. Okay." She should have known he'd think of everything. "They couldn't find out where Noelle's gone?"

His shoulders tensed. "Left this morning on a flight to Atlanta."

"I'm sorry."

He met her gaze. "Not as sorry as you will be."

She was tired of his threats. "The worst thing you can do is put me in jail. The next worst thing you can do is ruin my business. You're about to do one. I'm beginning not to care about the other."

After a beat of silence, he laughed, his real laugh that lit his eyes and erased the strain on his forehead and softened the set of his mouth. There was even a hint of the dimple under one corner.

"I'll do what I can for your business," he promised carelessly. "So long as you help me find your sister. And my, um, my studs."

"What can I do?" She spread her hands. "I didn't even know about her divorce. Why do you think I can help you?"

"Because," he said, pulling cigarettes from his pocket, "according to what I'm told, she always comes to you when she needs anything." His lighter flared. He drew on the cigarette, closed the lighter, and put it away while blowing out a thin cloud of smoke. "Everyone says so."

The sight of the capable hands in their simple task evoked an uncalled-for reaction in Amanda. She cleared her throat. "You aren't supposed to smoke in here."

"Sue me."

She picked up a magazine to fan at the swirling gray cloud. "If Noelle has as much money as you think, she won't need me for anything."

He ignored her pointed fanning. "She'll get dumped sooner or later." He cocked his head to appraise her. "And come crawling back to big sister."

She was irrationally annoyed at his casual dismissal of Noelle. More annoyed at his indifference to herself. "How do you know she'll get dumped?"

"Because she's the type that always gets dumped. You, now." He took a step toward her, reached out, and drew the back of his hand down her cheek. An assessing gesture rather than a caress. His cologne filtered through the smoke. "You're altogether different. I expect you've never let a man dump you in your entire life."

It took all her will power not to balk under the touch of those astute fingers, all her self-control to meet his eyes. "I expect you're right." She returned stare for stare, adding without emotion, "If you intend to give me bronchitis as well as destroy my business and put me in jail, you can keep blowing that smoke in my face."

"Should I care if you get bronchitis?" But he put the cigarette out, slowly, deliberately, while his gaze wandered to her mouth. "Give me a reason I should care."

His eyes fastened on her lips were unnerving.

Amanda licked them, and wished she hadn't. She recognized the signals, knew what was coming, but didn't try to avoid it. Didn't want to avoid it.

Her skin tingled and her breasts swelled while a longing started in her depths and spread upward, preventing her from looking away as he bent and touched his mouth, acrid with tobacco smoke, to hers.

His lips were gentle.

His tongue, if possible, was gentler, finding the parting of her lips and stroking, willing them to open to him.

As they did.

Her heart thumped in her ears and blocked out the hum of the air conditioner. His mouth took its fill of hers as he demonstrated his mastery over her will.

Their bodies never touched.

He drew his face away unhurriedly, satisfied.

"Why did you do that?" she asked hoarsely.

He gave her the little boy's smile, changed somehow. Saddened. "Because I wanted to."

"Don't do it again."

"You didn't stop me."

She crossed her arms over her breasts.

His smile twisted, mocking her. Or maybe himself. He opened his mouth but a knock on the door interrupted what he would have said.

"That's our supplies," he said instead. "Let's see what they've brought up and then go down to dinner."

* * * *

HE'D BEEN ABOUT to admit that he was stupid, weak and irrational where women were concerned and that he couldn't control his impulses. He had been on the verge of telling her he'd kissed her because she seemed fragile and looked like she wanted to be kissed.

No, those weren't the real reasons. He'd wondered if the sedate Amanda Jane would taste like the redhead he'd been so wild to possess in Houston.

*That's why I kissed her.* Not because, despite her show of composure, he'd sensed she was tired and uncertain, in need of comforting.

Not because her only crime was in caring too much about her damned sister.

# CHAPTER TWELVE

AFTER BATHING, AND donning new underwear and a dress chosen from several sent up by the boutique, Amanda looked into the mirror with, if not pleasure, resignation. Though she would have preferred a sober color, her choices had been pastels and rich jewel hues. Because none had price tags, she had steeled herself to select an aquamarine cotton with a discreet neckline and handkerchief hem that fell below her knees. The simple lines shrieked expense.

Noelle would have hated it.

She didn't want to think of Noelle.

Noelle had managed to lie to her and betray her. Someone had coached her sister. That was the only explanation.

What could have driven Noelle to do such a thing?

She wanted to blame Edward but couldn't. He'd tried, she was sure. But thanks to her disability, Noelle had no idea of how to deal with life.

Amanda knew the truth, though. Had she listened to her conscience, she and Noelle wouldn't be in such a mess.

In the crowded elevator, she was pressed inside the perimeter of Callaway's scrubbed masculine fragrance. Like Amanda, he wore fresh clothes from the hotel boutique. Creased khakis and a buttoned plaid shirt turned him into a tourist. The two of them blended in with everyone else milling around in varying degrees of casual and fancy dress.

They ate in the Chinese restaurant, at a secluded table beside a small fountain that issued a continuous soothing trickle of water. As electronic fireworks whizzed overhead, Callaway told her about Sonny Kirkman.

His nimble fingers manipulated the chopsticks with practiced precision. She wouldn't mind learning how to eat with them, but not tonight. "You think he's connected to Noelle? That he was her lover?"

"He knows, knew," he corrected as he put more lemon chicken on his plate, "my weakness for redheads. He was in a position to reserve your theater box. As Robert's assistant, he had opportunities to learn the safe combination that Robert, Claire and I all used. And Sonny's spent a lot of time here in Las Vegas lately, where your sister came." He brooded a moment. "Women liked Sonny. He could get them to do anything."

Amanda shivered. "And now he's dead. That's why you're so sure Noelle will get in touch with me. Poor Noelle. Losing her family and now her lover."

He wielded his chopsticks in chilly silence.

Should she tell him about the conversation overheard at Johanna's wedding? Yes, better not hold anything back. She put down her fork. "At the wedding, I was in the garden. I overheard some people talking. A man was blackmailing Senator Swift, and I think it was Sonny."

That startled Callaway so much he sloshed hot tea over the edge of his cup. "Matthew?" He wiped at the spilled tea with his napkin. "What did they say?"

Pausing, she tried to remember the conversation.

He caught her lower arm. "What? What did you hear?"

"Give me a chance to think. I'm trying to remember the exact words."

He sat back but kept his hold on her arm.

She mistrusted the way that contact affected her. "Sonny mentioned a diary." The rest poured out. "Something about the publicity if reporters got hold of it. The senator said he felt threatened, that he couldn't get that much cash on Sunday."

Callaway jerked away as if she were tainted and picked up his chopsticks.

The connection hit her, out of the blue. Her fork clattered on the table. "The book you're after. That isn't . . . ?"

"Isn't what?" He challenged her to say the words.

She rescued her fork and picked up shrimp and rice to avoid his accusing eyes. "Nothing."

"Go on." His chopsticks lay still. "Isn't what?"

The food in her mouth made her sick. "Is the diary the same book that was taken from you?"

"Stolen from me, thanks to you."

Cold enveloped her, so forbidding was his face. "I didn't know." She put the fork down, appetite gone. "I'm sorry."

"You should be." His countenance lightened as he sighed. "Oh, what the hell. I thought you were a hard woman, Scarlet, but you're putty in the right pair of hands. I'm beginning to believe you can be talked into anything."

His voice turned meditative. A questing forefinger touched her forearm, skimmed to her shoulder. "What kind of man can turn you all soft and yielding?"

Her heart jumped before she could draw away. "Someone a lot nicer than you. Someone kind and considerate and caring."

"Not selfish and manipulative like Noelle?"

Her neck grew hot. "It isn't that she's selfish. She just doesn't think. It's a disability. Noelle tries, really she does."

"Sure she does."

When their fortune cookies were set down, she broke one in half. Across the table, he watched. "What does it say?"

"'You will take a long journey and find your heart's desire at the end.' Pretty standard. What about yours?"

He broke it open, glanced at the strip of paper and tore it in half. "Beware of redheaded women."

She flushed.

Then, as lately he seemed prone to do, he did an about-face that threw her off balance. "Let's not talk about them anymore. Your sister, my diamonds, Sonny. We're stuck here till tomorrow in Sin City, a perfect place to kill a few hours. Let's forget everything but having fun."

True to his word, he kept to innocuous topics as they meandered into the huge casino. He pointed out a well-known TV star at one table, in full stage makeup. That brought up the review the actor was starring in and led to the pop singer headlining for another hotel. "Too bad we don't have time to see her."

With all the sights around them, his words barely penetrated. People streamed toward tables set with dice or cards, or roulette wheels. Other gamblers fed machines quarters, half dollars, and dollars. Circulating waitresses dispensed drinks.

Though most were enthusiastic, many players seemed grim, like they were unwillingly caught up in the game.

And the noise. Besides the chatter, the mélange of screams and falling coins when someone won at the slots made it difficult to hear.

A redheaded blackjack dealer caught Cal's eye, and Amanda couldn't resist a barbed comment as he steered her in that direction. "Remember what your fortune said."

"My what?"

"Your fortune. Beware of redheaded women."

"Oh." Blankness gave way to amusement. "You don't believe those things, do you? Besides, that's not what mine said."

"Oh? What did it say?"

He chuckled. "Go on." When he nudged her toward the redhead's table, his hand rested on her back so that they could have been a normal couple.

Amanda, staggered at the amount of the wagers, stood around for a while as he played.

What she could do with some of that money.

During a small flurry of excitement after Cal turned up three blackjacks in a row, she took advantage of his diversion to slip away and find the boutique which had sent up their clothes.

The saleswoman's cordiality cooled when Amanda explained what she wanted. "If the garments were put on the room account, I can't do a thing. I'm sorry."

Amanda smiled brightly. "Either they get transferred to my credit card, or I'll return them all. And I'll start right here, right now. Dress, sandals, petticoat, panties, everything."

She had to pull her dress over her head before the woman caved. Then papers were filled out, accounts were switched, and the clothes were charged to Amanda.

At least she had one thing off her conscience, even if her next Visa bill would be out of sight.

Back inside the casino, she stopped at the quarter poker machines and watched the action. Maybe she wasn't much of a gambler, but poker was a familiar game. After she got ten dollars' worth of quarters and sat down, two or three tries practically made her a pro. A pair of jacks or better would get her quarter back, and breaking even was as thrilling as winning.

Her roll of coins would last a long time at this rate.

\* \* \* \*

THE WINNINGS FROM hitting blackjack three times were lost before Cal remembered Amanda.

Gone, dammit. Where was she?

He abandoned the blackjack table.

While he'd been so distracted with his big win, she'd run away. Damn, when would he learn? She could be halfway to the airport . . .

No, Amanda was too intelligent to run. She wouldn't take the risk of her sister going to jail.

Still, the knot in his gut didn't unravel till he found her perched on a stool at the machines.

Excitement animated her, drawing in a man sitting beside her. He spoke to her. With a smile, she shook her head. He argued, pointing toward the slots. A gurgle accompanied another negative head shake, making the man linger. When she got four of a kind and squealed, he said something else that made her laugh.

*Why the hell is she letting a stranger flirt with her?*

Cal started through the crowd as her admirer headed off toward more productive machines, but by that time, an irrational emotion had taken hold of Callaway.

He wasn't jealous. Hell no.

But Amanda Jane possessed something special, that was for sure. No vamp tonight, no stiff-necked dressmaker, no worried older sister. She was an alluring woman, sending out vibes that made everyone around her feel good.

Making strangers want to pick her up.

He went over to the vacated stool. "Having any luck?"

She didn't hide her pleasure. "I am. I started with ten dollars in quarters and now look."

He wanted to flirt with her, make her laugh, but he had to remember she was a liar and a thief, for whatever reasons. "Oh, you must have twelve or thirteen bucks in there," he drawled, looking into her plastic container. "Wow."

"At least I won. How'd you do?"

"Ouch. Won some. Lost more. Ready to go up?"

"When I'm winning? Why should I have to leave if your luck's soured?"

"We've got to catch an early plane."

Her glow faded. Without further protest, she scooped up her plastic cup and followed him out.

Damn it, he was no bully who enjoyed ending her fun, but she didn't deserve pity or any other concession. Not after playing him for a sucker and turning Claire's life upside down.

They were the only occupants of the elevator taking them to the eighth floor. The rattle of her container of quarters beat time to the piped-in music.

He raised a brow. "You're easily entertained."

"I don't get to play electronic poker very much."

"You don't have a computer?"

"Sure, but that's for business." She might have been an indulgent parent speaking to an immature child. "I don't have time for games. It's too hard running the shop. And now . . ."

Her features clouded.

He guessed she was worrying about how her absence would affect business. "Claire has friends. She'll help you if you lose too many customers."

"That's kind of you, but she may not want to." Constraint lay behind the polite words.

Because she was afraid of him.

Why wouldn't she be, with his threats of jail and the way he'd manhandled her?

"Claire isn't vindictive. She'll help."

Her business meant a lot to her. She probably worked long hours if it was as successful as Johanna had implied. Her days were productive while his were empty.

So what? He'd learned to live with being useless. No reason to regret what he couldn't change.

Robert frequently needled him, and so had his mother when she was alive, about his carelessness and incompetence.

Amanda hadn't uttered one critical word, yet her silence turned him more defensive than any of their reproofs.

*Work hard and reap the rewards.*

That's what his fortune tonight had said, much the same advice Claire had always given. Maybe she was right. Maybe he ought to talk to Robert about doing something meaningful for a change.

Except Robert, arrogant ass, was already paranoid about plots to oust him as head of the company. Cal would have to find something else to give him purpose. A new hobby, maybe.

They came into the room and there stood the lone bed.

When she looked at it and quickly away, he read her mind. "We can make it if we're careful, sugar. But if during the night you grab something hard, don't blame me for what happens."

She rolled her eyes before laying claim to the bathroom. While the shower ran, he imagined her in a sexy see-through gown but wasn't surprised when she finally emerged in prim pajamas chosen from the boutique's offerings.

When she went to bed without comment, he felt sorry for her and angry with himself for feeling sorry for her. And because of that, he goaded her. If she snapped at him, he might forget his pity. "Why don't you sleep in your skin like last night? All soft and sweet and bare."

"Stop badgering me. If you'd been peeking last night, you'd know I was too petrified to take off my underwear."

He smothered a laugh as he entered the bathroom. She did have backbone, Amanda Jane.

When he came out, the room was dark. He left the light burning behind the closed bathroom door, so that its faint illumination joined that of neons creeping in from behind the shades. In bed, two of the three pillows stretched lengthwise down the middle. Under Amanda's head rested a sofa cushion.

He grinned. Despite her bravura, she was anxious. Despite his resolve, compassion welled. "What's the matter? Think you might feel the urge to reach out and touch someone?"

"Nope. Making sure you don't misunderstand the situation. Good night."

"Good night, sugar."

She lay on the other side of the pillows, smelling of soap and making every nerve in him aware of her tiniest movement. He stretched out and tried not to remember how she'd felt on top of him, how her curves fit against him.

He usually had no trouble dropping off to sleep, but he did this night.

\* \* \* \*

AMANDA ALWAYS FELL asleep the moment she closed her eyes, but Callaway was on the other side of her flimsy barrier. He made no effort to bridge it, despite his tall form taking up all his half of the big bed. She breathed in his male scent that cigarette smoke and faded cologne couldn't hide, and tried to calm her racing heart.

Think of something else.

It was eleven out here. That means it would be two in the morning at home. Tired as she was, she ought to be sound asleep.

When he turned onto his side, she felt the mattress quiver. His breathing became even.

He wasn't having any trouble getting to sleep.

He didn't care that he had disrupted her life, dragged her off to the other end of the country, put her in a strange bed where she couldn't get to sleep because he lay on the other side.

*Ah, Noelle, what did you get me to do?*

Nothing she hadn't agreed to do of her own free will. Noelle was her sister and all the family she had left. Despite everything, she loved Noelle.

But Callaway had a sister, too. Although he'd confided nothing, the missing diary must have something to do with Claire. He might be as worried about Claire as she was about Noelle.

There seemed to be no easy way out.

What could his fortune cookie have said?

\* \* \* \*

AS AMANDA HAD learned the first time she met him, Callaway could be charming. On the flight back to Atlanta, he exhibited his best behavior. Absent was the previous animosity. Instead, he showed a careless consideration that both perplexed and gratified her. By the time the plane touched down in Atlanta, she was almost at charity with him.

Maybe, somehow, things would work out. At least he knew the reason for what she'd done and that she regretted it.

She'd helped him every way she could. He no longer seemed angry so maybe he'd stop talking about sending her and Noelle to jail.

As they came off the unloading ramp, she gripped her shopping bag with her dirty clothes and took a deep breath. "I'm sorry, Callaway, I really am. I should never have done it."

He was preoccupied. "Hmm."

He took off for the train. She hurried to keep up with him. "And I appreciate you not telling Edward about what we did. If there's any chance for them to reconcile, learning about Noelle's part in this would have killed it."

"No use dragging him into it."

They boarded the train going to the main terminal and clung to a pole facing each other. "It's an imposition, but do you think you could have someone drive my minivan back to Atlanta from Fair Meadows?" Not yet four o'clock. If she hurried, she could get to the shop in time to close up. Her employees needed to be reassured that they hadn't been deserted.

Sleepy eyes were inscrutable. "Sure, if you want me to."

"Thank you."

Unhindered by luggage, they swept through the lobby to find outside skies overcast and drizzling. Callaway looked around.

Amanda pointed. "I'll catch MARTA there. Oh, and can I get my cell back from you?"

His head swiveled. One eyebrow arched as if he didn't believe his ears.

He was used to having taxis or limos waiting wherever he went. He probably didn't know anyone who actually used public transport.

"Don't worry," she said. "MARTA goes to Lenox, not far from my shop."

A second eyebrow joined the first. "I'm not worried, sugah. Why should I be worried?"

She didn't trust the way he strung out his words. When he drawled that way and got that mocking expression on his face, he was saying something she didn't want to hear.

*Careful, careful. Let him know you're still willing to help.* "If Noelle gets in touch with me, I'll let you know right away."

He scanned the crowd. Waving one hand in the air, he caught her wrist with the other.

A large car, glistening with rain, pulled up and stopped.

"Climb right in here, sugar."

Before she could protest, he had forced her into the cushioned leather interior. When he slid in behind her, she knew without asking that there was no going back to her shop. Not today.

"Sorry, Scarlet." The old indifference was back, but distant as though an afterthought. "We have to go to Fair Meadows. Then, well, we'll see." A determined jaw jutted. "One thing's for sure. You won't be going anywhere without me."

Despair surged. "That's unfair. My shop is my livelihood."

"Sorry."

"I don't want to go to Fair Meadows." She covered her face with both hands. "There's no need. I'll tell you if I hear from Noelle. I promise. Oh, please."

Entreaties and arguments failed to move him. "I don't know what you're upset about. Haven't you noticed I can be a very interesting companion? I've been told that my conversation is scintillating."

"Are you sure the word wasn't sibilating?" The gibe slipped out. "Sibilating as in snake-in-the-grass?"

"I am sure it wasn't simulating," he retorted, "as in sham and swindle."

She looked away.

He waited for a reaction. "What's wrong? Does the shoe fit too well?"

When no answer came, he gave a short burst of laughter that held no true mirth. She was glad when he settled his long body in the seat, leaned his head back against the headrest, and, to all intents and purposes, fell fast asleep.

\* \* \* \*

AT FAIR MEADOWS, the car stopped on the circular drive before the wide veranda. Callaway helped Amanda out. "Don't pout. Didn't your mother ever warn you your face will freeze in that position?"

She snatched her arm away. "I'm not pouting."

A grin softened his features. "Looked like it to me. Behave yourself if you want to go home today."

He had reached the top of the steps before she took in his words. *Home.* Did he mean it?

She rushed to follow him through the columned veranda into the house.

From the speed with which Claire appeared, she had been expecting them. Over gray slacks, an oversized white top with long tails fluttered ghostlike. "Oh, thank God—" On seeing Amanda, she froze.

Callaway's sister had aged ten years and lost ten pounds since Sunday. The shirt was cut big but the fitted slacks hung, far too baggy.

Shocked, Amanda put out a hand without thinking. "Are you all right?"

Callaway stepped between them. "She would be if we could find your frigging sister."

As though he blamed Amanda.

And she was to blame.

Claire gasped. "Cal, there's no need to be rude. I'm fine, Jane." She looked back at her brother. "Tip's lying down in his room. The shock of Sonny on top of everything else has upset him. Will you talk to him?"

Amanda didn't miss their silent communication. Her guess was right. The mysterious diary had to concern Claire.

"Is Robert here?" Cal asked.

Claire seemed to withdraw. "No, he had to meet the auditors in Roswell."

"Thank God for small favors. Let's go see Tip." Callaway put his arm around his sister's waist as they walked out. "It'll be all right."

Amanda watched them go. What she wouldn't give to have someone put his arm around her and tell her everything would be all right.

Mocking her daydreams, Cal's athletic form spun at the bottom of the stairs. Without releasing Claire, he pointed at Amanda. "You wait here."

For all the world like he was talking to a lap dog.

Amanda looked for a chair. "I'm not going anywhere."

"You'd better not be."

As he and his sister disappeared, a large yellow cat strolled out and inspected Amanda. She recognized it from the wedding, but it wore a malevolent glare today, eerily reminiscent of one of its family members.

"Nice to see you again, too."

Amanda's sarcasm was ignored. The cat sidled toward her chair until, without warning, it jumped onto her lap where it turned round and round, then curled into a ball.

"Well." Taken aback, Amanda scratched its ears. "Make yourself at home, cat." At least this particular animal didn't treat her as though she were beneath contempt.

* * * *

"STATE REPORTS AREN'T back, but preliminaries indicate Sonny died between ten and four." The bedspread on the rice poster bed was turned down, and Cal's stepfather, fully dressed, lay on the sheets.

Heavy blue draperies were drawn and lamps were lit to dispel the dreary day. "The sheriff and I used to hunt quail together," Tip explained his knowledge.

"Could it have been accidental?" Cal asked.

"With one of the bullets straight through the heart?" Tip looked at him over his glasses. "The lab tests aren't back, but no, it wasn't accidental."

Cal thought about who might want Sonny dead and didn't like the list of names.

"The thing is," Tip went on, his aged forehead wrinkling, "anyone could have done it."

Cal was wary. "An intruder, you mean?"

"Any one of us." Tip voiced Cal's concern. "We were all here, off and on, during the crucial hours."

"Matthew Swift," Cal said out loud. "Does he have an alibi?"

"No," Tip said as Claire simultaneously said, "Matt wouldn't have done it."

Cal ignored Claire. "Sonny was blackmailing Matthew, too."

Tip nodded. "Matt told me. He intended to pay."

Claire was stubborn. "Matt would never have shot Sonny."

"Claire." Sudden comprehension jolted him. "Don't tell me . . . Are you still in love with that man?"

"Oh, Cal." Claire's face contorted, dissolved. "Why must I be in love with a man to know whether or not he's capable of murder? Matt would either have paid the money or not. He would never harm anyone."

Cal stared, aghast at this unexpected shortcoming in his sister.

Claire paced. "I know Matt." She turned back. "Besides, no one here has an alibi except you."

As Tip nodded agreement, Claire rushed on, "I was here. Tip was here. Robert was here. We didn't keep tabs on each other, and most of the help were off after the wedding so they can't confirm our whereabouts. Stop trying to blame Matt. We had as much opportunity as he did."

"Ahem," Tip intervened. "I take it we agree Sonny was the actual blackmailer. Was he also the thief?"

"There's no one else, is there?" Cal couldn't think straight.

Claire, irreproachable, exemplary Claire, of all people, in love with a man not her husband.

Johanna's birth could be forgiven, chalked up to youth and an older man's seduction, but for her to still care for the man was incomprehensible.

Stick to the problem at hand. "I expect Sonny saw Robert open a safe, or maybe Robert gave him the combination. Robert trusts—trusted him implicitly. We all did."

Tip raised the important point. "But in that case, what happened to Lila's journal? It wasn't in Sonny's things."

"That's something else, Cal." Claire sounded as despondent as Cal felt. "Tip searched Sonny's room and luggage before the authorities got to them."

"It seemed best," Tip apologized.

"Good thinking," Cal said. "No journal, though?"

"No. But in his suitcase, I found a folder with ten bearer bonds. For fifty thousand dollars apiece."

Cal swung to look at Claire but she was shaking her head. "No, I never had a chance to give mine to him. And neither did Matt. Tip asked him."

"Five hundred thousand dollars. Where did they come from?" Then he knew. "That's got to be money for my studs."

Tip nodded. "That seems logical. I thought it best to take the bonds. Ahem. I saw no need . . ."

"Of course." Cal waved away his stepfather's admission to breaking the law. "Sonny got cheated. The stones by themselves were worth a helluva lot more than that." The others were silent as he chewed at his lip. "We may have to tell."

"No." Claire wet her chapped lips. "Johanna would die. Matt's life would be ruined, too."

"Better to face it. It depends on who bought my studs, whether the same person who connived with Sonny was the one who has them, and if he's the one who's got the journal. Was Miles here yesterday?"

"No." Claire followed his train of thought. "Tip and I thought of him, too. He and Sonny went off together at the reception, Cal. He could have given Sonny the money then."

"Had to be him. Damn his eyes," Cal muttered. He'd known Miles all his life. Miles had helped replace the father he barely remembered.

"Can bearer bonds be traced?" Tip asked.

"It depends," Cal said. "That still doesn't solve our problem, does it? Where's the journal?"

Claire sighed and stared out the window.

Cal sat down on the edge of the bed, clasped one knee, and rocked back and forth. "We need to talk to Matthew. He may have got it from Sonny and didn't tell Tip." He cut short Claire's beginning denials. "Before the murder, Claire. He may have paid Sonny for it before the murder."

Claire face brightened. "Do you think so?"

Best to evade what he thought. "We'll soon know."

But Noelle seemed the logical person to have the journal

He'd have to find her. One way or another.

A patient Amanda sat where he'd left her, encumbered by Johanna's cat sprawled over her lap as she thumbed through a magazine. They made quite a domestic tableau.

He refused to be taken in. "Snick sheds like crazy. I wouldn't let him sleep on me."

"Neither would I if I had a choice."

"I have to go see a neighbor. You stay here. If you leave, you'll be sorry."

She plopped the magazine on the table beside her. The sleeping cat didn't budge. "Stop threatening me. You're beginning to bluster and I'm getting tired of being told I'm going to jail."

He grinned. In spite of his attempts to keep his distance, he was warming to Amanda Jane. "All right. Stay put and we'll get you home tonight."

Her eyes flew wide open. "Do you mean it?" Her knee jostled the cat, evoking an admonitory meow.

He held up two fingers. "Scout's honor."

"Hah. You were never a Boy Scout in your life."

"Yes, ma'am, I was. Damn near made an Eagle." Honesty made him admit, "Except I discovered girls."

His mother hadn't approved of him quitting Scouts. She hadn't approved of his interest in the giggly girl who worked at the coffeehouse, either.

The cat in Amanda's lap flopped over onto its back and claimed her attention, but her lips twitched. "And they took up all your time from then on, I'm sure."

"Can't pull the wool over your eyes, can I? I'll be back soon." The image of her with the cat, in the aquamarine dress with her brown hair pulled severely back, followed him.

Fluffy blondes or dramatic brunettes or dazzling redheads were his thing. Particularly dazzling redheads. He had never looked twice at a woman with nothing to her credit but a pair of cool gray eyes and a smile that could light up the world.

Damn her.

Under Amanda's influence, all kinds of crazy ideas were taking root in his head.

Ideas like tackling responsibilities and doing something with his life. Ideas that hadn't crossed his mind in years, since his mother and Robert had tacitly decreed he was incapable of being entrusted with the most menial task for the company and had assigned him to his current irrelevant position.

What was Amanda Jane doing to him?

# CHAPTER THIRTEEN

CAL'S VISIT DID not surprise Senator Matthew Swift. Cal suspected very little would.

"I told Tip that Sonny approached me." Matthew poured a shot of bourbon for Callaway and another for himself into glasses before adding splashes of water. "He gave me until yesterday morning to raise half a million dollars."

Cal drained his drink and set the emptied glass down beside a vase containing fragrant jonquils and iris the same color lavender as the delicate tracing on the porcelain. "Did you pay him?"

"I couldn't raise that much money by then." Matthew sat opposite Cal, the piecrust table a barricade between them.

The two had never been friends.

Cal rested his elbows on spread knees and clasped his hands. "Then you didn't get the journal?"

"No."

"You didn't see him at all?"

There was nothing to be read in Matthew's face above the floral arrangement. The senator had been in public service for too many years.

Noting a wilted jonquil, Matthew reached out and lifted it from the vase.

"Oh, I saw him." Dry petals were plucked, one by one, and thrown down without regard for the antique Oriental rug. "I offered him two hundred thousand in cash. He took it, said he would be back after lunch for the rest." He twirled the naked stem of the flower round and round while Cal watched the revolving stem. "But he never came."

"There was no cash found on him."

"No." Matthew shrugged. "Perhaps robbery was the motive. I didn't ask Tip, but I wondered if he had another buyer for the journal."

"Another buyer? Who?"

The flower stem stopped its twirling. "Claire perhaps? Did he approach her?"

Cal hesitated, gave a curt nod.

Matthew expelled his breath. "I thought he might have. May he rot in hell." The viciousness with which the remains of the jonquil were thrown down belied the melodic voice. His fingers closed around the untouched drink glass so hard, his knuckles turned white.

"He must have been shot right after leaving here."

Matthew's face was guarded. "I didn't kill him. Though if I'd known he threatened Claire, I could have."

"I didn't ask if you killed him." Cal got to his feet.

"You were thinking it." The last strains of daylight mingled with the glow from the overhead candelabra to cast an aura about the senator's head. "Your jaw came from your mother. Claire's jaw has that same thrust."

The reference to his mother took Cal unawares.

Matthew went on, "I've often thought it a pity Lila was such a formidable woman. She set a wonderful example for Claire and Johanna. But not for you."

"Leave my mother out of this."

Matthew gave a small smile. "Your mother was stifling, Cal. I'm sure it was worse for you without a strong male figure to balance her unrealistic goals for you. It's a wonder you didn't turn to drugs or drink."

"I didn't." Just women and other diversions.

Matthew sat up straight. "Let me be plain. I don't care who killed Sonny, just so long as it was the right person." His words rose slightly, querying.

"What exactly do you mean, the right person?"

"I was walking down the hill that morning, not too far from the pond where he was found." Matthew picked up his drink. "I caught a glimpse of someone in a blue hooded jacket heading toward the pond."

"Who do you think it was?"

"I don't know. I couldn't tell."

"Man or woman?"

"I don't know. It was hard to see." The senator pressed his lips together.

"It wasn't Tip."

A split second passed. "Of course not. But if Claire needs help," Matthew said, choosing his words with painstaking care, "of any kind, for any reason, I'll give it without reservation."

"An alibi? Claire didn't kill anyone."

Matthew gestured with his glass. "The idea of Claire being under any suspicion, however slight, is unacceptable."

"I agree. But Tip and you could have killed Sonny as easily as she. Even Robert could have done it. Or this unknown person you saw. Are you sure you didn't see anything to identify him?"

"Nothing." Swift looked at the broken flower on the rug at his feet, and gingerly set his still full glass aside. "Claire looked ill Sunday. Had he approached her then?"

"No. But she knew someone would."

Matthew bent down, picked up the leaves and stem strewn moments before. "If I had my life to live over, the one part I'd change would be that autumn."

Cal snorted. "If wishes were horses, we'd be covered with horseshit."

"Ah, Cal." Matthew gave a slow smile. "Such a blunt person you always were. From the time you could talk. That's why you found it so hard to placate Lila. Wait, my friend. One day you may find yourself in a situation where you know what the consequences will be, but you send them to the devil and let yourself be damned."

"Was it worth it?" Cal asked tightly. "Your fling with my sister?"

"It wasn't a fling. And in terms of heartbreak, no, perhaps it wasn't worth it. But Claire . . . I can't talk about it." He turned, but not before Cal saw the naked pain. "Claire has you and Robert, but if she needs me, I'm not going back to Washington right away." He raised his eyes. "Tell her. If she needs me for any reason, I'll be here."

"It's no use us killing anyone until we make sure we can recover the journal."

"Such a pragmatist. My scruples would normally prevent me from participating in murder." Matthew rose from his chair. "But in this case, I'll do as I've done all along. Whatever's necessary to protect Claire and Johanna. Call if you need me. For whatever reason."

Cal went out the door, wondering if Matthew Swift would in actuality kill to keep their secret, and about whether the senator had had a part in Sonny's death. This man in the hooded jacket could be a fabrication to cover Matthew's own proximity to the pond.

\* \* \* \*

"SO YOU THINK she'll call Jane?" Claire asked as Amanda made a trip to the bathroom while the minivan was brought around.

Cal had filled his sister in on part of the story about Amanda's sister, but he'd deliberately let Claire think the seductive thief was Noelle. He hadn't stopped to question his motives, and skimmed over them now.

"Amanda is her first name, not Jane. According to all reports, Noelle always calls on Amanda when she's in trouble. With Sonny dead, she's in a lot of trouble." He wasn't protecting Amanda, he assured himself. No way. Amanda Jane could look out for herself.

"What if this sister doesn't have Mother's journal?"

Cal patted her shoulder. "Then she'll know where it is."

He hoped.

A steady drizzle fell as Amanda and Callaway left Fair Meadows. When the minivan swept around the curve of the driveway, Cal looked back at Claire, her face an indistinct oval through the rain's gray veil, keeping vigil by the porch columns.

Strange to think of her unconscious revelation. She'd always been so ethical, so strong. Her continued bond to Matthew was unfathomable.

If Claire of all people could be so susceptible, then perhaps everyone had weaknesses of some sort. Perhaps Cal wasn't alone. Perhaps the difference between him and other people was that they worked around their failings while he wallowed in his.

So. Something to contemplate.

The first part of the trip to Atlanta was accomplished in a chilly silence reminiscent of the plane ride to Birmingham.

Amanda was a careful driver, keeping her eyes on the road and traffic, and avoiding sudden stops or abrupt lane changes. Cal's presence clearly rankled.

After she merged the van into the interstate traffic, she vented her spleen. "It seems you'd have better things to do than terrorize helpless women."

Her defiance amused Callaway. Under other conditions, he might have liked Amanda Jane. A lot. "I've known a few helpless women, but you're a long ways from being one of them." He reconsidered. It might be best to stay on a good footing. "Look, Amanda, I've tried to be nice to you."

"Oh, sure," came her quick rejoinder. "Pushing me around like a madman."

Guilt flared. "Okay, I was pretty angry at first, but I had a lot to be angry about."

Her eyes stayed on the road. The windshield wipers flicked back and forth. "I never denied that. Not after I found out the truth."

"I'm happy to hear it. Well, I'm over being angry. I can even admire that quaint sense of loyalty that makes you want to defend your sister despite the way she set you up. But there's a limit to my admiration and certainly a limit to my tolerance. So let's try to get along, okay?"

He wasn't being drawn under her spell again. He was simply being pleasant.

\* \* \* \*

CAL'S CONCILIATORY WORDS didn't make Amanda any less uncomfortable. The jittery discomfort she felt around him accompanied a growing unhappiness she wouldn't confront. His request might be reasonable, but she wouldn't cave in to him.

"I don't want your admiration or your tolerance," she said, "and I don't want to get along with you. If Noelle calls, I'll let you know. What else do you want from me?"

"Sorry. You're stuck with me, at least until I find your sister. What I'm trying to say, in my scintillating or sibilating way . . ." One twinkle of his minuscule dimple chased away rancor. ". . . is that I think we should call a truce. I know I was rough with you and I'm sorry. But you didn't exactly treat me with kid gloves in Houston."

The windshield wipers beat a steady tattoo. His calm rationality shamed her. The telltale heat crept up her neck. "No, I didn't. Believe me, if I had known—"

"I do believe you. Otherwise I wouldn't be making these overtures. Let's try and get along until we hear from Noelle, okay? I'm not used to shoving women around. In fact, women are usually the ones who push me around. The feminine community at large thinks I'm a real pushover."

"All right." Amanda couldn't resist the way he gently poked fun at himself. "I don't much like being shoved around but on the other hand, I'm not used to shoving either."

Afterwards, they conversed like two civilized people. They might both still be guarded in what they said, but she relaxed, and the trip passed uneventfully.

About nine, armed with Chinese takeout, they arrived at her basement apartment.

When Callaway noticed the broken sidelight Melissa had managed to get boarded up, Amanda explained about the botched burglary. "Someone's coming Thursday to replace the stained glass."

He inspected the boards. "It happened early Sunday morning? About two or three o'clock?"

"Yes."

She wondered what was going through his mind, but he gave no hint.

When he finally came out of his preoccupation, he only said, "Check your answering machine."

There were several messages, but none from Noelle.

When she went upstairs to inspect the deserted shop, he came with her.

The familiar environment of white walls and varnished wood was comforting. Touching the rows of dresses, smelling the crisp fabric further settled her. This was her home, her haven. She could almost pretend she'd never met Callaway McIntyre.

Almost.

Back downstairs, they ate in reasonable harmony. He told her about the sailboat he was helping sponsor for the BOC and she told him about coaxing elderly grannies out of buying clothes meant for teenagers.

Then he talked about his race horse stabled in Florida and she answered with tales about the rabbit in the wooded strip behind her shop.

They didn't have much in common, but it didn't matter. He might not be the scintillating conversationalist he had claimed, but he was a good listener.

Afterward, she showed him the spare bedroom.

He glanced in, moved down the hall.

She followed, crossing her arms reflexively, guardedly, as he paused at her door. "That one is mine."

"Yes, I see." He entered anyway.

Wadding up fists, she trailed after him, saw him take the cordless phone from its cradle. The weight returned to her chest. "Why won't you trust me?"

He gave a cursory smile. Not the little boy's grin. No sign of the tiny dimple. "I do trust you. But not far. If Noelle calls while I'm asleep and I don't hear . . . Well, I've got your number, Scarlet, and your loyalty, commendable or not, seems to be unshakable in regard to your sister. I can't have you warning her."

Amanda stiffened. She'd begun to detest that name. "Don't call me Scarlet."

"What would you prefer? Thief? Tease? Chump?" But there was no heat behind the taunts. His face, not unkind, suggested weary amusement.

When she made no answer, he brushed past. She closed her door and wished she didn't feel hurt that he would laugh at her.

He didn't trust her. But then, he had good reason not to trust her.

Still, he'd been so friendly, so companionable tonight that she'd hoped he was beginning to forgive her.

"Fool," she muttered. If he decided to press charges, she was still in big trouble.

In bed, she lay awake. What was going to happen to her and Noelle? If Cal took legal action, they'd go to jail. Her career would be over. Noelle's marriage was already over. Cal . . .

He'd been kind to her tonight. Easy to remember the planes of his face and the way its hard lines turned gentle when he was with his sister. It would be nice to be looked at that way.

What was he? The jaded pleasure seeker Noelle had described or the ingenuous little boy with the hidden dimple?

She sighed, letting the drowsy mists of sleep envelop her. It had been a long time since she'd wanted a man. After Tommy, she'd put her body urges away forever. Finding out they were still active was hard to get used to.

Controlling herself might be harder.

\* \* \* \*

KEEPING HIS LUST under control was getting to be a problem.

Amanda Jane, when her eyes darkened to slate and the corners of her mouth turned up, was way more tempting than Scarlet Smith.

He liked her calm gaze and gurgling laugh, the way the aquamarine dress clung to the tiny waist and the way she'd stood up to him despite her fear.

Yeah, he could tell she'd been afraid.

But most of all, he admired her loyalty to her sister, who didn't deserve it. He tried to whip up outrage with thoughts of Noelle, but Amanda's smile kept intruding.

The short upper lip, the plump bottom lip. Begging to be kissed.

I'm a fool for thinking of her, he told himself. You're a fool for wanting her, he told his prick. She'd have you for an hors d'oeuvre and lick the toothpick if it would get her damned sister off the hook.

And on that titillating thought, he chuckled and drifted off to sleep.

\* \* \* \*

ON WEDNESDAY, AMANDA went to work. As he'd promised, Callaway tagged along.

"You'll scare away all my customers," she told him crossly when he took up a position in a chair beside the entrance and made as if to become a permanent lounger. "For heaven's sake, come back to my office and try and stay out of the way. And don't you dare light a single cigarette."

He scowled. "I can't smoke?"

"You're a big boy. If you want to get lung cancer, you know where the smoking lounge is." When he hesitated, she added in a maternal tone, "Need me to go with you? Does walking down that long hall alone frighten you?"

He sulked, but put away his cigarettes. Then he sat in her office and sulked some more. His actions were so like those of a small boy, Amanda had all she could do not to smile at him and coo the way she did with baby Teddy.

*It's all in how you handle him.*

Under other circumstances, she could have handled Callaway McIntyre. Oh, yes indeedy. Under other circumstances, he would have been eating out of her hand.

What nonsense. Why would she want an inconsiderate hedonist like Cal McIntyre eating out of her hand? Even if he did have a dimple that asked to be kissed.

She spent the morning making sure imminent deadlines were being met by suppliers and seamstresses, and calling to apologize personally for canceled appointments and to rebook them.

In her office, Cal took a seat at the drafting table where, bored, he turned magazine pages or talked on his cell. She saw him on it through the glass once, and later came in from the sewing room to hear the end of another conversation.

". . . Break-in could be connected. When will Robert . . . Yes, her apartment, but we're at the shop." He caught sight of Amanda. "Nicer than the exotic dancer and that water skier. But she isn't a redhead, so I don't know if it'll last."

Amanda drew herself up.

He listened and burst out laughing. "You're not fooling me. You just want to get a discount." He lowered his voice, turned his back to Amanda. "Don't, Claire. We'll manage."

After he hung up, his somber expression vanished beneath a wide grin. "My sister approves."

"Of you spending the night with me?" Her bitterness surfaced. "She must have a strange sense of values."

His jaw became rigid. "Claire's one of the finest people in the world. I don't think, after what your sister's done, that you have much room to criticize mine."

She had earned his rebuke. "No, I don't. I'm sorry."

The jaw loosened. "I am, too. Claire thinks you're nice, despite everything."

"In spite of Houston?" Her hands balled up. So Claire Winslow knew the whole sordid story. It was bound to happen.

"She thinks the thief is your sister."

"You didn't tell her about me?"

He made a lazy gesture with sun-darkened fingers, sleepy eyes falling to her fists and narrowing in amusement. "I thought her knowing would make all of us too uncomfortable."

She looked at him skeptically but left it for weightier matters. "You were talking about my apartment being broken into, weren't you? Why do you think that's connected to your diamonds?"

"It may not be. But if something had happened to you, there'd have been nothing to lead me to Noelle."

Ice encased her at visions of her small car bursting into flames.

He picked up on the change. "What's wrong?"

Sometimes, damn him, the brown eyes could see her every thought as soon as it formed.

She told him about the explosion that had totaled her car.

He heard her out. "Begins to sound more like someone intended to do away with you, doesn't it?"

"We don't know that."

His silence screamed at her.

"Noelle would never hurt me. Not Noelle."

"What about her boyfriend? Robert picked Sonny up at the airport around three that morning. Sonny could've flown in early, come here, and gone back to the airport in time to meet Robert. Would Sonny have been as concerned about your health?"

Her hands involuntarily wound together in the childish gesture she'd broken herself of. She separated them.

"When Sonny got to Fair Meadows," Cal went on, "he discovered I knew who you were. You being dead wouldn't do him any good. He decided to collect what money he could and leave for wherever Noelle was waiting. Maybe she's still waiting there."

She put up her chin. "If he's the one who broke in, Noelle didn't know. Noelle would never do anything to hurt me."

His expression said he believed otherwise.

"She wouldn't."

\* \* \* \*

CAL FUMED.

Amanda refused to see the truth about her damned sister.

At noon they ordered from a deli across the street. While they ate on Amanda's desk, Copland's Rodeo played in the background and Amanda offered excuses for Noelle's behavior.

After relating how she'd had to fill in for their dead mother, she ended, "You're right. Noelle calls me when she needs help. I tried to teach her that life is more giving than taking but she's never been able to understand. She's able to lead a mostly normal life, but sometimes she does idiotic things that don't make sense even to her. I shouldn't have dumped her on Edward when they married."

Cal knew all about feelings of inadequacy. Too bad he couldn't say something, do something to banish that disheartened air about her. The severe navy dress should have turned him off but didn't, not with her breasts mounding the knit fabric at each gesture of her arm. "When Sonny doesn't show up, she'll call."

Unhappy lips caught the straw. Iced tea made her throat ripple. "You're very confident."

"I am. She'll call." He felt his prick shift, pretended to be fascinated by the wall sketches.

She wasn't a redhead, she wasn't sexy, and she wasn't his type. Maybe he felt sorry for her, but this time primitive lust would not overwhelm common sense. He was through being some woman's pawn.

She put down her tea. "Thanks for not telling your sister about me."

"No problem. Are you going to eat your dill pickle slice?"

"No." She held it out for him to take.

"Tell me something." He considered the briny slab, knowing he shouldn't ask, shouldn't become any more involved with her. "I have a dossier on you."

"A dossier?" She dropped her napkin and bent to pick it up. "How flattering."

"It's very interesting." He wanted to laugh, as she sat looking for all the world like a woman threatened with the unspeakable, ready to defend herself to the death. Worse, he wouldn't mind doing the unspeakable, damn his rutting soul.

Except it wasn't his soul that wanted her.

"It's hard enough to live one's life without having someone else examine it through a microscope," she snapped.

"I wanted to ask why you changed," he said mildly. When he bit the pickle, he pretended he was biting her ear.

The erect back slumped. The thin mouth relaxed and the uneaten portion of her sandwich was pushed away. "Everyone changes."

"Not as fast as you. Cheerleader, homecoming queen, various club offices. But in your third year of college, you raised a 2.6 average to a 3.5 before you dropped out without graduating. No more social life, no more Miss Personality." He waved what was left of the pickle. "Your yearbook pictures changed, too. When you started college, you looked like a movie star. Like a real Scarlett O'Hara."

She flushed.

"Afterward, you looked like a librarian."

"Looks have little to do with a person's abilities."

"Most people make the best of their appearances. You did once.

You proved you still can if you want to. What made you not want to, Amanda?"

Her attempt to evade his questions didn't hide the pain. "Isn't it in my dossier?"

"No." His urge to understand was too strong to spare her memories. "What happened?"

Unwilling words came out, stilted. "I was engaged when I was twenty-one. At a fraternity party one night, my fiancé paid too much attention to another girl and I flirted with one of his friends to get even. Flirted a lot. Like, sat on his lap and let him feel me up. Tommy and his friend had words, and it ended up in a shoving match. Tommy hit his head on the corner of a marble mantle. He was dead before he got to the hospital."

Pity welled.

Her stoic veil returned. "It was my fault. All mine. If I hadn't been playing stupid games, Tommy would be alive."

"So you stopped playing games altogether."

How about that? Amanda had her failures, too. She atoned by retreating from the world into her career, just like he retreated from his career into his diversions.

He longed to pat her shoulder and tell her that life would go on.

She didn't give him a chance. "Games aren't worth anyone's life." Her chair lurched back from her desk. "I have to go. I have a fitting at one thirty."

He watched her go, back straight and chin up.

* * * *

SHE FELT HIS eyes on her as she left.

Damn him, damn him.

What had possessed her?

She hadn't talked to anyone about Tommy's death since it happened and had never intended to. Certainly not to a sardonic playboy like Callaway McIntyre.

He wouldn't understand. He couldn't. All his life, he'd been given everything. His future had never turned from gold to rust in one quick instant. No one he loved had ever died because of his foolish mistake.

Why had she told him? Because of his imagined empathy? She didn't want his commiseration or his pity. All she wanted was to be rid of him.

After bathing her face in cold water, she inspected it in the mirror.

A librarian, he had labeled her. That stung, though such vanities ought to be long buried. Stupid, stupid. What did it matter how he thought of her? Smoothing her hair into place, she tidied the discreet knot at the nape of her neck.

Some librarians were very attractive, but she was pretty sure they weren't what Cal had in mind.

A librarian.

# CHAPTER FOURTEEN

TOWARD THE END of the afternoon, Amanda's office phone rang.

On the other end, Noelle sounded hysterical. "Manda, oh, Manda, I'm in such trouble."

"Noelle! Thank God. Where are you?"

Callaway threw down his magazine and closed the glass door leading to the outer shop. Though he didn't rush, he was back in an instant to turn on the speaker and stand, every muscle alert, beside Amanda.

"Manda." Sniffling and crackling filled the room as Noelle hiccupped. "Manda, I-I—I just found out . . . Amanda, I . . ." her voice broke, "Sonny's dead."

Amanda's heart sank. Everything Callaway had said was true. Noelle was Sonny's accomplice. Noelle had tricked her.

*Oh, Noelle, how could you?*

At her side, Callaway's eyes glittered. He squeezed her elbow.

Noelle's fierce weeping filled the office. "I'm stuck here by myself with no money. I c-can't buy a ticket home and I c-can't speak the language and it's so awful. Oh, Manda, I'm in such trouble."

Years of habit kicked in. "I know, honey. But I'll help you, you know I will. Where are you?"

Noelle snuffled again. "Have you . . . talked to Edward?"

That note of withdrawal was familiar. Whenever Noelle did anything wrong and wanted to hide it from Amanda, she belatedly turned cautious. Noelle had behaved that way after getting her ring back, but Amanda had ignored the signs. She should have known better.

"Yes, I've talked to Edward." She had never lied to Noelle, would not start now. Callaway, thank heavens, made no effort to control the conversation.

"He t-told you. About the divorce."

"Noelle, it's all right, whatever you've done, it's all right. Do you hear me?" Amanda wanted to scream. "But I can't help you unless I know where you are."

Callaway nodded approvingly.

After a long pause, Noelle said, "The phone sounds funny, Manda. Like it's . . . Are you alone?"

"If you won't tell me where you are, I can't help you."

Noelle's breathing spanned the lines. "You're on a speakerphone. I can tell. Sonny's dead, Manda, and I don't know who killed him. I can't trust anybody, even . . . Who's there with you?"

She needed to comfort Noelle, to assure her nothing bad would happen. "Callaway was with me when Sonny died. He's—"

"Callaway?" Noelle's gasp was audible.

"Noelle! Don't hang—"

A click and dial tone followed.

Callaway's hand fell away. The spot where his fingers had gripped her elbow felt cold.

Triumph blazed in his face. "She'll call back. Edward won't send her money. Who else does she have but you?"

"No one." Amanda sank down on the sofa and laid her head in her hands. "No one."

* * * *

AT DAY'S END, a weary Amanda closed the shop and, with Cal at her heels, went downstairs.

"Noelle may not call me back," she said, falling into the upholstered wing chair in her living room.

"Yes, she will. Either on the work line or your cell, and we'll talk to her when she does." He headed to the kitchenette, saying after a few minutes, "This explains that emaciated look about you."

Amanda made herself get up and go to the opening between kitchenette and living room. He was surveying the contents, or non-contents, of her refrigerator.

"It's fashionable to be an emaciated woman nowadays."

"Not any more, with bulimia and anorexia so widespread among our female population. It's becoming much more fashionable to be pleasantly plump." His gaze moved over to where she stood by the bar, brushed her breasts. "Of course, plump's always been fashionable some places."

"That's a sexist point of view." She refused to acknowledge the giddiness his approval engendered.

"Sad and politically incorrect, but true just the same. You have eggs." He opened the carton and surveyed the eggs with distrust. "They expired last month but they look okay. How about an omelet?" He opened a cabinet door at random.

"If you know how to cook one, sure."

He opened more doors. "Where's your omelet pan?"

"Hey," she said with alarm. "I don't know what an omelet pan looks like. I use the microwave."

He brandished a black iron skillet rescued from the depths of a bottom cabinet. "This might work. Actually, my one culinary feat is an omelet. And I hate washing dishes." He aimed a meaningful stare her way.

Okay, she could take a hint. "If you cook, I'll clean up."

His omelet, after he'd found a can of mushrooms, another of olives, some minced onions, and a jar of pimientos to add, didn't taste too bad. Neither mentioned Noelle, though Amanda knew he, like she, was expecting the phone, hoping the phone, would ring at any minute.

After supper he looked for the television. "I can't believe you don't have one. Don't you watch the news? How do you know what's going on in the world?"

"There's a TV in the smoking lounge," she said, rinsing the skillet. "I read CNN on the computer and take the Sunday AJC." She didn't admit that the Atlanta paper was mostly for the comics. After she dried and put the pan away, she walked past the bar to check on what he was up to. "Besides, I have too many other things to do. I don't have time to watch TV."

"Oh? Go out a lot at night, do you?" He had found the iPod in its speaker dock and was checking out its contents.

She folded her arms and leaned against the living room archway while she thought about lying to him, and wondered briefly why. To make him aware she was a desirable woman? Too foolish. "I never go out. Usually I have designs to rough out, or billing to get out, or fabric orders to work up. There's always something to be done in the shop."

He *tsked* in either disdain or sympathy. "All work and no play makes Jill a dull girl."

"And all play and no work makes Jack a . . ." She stopped at his darkening expression.

"A what?"

She dropped onto the wing chair. "A playboy."

He laughed and the tension disappeared, but she could tell she had unwittingly struck some sort of nerve.

He started some music. "How's this?"

"Nat King Cole. Before your time."

"Yours, too," he countered. "Nice." He came to stand over her, holding out his hand. "Want to dance?"

"Dance?"

"You know. One two, one two. And don't say you can't dance. We've danced together before, remember?" He was smiling at her, the little boy's smile that revealed the unexpected dimple. His hand was held out.

She ought not.

She ought to stay in her chair, safe and intact and alone. The smart thing to do would be to run away and hide.

Instead, she got up and took his hand. "I remember."

Embracing her, he whirled her around and hummed with the song. At first she laughed, but when he pulled her close, when the tempo slowed along with his steps, she fell silent.

Being in his arms made her weak. Her heart hammered like a schoolgirl out with a boy for the first time. She'd forgotten how his fingers could touch her so lightly, yet start a hundred fires racing through her blood.

Too dangerous.

She pulled away, putting space between them. "Do you go dancing often?" Small talk should calm the inner turmoil his nearness caused.

"It kills time."

She wrinkled her nose. "Not enough to keep you out of trouble. You've been married three times."

"Yeah, never could hold on to a woman." He pivoted them around the small hardwood floor, drawing her back against him.

His smell was a blend of woodsy aftershave, cigarette smoke, and male skin.

"First time, I was still in school. She was looking for a meal ticket and I was available, but she could only hack it a couple of years. That divorce cost me a great deal of money and a great deal of self-respect."

The barest trace of bitterness hinted at how badly he'd been hurt. Beneath the hard surface there might just be that little boy she kept envisioning. "And the second?"

"An aspiring actress. I was twenty-four. She lasted six months before settling for more money and what was left of my self-respect."

Poor boy. She hadn't mistaken his hurt, nor did she mistake something else. He was hard against her. Moving away again, she tried to keep him at a distance.

His tone lightened as he pretended not to notice her retreat. "My absolutely, positively, indubitably last foray into matrimony was eight years ago. A stewardess I met in Palm Beach. That one was my record, time-wise. Two months. It wasn't quite as expensive as the others. Seemed she had a boyfriend waiting." He spun her around. "I may have to be hit in the head a few times, but eventually I learn. I'm as good at marriage as I am at cooking."

His cheerfulness invited laughter, and, lightheaded from his twirling and something else, she obliged. "Your omelet was wonderful. And it takes two to succeed at marriage."

He grunted although she wasn't sure whether in agreement or not. She could tell he blamed himself for his marital failures.

"Why do you prefer redheads?" she asked, and was instantly annoyed with herself for probing. She should leave him alone and not try to learn any more about him.

But she couldn't help herself.

Any more than she could help the lovely, languorous tingly feeling creeping up her arms and up her legs and down into her stomach and between her legs.

"Never thought about it." His mind was somewhere else. "Red hair just always seems to catch my eye."

"I'm honored then."

"What?" He looked down at her, bewildered, before the dimple twinkled. "Don't worry about it. You've got something I want more than red hair."

"Noelle."

"Exactly."

When he pulled her back to him, she had to stick her face against his neck or stare cross-eyed at his dimple. His beginning beard sanded her cheek, but she didn't care. She inhaled his aftershave and the smoky male scent, and felt his excitement growing. Something perilous awakened within her.

This couldn't go any further. In the middle of the song, she pulled away and turned off the music. "I'm tired. It's late."

The gleam in his eyes was all too familiar. She had seen the same gleam too many times in male eyes, had preened too often at the power it gave her.

The old exhilaration was gone. She didn't want this power over Cal, hadn't sought it, wouldn't wield it.

Her deceitful body trembled.

His voice was mild. Beguiling. "It isn't nine yet."

"But I'm exhausted. Thanks for the omelet." She spoke as coolly as she could. "You're a great cook." How had she been so foolish as to cling to him, mold herself against him? She knew what could happen.

Logic told her it would do her irreparable harm to go to bed with him. She wouldn't lightly sleep with a man, and his reputation was well-known. He joked about it. She could have captivated him once, but now he'd be too wary to trust her for anything other than a casual fling.

She was beginning to like him. A lot. And oh, how she longed to have him, even for one night.

So when he came to her and took her in his arms, she let him kiss her and run his hand down her thigh, returning his kiss with long-banked passion.

But when he clasped her breast, she pushed him away. "I can't," she whispered. "I'm sorry. It just won't work. Don't be angry." She turned to go before she lost the will.

"Why won't it work?" From behind, his hands caught her shoulders and his lips brushed the responsive place beneath her ear.

Her head fell to the side in longing.

His voice was low, persuasive. "Why not, Amanda?"

Desire made her dizzy. His mouth on her neck sent shock waves throughout her body. The imprint of his hands made fiery patches on her skin.

He turned her to face him, using his body to press her against the frame of her bedroom door as he'd once pinned her to the wall of his cottage. But now she wasn't frightened. Now the quickening in her heart echoed in her ears as his thighs followed her legs. His hardness stirred an answering heat in her center.

"Let me go in with you. Please." His fingertip traced the outline of her nipple through its protective layers. "You want me as much as I want you."

Her body, aroused to fever pitch, screamed at her to let him come into her room, into her bed.

Her better judgment won out.

"I can't."

"Why not?" Not angry, simply curious. He deserved a reply.

"I . . ." She sighed.

His tongue nuzzled her neck and moved down, so that his breath warmed the cloth of her dress and burned through to her swelling breast. His hand caressed her belly slowly, enticingly; sought her heated core. "You want this."

She couldn't. "I'd want more than you're prepared to give." This shaky voice wasn't hers. "To me or any woman. If I went to bed with you, it would be because I'm falling in love with you. And that won't do, Callaway. You know it won't."

He froze when she mentioned love. Then he lifted his head, the dim light from behind him making him a dark faceless silhouette. "You can't bring Tommy back."

The name on his lips shocked her. "Tommy has nothing to do with this."

"Doesn't he? Aren't you so wary of repeating the past you've forgotten how to live in the present?" His hand traced her cheek, rounded her ear to loosen the knot at the nape of her neck. "Have you fallen in love since Tommy? Have you let another man get near you, touch your heart? Or are you paying for an old mistake by turning into a dried-up prune, afraid to risk caring again?"

His directness made her gasp before she twisted her head away so that the thick coil of freed hair splintered and fell like a wall between them.

He pushed back the brown strands, caught her chin, and forced her to look at him. "Tell me, Amanda." When he stepped back to get his shadow off her face, she seized the opportunity to slip inside her bedroom and close the door. Though she shut it with deliberate softness and did not lock it, she fell against its frame and clung to the knob and used it as support.

His presence, still and silent on the other side of the wooden panel, pressed against her like a solid mass.

It wasn't true, what he said.

She'd learned to deal with her guilt at Tommy's death. Her life was full and satisfying.

Wasn't it?

Her body screamed for culmination, for consummation at this moment with this man, but she had turned him away and fled because she knew beforehand what the aftermath of loving would bring.

*I'll regret this.*

Over the thudding of her heart, she heard his steps going down the hall toward the other bedroom.

\* \* \* \*

AS HE TORE himself away from her door, Cal's heart thumped.

God, what was he thinking? He'd promised himself no more dumb surrenders to lust, no more mindless seductions. Dancing had merely been a way to while away the evening until Noelle's call. But Amanda had felt so good against him, so right. He wanted to make her laugh and forget her dead lover and conniving sister. He wanted to bring her back to life and change her back into the vital person she'd once been.

Oh hell. *Don't try to excuse yourself by dredging up some noble reason for seducing her. You wanted a woman and she was there. That's all it was, damn it.*

Amanda's face, shattered behind her hair's protective strands, haunted his sleep.

\* \* \* \*

AMANDA DOZED, UNABLE to sleep soundly because of seeing Callaway's dimple, feeling his embrace.

When she heard her cellphone's distant tone, she came instantly awake. By the time she stumbled out of bed, Cal was in the hall bringing it to her. His body was uncompromisingly nude, just as long, lean, and sinewy as she remembered from the night she'd met him, and deeply tanned with the one conspicuous exception.

Their eyes met. Hers dropped first. He'd already turned on the speaker.

"Manda, Manda, you've got to help me. I don't know what I'm going to do."

Amanda waited for the torrent of words to stop. "Noelle, I can't help you unless I know where you are. Tell me."

There. The words were easy to say. She didn't know why she'd been so frantic this afternoon.

"I can't . . . I don't want to tell you where I am because he'll find out. He's there, isn't he?"

"Callaway knows you talked me into drugging him, but it doesn't matter. He wants to help you."

"You said he was with you when Sonny died. You knew about Sonny before I called." The words were accusatory.

"Noelle, was Sonny your boyfriend?"

"He . . ." Silence. "I wanted to get married. I thought when I got my divorce . . ."

"Honey, you have to talk to us, tell us what happened." Amanda wasn't even conscious of using the plural.

"I know." Noelle's sigh was breathy and long. "You'll have to come to me, Amanda. I'm scared. I don't want to go to jail."

"Callaway isn't going to put you in jail." Amanda hoped her assurance was true. Callaway held her eyes, inscrutable. "He isn't," she repeated, challenging him to deny her words.

Noelle didn't know how daunting Callaway looked in his impressive male nudity. "Bring me some money, Manda. He can come with you if he has to. Okay?"

Callaway nodded for her to agree, and Amanda did. "Where do we come?"

"Cancun. Since he's coming, too, you might as well go to the McIntyre hotel there. The Firth of Clyde."

"All right." Amanda sank down on the sofa.

Noelle was rushing on. "I know there's a plane tomorrow morning. You can catch that. Will you?"

"Noelle . . ." Something about Noelle's suggestions seemed too pat.

Noelle wouldn't wait. "I'll call you tomorrow afternoon at the Firth of Clyde. I love you, Manda."

There was a click.

Way too pat. Noelle had practiced.

Amanda became conscious of Callaway's bare feet, long and narrow. They stood in front of her, waiting for her to do something, say something. An earthy aroma lay about him, of bed, sleep, and virility. The faint sweetness of aftershave cut with cigarette smoke.

She looked up. His hair was tousled, his features impassive. What was he thinking? What would he let her do? What would become of her and Noelle?

"I'll make arrangements," was all he said. He glanced at a wall clock. "You'll have to call Melissa first thing in the morning. Better not plan on getting back for a day or so. God knows what your sister will do once we get there."

All along she'd hoped in the back of her mind that Noelle wouldn't call back, wouldn't admit she was in trouble. Amanda had not wanted to hear.

He saw her eyes on him, reached out to rest his fingertips on the top of her head. Something in her expression must have touched him, because his hand and his voice were kind. "Go back to bed, Amanda. We can't do anything till morning."

His fingers sifted through her hair.

She stumbled back to her room, remembering when she was in bed what his body had been beginning to show.

* * * *

CALLAWAY, FULLY AWARE of his damned prick, couldn't put Amanda's distress out of mind.

*She's looked after Noelle the way Claire looked after me.*

Was he as big a disappointment to his sister as Noelle was to hers?

But Amanda and Claire hadn't let their failures govern their lives. He could learn from their examples, rise above his deficiencies so that a woman like Amanda wouldn't reject him outright as she had tonight.

As she had in Houston.

He jeered at himself. Amanda's kind of women were capable, confident and intent on worthwhile goals, with no use for affable incompetents like Callaway McIntyre.

Only she wasn't so confident and capable as she seemed, was she? Not below the surface.

He closed his eyes and tried not to think of her disappointment at the confirmation of her sister's betrayal.

It was hard, when he wanted to take her in his arms and kiss away her unshed tears and make her forget her imagined failings with Noelle.

*I want her, period.*

The old primitive instinct raising its ugly head. That's all it was. He beat at his pillow and tried to go back to sleep.

# CHAPTER FIFTEEN

CANCUN WAS HOT. Mid-May in Atlanta was pleasant, but in the southern seas, an ocean breeze saved the spring from being almost uncomfortable. Balmy gusts brushed the flat sandy spaces and daubed at corners hidden behind structures, moderating the sun's scorching beams and cooling overheated human bodies.

Amanda, who had never been anywhere farther south than Orlando, tried not to goggle as they navigated the long customs line that snaked between strolling armed soldiers. In the hotel's air-conditioned van, she watched palm trees, white sand, and flatlands go by.

And water. Always the water in the distance, a dazzling shade of blue she could never have imagined.

She pointed. "Is that the ocean?"

"That's the lagoon. The ocean's on the left and the Firth of Clyde is on the peninsula between them." Callaway was behaving as if last night hadn't happened, as if he didn't remember how near she'd come to yielding to him, or her ignominious last-minute retreat.

He might have forgotten, but Amanda hadn't. She'd led him on, letting him play that romantic music, letting him hold her close. Led him on despite her better judgment.

Long before Callaway had realized what was happening, she'd known he was aroused.

Better not think about last night.

"This is wonderful," she said. "I've seen pictures and movies with the sea and sky so blue, but being here in person is something else entirely different."

"Don't you go anywhere?" he teased. "I thought everyone had been to Cancun. It's a regular tourist trap."

"I don't have time for vacations. When I go anywhere, it's usually to New York or Europe on buying trips, and there's never time to sightsee. I'm a working girl, you know."

He looked out the window, suddenly aloof.

She'd forgotten how sensitive he was whenever work was mentioned.

The McIntyre Firth of Clyde was as splendid as the countryside, its lobby and hallways open to the outdoors in a delicious foreign flavor. They left the van, walked past the luggage depository, and reached the desk without opening a single door. As Cal checked in, Amanda checked out the large, airy lobby.

A huge floral centerpiece adorned the round coffee table in the middle of crisp cotton-covered sofas scattered around red tile floors. Tall tropical trees in planters made green splashes against white stucco walls. High ceiling fans turned lazily over people sitting singly or in chattering groups. One woman in a wide-brimmed hat tied on with a scarf, had chosen an inconspicuous corner away from the traffic to read a magazine.

As Amanda's glance passed over her, huge sunglasses were lowered for one split second.

Blue eyes locked on Amanda's.

Noelle!

With blonde hair covered by the large straw hat and delicate features shielded by instantly replaced dark glasses, Noelle lifted a warning finger. She looked scared to death.

Amanda bit her tongue to keep from crying out.

Her sister got up to join a noisy group passing through the lobby and, concealed in the midst of laughing chatter, made her way up a corridor to a large urn for cigarette butts. There, after checking around for unwanted observers, Noelle slid something into the sand. Then she looked nervously back over her shoulder.

At Amanda's imperceptible nod, Noelle fled.

*How does Noelle expect me to pick up whatever it is she's left there with Callaway dogging my every step?*

"All set." Callaway held up a keycard and took her arm, leading her toward the urn. "They'll bring our luggage up later."

When they neared the large urn, Amanda opened her purse. "Did I get my passport back at the airport? I hope so. It would be awful to have to go about trying to get a replacement down here, wouldn't it?" As she babbled, she rummaged through the contents of her purse.

They reached the urn. Her open purse lurched to the floor.

Compact, lipstick, lotion, ibuprofen, nail file, spray perfume, breath freshener, tampon, Sudoku book, ballpoint pen, hand sanitizer, sewing kit, tissue pack, and several condom packets clattered onto the tiles.

"Oh no." She rushed to pick up the condoms.

Callaway bent to retrieve the compact. When Amanda snatched at the tampon, she knocked the ibuprofen box one way while the lotion and perfume went up the corridor the other way. Straightening, she let her foot send the sanitizer and sewing kit skidding in another direction entirely. "Oh, my."

A hotel employee stopped to help, but Callaway was already

retrieving the sanitizer and sewing kit. By the time her things were collected, Noelle's wedged paper had been tucked away in Amanda's purse with no one the wiser. She thanked the bellman and Callaway with a brilliant smile.

Callaway suspected nothing.

It wasn't that she wanted to deceive him, but she knew Noelle. If Noelle thought she'd have to face Cal, she'd bolt, like the time she was caught smoking in school and hid out at a friend's house for three days rather than come home and tell their father she'd been expelled.

If she could reason with Noelle alone, she could convince her sister to tell Callaway whatever he wanted to know. Otherwise, nothing, including conscience or threat of jail, would keep Noelle from running. Not if she was panicky enough. And she'd looked terrified.

If she ran away, they might never find her again.

The open corridor led to an air-conditioned elevator, mirrored in front and padded with velour on back and sides. Upstairs, humid outside air flooded the corridor, but they entered a frigid suite.

Ceiling fans over the coffee table and the small dining table were stationary, unnecessary in the cold. Latticework shutters hid sliding glass doors that led to a balcony overlooking sugar white sands. The sea beyond was azure, the sky a shade lighter.

In slacks and short-sleeved tunic, Amanda shivered.

Callaway went straight to the thermostat. "Maids get hot working and leave the air turned down. We don't need it, do we?"

"I don't." Her teeth were chattering.

"My room's here." Cal motioned toward double doors on the right. "Yours is over there."

She followed him through the double doors on the left to her room with king-sized bed, built-in dressing counter, and bar. A balcony with a waist-high lattice brick wall held wrought iron chairs and tables overlooking the sands and sea.

Callaway unplugged the telephone by the bed and also the one in the bathroom. "You won't need these."

When he left with the phones, she went into the bathroom. Glass shower doors stood on one side and a jetted sunken tub on the other. An empty telephone receptacle hung beside the john, a hair dryer beside the sink. A small television stood on the counter.

Nice place. If it weren't for Noelle, she'd love being here.

With Callaway.

After using the facilities, she came back to the common area to find the bellman gone and the outside doors open to let in the outside warmth. "If I owned this hotel, I'd live here year round."

He shrugged. "Too crowded. Too many tourists. You'd get tired of it."

No, she wouldn't. She was sure she wouldn't. Perhaps that's what separated sophisticates like Callaway from ordinary people like her. When you had everything you wanted, there was nothing to look forward to. Maybe that's what was wrong with him, why he was so uncomfortable any time work was mentioned.

She was itching to read Noelle's note. "Is that my overnight case? I want to freshen up."

Locking the door of the bathroom and turning the TV to a program in Spanish, Amanda pulled out Noelle's message.

A ticket was attached to a flyer describing a guided bus tour of Chichen Itza originating from the Firth of Clyde the next morning. There was no note.

Noelle must mean for her to take the tour without Callaway. That would be hard since the only entrance to her bedroom led through the common living area. Although he didn't watch her as closely as before, he still managed to stay underfoot. She might be able to elude him, but when he missed her, he'd come after her. He'd be furious when she slipped off to meet Noelle.

Maybe she could get him accustomed to her being gone for short periods.

She went into the living area. "I forgot my decongestant tablets. Do you suppose the hotel shop has some?"

"Probably."

"I'll run down and get some."

"Have some sent up. Your cell stays here and if you're not here when Noelle calls, she sure as hell won't talk to me."

There went that idea. "You're right. I can pick some up later." She sat down. "So what do we do? Hang around and wait?"

He gave a ghost of a grin, letting his eyes touch her legs, ascend to her breasts, and settle on her mouth. "Unless you have a better suggestion."

He knew what he was doing to her, damn him. "I think we hashed that out last night."

"Is that what we were doing?"

She didn't miss the irony. She'd rejected him the past night after making a fool of him in Houston. No man enjoyed being made to feel ridiculous once, much less twice. He should be bristling with hostility and resentment, not sitting here smiling at her.

If they'd met some other way, Callaway McIntyre might be someone she wanted to know. There was a decent streak in him that sometimes peeked out. Like his dimple.

"Okay," he said when she didn't answer. "Guess that's out." His brow creased in thought. "There's a hot tub in my room."

"A hot tub? Really?" She jumped up, eager to take his mind off what hadn't happened between them. "Can I see?"

"Straight through and outside."

Sure enough, his secluded balcony ran the length of his room and was twice as wide as hers, allowing ample room to shelter a hot tub meant for several. It was hard to resist perching on the edge and dipping her fingers into the silky, inviting water.

The midday sun on her hair felt shamefully extravagant. When was the last time she'd been outside in the sun with nothing to do? Her free days were always spent running errands, but this, this lazy, magnificent, bright afternoon under the palms with its scent of salt and sand, was seductive. She could laze here and trail her fingers in the water all day.

Such luxury ought to be outlawed, even if there was something marvelous about the decadence.

"Clothes aren't allowed." Callaway, thumbs stuck in jeans pockets, strolled to the door. The golf shirt outlined his muscled chest. "Everyone strips before getting in. Management is very strict about the rules."

"I'll remember that if I decide to get in."

"You can use it anytime." He didn't move when she stood. "So long as you remember the rules. You can use my bed anytime, too. In case yours isn't comfortable."

"How generous." She wouldn't meet his eyes, knowing what they held, conscious of how they affected her.

He didn't step out of her way. "Of course there's a rule about that, too."

"I imagined there would be." She couldn't help but giggle at his blatant flirting. "No clothes in bed either?"

His minute dimple quivered, erupted. "No clothes. Oh, and I forgot the second rule. You have to share the tub or bed with me. Or both."

"What if a woman doesn't accept the rules?"

"Following the rules is the price of the fun." His gaze held the light she recognized from the night before. "We could have lots of fun together, Amanda."

Her throat closed up at the thought of basking in the water with him before lying on soft sheets beside him. "I don't think so. Your rules are too strict."

"Too bad." He stepped aside. "They sure do make everything a lot more . . . enjoyable. Think about it."

Carefully skirting him, she retreated into the safety of the common area before looking back and laughing. "Enjoyable for you, maybe. I'm not so sure about me."

\* \* \* \*

CAL FORGOT EVERYTHING when he saw the dancing eyes peeking over one shoulder.

*Hold on, dude. You don't need another public humiliation.*

What worried him most was the hollow feeling in his stomach. Amanda had qualities his usual choices never possessed.

Her loyalty to her sister. He'd never had that kind of loyalty from wives or lovers.

And she'd withdrawn from life because she felt responsible for some kind of freak accident.

A woman like Amanda ought not to have to deal with her sister, mentally handicapped or not. She ought to be protected from people like Noelle and left to run her shop to her heart's content. If he had his way, neither Noelle nor anyone else would cause her a moment's anguish. He'd make sure she never had to worry again.

Dammit to hell, what was he thinking? Didn't he have enough aggravation after she'd helped him nearly destroy Claire and Johanna? He couldn't run his own life, much less hers.

\* \* \* \*

AMANDA WISHED SHE had done things differently. If she'd managed Noelle better, she wouldn't be in this situation.

As she thumbed through magazines, Callaway paced the floor and examined her cell every five minutes, waiting for it to ring.

She was acutely aware of his physical presence the entire time she pretended to read: the long legs, the wide shoulders, the muscular arms.

What would he do when Noelle didn't call? And how was she going to get away the next morning?

She still had no plan when about five o'clock, her cell rang and he held it out to her.

Jumping up, she looked at it. An unknown number flashed up.

"Go ahead," he said impatiently. "Answer it."

As she pressed the answer button, he moved closer.

"Hello."

He pressed his head against hers to listen.

"Hello, Amanda." Noelle sounded calmer than she'd looked in

the lobby. Maybe she'd found her courage once her big sister showed up.

"Where are you, honey?"

"Here in Cancun." Noelle was cagy. "Did you bring money?"

"About two thousand dollars. All I could get." Noelle sounded too calm. What was she playing at?

"Thank you, Manda. I didn't know what to do."

"I know, honey. But you need to come out of hiding now. I'm here and you're safe."

"I don't want to talk to Callaway McIntyre. He's scary."

"He isn't going to hurt you." She looked into his dark eyes, daring him to say differently. "He hasn't gone to the police, Noelle, but he needs to speak to you."

"Why?"

Talking to Noelle was sometimes worse than talking to a five-year-old. "Other things were taken from him the night I stole your ring. Did you know that?"

She could hear Noelle clear her throat. "I wasn't there that night. I don't know anything about it."

"He still needs to talk to you."

Noelle inhaled. "All right. I'll meet you both at the restaurant on the street at the front of the first shopping center going into town. I'll be there at one tomorrow. But Manda?"

"Yes, honey."

"You won't let him hurt me, will you?"

"Of course not. He just wants to talk to you. Noelle, can't we meet earlier than—?"

Noelle hung up.

Defeated, Amanda put down the phone.

Callaway bit his lip. "Okay. Tomorrow."

"She's scared to death," Amanda said sharply. "You've got to be gentle with her."

"I don't normally hurt women."

"She's more a little girl than a woman. You'll be abusing a child if you scream at her."

"I don't plan to scream at her."

"Good." Time to start breaking away. "We're set up to meet her so there's no need to stay in the room. I'm going to run down and get some decongestant tablets. Okay?"

"Yeah." He pulled out his cell. "I'd better tell Claire, see if anything else has happened on her end." He called after her, phone to his ear, as she put her hand on the door. "You know what this means, don't you?"

Guilt made her jerk her hand back, and guilt made her heart pound. "What?"

The hard lines of his face had disappeared, making way for the dimple. "We have tonight and tomorrow morning to kill. I don't know about you, but I don't want to stay cooped up here."

"No." She managed a grin, hoped it didn't look too sickly. "I don't want to stay in the room either." Not with him.

"We could ride the bus to town, what do you say?"

She made herself unball her fists. "What can I say? This is your show." She went out, got into the elevator.

What could she say?

\* \* \* \*

CAL WOULD SAY things between them were progressing. Maybe a few hours relaxation would erase the worry lines on Amanda's face.

He filled Claire in on what had happened. "So," he ended, "after the meeting with tomorrow we'll know where the book is."

"I hope so." Claire sounded stressed.

"Everything all right there?"

"They have deputies dragging the pond, looking for the gun that shot Sonny. They've also been asking us all kinds of questions, but so far nothing we can't handle."

"What about Robert? Is he over the flu?"

"Yes. In fact, he's got an appointment with the auditors in Roswell today. Once they get a preliminary okay on everything, Robert thinks the Board will offer him Mother's job."

"Too bad. You'd be much better at it, Bags."

"Robert's earned it. He really wants it." Claire's weariness came through the phone. "I've got to go. Let me know what happens after you meet with this woman."

"Will do."

And God help Noelle if she didn't come through.

No matter how fond of Amanda he was becoming, her sister was another story.

# CHAPTER SIXTEEN

THE BEAUTY OF the late afternoon ocean made Amanda wish she had packed a bathing suit.

When she said as much to Callaway, his jaded air flickered. "What, you want to go swimming?"

"I've never seen a sea as blue as this one."

"So go down to the hotel shop and get a suit."

"No. I can't."

"Go on. I keep one in my overnight bag so if you hurry, we can get in before dark."

She gave in. This was another chance to get him accustomed to her absences.

Though he told her to use the room account, she charged the suit on her credit card and tried not to wince.

Her bank account would be out several thousand dollars before she was through with Callaway McIntyre. Or before he was through with her.

If that was all she was out, she ought to be grateful.

Amanda hadn't worn a swimsuit in years. Despite this one being more modest than most, with no robe and her hair caught in a topknot exposing her neck, she felt naked.

When Callaway met her, completely unselfconscious in sandals and revealing suit, she had to swallow. His shoulders were good, tapering to slim hips and well-shaped legs, and the nylon, though not snug, clung to places impossible to ignore.

Easing into a T-shirt, he looked her over. "Now that is one bathing suit that leaves a helluva lot to the imagination."

She interpreted that cryptic remark to mean he didn't approve, but she couldn't tell whether the suit or the body inside displeased him.

As if it mattered.

How long had it been since she worried about whether or not she appealed to a man? There was no reason to start at this late date.

The fine beach sands, soaked by the late afternoon sun, led beyond the white shoreline to an ocean that was the most gorgeous blue Amanda had ever seen. Wouldn't a dress in this color be . . . ?

*No. Don't think of work. Don't think about Noelle.*

Just for the moment, she forgot about Callaway's diamonds and book. Concerns of going to jail fled when the first step onto the beach turned her back into a carefree teenager who stood scrunching her toes through the dry sand. She couldn't hide her delight.

Cal, coming up with towels, ridiculed her. "Stop gawking, hayseed. Haven't you ever seen a beach before?"

"Not a beach like this."

When a girl in a tiny bikini and high heels minced by, Callaway automatically turned his head to check her out.

Amanda gave him a wicked nudge with her elbow. "Stop gawking, hayseed. Haven't you ever seen a bikini before? And don't tell me heels are part of the usual beach attire here."

"The usual attire for models." He nodded toward the beach. "See the camera outfit?"

Girls with full makeup and sprayed hair stood around as a photographer posed them for single and group shots. When she was done, each girl, grimacing from the sand sifting into her five-inch heels, made her way up the steps to the walk and picked up a satchel big as an overnight bag, containing heaven knew what.

Coming back to reality from the world of high fashion, Amanda looked up to find Callaway watching her. He was smiling, his friendly smile.

She beamed at him. "Are you embarrassed?"

"About what?"

"At me gaping like a tourist."

"No. I told you, Cancun was built for tourists." He walked toward the ocean. "Want to get in?"

They waded into the waves for a few moments. Then, beneath a towering dune, they flopped down in the sand where Callaway dug a hole that quickly filled with water.

Soaking up the enchanting late day sun, she rested her arm on her forehead and watched him. "What are you doing?"

"Getting set to make sand castles. Another of my small talents, besides omelets. Claire's boys love making them. Sand castles, that is. Not omelets."

"Looks like fun." She sat up. "Show me how."

His eyes widened. "You've never built a sand castle?"

"I've only been to the beach a couple of times in my entire life. The last time, Tommy and I . . ." She hadn't meant to talk about Tommy. She licked salty lips. "We went on spring break to Florida. His sister and her husband had a condo in Destin."

"Bet you didn't build sand castles."

"No." Talking about Tommy to Callaway didn't hurt as much now. "We didn't build sand castles."

"Poor lady. What you've missed."

He showed her how to dig a hole that filled with water, how to scoop up a handful of sand the right consistency.

She soon got the knack of letting the mixture dribble into a pile, the water draining out to leave patterned sand stacked higher and higher until a delicate tower soared. Absorbed, they built castle after castle, joining smaller peaks into battlements until a fort, one yard square, boasted a main center rising almost two feet high behind the expanding hole.

She was glad Callaway was enjoying their play. He'd needed to forget his problems, too.

\* \* \* \*

CALLAWAY WATCHED HER over the grains trickling from his fingers.

She deserved this. She needed a break.

Despite her hair in its inevitable knot and her sleek feminine figure, she was as absorbed as a child. It was his weak, lusting body that insisted she was all woman.

*Someone needs to teach you how to play again. Someone needs to make you laugh, show you life's more than regrets and hard work, make you wean Noelle from clinging to you like a leech.*

Not him. Nosirree, not him. He couldn't even sort out his own life, much less hers.

Waves neared their edifice.

"Surf's coming," he warned.

The sun had fallen behind the dunes, casting a shadow that crept toward the water. People were starting toward hotels.

Amanda sat back, kicking out long legs and flinging up a handful of sand that promptly rained down on her head and shoulders. "I don't care." Then pulling at her knot, she sent brown tresses flying in an attempt to rid them of sand. "The making of it is what's so much fun, isn't it? I can't believe we made anything so gorgeous."

Something deep inside him stirred. Something hinting at the vague discontent he'd felt before. But Amanda caused his restlessness this time. Amanda with her set goals, her fortitude, her refusal to be diverted.

So different from him, with his meaningless hobbies to fill the days and his haphazard attempts at love.

Amanda had measured out her life, building it as carefully as she had built the sand castles while he had built nothing.

Resentment grew.

He wanted to lash out at someone, anyone, and Amanda was at hand. This whole situation, the loss of his studs and his mother's journal . . . It was all her fault.

And she had rejected him, emphatically. Last night as well as that first time she'd led him on and run away. She had nothing but contempt for Callaway McIntyre.

He wanted to seize her, hold her, and prove he wasn't as bad as she thought. He wanted her to like him.

Jumping to his feet, he yanked her up so hard her hair slapped at his face. "You were going to swim in the ocean. All we've done is paddle around the edge."

When she drew back protesting, he swept on with her, anyway.

Snug in his arms, she was solid but not heavy. He pretended she was his, that he could use her certainty to overcome his failures.

"You're going to get baptized in Cancun's waters, Amanda Jane. Here and now."

She gurgled, and made a halfhearted attempt to escape. "The last time I got dunked, I was sixteen years old."

He walked into the surf feeling sixteen all over again himself, when he had thrown in the cutest girls and laughed at their squeals and made up with them later.

Amanda wasn't angry or squealing. She was an ebullient bundle against his chest, laughing so hard that he began to laugh, too. The breeze lifted her hair to screen his eyes and catch on his lips. The water covered his knees and thighs, drenched his suit and cooled his groin.

"You've needed a good soaking since I met you, Ms. Jane. Give me a kiss and I'll put you down."

She turned her head away and laughed harder. "I'm not afraid."

*I am.* The thought came without warning, and he wasn't sure what he was afraid of. His laughter fled.

"Kiss me," he said.

She shook her head. "Toss away, Mr. Macho. I can swim."

"You'll get your hair wet."

"It'll dry."

She was alive and vibrant, and he couldn't plunge her into the indifferent sea. Abruptly, he set her down on her feet. A wave slapped his chest, knocking her away.

She was surprised, but weathered the surf and hurried back to the beach. Her movements emphasized the outline of her butt, the flare of her hips from the small waist.

"I thought you were going to throw me in," she taunted. "Not as strong as you thought you were, huh?"

"No. The ocean might have carried you off and I'd have hated that." He grinned so she wouldn't realize he wasn't teasing.

He wanted her, damn, how he wanted her. He was almost sick with desire. He'd like to throw her down on the sand and let the waves break over them as he took her over the edge and turned her back into the woman she was meant to be.

She saw something in his face. Her smile faded, the glow in her eyes died, and she picked up her towel a shade too quickly. "I'm starved. It's getting late."

"Near seven," he agreed, relieved at her change of subject.

If he wasn't careful, he would lose himself in her. He could envision a mind-whirling trap springing closed.

And his head, where Amanda Jane was concerned, was already reeling.

\* \* \* \*

CALLAWAY KEPT CONFUSING Amanda. One moment he seemed jaded, the next an innocent. His changing moods kept her mind in turmoil.

After cleaning off the sand, they caught the bus into Cancun and got off at the restaurant where they were to meet Noelle—where Callaway thought they were to meet Noelle—the following day.

Amanda hated deceiving him, but she couldn't chance driving her sister away. She would force Noelle to talk to Cal.

Over dinner, Callaway's charm hit full blast. He advised her on the menu, joked with the waiter and entertained her with tales of Cancun's denizens.

In the face of such goodwill, Amanda's conscience kicked in big-time. But she had to stick to Noelle's plan. If she didn't, Callaway would never recover his things.

Once Noelle saw she had no choice, she would cooperate. There was no reason for her not to, now that Sonny was dead.

But Noelle couldn't cooperate if she ran away.

I'm doing the right thing, Amanda told herself as she and Callaway strolled around the mall behind the restaurant.

As she tarried in the shops, he trailed along without complaint. A weaver working in the upstairs aisle displayed tablecloths and napkins that she fell in love with. She debated on buying some and flipped through the different designs until a pattern in bright colors made her exclaim.

"Go ahead," Callaway said. "Get a set."

She put down the samples. "I've spent too much money already."

The moment she said it, she regretted it. Her finances were none of Callaway McIntyre's business. "Let's get something to drink."

Leaving her sipping her soda, he wandered off. On his return, he carried a large bag. From it he pulled a leather purse. "To go with your dress I got Claire for her birthday. Only six hundred fifty pesos," he boasted. "See, the hardware's real silver."

Envious of Claire for having a sibling who remembered birthdays, Amanda tactfully refrained from saying the purse was far too sporty for the orange gauze dress. She also left unvoiced doubts as to its worth.

On the bus, Callaway, pleased with his purchase, swung his shopping bag and chatted with the other passengers. Most of them were tourists, some staying at the Firth of Clyde. These he skillfully led into voicing opinions on the rooms, the staff, the shops, and the service. All without disclosing his own interest in the hotel.

As he listened to what the Firth's guests were saying, Amanda could almost see him making mental notes. He might pretend he wasn't interested in his family's company, but his actions said otherwise.

When they got back to their rooms, he opened the bag and pulled out a smaller sack that he handed to Amanda with a flourish. "This is for you."

Mystified, she looked inside to see the tablecloth and napkins she had admired.

When she found her voice, she said, "You shouldn't have done that." She folded the top of the bag down and handed it back. "It's very sweet of you, but it was my choice not to get them."

"You didn't let me buy your clothes in Las Vegas or a swimsuit here." The corners of his mouth turned down. "These cost hardly anything."

She recognized the beginnings of a sulk. "Thank you, but I can't take them."

"Look, I'm trying to make up for dragging you all over the country and then some. Let me give them to you."

"No. Sorry."

He shrugged, his jaw tensed.

She'd hurt his feelings. He took her refusal of his gift as another rejection. "It doesn't mean that much to you, I know." She touched his arm, trying to make him understand. "But it puts me in your debt, don't you see?"

"And you don't want to be in my debt?"

She thought of his stolen diamonds and book. "I'm already way over my head in debt to you. I can't afford to owe you more."

"Okay." He threw the bag on the sofa like a thwarted little boy. "Don't take them. Be that way."

Amanda could barely restrain a big grin.

I could handle him, she thought for not the first time. I know I could. If I only had the chance.

"Hey," she said. "It's nine o'clock. Almost bedtime."

He scoffed. "I can't go to bed this early. I'd wake up at three in the morning. How about going downstairs to the club? They've got a band there, we can dance." A faint scowl returned. "Don't worry. There's no cover charge for us."

Yes, she wanted to go with him. Anywhere. It would be heaven to dance with him, feel his arms around her, and put her arms around him. To gaze into his eyes and watch them light up with the laughter that lurked beneath the surface. Her kisses would tease away the frowns and charm the dimple out of its hiding place.

She wanted that. She wanted him.

No more evading the truth: it was too late for her and had been all along. Callaway McIntyre had come into her life like a cyclone and no matter how hard she fought being blown away, it didn't change a thing.

"All right. Let's go out." No more nerves, not tonight. It's for me to choose. She could dance with him and laugh with him and come back to her lonely room, her solitary bed.

Or not.

She could take him into her body, let a few hours assuage the need he evoked. Or she could sleep alone and wrestle with her demons in her own way.

Her choice. Seize the moment and have a few hours of happiness, or let it go by and regret it.

Maybe he'd be gone afterward, but she could have this one night.

It was her decision to make.

# CHAPTER SEVENTEEN

THE CLUB, A large area of the hotel's lower level open to the beach, was filled by colored lanterns and people gyrating to music played by a loud Mexican rock quintet. Callaway, in shorts and Hawaiian shirt, pushed his way to the bar, got their drinks, and elbowed his way back to her.

"Dance?" He had to shout above the din so Amanda could hear.

She raised her brows in imitation of the incredulous looks he so often used on her.

Recognition of her mimicry evoked his quick grin. "How about a walk down the beach instead?" he yelled.

She led the way outside. Her dress was loose-fitting and long, one of her few casual dresses. On impulse she'd thrown it in at the last minute because it didn't wrinkle and its vivid orange shade brought up images of exotic places. It looked good on her, too, even if its classic cut might not be to Callaway McIntyre's taste.

The moonlight fell like a satin sheet, turning the beach silver and leaving dark shadows in its hollows. As they sat on a concrete wall and sipped their drinks, the background music diminished, its hush overwhelmed by the roar of frothy surf hitting luminescent sands. When they joined hand-in-hand couples strolling on the beach, Callaway offered a steadying arm while she took off her flat sandals.

We're like the others, she thought. Or almost.

How nice it would be if they were just another pair of lovers.

The sand crunched pleasantly underfoot. They moved together, walking side by side, arms entwined around waists, hips brushing. His quiet presence evoked a tranquility she hadn't felt in a long while.

When he stopped and drew her to him, she didn't resist.

The moonlight shadowed the oval of his face so that she couldn't see his eyes, but his mouth was close, close enough for her to see his lips quiver.

"Amanda?"

She reached up and pulled that wonderful pliable mouth down to hers. Traces of his bourbon mingled with her piña colada as his very own odor, very own taste drowned all the extraneous flavors and scents wafted by sea and flowers.

He hesitated, but once he understood she had no intention of bolting, he curved her form to him, seeking to absorb her into his flesh, consume her body and soul until she was part of him. Once arranged, they were a jigsaw of arm over arm, shoulder over shoulder, mouth over mouth.

*Pop!* came an explosion from behind. *Pop! Pop! Pop!*

They drew apart.

Amanda, heart pounding, sensed something akin to her panic emanating from him. But her fear wasn't at the sudden racket. She had immediately recognized the fireworks.

What frightened her was herself and her feelings for Callaway McIntyre.

Tearing her eyes from his, she looked to the side where brilliant shooting lights sped skyward over the hotel, arced, burst, patterned, and faded.

He coughed. "It's a fireworks display at the lagoon. For the janitorial convention. They're taking up a lot of the rooms. Nice place to have a sales convention."

He was trying to pass the kiss off with trivialities. Her inner battle had infected him. After their history, he would find trusting her, even in a kiss, difficult.

As they watched, more radiant bursts came. More lights of silver and gold shattered into pinpricks. Palest sprinkles of green, blue and pink dotted the velvet night sky.

"We could walk past the hotel, over to the lagoon."

Callaway's husky voice betrayed him. Like her, he was fighting for self-control.

Her choice was quite easy after all. "No."

The throat flutter of his swallow showed against a brilliant bursting light. "We can see better from there."

"I can see fine from here." She drew him toward her.

He held back. "I don't need this. You've kissed me one time and left me in bed. You kissed me the other night and turned me away at your door."

"I know." He wouldn't understand her capitulation when she didn't understand it herself, but she wanted him the way she hadn't wanted any man in a long time. Whatever he would give her tonight, she would take. "Let's try it again. Let's walk to my door and go from there."

Wary, he still hesitated. After all that had passed between them, he couldn't bring himself to take the risk.

She couldn't blame him.

"Please."

"All right." The rasping words revealed his desire, made hers intensify. "We'll go from there."

I deserve this much, she rationalized. He'll be gone tomorrow or next week, but I'll have something besides Tommy's memory. I can hardly remember Tommy's face. I can't even remember the tone of his voice. I'm too full of Callaway. The concern when he looks at Claire, the dimple when he smiles, the cold stare that hides so much uncertainty.

He took her hand, tucked her fingers under his arm possessively, carefully, as though she were made of fine porcelain.

A small gesture, but executed in a way that made her feel precious, cared about. How long since anyone had cared about her?

When they reached the beach faucet, he took her sandals and bent down so that she could hold onto his shoulder to rinse her feet. Then he wiped away the water with his hand and slipped her shoes back on.

A child would have run into her on the steps except that Callaway's intervention meant his leg took the blow instead of her hip. At the collision, he caught the boy, kept him from falling. "Slow down, kid. You'll hurt someone." He chuckled as the wide-eyed boy ran away.

Under his protective arm, she let him steer her past a rowdy group on the walkway.

Had she ever felt as desirable, as safe as this? No wonder he'd been married three times. Why hadn't a fourth woman grabbed him up long ago? When she caught him looking at her in the elevator, she put up her hand and touched his jaw.

His nostrils flared, his eyes narrowed. Not from anger but from desire. Despite the dim light, his eyes spoke to her as surely as his voice. Inside the suite, he closed the door and turned the lock. He never took his gaze off her, yet he made no move toward her.

She stopped at the sofa. Ten feet of polished tile separated them.

He caught his bottom lip between his teeth. The sweet idiot expected she would back out and was giving her every chance to change her mind and save them both a bitter aftermath.

"Do I get the good night kiss-off now?" he finally asked.

"Not unless you want it."

Silence.

Exhilaration filled her. He didn't know what to do when a woman made up her mind to have her way. Callaway, she suspected, had always ensured he made the decisions in past relationships.

So she stood her ground, not making it easy for him. She'd chosen. Now it was his turn. He would have to bridge the separating tiles.

His thumbs and fingers rubbed together in a nervous manner at odds with his fixed stare. He wanted her. She could see his chest rise and fall, see the telling bulge in his shorts.

It seemed she would have to prod after all. "For heavens' sake. I never thought I'd have to resort to asking a man to show me his bed."

Confidence sparked, but insecurities and suspicion remained.

Amanda perceived every doubt running through his mind, and held out her hands in reassurance.

He ignored them and scooped her up. She giggled as she clasped his neck, and let her head fall onto his shoulder.

In his room he laid her on the bed and bent over, stopping at traces of a forgotten bruise on her wrist. "I did that. I'm sorry."

"I'm not." His remorseful apology stoked her need.

He kissed the purple spot on her skin. "I can stop now, but soon it'll be too late. This is your last chance."

How strange he couldn't tell. "Callaway, don't you understand? I never had a chance. Not from the first time I saw you. I've been fighting this as much as you, but it's already way too late."

His mouth found hers, claimed it, first in a hard, wild kiss that snatched away her breath and then, determined to subjugate his needs to her pleasure, by dancing his tongue in an erotic minuet on each tooth.

Somehow her dress disappeared. Her slip and bra soon followed. When his hand reached her panties and slipped inside, she shivered. He stroked her with one hand and stripped them down with the other.

How had she resisted his appeal for so long? Why had she denied this celebration of life for all these years?

Because she'd been waiting for Callaway's smile, his touch.

Her turn. She pulled at his shirt before tackling his zipper. Tearing off his shorts and boxers, she pulled him to her. Their nude bodies entangled before he pulled back, with a shuddering breath and an impassioned obscenity.

Desire left her dazed. "What's wrong?"

He chuckled, a half-hearted chuckle that turned into a peal of full-blown laughter as he rolled off her onto his back. "I knew damned well I'd never get you in bed, Amanda Jane. I was so sure you'd never, I'd never, we'd never . . . I didn't bring a single damned thing with me."

She understood the problem right away. "Why, Callaway, this is so unlike you. You're always so organized." She tried, but couldn't control her curving mouth.

"There are other ways . . ." He put his hand between her naked thighs and cupped her persuasively. "We can use them and then afterward . . . What are you doing?"

She shrugged into his discarded Hawaiian shirt. "Hold the thought. I'm not as high-minded as you."

After Houston, she had dumped the evening bag into her purse but never sorted out the contents. Tonight her actions made perfect sense: she'd intended all along to use the condoms.

What she'd told Callaway was true. She'd been lost from the moment she saw him.

He was sitting on the edge of the bed when she returned. "Didn't I tell you to stay put?" Discarding his shirt, she shook her plunder in his face. "Why can't you do as you're told?"

He realized what she held. "Oh, wow!"

"I've never heard of that brand. Here." She handed one to him, pushed him back, and fell down on him. "They may not be *Wow*'s, but they'll work."

He held her off. Passion had ebbed, leaving him chary. "This isn't a repeat performance of Houston, is it?"

Her passion had soared. She ran her hand down his chest. "You don't trust me."

Desire warred with cynicism. "I . . . No."

"I don't blame you." She found his navel, circled it with her thumb as she tried to ignore the clamor between her legs. "You want to trust me, though, don't you?" She licked his nipple.

His swallow was audible. "I don't know."

"Let's try that again." Her fingers trailed down to the base of his erection, tickled his scrotum. "You do want to trust me, don't you, Callaway?"

Beads of perspiration had collected on his upper lip. He opened his mouth, but only ragged breathing emerged.

Her hand caught and held him tightly. "Don't you?"

He groaned. "Yes. God help me, yes. I want to trust you."

"Hasn't anyone ever told you that talking during sex is a turnoff?" She lightly bit his nipple.

His chest lurched. "Put it on and I'll shut up."

An open packet plopped in front of her.

She looked at it.

A glint in his eyes dared her. "Afraid?"

"Not of you." She took a tighter hold to prove it, heard his sharp intake of breath, and saw his laughter flee. She stroked him. Slowly. Deliberately. "Never of you."

"Don't. Wait, before we're both sorry." His struggle for control was truly heroic. "Please."

She slid up, wiped the sweat off his face with her breasts. "Don't you want to feel good?"

"Yes. Christ, yes." He caught her hair, held her motionless. "But not without you."

All thoughts evaporated, leaving her terrible need in total command. "You make it awfully easy to love you, Callaway. Hurry."

She slid her face down his chest and laid her cheek on his torso to watch as he rolled on the sheath, smiling a little when his hand came back to caress her, and as he rolled atop her, smiling more at the knowledge he would soon be inside her, and then gasping when in fact he was inside her.

The friction, the heat, her need expanded. The ravenous part of her met his ravishment, until her exploding body recorded his answering tremors as he filled and fulfilled every part of her need.

Delirium gave way to an explosion and then a kind of exalted happiness.

They lay spent for long moments, the quiet after consummation all-encompassing.

"I can't move," he murmured next to her ear.

"Don't." She held him to her, and kneaded his relaxed bottom. "Stay right here on top of me."

"Amanda." His hands tangled in her hair. He sounded uncertain of himself. "You said you . . . you mentioned love."

"So I did." How contented she was.

She told him in extravagant terms how wonderful he'd made her feel, how skillfully he'd delayed his satisfaction, how precisely he'd gauged the moment, winding down with, "I've never known anything so perfect in my life. You were flawless, exemplary, magnificent."

"I'm glad." He nuzzled her neck. "That's pretty scary, you saying that. You know. About your . . . about love and all."

"I know." Poor Callaway. She did know. Three times burned, of course he was scared. Why should this time be different? "It doesn't matter. It's something to say during sex. And what I feel for you is my problem. Not yours."

He lay unmoving, his heartbeat steadying and his breath heating her neck. The fan above made lazy circles that ruffled his hair. The open sliding doors let in the sound of the surf. She was content to support his weight and embrace him while he rested.

He mumbled, "It does matter. You don't know me."

"I told you. It's my problem, not yours." She ran her thumbs beneath his hipbones, prying him up, finding and tweaking his nipples. "You feel so good. All nice and smooth and hard and . . . Um, what's happening down there? Maybe we'd better take this off and find a new one."

Then his hands began to roam, catching her shoulders, tightening around her waist, shaping her hips. His mouth began to roam, too, finding a pulse here, a vein there, sucking at her fingers, her breasts, and her navel. She lay enjoying his explorations, the heat building up again. When he reached their jointure, he used short circular strokes to rekindle her desire.

"Stop," she managed to gasp before he sent her soaring. "Wait."

She disengaged him, turned him so that he lay on his back, eyes grave and unblinking and fastened to her face. She bent over his tensed stomach and gave him a tweak. Then she straddled him and stared into his chocolate eyes.

"I think I do love you," she whispered as she took him. "In fact, right at this moment, I know I do, Callaway McIntyre. Otherwise, I'd never be here. You can't change a thing about how I feel and neither can I, so let's not worry about hurting each other or you not loving me back."

Damaged, she thought as his face shadowed. He looks like I've damaged him.

She wanted to retract her words.

When he touched his hand to her cheek and opened his mouth, she pressed his lips with her fingertips. "Let's take this night and forget tomorrow. Forget everything but this."

"Amanda."

"Please."

By then the rhythm had quickened, the thrumming in her ears crescendoed until only their bodies mattered, and when she saw his contorted face, the joy building up within her abruptly burst out to join his.

*I do love you, Cal, whether you want it or not.*

Satisfaction overcame melancholy.

\* \* \* \*

THE DARKNESS OUTSIDE the latticework shutters gave way to a pearly luminescence preceding dawn.

Amanda had dreaded morning. Callaway would be crushed when he discovered her gone. He'd understand and forgive her though, once she brought Noelle back.

Of course he would.

In the yellow glow of sunrise, she watched him sleeping. They had made love a third time during the night, and then a fourth, each interlude as miraculous as the first.

He hadn't been the lover she had imagined. She'd assumed he would be as impulsive as the little boy who sometimes peeked out, but he had surprised her. He had been patient and accommodating and tender. Everything a woman could hope for.

Sleep cleansed his face of cynicism, giving it innocence. She wanted to reach out and caress it, awaken the other side of him, the man revealed during the night.

Seven thirty. Time to get up.

Despite her caution, he stirred. "Don't go," he murmured, putting out a hand to touch her hip.

Sunbeams forked through the latticed shutters and landed on the disheveled shock of hair falling across his broad forehead. Coppery threads caught the rays and frolicked. Thick lashes opened on eyes dark with sleep.

"Stay with me."

She wanted to. She could snuggle down beneath the sheets and put her head against his shoulder and never get out of bed again. Instead, she combed back his hair with her fingers. "I'm starved. After I shower, I'm going to breakfast."

"It's too early for breakfast."

She kissed his nose. "Then go back to sleep."

He turned, squinted at the clock radio. "No, I'll go, too."

On the edge of the bed, she leaned over, brushed a hand over his morning beard, and pecked his mouth. "I have to shower and dry my hair first. Sleep another hour."

"Ummm." He touched her lip. "I want to kiss you, really kiss you, but your mouth looks swollen."

"I wonder why."

"From me." His thumb traced her lip's bow. "I'm sorry."

"I'm not."

Her reassurance contented him. He closed his eyes. "Come love me when you've showered?"

She shook her head, elated because he still wanted her. "I've got to have food."

Eyelids slitted to reveal a drowsy gleam. "All right. Call me five minutes before you go down. I'll come, too."

She kissed him, slid off the bed. He was already closing his eyes.

Too easy. He didn't deserve her doing this to him again. But she had no option. Not if she wanted to calm Noelle so he could recover his things.

By now, she knew the book could somehow hurt Claire and that Callaway was as anxious to protect his sister as she was to protect Noelle. He'd never care for Amanda as much as he did Claire, but she'd be happy with half the affection.

If not, well, it didn't make any difference.

# CHAPTER EIGHTEEN

WITH A START, Cal woke from a nightmare where a laughing Amanda had pushed him into a fountain before transforming into someone who looked a lot like his old girlfriend.

He sat bolt upright in bed. Cold sweat bathed his forehead and upper lip.

Christ, what was that all about?

An obvious comparison between Amanda and Serena. Was it also a warning that his involvement with Amanda would end the same way? Was his subconscious advising him that one night of passion means shit-all between a man and a woman?

He knew that. He couldn't trust Amanda, not really, not where her sister was concerned. But could he fault her for that? Hell, no. Loyalty to Noelle meant Amanda would be as loyal to anyone she cared about.

He couldn't believe after the past night that she didn't care about him.

She'd told him she loved him. He hadn't asked. She had volunteered, told him outright she didn't expect anything from him.

And he had wisely, for the only instance of his life in the same situation, kept quiet.

Before, uncertain of what he might find, he hadn't dug too deeply into a woman's mind. Or his own. He'd simply mouthed the usual words when appropriate.

With Amanda, he wanted to peel away the layers of brisk businesswoman and bewitching siren and discover what lay underneath. He wanted to reach down inside and pull out the best of himself and hand it to her on a silver platter.

Fool.

He had always been carried away in the throes of passion. "I love you," he had told his wives, apprehensive without knowing why. "Sure I love you," he'd answered Serena and the others who had coaxed the words out of him. How many times had he said them?

It was so simple to promise love, so hard to keep the promise when a woman revealed her vacuity, when she deceived and betrayed.

This time, with Amanda, he had learned caution. No matter how much he was tempted, memories of the past kept the usual words spoken so easily in bed, unsaid.

But he had wanted to say them. Christ, how he'd wanted to say them.

He cocked an ear toward his bathroom but heard no running water. She must be in her room dressing. He yawned. It had to be past time to get up, but after last night, he had an excuse for sleeping in.

Last night.

Amanda had given herself so freely that his throat clogged up thinking about it. He'd never known anyone like her, so restrained and so eager, so composed and so ardent. He'd wanted her and gone after her, but he'd never expected her to give in. Even last night, until he was inside her, he'd thought she would renege. The one thing he had never envisioned was the explosive power of their joined bodies, the flood of denied longing she'd unleashed.

In her arms, he'd felt good about himself. She'd enjoyed his body, his lovemaking, and had let him know it, so that all he wanted to do was satisfy her, pleasure her.

Now he found himself thinking weird things. Really weird things.

He wasn't making plans to take her to Greece or show her off to his friends. He wasn't even figuring out how not to get too involved. Oh, no, nothing so simple as those usual kinds of post-coital pursuits had crossed his mind.

Instead, he was devising outlandish ways to please her, such as incorporating her dresses into the hotel shops to give her a national and international outlet.

Which wouldn't be hard to do. His marketing skills were rusty from lack of use but still intact. They could allot her cheap space and give discount vouchers to guests. Or use her clothing in retail stores already established in the chain. It would be a simple matter of contacting tenants and working out terms.

Shit. He swung his feet off the bed to stop his runaway imagination.

He was crazy.

Simply because she'd looked at that frigging tablecloth and he'd seen how much she'd wanted it and he'd wanted her to have it but she'd refused to take it from him.

She couldn't refuse his gift after last night.

He grinned, feeling pretty cocky. On the whole, he'd acquitted himself pretty well, but Amanda had been wonderful.

Oh, hell. His stomach turned to water thinking about Amanda.

Out of habit he reached for his cigarettes but stopped. The smoke bothered Amanda, and it was an unhealthy habit. Maybe he should quit like Claire and Johanna kept nagging him to. A glance at the clock showed him the time was past eight thirty.

Eight thirty. He hopped up. She should be dressed. He went through the living area and into her silent room.

The shower was off. The bathroom door was open. The air around him held that vacant hush, the peculiar desolation that signaled the absence of its occupant.

He stopped, uncertain.

She wouldn't have left without him.

"Amanda?"

There was no answer.

Back in the living area, he found a note. *Callaway, You were asleep so I'm going on. Back later. I love you.*

He read the words once and again.

She went to eat. *She'll be back. She won't chance missing Noelle.* After last night, she wouldn't run away from him.

He showered. By the time he dressed, she still hadn't returned. She should have been back by then.

He hurried downstairs, looking first in the expensive restaurant before trying the other hotel eateries. No luck. Maybe she was at the pastry buffet. But when he crossed the lobby to the potted palms where uniformed employees set it up each morning, she wasn't among the customers milling around there either. As they opened one by one, he checked the gift shop, the jewelry shop, the boutique, the Mexican market shop, and all the rest.

Amanda was nowhere to be found.

When he asked at the desk, no one had left a message for him nor did anyone remember seeing Amanda. He turned away indecisively, to bump into a bellman who had heard him questioning the concierge, the same bellman who had helped recover items from Amanda's spilled purse the day before.

The man hesitantly asked, "You look for the lady with the beautiful smile, Señor McIntyre?"

"Yes. Have you seen her?"

"She go to Chichen Itza this morning." The bellman pointed to the area where daily tour buses loaded. "She wear a hat and red pants, and I do not know her except for her purse and the smile. I see them and I think, she is the lady with Señor McIntyre. The lady who drop her bag."

Icy hands clutched his chest. He was suffocating.

*She's gone to Noelle.*

Amanda had again deceived him. She had come to bed with him deliberately the past night so he wouldn't suspect she was meeting Noelle this morning. She had let him love her, had made love to him, intending all the while to run off with her sister.

She'd hoodwinked him as cleverly as she had the first time they'd met. And fool that he was, he'd let her.

His ears roared. A red haze eclipsed the sunlight. He could not remember suffering such a rage in his entire life. It filled him, debilitated him before leaving him almost insensible.

She'd never meant any of it, not the words of love, not the sweet caresses. Had she even enjoyed it?

He mastered the rage, pulled out his money clip and gave the bellman a handful of bills without looking to see what they were.

Then he went to the tour agency for the bus schedules. In fifteen minutes, he had made arrangements to get to Chichen Itza by air. Another twenty minutes found him climbing into a chartered plane which had to be at least half a century old and would probably crash in the jungle and kill him.

Not that he cared.

Still, grim satisfaction accompanied him. Anger ceased to be a cutting hurtful thing and became numbing cold.

When Amanda Jane and her sister arrived at the ruins, they were going to be in for an unpleasant surprise.

\* \* \* \*

DISGUISED BY A baseball hat and dark glasses, Cal sat on crumbling blocks at Chichen Itza to wait for the tour bus. Since it was a long trip by road from Cancun, he had time to kill, but he couldn't concentrate on his newspaper and instead, lashed his outrage into a controlled fury.

He would never forgive Amanda Jane for making a fool of him again.

Never.

He would never forgive himself for allowing another woman to make a fool of him.

Things could have been different.

He'd been prepared to overlook Amanda's enticing and drugging him. He'd been prepared to overlook her part in the theft of his diamond studs and the loss of the journal.

Criminal offenses all, and because he believed she was another person, a good person pulled into the mess by her sister, he'd been prepared to forgive and forget everything.

All because he'd gazed into those clear eyes and imagined something in them besides treachery.

Then this.

There was no reason to be surprised, knowing women as he did.

But he'd actually believed Amanda was different. He had come frigging near to trusting her, damn it.

What made him the sickest, what made him despise himself, was that he still wanted her so much that his stomach knotted into a ball thinking about her.

When she approached his post, keeping a little apart from the group getting off her bus, he wanted to go over and seize her, shake her and kiss her until she melted into him as she had the past night.

Instead, he hid behind his newspaper and watched her wander toward the big pyramid towering over them, its cold barbaric dignity a reminder of ancient human sacrifices offered up to the gods.

He wouldn't mind adding another to its list of offerings. Maybe that would ease the ache in his heart.

Neat in red capris and sleeveless knit top that outlined her breasts, Amanda strolled unaware of his observation. Though frequently stopping and scanning her surroundings, she didn't spare more than a passing glance in Cal's direction.

As she moved farther into the park, he got up to follow. He kept out of sight in the shade of the wild growth that, despite the park service's heroic efforts to keep eradicated, sprang up in sporadic clumps between the time-battered buildings.

The midday heat was stifling. He'd hate to be here in summer.

When Amanda paused to wipe the sweat off her forehead, he paused and lit a cigarette. She cocked her head to one side in perplexity.

Damn her. He watched the long neck twist as she searched the tourists. He'd kissed that neck last night, put his lips right on the pulse at her collarbone and felt her laugh gurgle up, her enchanting laugh that turned her eyes smoky and languorous.

In the end, he spotted Noelle before Amanda did. The slight form in puffy blouse and shorts came out from behind one of the nearby weatherworn buildings and, face protected by a big hat and sunglasses, came up to Amanda's back and touched her arm.

Amanda jumped, turned, grabbed her sister and hugged her.

Swallowing bile, Cal hurled his cigarette down.

Time for his big entrance.

"What were you planning to do?" Amanda's question was loud enough for interested bystanders to hear.

Cal loitered behind a palm tree and eavesdropped.

Noelle's voice, thin and querulous, echoed the nervous mouth and twitchy body. "Manda, I'll go home and never do anything like this again. I swear I'll be good."

"Listen to me and listen good. You and I are in a lot of trouble."

"I know, but I didn't mean us to be. And I don't know how to fix it."

Amanda, shoulders set with a resolve Cal recognized from the past few days, said with a firmness he didn't expect, "I do. Callaway McIntyre's agreed to buy plane tickets home for you and not press charges against us. But only if you tell him everything."

"Do you believe him? You don't know what he's like. He'll put me in jail." Noelle sniffled.

The crisp Amanda Cal remembered said, "Don't be ridiculous. He'll keep his word, but we have to help him."

Hah. All Noelle had to do was cry and Amanda would cave.

He started toward them.

"Noelle, you and I are in bad trouble. Do you understand that? If Cal had gone to the police, we could be in jail right now. But I've told him everything. He knows you lied." Amanda stopped for a deep breath. "Sonny Kirkman talked you into it, didn't he? So he could steal Cal's diamonds?"

At that moment, she saw Cal. Her mouth stayed open.

He would have laughed, except that Noelle, following her sister's gaze, yipped and took off running.

*Hell and damnation, she's not about to get away!*

He dashed after her, used a flying tackle to bring her down.

She shrieked as her hat and sunglasses flew off.

Several tourists gasped.

He smiled at them as he got up. "Iguana got after her." He yanked the protesting Noelle to her feet and, gripping her arm firmly, brushed off her shorts. "I told her you can't run from them, but women. They never listen." Turning to Noelle in a solicitous manner, he said audibly, "Stop screaming, sugar. The little fellow's long gone." He added, *sotto voce,* "You and your damned sister'll both be in jail if you don't shut up." An added pinch subdued her.

The group of senior citizens, excusably shocked by the exhibition, scurried to give Cal and Noelle plenty of room. One woman handed Noelle the dropped sunglasses and hat before backing off.

Several were upset. Cal reassured them by putting on a solemn face. "You can't run from iguanas, folks. If one starts toward you, hold your ground. If you're lucky, he'll respect you enough to back off."

"You mean they're dangerous?" a short, anxious man asked. "They're such cute little things."

"The tour people said not." His companion, made of sterner stuff, had recovered from her shock. Iron gray curls shook in indignation at being misled. "Wait till I see that agent. I bet I'll give him what for, failing to warn . . ."

"Letting us out among dangerous animals . . ."

"I told you they were looking at me funny."

"Is she all right?"

Callaway, assuring would-be assisters that Noelle was fine, led her, face ashen, out of the ring of disturbed onlookers and toward where Amanda stood.

Amanda hadn't moved.

When he brought Noelle back, he didn't hide his contempt. "I have a plane waiting. We'll discuss this in air conditioning."

Noelle whimpered and tried to pull away, but a jerk on her arm changed her mind. A docile Amanda followed. He looked back once, to find her with back ramrod straight and cheeks blazing.

He wished he was holding her instead of Noelle. Noelle might have instigated the theft of his studs, but Amanda had betrayed him personally.

Maybe he'd invited it, dammit, wanting to believe her, wanting to make love to her, but she had been the betrayer. He had willfully disregarded his record for misjudging women and see what had happened.

How wise he'd been to put aside the temptation to say, "I love you," and hold his tongue. Too bad his wisdom didn't help the hollowness in his chest.

He wanted to yank Noelle's damned arm out of its socket but didn't. No need to take his anger at Amanda out on her sister.

He'd never felt so foolish or been so furious.

\* \* \* \*

AMANDA HAD NEVER been so mystified. She'd known Callaway would be annoyed, but such rage?

Why? Because she'd gone to Noelle without him? When he calmed down, he'd see that her way had been better, otherwise they might have lost Noelle altogether.

Callaway, though he slammed the door of the ancient Jeep transporting them to the air strip, didn't touch her. At the air strip, he thrust her into the plane after Noelle with none of the gentle solicitude of the past night. His bulk crowded her against the tiny seat.

"We'll be a little tight, but you don't mind being squeezed against a man, do you, Amanda?" he asked with the mocking smile she hated. "Any man," he added with a certain bitterness. "We're all the same to you, aren't we? Expendable so long as we suit your purposes."

How had the tender lover of the previous night morphed into this hard stranger?

"Callaway," she started.

No, this was no place to discuss this. Not with Noelle sitting here listening to every word.

The plane was noisy and small. Noelle snuffled into tissues, Cal sat in icy silence, and Amanda's head began to hurt.

When they got back to the hotel, Noelle retreated to the bathroom.

Amanda spoke to him, one eye on the bathroom door. "I can tell you're angry."

"How perceptive of you." He was as remote as he'd been in the cottage at Fair Meadows.

"Is it because I went to Noelle without you? If I'd told you, you'd have insisted on going, too. And if we had both shown up, Noelle would never have come out. She would have run away again."

"You think so?" The rigid lines of his body said that he didn't give a fig for her opinion.

"You know she would have."

"You don't think if you'd bothered to confide in me, I could have worked around her seeing me?"

Before she could answer his scathing rejoinder, he went on, "Oh, hell, why should it matter? You know by now I'm a pushover when it comes to women. I won't make the same mistake again, though. Not with you. Johanna always says that I don't think straight when it comes to my prick. I guess you proved she's right."

"Callaway." Too late Amanda understood. He believed the past night had been another subterfuge on her part, a trick to make it easier for her to elude him. She touched his arm.

He jerked away.

"I wanted to be with you last night," she said, in a low tone that wouldn't carry to Noelle in the bathroom. "I chose to be with you. Whatever you think, I didn't go to bed with you to make meeting Noelle easier. I wanted you."

He snorted. Then Noelle crept out, subdued and frightened, to put an end to their brief conversation.

Callaway, still formidable, put Noelle on the sofa and sat down beside her. "You are a very fortunate woman, Noelle." His flat voice in no way hid the threat. "I'm not going to slap you around physically the way I did your sister. And I'm not going to have you charged with accessory to theft. Not yet. I'm going to listen to you. And if you tell me what I want to know, we might be able to forget Houston altogether. Understand?"

Noelle shrank back and wrapped her arms about herself. Fresh tears welled.

Amanda bit her lip. No wonder Noelle was terrified. Callaway would give anyone pause.

Five days earlier, this stony stranger would have terrified her, but she knew him now, as well as the considerate heart under the intimidating mask. She wanted to comfort her sister, tell Noelle everything would be all right, but couldn't bring herself to do it. Callaway had a right to question Noelle. Noelle would have to answer.

"It's all right, honey. No one's going to hurt you," she said gently. "Tell us how you came to think of using your ring to get me into Cal's safe."

Noelle trembled. "Sonny thought of it. He promised no one would ever know you were involved, Manda. You don't hate me, do you?"

"Of course not. Go on, tell us what happened."

Cal's lip curled. He would assume she was siding with Noelle.

I'm not, she wanted to cry. Can't you understand I'm trying to help you?

No, he was too busy questioning Noelle. "Did you get the combination for the safe from Sonny?"

Noelle plucked a cushion from the sofa, put it in front of her and held on for dear life. She gave one jerky nod.

"What did he want?"

"Your diamonds. He said everyone would think Amanda had taken them but that they wouldn't be able to find her so she wouldn't get in trouble." Tears filled her eyes. "He promised."

Amanda sat back. *Noelle, Noelle. After all the talks we had, all the discussions of right and wrong . . .*

Callaway kept on. "What did he do with the diamonds?"

Noelle shook her head. "I don't know. Somebody offered him a lot of money for them."

"Who?"

Noelle looked like a cornered deer. "I don't know. Some man who collected old jewelry."

Callaway changed tactics. "How much money are we talking about?"

"A lot, I guess. Sonny never said."

"Sonny had five hundred thousand dollars on him when he was killed," Callaway murmured.

Amanda straightened. "From the sale of your diamonds?"

"Who knows. They were worth millions. If that's all he got, he was gypped."

Nicole looked from one to the other. She kept hugging and releasing the cushion. "I just did what Sonny told me. He didn't think you'd care," she said to Callaway. "You've got so much money he said you'd never miss it."

Callaway clenched his jaw. "How did you come up with the idea of using Amanda?"

"One time I told him how Amanda used to wrap any man she met around her little finger, and he remembered."

*Oh Noelle.*

Amanda wanted to cry. Her sister was proud of her for being a flirt. The type of woman who could get a man killed.

"How did you meet Sonny?" Callaway asked.

"How did I meet him?" Noelle's blue eyes glistened. "Oh. Em knows him. Knew him."

"One of her friends," Amanda explained. "One Edward didn't approve of."

Callaway ignored her. "So you told Sonny about Amanda. And he thought of using her to get to me."

Noelle nodded. "When he started thinking of ways to get the diamonds, he asked if I thought Amanda could seduce you. I was sure she could."

"And you were right," Cal said tonelessly.

Amanda slumped.

Noelle said hesitantly, "It seemed like a good plan. I thought you'd never know who she was, but we'd have the money." She broke off, darting a glance at Amanda. "No one should have been able to connect you, Manda."

Amanda asked, "You didn't think it was wrong?"

"Wrong? When Callaway's so rich? Sonny says he spends more money on his wine every year than what his diamonds were worth."

"I believe the operative word is *said*, not *says*," Callaway said. "And that comment about my wines isn't true."

Tears welled, trickled down Noelle's cheeks. "I keep forgetting. Sonny's dead. What am I going to do? I'm sorry, Manda. I thought it was all right, I really did," she wailed.

Callaway didn't soften. "Do you know who killed him?"

Noelle, weeping, shook her head.

Callaway chewed at his lip.

Amanda almost reached out to stop him.

He quit of his own accord. "Sonny took more than my studs, Noelle. Do you know what he did with the other things?"

Snuffling, Noelle clung to her cushion. "What other things?"

"Think, Noelle," Amanda broke in. "This is important. Did

Sonny say anything to you about taking something else with the diamonds?"

"Like what?"

Callaway leaned over so that his face, ugly and threatening, was bare inches from Noelle's. Amanda had been terrified when he'd stuck his face up to hers that same way.

"If you're lying," he told Noelle in an icy, contained voice, "I'll see you spend the rest of your life rotting in prison. Down here. And a Mexican prison isn't nearly as sanitary as our own vermin-infested penitentiaries."

Noelle squeaked, tried to pull away.

He grabbed her chin, snapping her teeth together in the process of bringing her face back in line with his. "I'm efficient, Noelle. I know the right people to see you get put quietly away."

Amanda couldn't stand to see her sister bullied. "Callaway, please. She doesn't understand what she's done. She'll tell the truth, won't you, Noelle?"

Noelle nodded wordlessly.

Cal chewed his lip but leaned back. "Now," he said, pleasant as before, "back to the studs. They went to Miles de Graffen, is that right?"

"Maybe," Noelle stammered. "I don't know, but Sonny talked to Miles a lot. Does he collect old jewelry?"

"Yes," Cal said. "So they talked about the diamonds?"

"I guess so," Noelle mumbled. "I wasn't that interested. I just know there was a lot of money involved from some collector."

"It wouldn't have meant anything to her if she heard them bargaining, Callaway," Amanda said. "I told you, she doesn't always take in things."

Callaway was patient. "All right, let's try another tack. What happened to the other things Sonny took?"

"What other things?" Noelle threw a wild-eyed look toward Amanda. "What else would he take?"

Callaway stood, hands turning into fists.

"Noelle." Amanda didn't think he'd hit Noelle, but she wasn't going to wait and see. "For heavens' sake. Was there a book?"

"A book?" Noelle looked relieved. "Oh, yeah, there was something about a book. I didn't pay much attention, though. All I had to do was beg you to get my ring back." She burst into fresh tears.

Callaway's fists uncurled.

"Is that all you remember, darling?" Amanda asked quickly, before Callaway could start in again. "Did he say anything else about the book? Anything at all."

Noelle's forehead creased, she thought so hard. "Just that he found some kind of old book. He thought he could get some money for it maybe. I can't remember exactly what he said." She paused, her face brightening. "But that's why he stayed on after the wedding. He was supposed to leave right afterward, but he couldn't talk to anybody about it until Sunday and then he had to wait for them to get their money together."

Callaway nodded and sat back down. His voice was quiet as if calming a child. "Very good, Noelle." He gave her time to settle down. "Who did Sonny talk to about the book?"

Noelle began to twist the cushion again. "I don't know." She looked back and forth from Amanda to Callaway like an anxious rabbit. "Do you think whoever it was killed him?"

"Maybe." Callaway left the subject.

Amanda eyed him. *Doesn't he want to know who it was?*

But he was going on, "You've done very well, Noelle. I'm pleased with how you're cooperating. Where's the book now?"

Amanda held her breath.

"I dunno, I never even saw it. Honest."

"Noelle, this is very important," Amanda put in.

"But I don't know." Noelle's red rimmed eyes shifted to her sister. "I guess it's somewhere in Sonny's things."

They went to Noelle's hotel where Cal ransacked her room from top to bottom.

He didn't find the journal.

# CHAPTER NINETEEN

CAL QUESTIONED NOELLE until she was faint from exhaustion and he was ready to drop. Desperate to find his mother's journal, he used threats and persuasion but nothing worked.

Amanda finally beseeched him, "Can't you see she doesn't know any more?"

He could. And he could see Amanda was drooping as much as her sister. He stubbed his final cigarette into an overflowing ash tray and walked over to the window.

Afternoon had changed into evening. Looking out at the lights lining the path to the sea, he could ignore Amanda's glazed eyes. Her head must be hurting as bad as it had in Las Vegas.

Too bad. She'd have to get over her headache as best she could. The day had been exhausting for all of them. For him, it had been educational as well. He'd learned how gullible he was, despite years of bitter experience. He'd also learned redheads held no monopoly on deceit.

"I'm tired," Noelle whined. "My feet hurt from all that walking and I haven't had a thing to eat since this morning."

He turned toward her.

Noelle shrank.

Amanda intervened. "Will you eat with us?"

"I prefer my own company. If you want to run away, feel free. If you want air fare home, the airport bus leaves at nine tomorrow morning. Be there."

"Callaway." Amanda started toward him.

He turned on his heel, his glance stopping her in mid-step.

He wanted never to see her again, never think of her again. He should have left her alone from the beginning.

\* \* \* \*

AMANDA RUED TAKING Callaway to bed before she met Noelle. If she'd waited, he wouldn't be so disillusioned. But she hadn't thought of anything except her own desires. Every other consideration had fled.

She ordered from room service for her and Noelle. The grilled salmon looked appetizing, but Noelle sniffled throughout the meal and barely ate a bite. "I'm sorry, Manda," she kept saying. "It sounded like a good idea."

Amanda picked at her fish, too. She couldn't soothe Noelle but she couldn't fuss, either.

After they ate, she told Noelle she was going to bed.

"Can I take a sleeping pill?" Noelle asked anxiously. "I've had to take them so I don't toss and turn all night, but if you think I shouldn't, I won't."

Whenever Noelle made a bad decision, she hesitated to make others that might be wrong, too. Her confidence had to be restored.

Not that Amanda cared. But Noelle was her sister and old habits die hard.

"Go ahead. A sleeping pill's a good idea."

When Noelle went to bed, Amanda went looking for Callaway. She needed to talk to him.

He wasn't in the common area. After hesitating, she knocked on his bedroom door but got no response. An ear against the panel heard no sounds so she pushed on the door.

It was unlocked, but he wasn't there.

Thinking, she stood looking at the neat bed and used towel tossed on the floor. She had to convince him she didn't make love to him because of Noelle.

*Okay, I know what I can try.*

Wheeling, she went to her bathroom, showered, and donned the pajamas bought in Las Vegas. Of fine but unadorned cotton, they were plain classics.

Turning in front of the mirror, she checked several angles before shaking her head. "Nope. These won't do the job."

In the bedroom, Noelle's steady breathing confirmed the effect of the sedative. Good. This was no time for Noelle to interfere.

Re-dressing, Amanda went downstairs to the sundries shop. As she passed through the lobby and hallways, she looked for Callaway but didn't see him.

Probably at a bar, drinking away his cares. Stupid man.

Maybe he wouldn't be picking up any slutty women.

Back upstairs, she pulled out her travel case and took out the French-made silk slip she'd worn under her dress the previous night. It laced up under her breasts to push them up and show them off.

Rummaging in her purse, she brought out the perfume used in Houston, a light expensive scent bought from a perfumery near Lenox Square and hoarded for special occasions. She lavished the citrus fragrance behind her ears and knees, on her neck and the insides of her wrists, elbows, and thighs.

Individual ringlets were coaxed out of a topknot to fall in soft clusters round her face. After foundation and blush, she used a liberal hand to apply newly purchased eyeshadow, eyeliner, and mascara. A startling magenta shaded her lips. Hanging prism earrings, also chosen downstairs, caught the light and broke it into rainbows.

She turned back and forth in front of her reflection.

There. Provocative, cheap, and available. Everything that turned Callaway McIntyre on except red hair.

This was as good as she could manage on such short notice and without the proper equipment.

Maybe it would be enough.

\* \* \* \*

THERE WASN'T ENOUGH beer to make him stop thinking of her.

"*Jésus.*" Cal tapped his empty glass. "*Un otra cerveza, por favor.*"

In the dim main floor bar, he lingered on a stool, chain-smoking while the doleful bartender grumbled between customers.

Jésus, according to Jésus himself, supported a wife and thirteen of his nine children and ten grandchildren. One son was in prison. Jésus suspected two of his grandsons were headed there. Three of his girls had married and gone up north across the border, but they were ungrateful females, seldom sending home as much money as dutiful daughters should.

Cal nodded or shook his head. Jésus had obviously never heard that bartenders were supposed to listen and commiserate.

Why did people always have to talk to him? He hid his disinterest in Jésus's burgeoning monologue by a polite "*Lastima*" put in now and again as his mind mulled his own problems.

Noelle's scanty information might have confirmed that Miles de Graffen had bought his diamonds from Sonny, but if he believed her, the whereabouts of his mother's journal remained a mystery.

Could Miles have killed Sonny and taken the book?

Cal didn't think Miles was a killer. Miles was avaricious about his jewels, but he wasn't a murderer.

What if he was threatened with exposure?

No, Miles couldn't kill anyone.

But if not Miles, who? If something didn't turn up soon to lead to the journal, Cal would have to go the authorities, and that would make Claire and Tip prime murder suspects.

And involve Amanda.

Overshadowing all his worries was Amanda.

Not that Cal would have admitted to Jésus or anybody else what a fool he'd been over another frigging woman. Why couldn't he learn? He downed his beer and lit another cigarette as Jésus droned on. One more beer, he decided, signaling Jésus. One more to delay going up.

He'd stay away from the suite until they were asleep, the two she-devils who'd brought him to this sorry pass. He could imagine them huddled in the bed together. Maybe one of them was a restless sleeper who would kick the other.

It wouldn't be Amanda.

She slept the way she walked, softly, gently, moving so lightly he'd never have felt her get up this morning if he hadn't already been half-awake, trying to make some sense out of what had happened between them the night before.

They'd been so perfect together. He'd begun to believe he could change, turn his life around.

*Fool.* He swore under his breath.

Jésus set a foaming glass before him. "Your beer, Señor Cal."

Cal looked at it, puffed on his cigarette, looked at his watch, listened to Jésus, looked at the clock, and waited for the moment when he could down the beer and go up to bed and crash.

When the time finally came, the alcohol had numbed him and he was glad. He wanted to be numb. He didn't want to feel anything ever again. Though this misery was no more than he deserved. He'd yielded to his old instincts and failed Claire.

So what else was new?

The elevator ascent was interminable. The hallway leading to the suite was deserted, and once inside he crossed the living area quietly so as not to wake the two women. No sound of television or any other noise filtered through their closed doors.

Good. He didn't want to see or hear Amanda. Once the plane trip tomorrow was over, he'd never have to see her again. That ought to make him happy, so why was his heart aching?

The bed was turned back, the overhead fan was on, and a single floor lamp burned in the corner by the sliding doors.

No mints on the pillow as per McIntyre protocol. He made a mental note to talk to the manager about housekeeping quality. The tourists on the bus had mentioned not enough towels, too. And one had said something about the mini-bar being inadequately stocked.

Hell, what did it matter?

In the bathroom, there was no need to shower because he had washed away the grunge from the Chichen Itza trip before dinner.

Too bad he couldn't wash away Amanda's memory as easily.

He started undressing until, barefoot and shirtless he sat on the side of his bed, trying to figure out who might have the journal, trying to keep from remembering the past night, trying to think of Claire, trying not to think of Amanda.

He kept imagining the odor of oranges drifting through the air, reminding him of the delicate perfume she had worn the first night they met.

When he tried to make plans about confronting Miles, that imaginary scent kept dredging up unwelcome images of her lovemaking.

Damn, why couldn't he forget it, forget her?

He flung his socks and shirt across the room. The hurt roiled inside anyway, each memory a fresh jab at his bowels. Amanda's hand sliding on his chest, her breath at his ear, her low laughter as her body smoothed against his, fitted to his in effortless conjunction. Her sighs afterward.

He cursed and lay back on the coverlet to watch the blades of the ceiling fan revolve and let the pain take him until it was nearly unbearable.

When he got up to close the sliding door shutters, orange fragrance drenched his nostrils. A spot on the balcony caught his eye, an oval bleached ivory by the moonlight, floating above the top of the hot tub.

The oval was so still that at first he thought it a ball or balloon. He stepped outside, realized the oval was a face and that the face belonged to Amanda.

She lay motionless in the water, arms and shoulders in shadow.

He couldn't think of anything to say.

The first rush of joy sped away under outrage that she had used him and he had let her. Had she been there all this time, watching him when he'd sat on the edge of the bed, when he had thrown his shirt and socks across the room, when he had cursed aloud in the quick sharp ache of fresh pain?

She broke the silence. "You said I could use the tub."

*Don't do this. Stop being a fool.*

He moved without volition, near enough to see thin white shoulder straps and outlined eyes and breasts thrust up in frank invitation.

This was the last thing he needed. "I put conditions on your using it. I told you the rule. No clothes allowed." He couldn't stand here, imagining her nipples patterning the wet cloth, pretending he had something to say to her.

"I can take it off, but I've always thought a covered body was a lot more titillating than a nude one."

His foot took another step toward the tub, entirely against his will. His body shuffled, ponderous and heavy, as though the flesh didn't belong to him, and he were a shell encased in steel.

She was a magnet.

His throat clogged. "Do you want to be titillating?"

"Yes," she said, with bewitching simplicity.

"Why?" With no recollection of getting there, he stood at the edge of the hot tub, where the moonlight played with her cleavage and turned the tinted mouth incredibly wanton. "Is there something else you want from me?"

"Yes."

The need curled within him though he struggled to bring back the bitterness, to make the anger overwhelm the escalating desire to join her in the water and lay his head against her breasts, to let her caresses chase away his wretchedness.

"What is it you want? Tell me and I'll do my damnedest to give it to you so I won't get my guts strung out again. I'm tired of being a football in your mind games."

His cruelty didn't deter her. "I want you to make love to me, Callaway. The way you did last night."

He had to clear his thickening throat. "It takes a certain mood. I'm out of it."

"That's too bad." Her mouth, its provocative lines highlighted by the deep lipstick, drooped in reproach. So did the dark fringe of eyelashes. "No matter what you think, last night was wonderful. And the only way I know to convince you how wonderful it was is to make love to you again tonight."

What audacity. After what she'd done, she expected a roll in the hay would make everything right. His jeans were already catching and holding his erection. His heart was already pounding. His damned carnality was yanking at his gullibility, whispering that he should let her convince him.

"I love you, Callaway. I want you." The tempting mouth puckered, curved in the beginnings of smile. "Oh, don't worry. I'm not asking anything from you. A night of sex. No strings attached. What do you have to lose?"

He bit.

*You damned sucker. You stupid damned sucker.* He despised himself for letting his weakness overwhelm his reason, despised himself even as he said, "I thought last night was for Noelle."

She shook her head. "Last night was for me. No matter what you believe. If I'd realized you would think I used you to save Noelle, I'd have waited to make love to you. Noelle means a lot to me, but not that much."

She was strong and confident and tempting.

So tempting.

He was tired. Looking at her drained his resentment, his willpower. He had no defenses left.

"Please, Callaway. Let me make love to you again."

When she settled herself lower in its embrace, the water lapped over her, kissing her shoulders, her breasts, the secret places between her thighs. He wanted to be the water, feel himself losing all form against her skin, feel himself wrapping around her body, filling her, possessing her.

The weight of such want was stifling.

He fastened on what she had said, in one last desperate attempt to save himself from that cursed driving elemental force barely contained by his jeans. "Was it love you made last night, Scarlet? I thought it was something else." His drawl came out hoarse with longing rather than irony.

"It may have been something else for you." Her arms were bright with glistening droplets. "But it was love for me. If you can't see that, Callaway McIntyre, you're a lot dumber than I think. Please. Come and love me."

*God, I'm lost.*

There wasn't a man alive who could withstand that sultry voice, that humble plea. Why didn't he give in and be done with it? What else could she do to him?

Nothing.

She'd done it all. She'd led him on and rejected him, destroyed his ego and Claire's happiness. Because of her, people he loved were suspects in a murder while an old friend was now an enemy. She'd taken him to the heights, made him believe he was capable of changing and becoming a better person. Then she'd shattered his fantasies and left him the shards.

There was nothing else she could do.

The weight lifted off his shoulders, leaving him buoyant and free to give in.

He sat on the edge of the tub and swung his legs over. The water splashed. A wave rolled over the top and out of the tub.

He fell on her.

He wrapped his arms and legs around her and found her startled mouth and ran his tongue between her lips. He wrapped her hair around his hand and tipped her head back and tasted the water on her neck. He slid his hand down her breasts, sliding it over her stomach and between her legs where he caught and held her.

After a stunned gasp, she burst into laughter. "Callaway."

His name on her lips was sweet, seductive. Loving.

"You're breaking your own rule." She reached out, plucked at the band of his waterlogged jeans.

"I can remedy that." Her laugh had destroyed the tension and anger, the burden he hadn't realized he was carrying.

*One day you may know what the consequences will be, but you send them to the devil and let yourself be damned.*

He'd snorted when someone said that to him. Who was it?

It didn't matter.

Nothing mattered.

He would pay for this moment, but he didn't care. Being with her here, now, was worth everything it would cost him afterward. To see her smile, have her look at him, let her touch him with such tenderness . . . She chased thoughts of consequences away.

Precious minutes flew by as he undressed, while she laughed at him and with him, waiting patiently while he wrestled to divest each sodden leg and his underwear. Then he wrestled with her, rolling the wet chemise up to her waist, pulling the thin straps down to bind her elbows so that she couldn't lift her arms to stop him from licking her shoulders, the curve of her breasts, their divide.

The bodice was laced by a ribbon, soaked and hard to untie. He worked the strand out of each eyelet, taking his time until the ribbon was free and the chemise could be dragged over her head. Holding up her wrists, he kissed the faint bruise on one and then the other. "I wasn't sorry about this today."

"Weren't you?" Her tone forgave him, let him forgive himself. "You are now."

"Yes." The ribbon was long, and he took it, stretched it around her back, bringing it beneath her breasts and crossing it between to tie at her neck. Lifting her hips out of the water, he delved his tongue into her navel, running it down her belly and into the soft mound beneath the wet curls.

The spot was there, heated and moist with water and her.

She let him plunder, her fingers tousling and entangling his hair. "Does a ribbon count for clothes?"

He needed the interruption. Reining his lust, he let her slide back into the water. "I can take it off." He tugged at the ribbon, then pushed up her breasts with his hand and covered her nipples with the thin strand. "But you're right. Clothes are more titillating." His fingertips moved along the ribbon, tickled her nipples protruding through the satin.

"How long do you intend to play around with that?" Her breathing was labored.

His body was wild, but she was his tonight. Before he was through, she'd know it. "I thought we'd go slow. The way you like."

She tried to giggle and rise up.

He kept her down. His hand went through the water, to her stomach, to one hip. Rested there. "Very slow."

"Callaway." Her hand found his, guided it. Her sighs echoed on the water till she caught him, held him, stroked him.

"I don't want to get off without you," she murmured. "Please." Her hand moved languidly. The water became a silken sheath sifting through her fingers.

Too arousing. "If you don't want me to do something dangerous, you'd better stop."

Her head fell back so she could look up at him from beneath mascaraed lashes. "They're by the bed."

He lifted her abruptly.

She squealed. "It's cold."

"Because you're wet. I'll warm you. Directly."

He set her on the edge of the tub and climbed out. He would have carried her inside, but she slipped down to run ahead.

"If we keep doing this, we're going to have to try something else," he said as she circled the bed to meet him at the dresser. "Something easier to get to."

"All right." She stepped up and it was his turn to gasp as, without warning, she caught him. She unfolded her other hand to proffer him the packet. "If we keep doing this."

Trembling fingers barely fitted the condom before she was at him. "Amanda." He picked her up. "Slow down, slow down. You're rushing it."

"I can't wait, I want you now."

She wrapped her arms about his neck and her legs about his hips so he could slip into her as easily as though they'd been made for each other.

No time to reach the bed. His painstaking control fled.

He shoved her onto the dresser, knocking aside vases and books and glasses that tinkled as they broke, and held her there as he thrust against her, over and over until it was too late to hold back the flood. As he poured into her, all thought, all his body dissolved into a mind-bending sweet madness. She arched back and screamed.

Her spasms enveloped his. *Hers!*

Hers.

# CHAPTER TWENTY

AMANDA LEFT HIM before dawn, but not without giving an apologetic warning. "Don't let Noelle know about us. If she finds out, she'll be confused. And she might try to take advantage of you because of it. I've got to help her see she has responsibilities other people can't fulfill for her."

Cal didn't need her warning. He had no illusions about Noelle. Amanda thought her sister was telling them the truth, but he wasn't so sure. Not only was Noelle easily led, but she had no sense of right and wrong.

Amanda might not abandon Noelle, but was Noelle as attached to her sister?

In the Cancun air terminal, Amanda wandered into a shop where she browsed through the souvenirs. Soon she was holding up one tiny T-shirt after another.

Cal, seeing her safely distracted in buying shirts for her nephew, accosted Noelle. "Amanda's car exploded, Noelle. She's lucky she wasn't in it."

"Her car exploded?" Noelle had taken a step away at Cal's approach but stopped at his words. Her surprise seemed genuine. "Why did it explode?"

"I thought you might know."

"Me? How could I? I haven't even seen her until she came down here. She didn't say anything about it to me."

"She probably didn't want to worry you." Cal watched for a sign she was lying. "Someone tried to break into her shop, too. She could have been hurt, maybe killed."

Noelle's mouth gaped. "Her shop at Lenox? Who broke in? Why would anybody break in? Was it burglars?"

"I don't know that, either. I was hoping you could help me. Did Sonny say anything to you about Amanda?"

"Sonny?" Noelle looked worried. "He's dead. You think Sonny tried to . . . Why would he want to break into Amanda's shop?"

To clean up his trail.

Could Sonny have planted the bomb in Amanda's car? Maybe. The night of the break-in, he was supposedly late getting in from Las Vegas. Robert had complained about it.

But now Sonny was dead.

Noelle frowned. "I can't think of anybody who'd want to hurt Amanda. She's one of the nicest people I know."

"Yes, she is," Cal said slowly, "I can't think of anyone who'd want to hurt Amanda, either."

"Oh, look at that bracelet. It's so pretty." Noelle espied a silver bauble in an adjoining shop and went to peer into the window. "I wish I had enough money to buy that," she said wistfully. "Manda says I'm going to have to be frugal, though, now that Edward and I are divorced. It sure is pretty, though."

He went to stand beside her. "If Amanda had died, I'd never have caught up to you and found out about Sonny. Are you sure Sonny never said anything about getting rid of Amanda?"

"If she'd died?" That surprised her again. "Get rid of Manda? Why would Sonny want to get rid of Manda?"

Her ignorance was too real to be faked. "Because Sonny may have thought Amanda was a liability."

"A liability? What do you mean, a liability?"

"Everyone thought Amanda took my diamonds. As long as she never said anything, no one would find out Sonny was the thief. If she was dead, she couldn't lead anybody to him."

Noelle looked uncertain. "So you think he . . ." A new expression came into the blue eyes, one of dawning comprehension. She looked away. "Sonny wouldn't do that."

He pounced. "What is it, Noelle? What did Sonny say?"

"Nothing. Sonny wouldn't have hurt Amanda." Tears welled up. "Amanda's my sister. He wouldn't have hurt her. He wouldn't have. He knows . . . he knew I love Amanda."

Callaway thought he had his answer.

Amanda had emerged from the T-shirt store in time to overhear the last of his conversation with Noelle, enough to understand the implications. He saw her momentary shock, admired her quick recovery. "Look at what I got for Teddy, Noelle. Isn't it cute?"

She chattered with her sister, but Callaway wanted to throttle Noelle.

When they finally got on the plane, the flight to Atlanta was crowded. Callaway had managed to get two tickets together, but the third one was separate. He used it himself because Amanda wanted to sit with Noelle.

As the plane took off, he tried again to figure out where the journal might be.

If he knew who'd killed Sonny, he might know who had the journal. While Claire had ruled out Matthew Swift, Cal remembered the senator's face when he'd said he would do whatever necessary to protect Claire and Johanna. And Swift had seen someone at the pond. Matthew was hiding something, but Cal couldn't figure out what, unless Swift had recognized Tip and refused to admit it.

But Tip wasn't a murderer.

Then there was Miles.

Sonny might have tried to blackmail Miles. Or what if Miles had decided to recover the money he paid Sonny by killing him? Cal didn't think his former mentor was capable of shooting a man but now, certain Miles had commissioned the theft of the diamonds, Cal couldn't discount him.

Miles's alibi for Sonny's death. One more thing to look into.

Claire, Tip, and Matthew Swift were obvious suspects because of the journal, and Miles because of the studs. Neither Claire nor Tip was a murderer. If Cal had to choose, he'd rather Matthew be guilty, but Miles would serve. As far as he was concerned, it might be best if Sonny's murderer was never caught. Except then how would he find the journal?

Everything came back to the journal.

Cal couldn't see Amanda, but he knew she was three rows up, sitting in the cramped middle after giving Noelle the roomier aisle seat.

How could she bear to talk so placidly to her sister after what Noelle had done to her? He sat by a window, trapped by a whining child and his father. The father tried to restrain the toddler but the boy was much too active. Had it been Cal's child, he would have set him down and made him stay.

When the small feet whapped his thigh for the hundredth time, he fumed.

"He's tired and cranky," the father said in an offhand manner, doing nothing to stop the attack.

*Aren't we all?* "I can tell." Cal almost gave the man a lecture about parenting methods. He would have, except that the child hadn't caused his foul mood. He was exhausted and dispirited, and hated to think about parting from Amanda.

But until he figured out what had happened to Lila McIntyre Lathen's journal, he couldn't worry about his own affairs. Maybe by the time the journal turned up, he would have forgotten Amanda.

Sure. As easy as he could forget Claire and Johanna and how much they meant to him.

There was no time to think about Amanda. He had to deal with Claire's future.

Once he confronted Miles and collected his diamonds, more of the pieces should fit together. Miles could have shot Sonny and taken the book, or, Cal thought with returning optimism, Sonny might have let something about the book slip to Miles when handing over the diamonds.

You never could tell.

At the Atlanta airport, bidding a relieved farewell to the cranky child and his doting father—okay, the kid was pretty cute so maybe the father had reason to dote—Cal walked with the sisters to a waiting car that took them all to Amanda's shop. There, he and Amanda shared a reserved farewell under Noelle's disinterested gaze.

"You'll let me know?" Amanda's eyes said what her words didn't. "If, I mean, when you get your things back?"

"Sure. Thanks for going with me."

"I didn't have much choice."

"Guess not." He wished Noelle would vanish so he could kiss Amanda, hold her before he had to leave.

Unfortunately, Noelle was present, and Amanda had told him to cool it. Instead of kissing her, he got back into the car and left.

As the car drove past Lenox Square, he used his cell to contact the local detective agency Tip had recommended. "I want twenty-four hour surveillance on a woman." He gave them Amanda's address and Noelle's name. "You have a photograph and description of her in your files."

He knew damned well Noelle was frigging holding something back.

\* \* \* \*

NOELLE SEEMED PREOCCUPIED, but Amanda had no time to question her sister.

After Callaway left, she changed and went upstairs where the Saturday afternoon rush was underway. She wondered when she would see him again. If she would see him again.

The look in his eyes had promised she would, but a few days apart could cool passion.

No matter what he felt today, he could find a replacement for her tomorrow.

Probably a redhead. A sultry redhead wearing too much makeup and a revealing top.

Then her work kept her from thinking about him.

Coming downstairs after the shop closed, Amanda found Noelle had made herself at home.

Belongings were strewn over the entire apartment. Shoes left where Noelle had stepped out of them in the hallway, a wet towel crumpled on a kitchen chair, half the contents of a purse spread out on the coffee table beside the cordless phone from Amanda's bedroom, a coat tossed on the sofa, and used tissues everywhere.

Annoyed, Amanda carried the cordless phone to its cradle. Noelle would have to see to the other mess herself.

She wanted to call Callaway but didn't. She couldn't talk to him with Noelle listening to every word.

Besides, she wouldn't have called him anyway. An overeager woman would lose her prey because most men preferred doing the pursuing, even when they were the ones being pursued.

Especially when they were the ones being pursued.

So she went into the kitchenette to see about supper.

As she toasted bread and opened a can of chunk chicken to make chicken salad for sandwiches, Noelle, in leggings and a big shirt, picked up the damp towel left on the dinette chair and cleared her throat. "I need some money to go to Birmingham, Manda. Loan it to me?"

Hope filled Amanda. That was why the cordless phone was left in the living room. "You've talked to Edward."

Noelle swung the towel. "Yeah. But we haven't made up. Not yet. I want to see Teddy. I've missed him. I'll take him that shirt you got him if you want me to."

"Edward doesn't mind your coming?"

"No. That was the deal we made, that I could see Teddy whenever I wanted to. Will you loan me plane fare? I'll pay you back when I get my settlement."

Amanda looked at her for a long moment but saw nothing that suggested Noelle was lying.

"Sure, honey." She couldn't stand in the way of Noelle seeing her child and maybe, just maybe, Edward might reconsider his decision. A little voice in the back of her mind asked why Noelle was really going to Birmingham but faded with thoughts of Callaway.

She wondered if he would ever forgive her and Noelle.

\* \* \* \*

THAT NIGHT, CAL broached his thoughts about expanding Amanda's business to his brother-in-law.

"It's a ridiculous idea," Robert said over after-dinner drinks Saturday evening. Heavy curtains in the study were drawn while the tiny fire on the hearth was for effect rather than heat. "The kind of boutique you're talking—"

"Not a boutique," Cal interrupted. "A shop."

Recovery from the flu had brought back Robert's normal impatience. "Whatever." He flapped a hand. "Setting up that kind of project is expensive, and we already have contracts in most places. Besides, while the shop may do well in the local Atlanta market, for our purposes the name would mean nothing. You may not realize that nationally known brands do better in our hotels than unknowns."

This last insinuated that Cal knew nothing about the hotel business or marketing.

Cal said mildly, "The idea is to make the name mean something."

"Ridiculous."

Claire, usually supportive of her husband in business conflicts, spoke up. "It could work."

Sitting in the shadows and dressed with her pre-Houston neatness, she'd said little as Cal sketched out ideas for Amanda's designs. She looked better than the past Tuesday, with plumped cheeks and regained color. "We could use the upscale resorts. Jane's prices would never work in the others."

Trust Claire to understand. "That's what I thought. A small place, like she has now, but using her ready-made line for the floor with a seamstress-manager to make alterations."

Robert jumped up. "The idea's asinine. Listen to the both of you. Jesus H. Christ, don't I have enough on my goddamned mind without having to listen to the two of you prattle about dress shops?" He turned on his heel and left.

The obscenity was so foreign to Robert that Callaway looked askance at Claire.

In a colorless tone, she said, "He hasn't been feeling well. Dealing with those Virginia investors wore him out. And the auditors have been more critical than usual. He's under a lot of pressure."

"That's a good reason to bite our heads off?" Cal moved his chair close to hers. "I have an appointment with Miles in the morning. He may know something about Mother's book."

She laid a hand against one side of her face to shade it from his eyes. "What if he doesn't?"

He had no answer.

She lowered her hand. "I've talked to Matt."

"And?"

"He says . . . He's been very reassuring. He says I mustn't consider him or his son, or even Tip. That they can take care of themselves. He thinks Johanna is the only one to worry about."

"Johanna's pretty level-headed." Cal wondered if the conversation with Matthew was responsible for Claire's resurging vitality. "I'm sure she'd be upset, but she's strong, Bags."

"Matt said that, too." In the flickering firelight, Claire reminded him of a druid in a forest, waiting for the tree spirits to respond to her prayers. "Matt said that if Johanna did find out, he would almost be glad." A secretive smile played on her lips. She put fingertips to them as if reliving a kiss.

Cal was outraged. "He should have said that twenty-three years ago. Claire, you can't—"

"You know Matt couldn't have married me." Claire's smile remained. "He could never have abandoned poor Ellen. I would never have let him. It wasn't his fault."

"Hah. He had a choice. He didn't have to take advantage of you. You were too young to know what you were doing."

"Why, Cal, is that a puritanical streak in you?" She laughed, a low laugh rich in some instinctive gender knowledge that he would never possess. "It's nearly always a woman's choice. Don't you know that by now? Matt thought he was to blame, too, but I wanted it. I just didn't plan to get pregnant."

A woman's choice. He thought of Amanda, how he'd found her waiting—had it really happened just the past night or had it been a dream?—how she'd swept away his defenses. Something deep inside him stirred when he thought of Amanda deliberately choosing him. "If Mother and Tip hadn't married and wangled Johanna's birth certificate, what would you have done?"

"Something. Anything. I wouldn't have given her up."

"What are you going to do about Robert?"

Some of her serenity went away. "I don't know. I loved him once. I'd never have married him if I didn't."

"You don't anymore?"

A long sigh shuddered in the firelight. Her, "I don't know that either," when it came was almost inaudible.

\* \* \* \*

MILES DE GRAFFEN was tied up until Sunday afternoon. His daughter, Lynette, her shy prettiness faded and the creamy skin blotchy, opened the door of their North Atlanta home to Cal. "Dad'll be right down."

He noted the puffy eyes. "Have you been sick?"

"A little. Sonny and I . . . His death hit me hard." Tears welled, were hastily swiped. "It was all so shocking. He and I were planning a trip together, and then . . ." She looked away and waved a hand for him to go into the library. "Dad'll be right down," she repeated. "It's good to see you, Cal." Before her sobs became audible, she retreated.

Lynette and Sonny.

He had suspected Sonny was flirting with Miles's daughter, but he hadn't realized the affair had gone so far.

Was Noelle aware that her lover had been involved with another woman, and one with money? Lynette had inherited a fortune from her mother. Since she was de Graffen's only child, he would one day leave her more. A lot more.

Cal didn't feel sorry for Noelle, but he wouldn't be the one to tell her about Lynette if she didn't know.

The following interview among the smells and surroundings of books and leather chairs proved to be as unpleasant as he'd imagined.

Miles, tall and tan in casual slacks and golf shirt, strode in smiling and holding out his hand. "Cal. How are you?"

Cal didn't bother to sit down. He ignored the greeting and snubbed the outstretched hand. "Miles, my studs were stolen at the opening in Houston."

A telltale second elapsed. "My God, you don't mean it. Was it the redhead? Patrice tried to warn you." Miles gave a nervous laugh.

"If you mean to continue on your current path, you need to take acting lessons."

"What?"

"The redhead was meant to be blamed, but Sonny was the thief. As you know."

He didn't miss the sudden tremor, the paling under the tan. "You thought you were safe, didn't you? Sonny planned the entire thing. His girlfriend helped, but she spilled everything to keep from going to jail."

"I . . ." Miles coughed. "I hardly know what to say."

"I don't want to spar with you. I know you paid Sonny to steal the studs."

Miles tried to bluster.

"I don't know if you approached Sonny or if he approached you. It doesn't matter. What does matter is that I have the bearer bonds you gave him, and I want my studs back. And anything else he gave you." Cal kept his voice flat.

Miles avoided his eyes. "If this is a joke, it isn't very funny."

"The police haven't been brought in yet, but I can't keep them in the dark much longer. Sonny's death may be connected. Unless I get the studs back, I'll have to tell them."

"Sonny's death connected to your studs?" Miles turned pasty. "That's nonsense."

"If not connected to the studs, then to the book he stole along with them. I'm prepared to return your bonds for my studs.

Otherwise," Cal ended in the same flat tone, "I have no option but to take my informant to the police and make a clean breast of the whole thing."

"You should have gone to the police in the beginning. I can't help you. I don't know why you think I can." The frozen lines of Miles's face confirmed his guilt.

The man had been like a father to him.

If Miles of all people could do this, how could he trust anyone? Could it be worse? Could Miles be a murderer?

Maybe he should throw up his hands and go on to the police.

"I can't help you," Miles repeated woodenly.

No. There was Claire and Johanna to consider, as well as Tip.

And Amanda. Amanda who he wanted to love.

Taking a deep breath, he said, "Yes, you can, Miles, but we'll skip that for a moment. The reason I didn't report the theft is because the book that was stolen is one I need back without publicity." He was careful in choosing his words. "I've had no luck tracing it."

A blank look said that the journal meant nothing to Miles. His shrug concurred. "I have no idea what you're talking about."

Hope, faint as it was, withered. "Since that's the case, I have no reason for not going to the police. My witness is willing to testify as to your involvement with her and Sonny."

"Balls!" Miles bluffed. "The word of some two-bit whore won't mean a thing to the police."

"Don't put it to the test. I'm tired. I really don't want to have to prosecute you. God, you've been a friend of the family since before I was born. You've been my mentor, almost another father. I learned about antique jewelry from you. You taught me poker, golf, how to shoot . . ." He couldn't go on.

Miles held up one hand to examine a two hundred-year-old sapphire ring his middle finger sported, but his eyes didn't focus on it.

"Miles." One last appeal. "Don't make me go to the police. Don't make me have to bring all our dirty linen out in public."

Miles twisted the ring. After a long while he gave a little shrug of resignation. "All right. Suppose what you say is true? What do you want from me?"

"Give me my Antoinette diamonds and I'll return the bonds. There'll be no police, no ugly questions, and no nasty publicity. Not even any retribution such as a flat exclusion of McIntyre's business." Cal managed a smile. "Give me whatever Sonny gave you and all will be forgiven."

The fist with the sapphire went to Miles's forehead. His eyes closed. He took a deep breath. "When?"

"Now."

Miles's eyes opened. "You have the bonds with you?"

"There was no reason not to bring them. I've made copies and my witness can testify about your involvement."

Defeated, Miles dragged himself out of his chair and went upstairs. He returned within minutes holding a flat case. "Here."

"But no book."

"What kind of book? And what would I want with a book?" Miles asked, annoyed. "This is what I bought." He handed Cal the case. "All that I bought."

When Cal opened the case, his six diamonds winked out at him and behind the preserving glass in the lid lay the ancient bill of sale. "Thank you," he murmured, the politeness ground into him kicking in. "They're really unlucky for everyone except me, it seems. Guess my luck is so bad, they can't make it any worse."

Miles didn't smile. "Where are my bonds?"

Cal reached into his pocket, brought out an envelope and gave it to his one-time friend.

Color returned to Miles's face, along with some of the old arrogance. "Can't blame a man for trying."

Cal smiled. *Oh, yes, I can.* In his life he'd done a lot of things he regretted, but he'd never betrayed a friend.

Miles seemed to feel their relationship could be patched, that this was another sporting match between them. "I thought when Sonny died, I was safe."

Cal would never forgive him. Never. "Did you kill Sonny?"

"Me?" Miles's mouth dropped open. "Certainly not. How could you suggest such a thing? Why would I?"

"So he couldn't tell who he'd sold the studs to. Where were you last Monday about noon?"

"Last Monday?" Agitated, Miles drew back. "You're serious. You think I killed him."

"Do you have an alibi?"

"Monday." Sweat popped up on Miles's forehead. "I was in the office as I always am during the week." His shoulders relaxed. "And ten or twenty people saw me there."

"It never hurts to ask." He would have Miles's alibi checked, all right. "So Sonny never offered you a journal or anything else when he gave you the diamonds?"

"All I wanted was your studs. That was the deal and that's what I got." Miles opened the envelope and riffled the bonds, then counted them carefully. "Five hundred thousand dollars?" He blanched. "Five hundred thousand? Where are the rest of the bonds?"

"Were there more?" Noelle hadn't known the amount. "These were all we found."

Miles sank into a nearby chair. "Out of five million dollars, this is what you bring me back?"

"Five . . ." Cal's mind stopped working. "You gave Sonny five million dollars in bearer bonds?"

"Yes, damn it! Where are the rest of my sodding bonds?"

Cal breathed again, his mind worked again.

Four and a half million dollars in bonds were missing, along with the two hundred thousand in cash Matthew had supposedly given Sonny.

Noelle had either lied or really hadn't known the amount of money involved. But then Sonny would have told her as little as possible.

Now Miles was left with a fraction of his payment.

What a lovely comeuppance. "I'll do what I can to get the rest of your money back, but I don't promise anything, Miles. Consider it a lesson in morality."

As Cal drove away, it occurred to him that he wasn't that far from Lenox Square and Amanda's shop.

It would be rude to be so close and not go by to see her, find out how she was feeling after her trials of the past week. He could talk to Noelle, too, see if he could dig anything out of her about the big discrepancy in Miles's bonds.

And something else bothered him. Lynette and Sonny.

Had Noelle known about Lynette? Would she get mad enough to kill Sonny if she found out he was seeing another woman?

Or wait . . .

Admittedly reaching here but . . . What if Lynette found out about Noelle? Would Lynette kill Sonny?

No. Not Lynette. Maybe Noelle though.

His car turned of its own accord.

He got to Amanda's shop about four. Since it was Sunday and the shop was closed, he went directly to her basement apartment. The boarded up sidelight at her door greeted him.

She should have had it repaired by now. He'd get it done. Tomorrow, he promised himself. First thing, he'd call someone.

Amanda herself came to the door in sweats. Her hair was pulled straight up and tied in a ponytail at the crown of her head like a teenager instead of the ravishing woman she was.

He liked the way her mouth parted with delight when she saw him standing at her door, liked it as much as he liked her in the grubby outfit, as much as the glow that filled her gray eyes.

He knew he was a fool. Her sister was a liar, and Amanda might be as bad. He was crazy for trusting her, crazy for wanting her, but he couldn't help himself.

Matthew. That's where he'd heard about not caring for the consequences. And as the other night, that rush of sudden understanding was as exhilarating as it was frightening.

*I know what the consequences will be but I don't care. I'm set on the course and it's way too late.*

"Did you find your book?" she asked.

His preoccupation faded. Caution prevailed. "No, but I found my diamonds. I want to talk to your sister again."

"Noelle isn't here." Perspiration lay in a faint sheen over her upper lip, drawing his attention to its enchanting "V" and reminding him of the first time he'd seen her, of the last time he'd been in bed with her. "She went to a movie."

He ought not to want her so much this soon. He ought not to want her so much, period. "I found out something this past week."

She motioned him to enter. "What?"

"I found out that brown hair grows on you. It's easy to get used to it."

She laughed, looking up from under her lashes in the flirtatious slant that turned his insides to water. "I think Johanna was right. I think you like anything in panties."

"Preferably without," he replied, the teasing automatic.

She led him past a bad reproduction of Van Gogh's Sunflowers in the foyer and into the living room, white with glossy wood like her shop upstairs. A vacuum cleaner in the middle of the rug testified to interrupted cleaning. A dusting rag lay on a table.

He enjoyed following Amanda, watching the way the sweats clung to her hips as they moved back and forth. He wondered, as they sat down in a sedate side-by-side position on the sofa, how long Noelle would be gone.

Not long enough, damn it.

"Amanda, I think Noelle's hiding something."

"Yes, I think so, too."

He had prepared himself for the usual denials emanating from her misplaced loyalty to her undeserving sister.

But she agreed with him.

He wanted to kiss her, but Amanda didn't give him a chance. "Noelle says she's learned her lesson. She says she'll never gamble again." The smooth forehead puckered. "She says, oh, all the usual things."

"But you don't believe her."

The full mouth pouted with concern. "I don't know. I want to, but I just don't know. I think she's holding something back."

He did kiss her then, a deep, prolonged kiss, unsatisfying because he didn't want to stop.

Since she had voiced her doubts about Noelle, he told her about the amount Miles had paid for the studs and the amount found in Sonny's luggage. "Which leaves four and a half million dollars in bonds missing," he ended, "along with two hundred thousand cash we know Sonny had when he died."

Like him, she didn't understand the discrepancy, but her first thought concerned her sister. "Do you think Noelle knew? No, I don't think she could lie as well as she did if she knew."

Hell, Noelle had managed to lie about everything else. Why not this? "If Noelle didn't take the rest of the bonds herself, then maybe Sonny didn't tell her how much he was getting."

"She can't have taken them. She wants to borrow money from me for a ticket to Birmingham," Amanda said. "If she had money, she'd use it."

"Birmingham? Why's she going to Birmingham?"

"She wants to see Teddy. I'm hoping Edward will forgive her."

Fat chance.

But Amanda was an optimist. He liked that.

In the back of his mind the theory, nebulous and unsubstantiated, solidified. The theory that included Lynette, Noelle, and Sonny. A theory he took care to withhold from Amanda because she would never believe Noelle could kill anyone.

When Noelle didn't return right away, he left. Better to look for more proof before confronting Noelle.

And figure out how to do it without turning Amanda against him.

# CHAPTER TWENTY-ONE

AMANDA THOUGHT CALLAWAY had forgiven her. He couldn't have been acting just now, she told herself after he left.

Satisfied, she resumed dusting her thimble display.

Noelle came in. Her sister, forehead lined with anxiety, let the door slam. "I saw Cal McIntyre leaving. What was he doing here?"

"Looking for you."

"Me?" Noelle's cheeks reddened. "What did he want with me? I thought he was through with me. I've told him everything I know."

"He thinks you may have forgotten something, honey. He found out that Miles de Graffen paid Sonny five million dollars for those diamonds."

Noelle blinked. "Five million dollars?" Her eyes grew wide and her mouth rounded. "That's a lot of money."

Her sister wasn't acting. Noelle really was shocked.

"Part of it was found in Sonny's things, but only a little part." Amanda took a deep breath. "Noelle, do you know where the rest of that money is?"

"Me?" Noelle shook her head violently. "No way. Maybe Cal's lying. Who'd pay that much for a few diamonds? Sonny said they'd bring a lot of money, but it couldn't have been that much."

"Can you remember anything else Sonny said that might help find the money? Anything at all?"

Again Noelle shook her head. "I'm sorry, Manda. I've told you everything Sonny told me. We didn't talk all that much except for going over what I had to do. What are we having for dinner? Do you want me to walk over to that Thai place and pick up something?"

She'd get no help from Noelle for Callaway.

\* \* \* \*

THE BRIEF INTERLUDE with Amanda had brightened Cal's day, but his mood fell when he entered Fair Meadows through the rear gate and saw a familiar figure on the adjoining property.

Matthew Swift.

On impulse, he stopped his car and walked the short distance to Matthew's boundary.

As he approached, he tried to look at the senator from a

woman's viewpoint. The graying temples and strong face could be attractive, he supposed. His sister evidently thought so.

"Claire told you," Matthew said, picking up on something in Cal's bearing.

"I don't approve of your seeing her, but I guess it's not my place to approve or disapprove, is it?"

A big hand swept back a silver lock of hair. "I don't approve either. Talking is one thing but trying to revive the past . . . I've told her it's up to her where we go from here."

"She knows that."

The men fell into step on the dense green turf that followed the boundary between Matthew's home and Fair Meadows.

"The journal may be lost for good," Cal said. "All the mess, all that about you and Claire and Johanna may never come out."

Matthew's lips drew tight. "Cal, Claire and I are prepared for whatever happens. Right now the book doesn't matter. The authorities don't know about it. They think Sonny's death had to do with the money I gave him."

"You told them about the money?"

"They found that Claire and I had both been converting securities to cash."

Cal came to a halt before a stand of dogwoods.

Hell, he should have thought of that. "Do they—?"

Matthew waved a hand. "It's all right. We told them that McIntyre Resorts had a chance to buy some choice land in Virginia. If they bought openly, local interests could block resort zoning so money had to be used that couldn't be traced back to the chain. Sonny was to take the cash, put it in an account of one of our proxy companies, purchase the land, and get it rezoned before the name McIntyre came into play. My portion was an investment, as was Claire's. Her being an officer and me a member of the Board gives us that prerogative."

Cal was incredulous. "They bought it?"

"Every word. Claire thought of it," Matthew said proudly. "She'd already thought of it when she got her money for Sonny. In case she needed to explain her actions."

God, his own sister was as devious as the rest of her sex. How the hell did females get such convoluted minds?

"I see. Okay. Good for Claire."

They resumed their stroll, heading back the way they had come. "So the theory is that somebody killed Sonny for the money. Right?"

"Right. Let's leave it at that."

Something didn't ring true. Suspicion returned. "Why?"

They came to a second stop. Involuntarily, the senator glanced up and over Cal's shoulder. Cal turned and saw in an opening between the weeping cherries and dogwoods, a man moving on a hidden path.

Though he saw only the back of the man for the merest instant, he recognized Tip. Tip was walking on the gravel path leading from the road toward the pond.

The pond where Sonny Kirkman's body had been found.

He said slowly, "You saw someone when Sonny was killed, you said. You also said you didn't recognize him but you did, didn't you?"

"Don't go there, Cal."

"You let me believe you thought it was Tip, but it wasn't, was it? Who did you see?"

"I told you I didn't . . ."

"Who did you see?"

Matthew threw up his hands. "A woman. It was a woman's back. In slacks and a blue hooded jacket. I'd been walking, trying to decide what to do about Sonny's demands when I saw her. It was Claire. I almost went over to her."

"You didn't?"

"No." He shrugged. "I wanted to, but I didn't."

Cal tamped down panic. "Why did you think it was Claire?"

"Right size. Right build. The kind of clothes she wears outside."

"But you only saw her back."

"Yes, but—"

"It wasn't Claire."

Matthew turned away. "Of course not."

They walked in silence before Cal offered, "The jacket was blue, you said. Claire has a hooded jacket, but it's black. Besides, she couldn't have killed Sonny. She can't kill a spider."

Matthew took a long time answering. "I know that."

The senator wasn't as certain as he pretended.

"I could have, though," Matthew added, still without looking at Cal. "If I had thought it would help. I told you before, I can do whatever's necessary to protect Claire."

Cal believed Matthew might kill someone for Claire. What he didn't believe, was that Matthew had.

\* \* \* \*

THE NEXT DAY, Monday, Cal went into McIntyre Headquarters near Georgia Highway 400. As he got off the elevator on the twelfth floor where the executive offices were located, he saw Robert in the copier nook, emptying a shredder into the recycle bin. Robert started at the sight of him, but greeted him affably.

"You must be feeling better," Cal said. "Never saw you do your secretary's work before."

Robert held up the bucket. "Martha's busy. The auditors finally finished and we have a clean bill of health, you'll be pleased to know." He grinned. "And I got my contract offer from the Board this morning. Thought I'd clean up the office a bit before my attorney and I meet with them."

So Robert would be the new CEO. "Great." *The contract probably has a golden parachute clause, too, dammit.* "Anything new about Sonny's murder?"

Robert lost his affability. "No. As far as I know, they're still investigating. I think it'll turn out to be some tramp or someone else passing by. Maybe Sonny saw someone on the estate and warned them off and they killed him."

"Maybe so."

"What brings you in?"

"I have to pick up my golf clubs."

"Cal, Cal." Robert shook his head, but he was smiling again. "Spare a little time for work, why don't you?"

In his office, Cal called his detective agency and discovered that Noelle had taken a taxi that morning to the Atlanta airport where she had been observed boarding a plane.

Noelle was supposed to go to Birmingham, but he phoned Amanda anyway to make sure.

"Yes," Amanda told him. "I told you I loaned her money for plane fare. You don't need her, do you? She thinks she and Edward might work things out."

Callaway rolled his eyes, glad Amanda couldn't see. He couldn't stop himself from saying, "Strange she never seemed to care about her family before now."

"Cal, I've explained. Her handicap means she doesn't realize what her decisions involve. I think she really misses Teddy and Edward."

He snorted.

She huffed. "She's my sister. If she were paralyzed or had Down syndrome, you wouldn't expect me to abandon her."

"No. You're right." He might as well resign himself. Amanda would never stop trying to help the dim-witted Noelle.

Hanging up, he lit a cigarette. That would give Robert something else to carp about, since the building was non-smoking.

Noelle's dependence on Amanda frustrated him, but it wasn't his concern. Why should he care?

Because he cared about Amanda.

Because he was terrified that when it came to choosing between Noelle and him, as he judged it soon might, Amanda would choose Noelle.

He smoked defiantly, alternating between erotic images of Amanda, annoyance with Noelle, and worries about Claire and Johanna.

The detective agency had instructions to report everything concerning Noelle. From them, he already knew, though he hadn't told Amanda, that Noelle had bought a ticket to Las Vegas.

Not Birmingham.

From the time he'd discovered the money discrepancy, he'd worked out a scenario about Sonny's murder. A scenario he didn't much care for.

In it, Sonny met a woman at the pond, a woman who was his accomplice. Maybe Noelle had kept the other bonds for herself and they had quarreled over them. Or maybe she had found out Sonny was dumping her for Lynette de Graffen, and shot him in a jealous rage.

Whatever the reason, Noelle had killed him, then taken Matthew's cash and the journal.

The scenario played pretty good.

Except that Noelle had been in Cancun waiting for Sonny when he died, so low in funds that she'd had to call Amanda for help.

At least, that was her story. He had the agency checking on when she arrived in Mexico. If Noelle was anywhere near Fair Meadows that Monday afternoon, he'd go to the police.

Right now, he needed to figure out how to tell Amanda her sister might be a murderess.

As he was driving home from work that afternoon, the agency operative called. "We picked the subject up at the Vegas airport."

If Noelle wanted one last fling at the tables, there were places closer than Las Vegas. Perhaps Edward's settlement had come through, and Noelle was celebrating.

Or maybe she'd stashed Matthew's cash away and was using it.

The man was still talking. ". . . Went to the Sun Strip Bank near the airport and got into a safety deposit box there. Then she checked into the Marriott. She's booked on a flight back first thing in the morning."

A safety deposit box.

*Think, think. God, why can't I think?*

Okay, Sonny had gone on to Las Vegas after the theft. Could he have stashed the journal in a bank there? Could Noelle be retrieving it?

He had to find out what Noelle had got from the bank and where she was going with it.

He told the agency to make sure they had enough men to cover any contingencies. "I don't care what it costs. Don't lose her."

When he disconnected, a welcome thought struck. With Noelle tucked away in Las Vegas till tomorrow, Amanda would be alone.

He'd go home, get some clothes, and then spend the night with her. Keep her from staying by herself. Check on whether or not the glass company he'd called had put in a new sidelight.

\* \* \* \*

LEAVING HIS CAR out in front of his cottage, Cal went in to change into Hawaiian shirt and jeans. When he came out, Tip caught him on the porch. "Claire isn't here, and I need some help."

"Will it take long? I'm on my way in to Atlanta."

"Just take a moment. I was talking to R.T., the outside auditor, this afternoon, and he said something I don't understand. About the employee bonus account?"

Cal slung his hanger bag over his shoulder. "Do we have an employee bonus account? I seem to recall some discussions about starting one a few years back, but I also seem to recall Mother felt profit-sharing for everyone was a better incentive than giving bonuses to a few. And Mother always prevailed."

Tip ignored the sting in the last sentence. "I remember. Lila was emphatic about it. That's why I thought it strange when the auditor said the bonus account's built up to over three million dollars."

"That doesn't make sense."

"That's what I thought. Unless Robert's instituted some changes I haven't heard about. Of course," Tip added neutrally, "he may very well have done so. I don't pay as much attention as I should to goings-on at the company."

Callaway folded the garment bag over his arm. "If that's the case, he never brought any such action up before the Board."

"You look almost pleased."

"If Robert's gone against policy and set up this account on his own, we have cause to confront him. Why, something this bad might make the Board force him out. Three million dollars, you say?"

"Then Claire could assume responsibility for the company's future. She'd make a good CEO."

Cal clapped Tip's shoulder. "She would. She's calm, practical, and a born compromiser. And a much better leader than Robert ever could hope to be."

"Do you think this might be related to Sonny and his scam?"

Cal blinked. "I don't know. The amount of money's close, but what would Sonny have to do with a bonus account? He doesn't write checks or approve vouchers. No, Robert would have to be the one to instigate a new account."

Still, this new information was as puzzling as the missing bonds. As he drove toward Atlanta, Cal tried to put the pieces together but couldn't think of anything except getting to Amanda.

Hell, let his subconscious work on it.

He drove past the small sign that said *A. Jane, Dressmaker* and parked beside the locked garage leading to her basement apartment. The plywood boarding, he was satisfied to see, had been replaced with new stained glass. Though the draperies were drawn, a welcoming light shone out from the windows.

After he rang the bell and heard her quick step, he grinned at the peephole and held up the Chinese takeout sack. "It's me."

There was a second when the wild thought came to him that she wasn't going to let him in—that she knew he was suspicious of Noelle and had chosen her sister over him.

Then the door opened and she stood before him, backlighted from the subdued glow of a lamp on a desk where she'd been working.

A pink cotton robe wrapped and tied round the waist, and her brown hair fell in loose curling clusters specially arranged for his hungry hands.

He stepped inside and set down the wine and paper bag, and took her in his arms where, for a while, he sloughed off worries about Claire, Noelle, and everything else.

\* \* \* \*

AMANDA FORGOT NOELLE when she held Callaway. He absorbed her, made her cares vanish. At least while they made love.

Later, they sat across the kitchen table covered in the cheerful blue and fuchsia tablecloth from Mexico, and grinned at each other like kids who'd just discovered sex.

Amanda's body ached, but the ache was a good one. No matter what happened afterward, she'd have this.

She savored his nimble handling of chopsticks. "I'm glad Noelle decided to spend the night in Birmingham."

His fingers froze, and then recaptured the rhythm.

She didn't miss the falter. "What's wrong?"

"I'm out of practice."

She didn't miss his evasion, either.

"Callaway. What is it?"

He looked at his food, at his chopsticks, at his bright fuchsia and blue napkin. Everywhere but her. "Noelle didn't go to Birmingham."

"Where did she go?"

"Las Vegas."

Her mind went blank. "Las Vegas? Why?"

Finally, he looked at her. "I don't know but she's coming back tomorrow."

"Damn! Damn, damn, damn." Flinging herself out of her chair, she paced back and forth. "What is wrong with her? I can't believe she lied to me again. I can't believe I couldn't tell she was lying. I really thought . . ." She stopped short. "Noelle didn't have any money. I had to loan her money for plane fare to Birmingham. She wouldn't have money for gambling. Why would she go to Las Vegas? Oh."

Wheeling, she went into her bedroom and checked a decorative pot set up on a high shelf by her dresser. "I had a couple of thousand here strictly for emergencies," she told Cal who had trailed in after her. "It's gone."

Her bureau was old, with one central mirror and two smaller panels on either side that needed resilvering. In the muddied glass, she saw him approach, sympathy etched on the dark face. When he put his arms around her, she could only stand stiff and unbending.

He didn't give up but kept holding her, murmuring endearments under his breath meant for her ear alone, kneading the tension out of her neck and shoulders. At length, she allowed her head to loll against him while she thought how right their distorted reflections looked, with his arms around her and her hand against his chest. If only they could forget Noelle and his sister's diary and stand together this way forever.

"I'm tired, Callaway," she whispered into his shirt. "I don't want to worry about Noelle anymore, or have to watch out for her all the time. I don't want to be responsible anymore."

"No," she heard him murmur. "I know, sugar. I know. And you shouldn't have to be. You've done enough for Noelle. More than enough." She felt his kisses, butterfly-light, grazing her forehead, her cheekbones. She reached out blindly to him, squeezed back the tears. He held her tenderly for a long while, trying to overcome her grief with his caresses.

She was the one who initiated the lovemaking, when her body tired of his gentle stroking and began to clamor for more. She was the one whose lips became urgent, whose need rose to a fever pitch, who begged for his body to slide inside hers.

He was the one who joined her in the flight, who took her over the edge with him, and who held her tightly as they descended, sated.

Sometime near dawn she awakened, feeling that some word, some detail concerning Noelle had slipped by her. "There must be something in Las Vegas she needs," she murmured. "She must have forgotten something when she was out there before."

Callaway gave a sleepy sigh. "What?"

"I don't know."

He tightened his grip around her waist. "Stop thinking about Noelle. Think about this."

She nestled back against his warmth, pressing her hip against his erection, allowing his hands free play over her body until they orchestrated her need to near-delirium before they rocketed upward in unison again.

\* \* \* \*

AS SHE GOT ready for work, Callaway, bathed and dressed in navy suit pants and white dress shirt, prowled the apartment. When she came out of the bedroom, putting the last modest pearl in her ear, he was scowling at a note beside the telephone in the living room.

"Was last night that bad?" she asked, and was rewarded by emergence of the dimple.

He took two steps and enclosed her in his arms. "Last night was perfect. I could get used to sleeping with you."

"Don't muss me," she said, unable to keep from laughing. "Half my clientele already suspect I went away last week on some kind of orgy. They'll be convinced of it if I come in all wrinkled with my hair falling down."

He kissed the tip of her nose. "Why don't we go away on some kind of orgy and let them say, *Aha, I knew it all the time!*"

She slipped out from his arms. "I can't. I have a business to run and you, you have a job to go to."

His smile faded.

"Don't be so sensitive." Sooner or later his problem would have to be dealt with. "You could work at something besides the hotel business if you hate it so much."

"I don't hate it."

"No?" She put a hand up to touch his clean-shaven cheek. "I'm tired of tiptoeing around when I talk about my shop. If you don't like your life, change it. But for heaven's sake, stop making me feel guilty every time I mention my business."

He was taken aback. "Me? Make you feel guilty?"

"Yes, babe," she said patiently. "I don't know how you do it, but you do."

"Sorry." He looked as if he wanted to say something.

She waited.

"I've never . . . When I got out of school, I went to work for Mother in accounting and, to make a long story short, I screwed up, forgot to get some papers back to the company attorneys because my wife, my first wife," he qualified, "was about to leave me and I was distracted no end. Anyway, my carelessness cost us a lot of money and Mother was pissed. She put me in Future Growth Projections, a department that does absolutely nothing. A good place for a useless member of the family. I hate it."

"Of course you hate it," Amanda said with quick sympathy. "That kind of job would be all wrong for you. Don't call yourself useless. You're one of the most efficient people I've ever known."

"Efficient? Me? Hah!"

"You are. You trapped me, carried me off to Birmingham, got us to Las Vegas, back to Atlanta, and then Cancun and back here. All without turning a hair. The only bobble was the separated seats coming home when you couldn't sit with us on the plane."

"That wasn't a bobble. I had to bribe someone to take a later flight to get that seat, I'll have you know."

She wrinkled her nose at him. "If that isn't efficiency, I don't know what is. And anyone with half an eye could see you belong in public relations."

His eyes narrowed. "That's what Claire keeps telling me."

"Then listen to her."

The man simply needed someone to point him in the right direction, and he'd be fine. The only question was whether the person to point him would end up being Amanda. Once he found his journal, interest in her might fade as suddenly as it had grown.

She shivered, refused to think of it.

He didn't notice. "Hmm," he said, sunk in thought. "Maybe."

They looked at each other and burst into laughter. Amanda felt as though she were in love for the first time. How had she managed all these years by herself?

*How can I manage again if he leaves?*

I don't care, she said to herself. At least I'll have something of him to remember.

"I've got to go open the shop," she said.

"I've got to leave, too," he said regretfully. He reached over, picked up the paper he'd been holding when she came out. "I found this by your phone. Is this your writing or Noelle's?"

She took the paper, turned it over and saw it was an itinerary with a telephone number scribbled on its back. "Noelle's. Why?"

He took the itinerary back and looked at it. "She left for Cancun Tuesday morning."

"Is that important?"

"I don't know." He didn't meet her eyes.

Wondering what he was hiding, she followed him as he took his necktie to the foyer mirror. "What are you thinking?"

He turned up his collar. "The phone number. I recognize the sequence. It belongs to one of the offices in our Roswell office. I don't know whose it is, but it's a company number."

"Probably Sonny's, don't you think?"

"Well, duh. Am I dense or what?"

"You're not dense. Stop putting yourself down."

He looped, pulled, and finally knotted his tie. "Look, I'm meeting Claire in Roswell this morning. If we get through by lunch, do you want to go out to eat?"

"I won't have time." It was her turn to be regretful.

"All right. Dinner for sure, though, okay?"

"Okay." Happiness rushed through her, then dimmed. "Noelle may be back."

"I thought you were through worrying about Noelle." He moved away from her and picked up his suit coat, putting distance between them.

"I can't be, not really." How could she explain that she was worried more about him than Noelle? "I don't want her to mess up things with you."

The smile she disliked glinted. "Fat chance. You let me worry about Noelle. I'll take you out to eat. We'll leave her here."

She agreed because she was too much in love not to.

Something had to be done about that cynical smile, though. It didn't fit his character at all.

Not until he had gone did the anomaly strike her.

That airplane itinerary hadn't been there by the phone when she'd cleaned Sunday. Why was Noelle calling Sonny's office when Sonny had been dead since last Monday?

Going back to Noelle's itinerary, Amanda picked it up.

Atlanta to Las Vegas last Sunday. On Monday morning, a red-eye flight from Las Vegas back to Atlanta. Finally, Atlanta to Cancun Tuesday morning.

She frowned.

Noelle's time in Las Vegas had almost overlapped her and Cal's visit. While she and Cal had been asleep in the Mont Grande that afternoon, thinking Noelle was there, Noelle had arrived in Atlanta. The next day, she'd turned around and left for Cancun.

Now Cal said she was in Las Vegas again. What did Noelle think she was doing?

# CHAPTER TWENTY-TWO

USING ONE OF the company jets, Robert had taken the Virginia investors to the McIntyre resort near Orlando for the day.

His absence left Cal and Claire free to closet themselves with the controller and go over the books. Claire understood that the employees' bonus account had never been officially approved, but she didn't understand what the figures meant.

After several hours of tracing back entries, Cal did.

"Robert's been juggling funds," he explained in the privacy of his office where he and Claire had retreated.

"Robert?" Her blank face said she couldn't take it in.

"Uh huh." Over three million dollars paid out for supposed bonuses through an unauthorized account accessible to Robert Winslow and no one else. And then put back.

"I can't believe it."

"He's been shuffling money for years. Looks like he used the money to cover overrun costs for this building, but I can't tell for sure at this point. We need an audit."

The money from the sale of Cal's diamonds may have covered the shortage, but the trail remained and could be followed once the auditors knew what to look for.

Claire got up to pace. In her simple knit dress, she looked more like a distraught housewife than a capable businesswoman. "You don't think there's a mistake? Robert's too ethical to do that kind of thing."

"A reputation for being ethical makes it easier to get away with that kind of thing. A lot of people felt in the beginning this building would cost more than estimated. I imagine Robert wouldn't want to botch his first big project without Mother. It was probably very tempting to cover up fiscal miscalculations."

Claire put a hand to her throat. "Oh God, what a mess. What will we do?"

Cal shrugged. "That's your call, Claire. He's your husband."

She closed her eyes. "We have to know."

"I agree." He didn't bring up the other stuff he was thinking because she'd had enough shocks for one day.

But Robert must have planned the theft with Sonny. He could have given Sonny the safe combination and used Sonny's affair with Noelle to bring in Amanda.

The bonds in Sonny's suitcase would have been his fee. Strange Sonny was so stupid as to settle for a few hundred thousand instead of a million or two. But . . .

Sonny had asked Claire to run off with him. Maybe he did get more from the theft of the diamonds. Maybe when Noelle found out about Lynnette and killed him, she took the rest.

No. Why would she leave five hundred thousand dollars in his suitcase?

Because she couldn't get to the suitcase in the house. She'd taken the cash Matthew had given Sonny, though.

Or maybe Sonny had stashed the rest of the bonds in Las Vegas with the book. Maybe Noelle went there to pick it up.

Yeah, that made sense.

No matter. Robert was involved, and Claire would be hurt.

But not as hurt as Amanda if Noelle turned out to be a murderess.

* * * *

AMANDA'S HEART LEAPED when she found Callaway waiting for her after work. His necktie had been discarded along with his suit coat, but the open collar of his white shirt against his tanned throat looked downright seductive. As he listened to piano music she hadn't downloaded, his familiar presence filled her small abode.

She could get used to this.

"Is Noelle not here?" he asked.

"No. Just you and me, babe."

The answering twinkle before his kiss reassured her. He was as glad to see her as she was to see him.

"Too bad she'll be here soon," he said, coming up for air. "Her plane was due in an hour ago. Ready to go to dinner?"

That reminded her of Noelle's itinerary. "Callaway, look." She brought it over. "This number you said was to your office, the one we thought was Sonny's number? It wasn't here when I cleaned Sunday. Why would she be calling Sonny when—"

"—when Sonny was already dead," he finished. His face turned grim as he studied the itinerary. "I don't know. Look, do you care if we put off eating till Noelle gets here? I need to talk to her."

"I guess I'd better order pizza, huh?"

He glanced up at that, grinning so hard that the minuscule dimple was in full-blown display. "I'm sorry, Amanda," and on his tongue the name was an endearment. "I'll take you out to eat another time. I promise."

"It's a good thing you have more to recommend you than your taste in food."

He didn't hear. He was frowning at the number Noelle had written as he drew out his cell phone and dialed.

"No answer?" Amanda asked when he disconnected.

"No."

"It's six o'clock. Everyone's gone home. No voicemail?"

"Our top people don't use voicemail. We have assistants to screen calls. Mother insisted on the personal touch."

Why wouldn't he look at her? What was he thinking?

*Noelle.*

By seven o'clock that evening, when Noelle still hadn't shown up, Callaway called the airport and then his investigation agency.

"The flight got in at five thirty?" He listened. "A taxi. Where to?" He listened again. "Could be. I'd better get over there."

When he hung up, he picked up his suit coat. "I have to go."

Why wouldn't he tell her what was worrying him? "Where's Noelle?"

"Something's come up. Something about, uh, about the journal. I'll be back." At the door, he hesitated, looked at her in a way she didn't understand. "I'll be back."

He opened his mouth but shook his head and abruptly left.

What had he been about to say?

She picked up Noelle's old itinerary and studied the number on the back. Maybe she could find out who it belonged to.

She turned on her computer and used reverse lookup to put in the phone number. The name came up under McIntyre Resort Headquarters in Roswell as Callaway had said.

But he'd agreed it couldn't be Sonny's phone.

Okay. How about plugging in McIntyre Resort Headquarters? Their home page didn't have a directory, but there were other hits to check. After reading for a half hour through all kinds of legalese and lists, she found a phone number identical to the one Noelle had jotted down.

Office of the Chief Executive Officer.

Noelle was calling Robert Winslow?

\* \* \* \*

CAL PULLED INTO the parking lot of the Roswell building. A handful of cars remained this time of night, but they were empty.

As he drove around to the back of the twelve-story building, he spotted a nondescript Chevrolet parked alone with someone inside and stopped the Mercedes so that his door was next to the driver's side. The African-American woman of indeterminate age was expecting him.

She rolled down her window.

He did the same. "I'm Cal McIntyre."

"I'm Coronella. From Footwise Investigations. The subject got off the shuttle at the corner, walked across the lot, and went in the side entrance about twenty minutes ago."

Noelle needed a keycard to get into McIntyre headquarters after hours, but if she'd arranged to meet Robert, he might have met her and let her in.

Cal said, "I asked your boss for three more people. I'll stop at the front and tell them to let you through. When the others get here, bring them up to the twelfth floor and wait in the corridor. I'd guess we'll find her in the office at the far end."

The CEO's office. Robert's office.

"What do you expect to happen?"

He expected to find Noelle selling Robert the journal.

She'd shot Sonny, recovered his payment, and now she'd found a buyer for the journal. "I don't know, but it could be bad. I think we should be prepared."

Coronella looked doubtful. "Guess it never hurts to have some extra hands."

At the front desk, Cal recognized the guard monitoring the front cameras as a longtime employee who had been there in his grandfather's time. What was his name? Harold? Howard?

Horace, that was it.

"How're you doing, Horace?" After going through the obligatory what've-you-been-up-to and how've-you-been's, Callaway got to the point. "Say, you didn't happen to notice a woman come in the north entrance, did you?"

"Sure did. Got her on film with a record of the breach right here, Cal. This machine tracks everybody what comes in after hours." The elderly guard hit a key on his computer with a flourish, showing off his relish at the newfangled technology. "Yep. Come in at seven twenty-five. VIP keycard, according to the listing. She could of been one of them Virginia visitors we been having this week." His leer showed he didn't believe it.

"I'm expecting some more people shortly. Send them up to the CEO's office, will you?"

A wide grin cracked Horace's leathery face. "Heard the Board wasn't too happy with the way things're going. You here to have it out with Mr. Winslow?"

"Maybe." Cal grinned back. A person could say any outrageous thing after a certain age. "Or maybe he'll have it out with me."

"Nah, he ain't got the balls." Horace dug in his desk drawer and came out with a keycard. "Executive floor's locked up tight at night. Not even your card'll work. Better take this master."

"Thanks, Horace." Catching the card in midair, Cal strode toward the elevators while the grizzled security man was still cackling.

He'd be damned if he would let Robert get hold of the journal. With any luck, he'd catch Noelle in the act of selling it but hated to think about what would follow. He could see them explaining to the police, Noelle being arrested for Sonny's murder, Amanda's face when she found what her sister had done. And he could imagine Amanda's reaction, bristling with that strong protective instinct she had for Noelle.

God, she could turn on him and blame him for everything. She'd be too upset to see Noelle had brought this on herself.

He wouldn't think about Amanda, or what Noelle's guilt would do to his and Amanda's budding relationship. Not now.

The twelfth floor was devoted to executive offices, all empty this time of evening as was the rest of the building. Double doors in the hallway led back to the top offices, but they were locked. Cal fished out the keycard Horace had given him.

A fringe benefit from being a McIntyre, he thought in brief triumph, is that the guard will hand over the key to the entire building without question.

He hoped to heaven he'd get to Robert's office in time. Bad enough the man was going to be arrested for embezzling. No need to rub his face in Claire's past.

Quickening his pace, Cal went past empty assistants' desks to where a thin strip of light showed beneath the door to Robert's office. This door was, as were the outer entry doors, locked. He put his ear to its solid wood, heard voices indistinguishable except as those of a woman and a man.

Muffled squeals broke through the heavy wooden door, followed by a loud thump and the noise of more heavy objects falling.

What the hell was happening? It sounded like a maniac was wrecking the office, pushing over all the furniture in his path. Or like someone was struggling for his life.

Callaway froze, but no further sound came from Robert's office except an unexpected and sinister quiet.

He couldn't wait for reinforcements.

\* \* \* \*

WHEN THE PHONE rang, Amanda put down leftover pizza she was wrapping in plastic. The caller was from Callaway's investigative agency, asking for him.

"He isn't here, but I have his cellphone number."

"We've tried it but he isn't answering. Since he called earlier from this number, I thought he might be there."

"He isn't but he'll be back. I can take a message." Amanda licked pizza topping off her hand and scrabbled in a drawer for a pen.

"Hmm." A pause came from the other end. "Maybe you can help me. Did Mr. McIntyre mean he wanted another three operatives over at the Roswell headquarters? Or did he just need two? The person we've got on Ms. Parham now will be one, and if we send two more, he'll have three altogether."

"At the Roswell headquarters?" Amanda repeated stupidly. Noelle at the Roswell headquarters? What was Noelle doing there?

"Maybe I'd better wait and talk to Mr. McIntyre."

Panic coursed. "No," Amanda said sharply. "He's already over there. Send three. He'll need three more."

Noelle and Callaway were converging on the McIntyre building for some sort of showdown. She didn't know how she knew but she did.

Callaway hadn't wanted to tell her that something awful was about to happen and that Noelle was involved. He had left her, had gone off and left her alone while he confronted Noelle and somebody else.

Sonny's murderer?

Her thoughts when she had briefly awakened during the past night came back.

Noelle had gone to Las Vegas for some reason. Maybe to get something she'd left there earlier. That meant Noelle had stored something in Las Vegas, something that Sonny had given her perhaps, something that she had hidden away.

The book Callaway was so desperate to find.

Why did Noelle want the book now? Because someone at the Roswell building, someone at the telephone number Cal had dialed to no avail, was about to give Noelle money for the book.

Robert Winslow. Noelle was selling it to Claire's husband.

Dear God. Anger at Noelle's gullibility and duplicity flooded her, anger and a profound shame. And then horror.

What if Robert had killed Sonny because of the book? If he had, he could kill Noelle, too.

Noelle wouldn't even realize she was in danger.

That's why Callaway had looked at her so strangely when he left, because he hadn't wanted to tell her that Noelle knew the whereabouts of the journal and was trying to sell it.

Even if Robert wasn't a murderer, Amanda still wasn't about to let Noelle sell that journal to him, not if it contained something incriminating about Claire.

Grabbing her purse, she went to the garage and got into the shop's minivan and started toward Roswell.

She didn't know who she was most anxious for, Noelle or Callaway.

\* \* \* \*

CAL DIDN'T KNOW who he was most worried about, Robert or Noelle.

Heart pounding, he inserted Horace's master keycard into Robert's door lock.

The click of the latch sounded ominous after the sudden quiet following the crashes.

He entered a room which, because of a single green-shaded desk lamp throwing weak illumination across the office, conveyed an eerie underwater-like atmosphere. The musky odor of sex saturated the air. Articles of clothing, male and female, were scattered over the carpet and on the furniture.

Amid paper debris and strewn books, two leather guest chairs, a small file cabinet, and a round meeting table rested on their sides, doubtless the source of the heavy thumps.

As Cal stopped short, the couple on the desk sprang apart from where they'd been grappling.

"What the hell!" Robert hit the floor, his hair flying wildly around his head. He wore only a pair of dark socks and held his belt like a whip. His prick wilted.

Noelle, in a teensy black garter belt, black net hose, and nothing else, shrieked as she slid off the desk to cower behind the overturned table. "Omigod! Who is it? Robert, do something!"

Robert began to crawl on hands and knees to the side of his desk where various articles of clothing lay. After grabbing his pants, he thrust one leg in.

Oh shit.

Cal had thought Robert was killing Noelle, but all he was doing was humping her. "Sorry."

"Cal?" Robert looked ludicrous, hopping around on one leg as he tried to get his pants on. Without his glasses, he blinked in the dim light. "Is that you? What the hell are you doing here?"

The odd coupling didn't change the facts.

Noelle had the journal.

Callaway was sure she had it. "I came for Mother's diary."

Robert and Noelle were making it on Robert's desk.

Pieces, obscure and irregular, began to fall into place. The pattern had been laid, but he'd been too stupid to decipher it.

Robert, not Sonny, was Noelle's lover.

His voice sounded strangely far away. "Noelle, you lied."

The weeping Noelle, who had plucked up a denim blouse embroidered with garish red, yellow, and purple flowers, struggled to turn it right-side out.

"This is outrageous." Robert fastened his pants before slipping on his shirt. "How dare you break in here? Who the hell do you think you are?"

Cal concentrated on Noelle. "Sonny was never your lover, was he?"

Noelle's hands shook as she buttoned her blouse. "Sonny?" Trapped eyes flickered from Robert back to Cal. She choked back a sob. "I never said he was. Why would you think that?" Sniffle. "Robert—"

"Don't say anything else, Noelle. Get out of here, Cal. This isn't your affair. I'm going to call security, I'm warning you."

"Go ahead. Call security. You stole money from the company to make up for the budget shortfalls on this building and then you stole my diamonds to cover your theft. Did Sonny help or was he the innocent intermediary he claimed?"

Robert had to unzip his trousers to tuck his shirttail inside. "You're out in left field, Cal. You should stick to redheads." He put on his glasses and smoothed his hair back. Like Noelle's, his hand shook, but being clothed restored his composure. "You're making a fool of yourself."

Noelle was hysterical. She had problems with the zipper of her jeans, and wept harder.

"I don't care whether you tell me or not," Cal said for her benefit. "Everything will come out before you and Noelle go to prison."

"Prison?" Noelle squealed. "Why would we go to prison? Sonny was the one who thought of stealing your diamonds. I didn't do anything except whatever he and Robert told me to do."

Robert never took his eyes off Cal. "Shut up, Noelle."

She bit her lip. "But Sonny's the one to blame for everything. Not us."

"Shut up."

She snuffled and bent over to retrieve her shoes.

Cal could break her. "Someone saw you meet Sonny at the pond, Noelle. Did you go there intending to kill him?"

"Kill him!" She straightened, shoes in hand, eyes as wide as a child caught in a lie. "I never killed anybody."

"Why were you there at the pond?"

"The pond at Fair Meadows? I wasn't. Robert called, said Sonny was ruining everything and we had to talk him into pulling back."

Robert moved. "Shut up, damn you!"

The interruption had no effect on Noelle, busy explaining herself.

"Robert told me to bring his gun to him and that's all I did. I met him on the trail and gave it to him. He went to see Sonny but I don't know what happened. He came back in a few minutes and gave me the gun to take back to the apartment."

Robert dived toward the credenza and fumbled in its shelves. The sound of breaking glass preceded the smell of scotch creeping over the room.

Noelle babbled on. "Then I went to Cancun like I was supposed to."

"Did Robert give you a book, too?"

"No. Sonny left it in Las Vegas. I had to go get it. It's over there." She waved vaguely toward Robert's desk. "Robert's going to mail it back to Claire."

Robert turned, unzipping a soft pouch. "For the last time, Noelle, shut up."

She pouted. "But you said when Claire got the book, Cal would stop asking questions. You said now that Sonny's dead, everything would be all right."

"Did you try to kill Amanda?" Cal asked Robert. "You were once a mechanic so you'd know how to fix her car to blow up. And you waited after the rehearsal dinner to pick up Sonny. That gave you plenty of time to break into her apartment."

Noelle's mouth dropped. "You tried to kill Manda? But why? She didn't do anything."

"I'm warning you, Noelle. If you don't shut up . . ."

Noelle wouldn't. "But it was Sonny's plan. Manda didn't have anything to do with it. I can kind of understand why you had to kill Sonny, but Manda?"

Cal saw Robert's hand swing up, saw the lethal dark barrel aimed at Noelle.

Move, move.

His feet were two chunks of lead.

He opened his mouth but couldn't speak. His hand came up,

much too slowly, as Noelle said, "You wouldn't hurt Manda, would you, Robert? He's lying, isn't——?"

The gun spat.

Noelle's mouth remained open, but any words turned into a whimper. A red blossom joined the other flowers on her embroidered denim shirt.

Her hand went to it without understanding.

"It wasn't my fault." Her disbelieving eyes swung from Cal to Robert, begging one of them to comfort her. "It wasn't. I did everything Sonny and Robert told me to."

Cal froze.

Robert, face contorted, looked at the blood on her shirt. The gun fell limply to his side. "Jesus Christ, Noelle, I just wanted you to shut up. Why couldn't you just shut up?"

*Robert shot Noelle. How will I tell Amanda?*

The police. They'd have to get involved now.

Robert was a murderer.

*How will I tell Claire?*

Amanda. Claire.

As Noelle started to crumple, Callaway's paralysis lifted. He bounded two steps, caught and lowered her to the floor. "Call 911, Robert."

She was conscious, but her pulse was erratic. Shock glazed her expression. "I shouldn't have believed him, should I?" she whispered. "Manda always tells me to think before . . ." And then, fainter: "Manda. I want Manda."

Supporting her head, Callaway looked over at Robert. His brother-in-law stood immobile, feet spread apart and pistol dangling.

For an interminable moment the tableau endured. Cal kneeling on the floor beside Amanda's bleeding sister and Robert towering over them.

"Cal." The gun at Robert's side wobbled, and began a sluggish ascent as if reluctant to do the deed its owner required. "Now I'll have to kill you, too."

"I have people on the way, Robert." Strange how he could speak with such detachment. "They know everything. About the building overruns. About you and Sonny working together. You can't get away. It's too late. Call for help before Noelle dies."

"Other people know?" The pistol, partially raised, stayed suspended. "Who knows? Claire?"

Cal stared at the barrel aimed toward him.

Detachment fled. He didn't want to die. Not now, not with Amanda . . .

He nodded.

The gun was lowered as slowly as it had been lifted. "Claire knows?" Consternation took the place of resolve.

With the gun moved, Cal breathed again. "Yes, and so do the detectives I hired. They all know. Let's get help for Noelle, Robert. Don't make it any worse on yourself."

Agonized eyes darted from Cal to the door and back to Noelle. Robert's eyelids squinched together.

Trying not to cry. Or maybe not wanting to look at what he'd done.

"I don't think . . ." Robert whispered. "I don't think it can be any worse."

Robert wasn't going to shoot him. He had to believe that.

"We need a blanket." A nearby cart for coffee accessories held a basket of napkins. Cal snatched up a handful to stanch the flow of blood from Noelle's chest. "She's going into shock. Give me her coat to cover her, Robert."

"Jesus Christ." The gun fell to the floor with a thud.

"Robert, you have to help me."

Robert sank into a side chair. "This whole thing has been a nightmare. All I wanted was to show Claire, show everyone, that I could handle Lila's job. I never meant for it to go so far."

Cal left Noelle, went toward the phone on the desk. "I've got to call for help, Robert."

"I should never have listened to Sonny. He kept after me and kept after me, telling me Miles would pay through the nose for those studs. And the building was costing so much more than I'd thought. Everyone said it would, but I was sure I could bring it off at budget. I'd staked my career on it. If I hadn't, the Board would never have given me Lila's job."

Cal picked up the phone. "I've got to call before she dies."

Robert ignored him. "I had Noelle to think of, too. She needed money for her clothes and her trips . . . everything."

Cal got Horace, told him there'd been an accident. "Call 911 and find some blankets."

As he hung up he heard Robert groan. His brother-in-law, arms wrapped around himself, rocked back and forth.

A book lay on the corner of the credenza. Without triumph, Cal slid his mother's journal into his jacket pocket before going back to the woman on the floor.

Noelle was unconscious.

He took her long denim coat, embroidered with the same gaudy flowers as on her blouse, and laid it across her. When he touched her wrist, before tucking the coat under her sides, he found a thready pulse.

Robert stopped rocking. "How did you know to come here?"

"I had Noelle followed. I never believed her story."

"Why not? I went over and over it with her. It made perfect sense that Sonny would be her lover. He could have planned everything, carried it all out. Most of what she told you was true. She didn't even have to lie very much."

Cal tried to smile, grimaced. "Yes. But I've been lied to so much, I guess I've come to expect it."

Robert took a deep, shuddering breath and sat erect. "If Sonny had left after Johanna's wedding when he was supposed to, none of this would have happened." Remnants of his old authority returned. "I couldn't understand his staying on until I overheard him talking to Claire about selling something. Then I heard her and Tip discussing Sonny. That's when I realized Johanna was Claire's child and that Sonny was blackmailing her."

"So you didn't know about it till then."

"My God, no! I wouldn't put Claire through . . . Sonny was an asshole. His share from your diamonds should have been plenty for him to get Lynnette de Graffen. If he'd left the goddamned diary alone, no one would ever have known what we'd done. "

"You were worried he'd get caught and expose you."

"I was furious that he was blackmailing Claire. She should never have been involved," Robert cried. "I just wanted to scare him. I called Noelle once everyone left Monday, got her to bring my gun. When I let her inside the back gate, Sonny was coming back from Matthew's. I met him by the pond."

"Met him and killed him."

Robert slumped. "I didn't want to. He laughed, said he'd got money from Matthew as well as Claire." He put his head in his hands. "Greed, that's all it was. I gave him half the money from your studs."

"So you murdered Sonny, stole his share of the bonds and also the cash Matthew had given him earlier."

Robert wouldn't meet Cal's eyes. "I didn't mean to kill him. It was an accident. He tried to get the gun away from me and it went off. I thought if I left some of the bonds, you'd blame him for the theft and wouldn't look any further. Especially if you thought he was Noelle's lover. When I got his share out of his suitcase, I found copies of Lila's diary with a safety deposit key and receipt from the bank in Las Vegas."

"So you sent Noelle to pick up the journal."

"I was going to give it back to Claire." A bit of spittle had dribbled out of the corner of Robert's mouth. He wiped it away with an apathetic hand. "What are you going to do?"

Cal looked at the bloody handkerchief. Noelle's face was waxen. "Wait for help."

"Is she still alive?"

There was no pulse beneath his fingers. The glassy eyes stared without focus.

Cold hit him all over. "I don't know."

But he did.

As did Robert. "She's dead. I can tell. She looks like Sonny did after . . . I loved her, Cal. Not like Claire, no, never. But Noelle looked up to me, needed me. She did things I'd never ask Claire to do. Golden showers, bondage, leathers . . . Noelle let me do anything to her because she needed me. Claire never needed me. But Noelle did."

"How'd you meet her?" Surely to God help would arrive soon, before Robert changed his mind and decided he had nothing to lose by shooting someone else.

Someone like Cal.

The gun lay on the floor between them, but he left it. No need to remind Robert it was there.

"I picked up Johanna last year from a fitting at Jane's. While I was waiting, Noelle came out. We struck up a conversation and it was one of those things. She was so artless, so giving. I love Claire, I've always loved Claire, but Claire knew my background, what I had come from. She never said a word but I knew she looked down on me. Nothing I did would ever make me good enough for her. But Noelle didn't care what I was or wasn't. I could do anything to Noelle and she didn't care. She loved me."

"Claire never looked down on you."

"All of you did." Reaching a decision, Robert got up and stooped for the gun.

Cal tensed but Robert turned. The cushion of the padded executive chair behind his desk whooshed as he sat down. The sound died away as the casters swiveled in the unnatural hush. "I could never live up to the McIntyres' reputation, Cal. Lila divided her shares between Claire and you. Not a one to me. Even though I'd worked my ass off for the company."

The revolver fell with a thud onto the desk's mahogany surface. His hand took up a pen in its stead. "Everyone constantly compared me to Lila, to Claire. Even to you." He let out a thin laugh. "To you, with all your women and partying, all your expensive hobbies. Pretty rich, isn't it? I do all the work, but you're the one who gets a free pass."

Sickness filled Cal. How many times had he dealt with those same inadequacies? How many times had he tried to please his mother and failed? "No one compared you to anyone, Robert."

Robert ignored him. "Not that it matters now. I guess I blew it." Pulling a yellow pad to him, he began to write busily beneath the beam of the shaded lamp, write as if he was working on an important memorandum that had to be finished right away. As if he had not killed a man and a woman.

Callaway covered Noelle's face with her coat. She had infuriated him and he had despised her, but he couldn't stand to see the vacant eyes. Amanda . . .

Fresh pain washed over him. God, how would he tell Amanda? How would she react? Would she hate him because he hadn't saved Noelle?

A page ripped from the yellow pad. Robert carefully placed it in the middle of his desk blotter.

"My confession." He showed a ghastly smile. "Don't worry. I didn't give details about Johanna or the diary, just that I shot Sonny and Noelle to cover up my embezzlement. You'll want to leave now," he went on like they were having an ordinary conversation. "Tell Claire I'm sorry. And the boys. Tell them I love them all. Ask them to forgive me. Maybe one day they can."

Not until Robert picked up the gun and said again, "You'll want to leave," did Cal understand.

For one moment, he nearly broke under the pressure of Robert's unnatural calm. But he didn't. Somehow he stood upright. "Robert. No. This isn't necessary."

"Tell Claire and the boys that the strain of being named CEO was too much, that I snapped. You'll know what to say. You always know what to say."

Not this time. But he tried. "You don't have to do this, Robert. Too much stress can break anyone. They'll understand that. We'll get you lawyers."

Robert didn't listen. He was intent on the gun, cradling it in both hands and turning the barrel. "Yes. That's it. Too much stress. Tell them that." He jerked his head toward the door. His eyes remained on the gun. "Go on, Cal. You won't want to be here. If you stay, I'll have to kill you, and then Claire won't have anyone."

Cal tried to speak.

He couldn't leave. He ought to stay and try to keep Robert from harming himself.

But his feet meekly obeyed Robert. They took him past the leather guest chairs, two upright and two on their backs beside the overturned round table, until he found himself walking across the deep brown carpet to the thick wooden door that he barely got closed before he heard Robert's final act.

The door muffled the shot.

Horace, hurrying down the hall with his arms full of blankets, saw Cal's face and froze.

# CHAPTER TWENTY-THREE

AMANDA SQUEALED THE tires of her minivan as she pulled up to the McIntyre headquarters in Roswell. Whirling red and blue lights blocked the entrance to the twelve story building. People rushed in and out.

Her throat trapped her heart and refused to let it loose.

What was going on?

Parking as close as she could, she got out and ran.

A van screeched up. Its doors crashed open, people popped out. They carried television equipment.

Something bad had happened.

*Hurry, hurry.*

Inside the lobby, a modern architectural delight of glossy pink granite and polished gray marble and lustrous black metals, a weathered security guard talked to a policeman and a petite African-American woman. He gestured with both arms as he spoke. ". . . So I went up top with the blankets and next thing I knowed, bam! Dead, right there in Mr. Winslow's office."

Dead?

Callaway!

Amanda stopped sprinting. "Who? Who are you talking about? Who's dead?"

They turned, looked at her in disbelief.

"You aren't allowed in here." The policeman shifted so that he was between Amanda and the others. "All reporters outside."

"I'm not a reporter." An image of Callaway hovered, his face as he had gone from her apartment such a short time earlier.

He had known the danger, known what to expect when he had left her. He had almost told her. She had almost read something from what he wouldn't say. But he had held it back and she hadn't wanted to nag.

No, surely, it wasn't Callaway dead. Not him.

"Who is it?" she all but screamed. "Who is it that's dead?"

Somehow, without realizing it, she had put her hands out and they were bunching up the policeman's lapels.

He tried to undo her hands gently. "I can't say, lady. Hey, now, you calm down."

He was annoyed, but she didn't care. "Tell me." She yanked at his coat. He shoved her back so hard that she stumbled and slid out of his grip onto the slick marble floor.

He held out a cautious hand to help her up. "Come on, lady, calm down. We'll find out in a minute what's happened. You just calm down till we hear something, okay?"

He wasn't going to tell her.

A rustling sound came from the side. Gleaming black elevator doors opened and the back of a uniformed man emerged wheeling a stretcher.

With a moan, Amanda flung the outstretched hand away and started down the length of the lobby.

The startled policeman called, "Hey," and belatedly lumbered after her. "Come back here!"

She ignored his shouts. She had to find out whose body lay beneath the covering.

Noelle or Callaway.

Callaway or Noelle.

*I'll make it up*, she promised. The lobby seemed a hundred feet long. Her legs were sticks that refused to obey. *I'll make up for whatever I thought about getting tired of her. I didn't mean it. She's my sister. And* Callaway. *I never meant to hurt him. If he's all right, I swear I'll let him go without a word. I won't try to hang on when he's ready to leave.*

*Dear God, don't let it be Callaway. Don't let it be Callaway.*

"Not Callaway," she mumbled as she ran. "My fault. I promise I'll never see him again. Not Callaway. I'll let him go, I will. Not Callaway."

The EMTs saw her coming and moved to block her way.

"No!" She tried to dodge them and reach the gurney.

The policeman's hands came from behind and caught her by the shoulders and wrested her away, hard, as she fought to get free.

As she twisted and kicked, she saw Callaway step out of a second elevator and shrieked in thanksgiving and then he was at her side, saying something to the policeman, taking her into his arms, kissing her, holding her, calling her name over and over. "Amanda, Amanda, don't, Amanda . . ."

"I didn't know who it was." Her words flattened against his neck, as, unable to stop, she kept crying and crying and crying. "They said someone was shot and I thought it was you and, oh, Callaway, I thought you were dead, I thought you were dead. I couldn't have stood it." She held him tightly while great choking, wrenching sobs shook her entire body. He held her back tightly, murmuring in her ear and stroking her as she regained control.

"Amanda," he said after a bit, when her frenzy had turned to soft weeping and she no longer trembled. He sounded distant. "Amanda. Oh God, Amanda, I'm sorry, I'm so sorry. I have to tell you but I don't want to tell you. Oh God."

She knew. In one lightning flash of intuition, she knew what he was going to say.

Noelle. She had forgotten Noelle in the terror of thinking Callaway dead and in the joy of finding him alive.

She jerked her head back convulsively so she could meet his eyes. They were anguished, full of dread.

She didn't want to hear his words.

"Amanda." He caught her face in both hands so that she couldn't look away, couldn't move. "Amanda. I'm so sorry, Amanda. Noelle's dead."

Then her knees gave way and she sank into the comfort of his enfolding arms again. He didn't let her go but held her as she keened for the little girl who had been her sister.

* * * *

ATLANTA'S HOTTEST SEPTEMBER in twenty years parched the trees and shrubs, and turned the concrete parking lots around the big shopping malls into gigantic heat collectors. May, then the rest of summer, had passed with a dreamlike depleting quality.

Somehow, despite the stupor of grief, Amanda had managed to do nine weddings, attend a New York fashion showing, renegotiate a long-term mortgage on her shop, and clear out belongings from the Perimeter apartment Noelle had shared with Robert Winslow.

Noelle was gone, but the emptiness she left behind sometimes overwhelmed Amanda.

"She made her choice," Callaway would say when Amanda began reproaching herself for things she had or hadn't done that might have led to Noelle' death. "You did everything you could, Amanda. You are not to blame for what happened. If anyone is to blame, it was Robert."

His blunt counsel didn't absolve her guilt. She knew in her heart that she had traded Noelle's life for Callaway's.

When she'd rushed into the McIntyre building, she had wanted, she had hoped—no, she had prayed—that the person lying dead wouldn't be Callaway.

Her prayer had been answered. Callaway had lived while Noelle had died, and Amanda would keep her bargain to let him go.

It would be hard. She'd only maintained her sanity the past months because of him.

She couldn't have endured the long weeks without his fortitude and patience. Dividing his time between her and his sister, he'd managed to bring order out of chaos, make sense out of gibberish, and establish calm in the midst of turmoil.

Never in her wildest imaginings would she have suspected Callaway McIntyre of being so strong, nor herself so weak.

With his help she had survived the embarrassment of the media's spotlights. Day by day, he had helped her regain her focus as she became accustomed to a life that would never again hinge on saving Noelle from disasters.

Her dress shop hadn't suffered.

There had been a burgeoning crowd of inquisitive customers immediately after the tragedy that had led to an unprecedented profitable quarter. Now curiosity had faded, but business was markedly better than before.

The old saying "any kind of publicity is good publicity" seemed to be true.

After a busy Saturday, Amanda waved goodbye to Melissa and locked up. Soon she'd see Callaway for the first time in several days. He'd pleaded pressing business, but she suspected his neglect was the first sign of boredom with her.

It was bound to happen. She'd been steeling herself.

Going back through the workroom, she stopped at a design her seamstress had finished that morning.

Then she reached for it. No reason to hesitate. She'd known all along she intended wearing the flamboyant outfit herself. When she'd first seen the material, as clear and blue as the Cancun sea, she'd envisioned something cheerful and eye-catching that would flatter her cleavage and show off her hips.

Something wanton and risqué that Callaway would like.

A jumpsuit, she'd decided. She'd cut out the middle from bra line to navel, leaving four wide strips to hold top and bottom together. When she put it on, the bottom clasped her hips snugly while the neckline revealed the cleft of her breasts.

No way to wear a bra with it.

Callaway liked racy clothes.

He also liked fake eyelashes and pastel eyeshadow and dangling earrings so she used them.

Afterward, she looked at herself in the mirror and was satisfied with her made-up face and freshly manicured nails. She pinned up her hair, disengaging only a few curls. She'd give him the pleasure of pulling it down.

He enjoyed taking her hair loose.

Thinking of that made her smile, but her reflection showed the smile fading.

No matter how she tried to please him, no matter how she planned her outfits and her hair and her makeup, the bottom line was that Callaway bored easily.

And the past few days he'd barely called.

*I won't try to hold him. I knew all along how it would end. I promised I'd give him up and I will.*

She'd keep her promise made that terrible night when she thought she'd lost him forever.

Callaway had lived. Noelle hadn't, but the rawness was beginning to go away, mostly due to Callaway. He'd been so good afterward, advising, comforting, and being there whenever she needed him. He'd put all his plans on hold, plans made long before she'd entered his life and turned everything topsy-turvy. He'd swept them aside because of what had happened with Noelle and his brother-in-law.

His absence the past week probably meant he was ready to resume his old life.

She couldn't blame him. The past spring and summer had been a nightmare for him and her and too many others. It was time to start forgetting.

So that night she met him at the door with a smile and held up her face for his kiss.

He kissed her, but he seemed preoccupied.

Uh oh, she thought, schooling her features. This is it. The old hasn't-it-been-fun, but-we-just-aren't-right-for-each-other routine.

She'd always been the one to say it in the past, never wondering how the man on the other end felt.

Now she knew.

No need to put a guilt trip on Callaway. She owed him that much. After forgiving her for Houston, protecting her from jail, proving to her she could love again, she owed him more than she could ever pay back.

"Are those for me?" She indicated the hydrangeas he carried.

"Yeah." He inspected her approvingly. "They clash with your outfit though."

"I don't plan on wearing them. Come on in."

Going to the kitchenette, she arranged the hydrangeas in water while listening to him pace the small living room. When she returned with the filled vase, he stopped and watched her set it down.

Okay, she told herself. This is it.

There was no way she could spend the night with him, not knowing what was coming in the morning.

Better not to drag things out. Better to cut them short. Like yanking off a Band-Aid.

"Look, Callaway," she began, at the same moment he said, "Amanda, I . . ."

Both trailed off and exchanged sheepish smiles.

"You first," she said.

"No, go ahead."

"I was going to say that you look tired, and I am for sure. We don't have to go out, we can get something delivered."

He looked blank. "I wasn't planning on going out."

She kept her smile fixed. "Fine. We'll stay in. Unless you have something else you'd rather do."

Suspicion clouded his face. "Did you want to go out?"

She shook her head. A heavy mass settled in her chest. "No." She couldn't do it. She couldn't say, It's been nice, sorry it has to end, let's do it again someday.

She couldn't.

"Good," he said. "I wanted to talk to you."

"Okay." She put the flowers on a table by the door. An old armoire she'd turned into a computer center stood directly beside it. She braced a hip against it because her legs felt unsteady.

*Never let a man dump you. Always make the first move. Always be the one to leave. That way, he's the one hurt, not you.*

Not this time. Callaway would be relieved if she broke it off. He could go away without guilt.

Dismissing a man had always been easy before because she'd never sent away anyone she cared about. This hollow pit in her stomach was unknown territory.

She made her smile bright. "I wanted to talk to you, too, Callaway. Let's sit down."

He did, looking more suspicious if that were possible.

*He thinks I'm about to lie to him again.*

After she sat down in a chair facing him, she studied her hands. "Callaway, I want you to know how much I appreciate what you've done the past few months."

The words came out smoothly. They should. She'd practiced them for weeks, knowing their affair could come to this sooner or later.

She wanted to say the right thing so he'd know she didn't begrudge him his freedom.

Pleased at her rational voice, she told him how much his support and advice had meant to her after Noelle's death and the subsequent uproar, said that she could never have managed without him. "I can't tell you how much your generosity's meant to me. I'll never be able to repay you for—"

He cut her off in the middle of a sentence with one short, sharp, obscene word.

She stiffened.

"This sounds like the old brush-off to me, sugah," he drawled. "I thought we'd got past the point where we were playing games, Scarlet."

She shot up. "Don't call me Scarlet."

He stood up, too, more slowly. "Then drop the act, Amanda. Say what you mean. That it's over, that you're dumping me, is that it?"

He was close to her, his breath mingling with hers, his scent overwhelming her.

"Yes. No." Was that hurt underneath the annoyance?

Her shoulders sagged. She touched his chest, felt his heat beneath the linen shirt.

It was no good. She could have carried it off once, but not now. Not after mapping his body so intimately, figuring out the workings of his mind as she had, loving him as she did.

"No. I'm just thanking you for being there for me." She looked up into his face, found him exasperated, glaring, and something else.

Vulnerable. And afraid.

Callaway was never afraid of anything. Suspicious, wary. But not afraid.

When he took her in his arms, she didn't resist. His whisper warmed her ear. "Listen, I've gone over and over us these past weeks and I keep coming up with the same thing. I hate being apart from you, not knowing where you are, what you're doing, what you're saying. I think about you every minute. I've got used to having you to talk to, to laugh with, make love to, and just to be with."

What was he saying? Amanda held her breath.

He licked his lips. "This past week, it was awful not seeing you every day. I know I'm not much, but I've been working with Claire, helping her get the company straightened out, and, well, she says she needs me, the company needs me. Maybe it's true. I don't know, but I'm going to try to help her. Maybe I'm not the type person you want to spend the rest of your life with, Amanda, but I'm changing. I'm trying, and if—"

The first disbelief wore off. "Callaway, what exactly are you trying to say?" She thought she knew, but she wanted to be sure. She needed him to be sure.

When he took a deep breath, she felt his chest rise and fall. "I'm a three-time loser. You could do a lot better than me. I'm thoughtless,

I don't always think things out. I'm easily led astray. I've got a temper, too. Sometimes."

She put her face against his shoulder to hide a smile. "I know all that." She also knew he was loyal and caring, not to mention tenacious, organized and sometimes terribly naive. "What is this leading up to?"

He pushed her away. "Do I have to spell it out for you?"

"I think you do." She was proud how composed she sounded considering her heart was jumping up and down.

He ground his teeth. "I guess I want you to marry me."

"You guess?" She lifted her brows. "You guess you want me to marry you? Don't you know?"

"Give me a break. I've tried it three times and look at what happened. I don't know if I'll ever be able to make it work." Panic underscored his admission.

She took his hand and patted it before interlacing her fingers with his. "It'll be all right, Callaway. I promise."

She wasn't lying. She'd make sure everything would be all right.

There'd be no more traipsing around picking up redheads for Callaway McIntyre, no more dunkings in Paris fountains, and no more throwing huge sums of money away at the gaming tables.

Callaway might not know it, but his lifestyle was about to drastically change.

"You'll have to stop smoking." She took him and led him to the sofa and sat down close beside him. "And I'll want a pre-nup agreement. My shop's doing fine and I don't want you interfering in how I'm running it." She squeezed his thigh.

"Me? Interfering?" Thunderstruck, he realized what she was saying and before she could continue, pressed her down against the sofa, kissing her as if he didn't intend to stop.

She managed to escape for air.

"Does this mean you're going to marry me?" His breath in her ear was heavy.

"I'm willing to discuss it." Her own breathing was pretty heavy. She put a hand up to her hair, found it intact. "Really, Callaway," she murmured. "Show a little enthusiasm, can't you? My hair's still up."

In two seconds it wasn't.

Other Fiction

by

Cheryl B. Dale


*Romantic Suspense*

Intimate Portraits
The Man in the Boat


*Paranormal/Gothic Romance*

The Warwicks of Slumber Mountain
Treacherous Beauties


*Light Mystery*

Taxed to the Max
Overtaxed and Underappreciated


*Vintage Mystery*

Losing David

Thank you for reading this book. If you enjoyed it, please consider leaving a review to help others discover it. Among sites that offer places for reader reviews are:

http://www.amazon.com

and

http://www.goodreads.com

If you do have the time and take the effort to leave a review, please accept my sincere appreciation and thanks.

www.cherylbdale.com
cherylbdale.blogspot.com
cherylbdale@hotmail.com